Seed of the Fire

Virginia Warner Brodine

Seed
of the
Fire

by

Virginia Warner Brodine

International Publishers

New York

Maps for Parts I and II by Cynthia Snow
Drawing for Part III by Gina King

Poem quoted in Chapter 25 is "Kilcash" from *The Wild Bird's Nest:
poems from the Irish* by Frank O'Connor. The Cuala Press, Dublin, 1932

Library of Congress Cataloging-in-Publication Data

Brodine, Virginia.
    Seed of the fire / By Virginia Warner Brodine.
        p.   cm.
      ISBN 0–7178–0721–5 (cl : alk. paper). –– ISBN 0–7178–0722–3
(pb : alk. paper)
      1. Irish-Americans--Ohio--History--19th century--Fiction. 2. Ohio
and Erie Canal (Ohio)--History--Fiction.   I. Title.
PS3552,R6223S44   1966
813' .54--dc20   96-30543
                                         CIP

Contents

To all my collaborators

acknowledged at the end of book

Seed of the Fire

Part One

From the Hills of West Cork

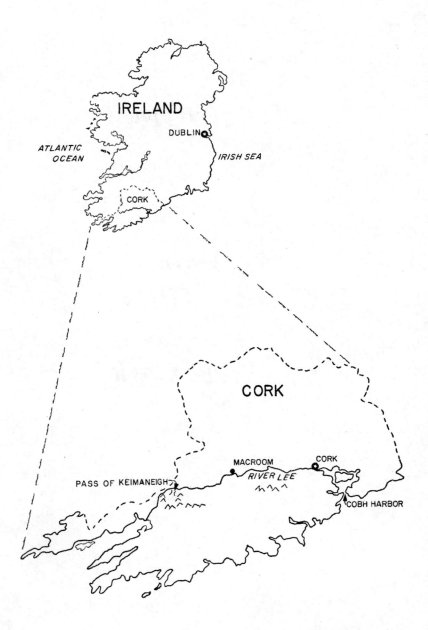

Chapter One

MARY GRIFFEN looked out across Cobh harbor toward the headlands that protected it from the open sea. Some of the ships on the water had their sails up and were moving swiftly before the April wind. Some of them were at anchor, rocking on the incoming tide, their masts sticking up like dead trees with no leaves on them. She would soon be on one of those moving ships. Everything was moving, the water and everything on it. She moved her own feet to feel that they were still on solid ground and looked back at the hill that rose steeply behind the wharf, all built over with houses and shops.

The hill was solid, unmoving, but there was no comfort in it. It shut her off from all that was behind it, shut her off from the road they had come down through the hills, along the River Lee, through Cork city and all the way from the city to the harbor. It shut her off forever from her twenty-eight years of living in that part of County Cork that was Ireland to her.

Where are the words now I've been flinging out so freely this whole winter past and more than a year before that? It was bitter words I had then on my tongue for the way life had turned on us in our own place and bright, careless words for the way we would fly across the sea. Now I'm far from home. Far from home . . . There is no comfort in such words as that. It is never known, till the cut is made, how cold and sharp is the knife that severs the slice from the loaf.

The worst of it all is, we came away without Ellen. It might be years before I see my one daughter again and maybe I'll never see her again in this life. When it's only three children left to me out of my five, what devil put it into our heads to leave the little one behind? Didn't I near pay for the child with my life . . . and four years I've been barren till it looks like there'll never be another child coming. What was the good of standin fast against Dan goin off to America alone, when the family will be divided by the water that will widen and widen till there's an ocean between me and Ellen? It's bad enough cuttin ourselves off from all my own people and Dan's people without cuttin the child off from ourselves.

Tim and Danny were standing close to her as if they were little bits of bouchaleens instead of big fellows of ten and nine. Dan had paid over the passage money to the captain of the ship they would be sailing on and had gone off to one of the shops to buy a sea chest with a lock to it to keep their things safe on the long voyage. He was coming back now with the chest on his shoulder. They would have to gather up their bundles and find a lodging place for the time they would be waiting till the sailing of the ship. The captain had told them it would be in the harbor the next day and the day after but would then sail with the first fair wind.

The boys caught sight of a ship that was coming in close with men on board and men on the dock shouting back and forth while they made it fast. Tim and Danny edged away from their mother toward this special excitement standing out of the mass of strange confusion.

Dan set the chest down. "Sit here on it," he told Mary, "Give your tired feet a rest after the long road we come from home." He put his hand on her shoulder and looked out over the water so his words would give her some cheer that would not be taken away again by the bleak look in his own eyes. "Don't grieve, don't now. We'll be sendin for Ellen before we've been a year in America."

The warm words broke through the cold only enough to let Mary's tears come

The captain came walking along the wharf. He clapped Dan on the back.

"Don't pull such a long face and tell your missis not to waste a tear on Ireland." His loud voice was hoarse with all the salt winds he'd shouted into. "This is the best day of your life, believe me. America is a great country and you'll never be sorry for leaving. I've carried many a shipload of folks to America and never a one regretted it."

Mary wiped her eyes and thanked the captain for his kind words and Dan said, "The tears isn't for the leavin, though God knows it's a far journey. The passage money wouldn't stretch over all three of the childer. The boys are big enough to work so our Ellen that's a small girl had to be left behind. Ellen it is that Mary's cryin for."

The captain walked off down the dock. But he had gone only a few steps when he was back, asking, "Where is this girl of yours?"

Dan told him, but Carrignahown meant nothing to an American captain that knew nothing of Ireland behind its ports. When Dan told him it was more than a day's journey, the captain said, "If you can bring your girl here before we sail, you can bring her along and not a word said about passage money."

Dan was poised to start before the captain was through talking, all the good sense forgot about Ellen being too small and frail for the long, hard journey, all his mother's pleadings that one of the children be left to lighten her loneliness. Still, he looked down at Mary and Mary up at him, considering. Both were thinking how there is nothing so sure to bring ill luck to a journey as turning back once that journey was started. And that wasn't all that was in it. The spring breeze was blowing the clouds away from the sun, showing how high it was in the sky. There were lodgings to find and a tin box to buy and stuff with provisions for the voyage. It would be past noon before Dan could be on his way.

"Can you make it all the way to Carrignahown and back before the ship sails?" Mary's voice shook with that question and her lips trembled, getting it out.

Dan looked back the way they had come, calculating the hours   "It will be a swift journey home, not like the four of us coming with our bundles   Many miles

I can run when there's no need to slow to the boys' pace. I'll be there on the morrow and here again by the next nightfall with Ellen on my back."

Mary stood up off the chest and pulled her cloak more closely around her small thin body, wrapping herself tightly in its folds. Its hood fell back on her shoulders. The sun shone redly on the chestnut braid that circled her head. She drew a deep breath and held her lips tight together. Making her voice loud and firm she said, "Go then, and I'll pray to the Blessed Virgin and all the Saints to keep the two of you safe and bring you back to me while there is yet time."

It was a big, empty, quiet morning. Hardly a sound was in it. Ellen made a small place for herself between the hawthorn bush and the cabin. She took the bit of rag Gran had given her. She would make a bundle of it and tie it to a stick she found under the bush. She had some small stones and bits of earth to put in the rag so it would be a real bundle, just like those that had been sitting plumply on the bench by the door and were now gone. She had to get up every few minutes, though, and go to the door to peep in and see was Gran still there Gran was there, indeed, but all alone in the empty cabin.

Ellen wanted things back the way they were, with Da's hat by Uncle Sean's hat on the pegs and Maimie's cloak next to them; with Tim and Danny making a yell and a clatter till Gran chased them out from under her feet.

Ellen dragged her toes slowly through the dust by the doorstep and crawled in behind the bush. She began again with the bundle but she couldn't make it behave the way the big bundles did for Maimie. A quick twist of hands, this way and then that way, and there it was, all round and fat with small ears sticking up. Ellen twisted her bit of rag this way and that way but it wouldn't stay properly She picked it up and the stones fell out, knocking against each other with a very small sound in the empty quiet.

She pushed up against the wall and opened her mouth and such a big noise came from the hard place inside her that it broke the quiet in pieces and brought Gran to the door. And then Gran's hand was over her mouth and Gran was saying whisht your noise, but not in her cross voice and not looking at her. Looking out and away. Ellen stopped noise and heard what Gran was hearing: the thud, thud of feet running, the feet of a big person.

Gran took her hand away and the thud, thud came louder and closer and here he was. It was Da himself and she was up in his arms and holding on to his shirt with her two hands. The hard place inside her melted and ran out of her eyes and made a wet place on Da's shirt where she was resting her face against his chest. His chest was going up and down with his big breaths from all the running. He sat down in the doorway, but he held her with one arm while he drank the cup of water Gran brought him. Uncle Sean came in from the field, saying he couldn't believe it was his brother in the flesh that he thought was gone from Ireland altogether

Gran called Da 'son' and cried for his leaving her and taking Ellen away Da promised Gran that Sean would give her a whole clutch of children to take Ellen's place.

That made Sean laugh and Ellen laughed, too, thinking of him carrying his big hands full of children like eggs from the hen's nest.

The talk of the big people came loud and went away soft . . loud . . . soft . . and Ellen was asleep. Then there she was on her two feet with Gran wiping her face and kissing her and smoothing her hair and kissing her again and Da saying quick now, we've a long way to go before dark and we must be at the ship on the morrow. Gran went to the bed and took up the old shawl that she wrapped Ellen in when it was cold but Da said No and Gran said Yes, it will be cold on the water and she made Ellen a real bundle of her own. Her hands weren't quick like Maimie's but they made a proper fat bundle of the shawl with oat cakes inside for their hunger on the road and ears sticking up where the shawl was tied to hold all in.

Da tucked the bundle inside his shirt and put Ellen up on his shoulders with her two legs hanging down where he could hold on to them with his hands. She put her arms around his head with the grey knitted cap on it and away they went, thud, thud, down the road, past all the people who were staying behind.

She rode high on Da's shoulders, waving her hand at Gran and Uncle Sean, at Seamas and little Peg who came out in the road and Peg-their-mother who stood in her door, at Terence, who straightened up from his work and stared at them, his spade dropping from his hand in surprise.

Then there were no more people, only the road. Away they went, thud, thud, down the long road to where Maimie and Tim and Danny were waiting so they could all go on the ship to America together.

They were gone from home, gone even from the strange, crowded city that clustered round the harbor. The ship had let the land go. It had taken away from them even the last sight of land. There was nothing but the water. They were alone in the midst of it.

Yet they were not really alone in their going. The five of them were among many from Ireland who had said goodbye to home and kin and country: Sons of farmers whose holdings were not large enough for dividing into holdings for sons and dowries for daughters, weavers from the towns whose looms and potato patches put together could no longer keep their families, tradesmen from the cities whose skill was going begging.

There were more this year of 1826 than ever before, thousands this year and more thousands next year and hundreds of thousands in the years ahead, as long as England kept Ireland poor in everything but people and for those people made it a more and more bitter struggle for a smaller and smaller piece of the Irish earth. America wanted them for the work they could do, for in America there was more work than people to do it. It was the work and the wages and the hope that beckoned.

There was little in their pockets once the fare was paid; little in their bundles and boxes when the journey was done. They brought riches with them all the same. They brought the children who would be part of the future across the water They brought a way of speaking and a way of singing, a way of struggling and a way of surviving. It would all be woven together with other ways of living and working being carried along the roads through other countries to other seaports and with ways of living and working that were already growing in the new world

Chapter 2

T HEY CAME OFF the ship in New York on to the unmoving wharf. The earth beneath it was rock-solid, unshaken by the spring wind that was spanking the water in the harbor up into peaks and ridges, sending the little boats scudding before it, getting a nod even from the tall ships tied to the wharves with their sails furled and their masts a winter forest of bare wood.

"Never . . ." Mary put her feet down, planting them on this earth that accepted her without a lurch or a quiver, "Never, as long as I live, will I ever go on the water again

She turned her back to it wanting a look at the city, but she couldn.t see a thing for all the people that were coming off the ship and those that were meeting them and the men calling out lodgings to be had and ship's passage to somewhere else and the carts that were being piled high with trunks and boxes.

Though the wharf was firm under their feet, between the planks they could see the water sloshing back and forth below. Little Ellen couldn't steady herself. She rocked back and forth, too, as if she were a babe just learning to put one foot in front of the other.

"Look at her now." Dan put a hand down for something she could get a hold on. "Her legs haven't been on the land for so long they don't know the way of it."

Mary had to laugh at that. Her voice tossed out on the sunny salt air that was blowing away the weeks on the ship—the frightening, shaking storms of it, the bad smells of it, the sickness and the crowding and the day-after-day sameness of it. But even the wind couldn t blow away the dirt that stiffened their hair and their clothes and soiled their bodies.

The people who had shared their journey had poured off the ship in a single stream. The stream had divided at once into streamlets and single drops and had been engulfed in the life that surged out from the city. They were left alone in its midst, a small island in this foreign sea.

They put their chest and their bundles down and sat on them to keep them out of the hands of the runners who wanted to drag them off to one lodging house or another It was their good luck that they didn't have to be a prey to these strange folk but had a good Irish house to be going to and a letter from a Carrignahown man to guide them. In all this confusion, though, the guidance seemed uncertain

Dan went off to ask the way from the dock through the streets of this big city. Mary put the hood of her cloak back and kept a good watch over the children and the things while he was gone. She spit on the corner of the rag that was all that was left of Gran's old shawl and vainly wiped at Ellen's face with it.

Dan was soon back with the word that they didn't have far to go and that was a piece of luck, too, for the sun was dropping low behind the city. After dark, they would be lost indeed Dan put the sea chest up on his shoulder, the boys and Mary managed the rest of it. Ellen followed after, walking sturdily now as a four-year-old should but holding tightly to her mother's cloak.

For two years, Dan and Mary had been hoping for this, talking of it, planning, saving a penny here and a penny there, sometimes doubting that it would ever be

Almost every letter Jamie McCarthy had written home to his father and mother in his eleven years in America had come from a different place. He always said he was doing well and Dan could do the same would he come but Jamie always seemed to be on the move. Dan and Mary, coming now with his help, had to find him somewhere, not in this city, but somewhere in the coutryside, as far as Carrignahown was from Cork, it might be.

It had been like an answer to a prayer, the letter from Jamie that brought the offer of passage money for Dan Still the journey seemed to be possible only if Dan went alone and sent for Mary and the children later Mary had her face set against that.

"If you go over the water by yourself, I'll never see you again. I know it," she said over and over. It was the fear for Dan's life that had come to her at the time of the fighting put that thought in her head. "You came safe through the troubles without bein shot and without bein transported to Australia or one of them other far places. You won't be transportin yourself now, in a ship to America, leavin me and the little ones behind," she told him.

It was the fighting and what came after that had pried them loose from their own place and sent them out across the water.

There had been some good years in the West Cork hills when England was busy with wars in other parts of the world and had need of all the Irish land could produce. There were small misfortunes, as always, but they could be shrugged off like the rain that passes when the mist lifts and shows the peaks again. At the war's end there was no break in the ill luck that pelted down, hard and cold. Prices plunged till the crops would no longer bring in enough to pay the rent. When Dan and Mary went down from the hills to work on the big farms below, hoping to make up the rent out of the wages, they found that jobs were few and workers many. Others, with a weaker hold on the land than they, had lost that hold altogether. The ranks of the wandering workers were swelled, too, with the men who had taken the king's shilling, lived through the king's war, and now were home again

In the winter of 1821-22, the uprising that had begun earlier in Limerick swept into the hills of West Cork. Its leader was called Captain Rock

The plain name of Captain Rock was a native weapon, dug out of their own earth, cut to fit their own hands. It came out of the action that was growing against those who used the land, not for a living but for the profit they could get out of the work of their laborers and the work of their tenants. Captain Rock could never be shot by the soldiers or tried by the courts, and the fight would go on whoever might be captured or killed, for there was no Captain Rock yet there were many. Dan Griffen was one.

By winter's end all the hills between the River Lee and the River Bandon, westward from Macroom, were in the hands of Rock's men, with scouts out day and night to warn of coming danger Against Captain Rock were the gentry and their yeomen, the English redcoats and that worst enemy of all—hunger A man can fight on one meal a day but he cannot work all day on a mouthful of nettles and a little blood drained out of the cow and then fight. A new crop had to be planted in March and April. As the hunger and the work increased, the struggle subsided.

It left the people maintaining their toehold on their rocky hills. Some rents were reduced, some tithes forgiven. When such concessions were not made, the fight briefly flared anew. Yet those who had lost land never regained it and for those who had held on, living in the hills remained hard. The risk of a bad harvest was always with them. The pressure of growing families on smaller farms intensified. Those who had come to be known as Captain Rock's men were still in danger.

Hope for the future that had blossomed in the Rockite winter faded. As the summer sun shone on the Big Houses of the gentry and the castles of the lords and the wide fields of the strong farmers and the small plots and thatched cabins of the peasants, it revealed a landscape little changed, a power unbroken.

As the seasons passed, Dan and Mary, like others in County Cork, turned and looked in another direction, hearing a new sound coming from the sea, carried all the way from its western shore: The sound of a way out of all this, a new life in a new country. Each family that heard that sound listened with its own ears, pulled its roots painfully out of the soil of home in its own way, for its own reasons, reached for a lifeline thrown from that distant shore by brother or sister or friend already there.

Jamie McCarthy had come up in the world since he crossed the water. He had begun years back to work on the Erie Canal. Now men worked for him on a new canal. He would make a loan of the money for Dan's passage and Dan could go to work for him and work off the debt. Since Dan's brother was to have the farm, it was only right Dan should have something for his share, even if Sean had to borrow. That would make it possible for Mary and the boys to go, too. Dan had written to Jamie the promise to work and Jamie sent the money for his passage.

It wasn't much of a letter that came with the money, only that they were to go to Pat O'Connor in New York, where Jamie had lodged when he first came to America, and Pat would have the word for them what they should do from there out.

For the seven long weeks of the voyage, New York had looked like the end of it but now they saw it was only the beginning. They were walking into an unknown world, filled with the clashing and rumbling noises of many wheels and hoofs on the cobblestones, of many human bodies moving back and forth around them— but none they knew, of many voices speaking in strange rhythms, but none speaking to them. As they went down the streets, the buildings closed the harbor away. The familiar little world of the ship was lost to them behind the shops and houses that leaned against each other along both sides of the street.

The man on the wharf had made it sound as easy as going to the neighbor down the road but in a strange city how did they know did they turn the right corner? They looked at each house with eyes to see only was it or wasn't it the place they were seeking. Still they might have passed the place without knowing it if Judy O'Connor hadn't been standing in the door. A big woman she was, almost filling the doorway She saw them peering this way and that and asked what they were looking for. When she found it was herself they wanted, she made them kindly welcome and in less than a minute they were inside. The small warm place closed around them, the clashing and rumbling receded. The sound of Judy's voice was the sound of home.

While she pushed and shoved the barrels and sacks to try to make room for all of them in her bit of a shop, Judy was asking the news of home, but she was a Skibbereen woman, too far from Carrignahown to have the same news. She didn't stop talking to listen anyway but went on telling how her husband had it in a letter from Jamie McCarthy that they were coming. They hardly had a word out in answer before she was pushing them out of the way of a man who came in to buy. They didn't mind that, for Judy O'Connor's talk was mending the frayed rope that tied them to the home they had left.

With the man gone, Judy was calling out the front for her son Mike to come in off the street and help with the Griffens' things and out to the room at the back to her old mother to put more potatoes on the fire and send one of the girls in with a dipper of water. "I know you must be thirsty, for it's the way on all the ships that toward the end of the voyage, they dole out the water by the drop."

Thirsty they were, indeed. Katy brought in the bucket as well as the dipper so they could drink their fill.

"Don't stint yourselves," Judy said. "The pump is only a step away from the door."

While they were drinking, she was looking behind the jugs on the shelf for Jamie's letter. They watched anxiously, for that would tell them if they were near the end of their journey and what would be there when they got to the end.

"Pat has it or he has the words of it in his head," Judy said. "What it is— Jamie's got the work for you, Dan Griffen, and it's Pat can tell you all about it. As for your lass there, and the childer, Judy O'Connor will take care of them."

Mary didn't like the sound of that. She smelled a separation in it. It had been a big chance they took when Dan went back after Ellen and now that they were all together, there were to be no more separations. Before she could ask a question, Judy was off on the story of her own voyage from Ireland, years before.

The next thing was to get the Griffens' things out of the shop and into the back where the O'Connors lived. Mike, a boy about the size of Tim, helped with that.

It made things a bit easier in the shop and a good deal more crowded in the back where the grandmother and the two girls were cooking the supper. Judy thinned out the crowd by sending Tim and Danny along with Mike to get the pig in off the street while she went back to the shop herself.

"Find the pig or don't come back yourselves," she called after them. "Leave it out all night and we'd have no pig in the mornin with the thievin gaumers we've got about here."

The boys went reluctantly, with glances over their shoulders at the slices of meat roasting over the fire. Indeed, all the Griffens now found their thoughts of the future narrowed down to the supper that would be coming. They had been on short rations all the last week and once in sight of land had finished what was left, so they had eaten nothing this day but the last of the ship's biscuits in the morning. Ellen could hardly be kept away from the hearth till the old woman gave her a cup of milk. She drained it in a minute, the first milk she had tasted for seven weeks, and held out the cup for more. Mary would have taken it from her, but the old woman pushed Mary's hand aside.

"If it's a sup of milk she wants, don't say her nay," and she filled the cup again. "The jug's not empty yet and she's such a wee thing, you could blow her off your hand."

It wasn't long before the boys chased the squealing pig through the room and out into the shed that leaned against the back wall of the house. Mary borrowed a bucket from Judy and sent the boys out again to the pump to fill it so she could get the ship's dirt off their hands and faces.

Pat O'Connor came home and made them such a speech of welcome he might have been the lord mayor himself. Then Judy locked up the shop, the girls raked the potatoes out of the ashes and the old woman took the pork off the fire. Soon they all had their fill of the meat and potatoes, the Griffens wondering to themselves was it a bit of luck they came on this day, or did the O'Connors eat meat every day of the week.

Supper over, Pat O'Connor took Dan into the shop where they could talk over the business, closing the door after them. The three women sat down at the table for a cup of tea while the children tumbled about on the floor.

The hot strong tea tasted good but Mary's eyes were on that closed door, her mind on what was being said behind it. Still she kept an ear open toward Judy's talk. Judy was saying how glad she would be, could she give them all lodgings upstairs.

"There's not a bed left up there for the night," she said, "but we'll make a place for you down here. There's two men upstairs will go off to the west with your Dan to work on the canal. When they're off, it's a nice little room I can give you and the chiselers up there. No one else in it but a decent Skibbereen family."

Mary put her mug down and gave Judy her whole attention. "But we all go together, wherever it is Dan goes."

Judy shook her head. "Oh, Mary Griffen, honey, that's no place for a woman like yourself." She patted Mary's arm. "You'll be better off here with us, indeed you will, and your man can send for you when he's a bit saved."

"Is it far off Dan will go?"

"Oh, very far off. It's away off out in the west, you know. That's the wild part of the country. They tell me you can travel for days and days without the sight of a house or a human face."

The old woman shook her head over it. "Indians, too," she said.

"There's a true word spoken," Judy agreed. "Bloody Indians. Red Indians. No, Mary Griffen, honey, that's no place for you."

Every word they said made the new country more fearsome and Mary more determined. She threw all her thoughts against that closed door and Dan behind it

Red Indians or no, wild beasts or no, a far journey or no, it's together we go to the west, Dan Griffen. Can you hear me?

Dan could hear Pat, sitting there on the barrel in the shop, with a candle lighting up his square body in its American clothes. He was dropping the hard facts out of the straight mouth in his smooth city face.

Dan sat on the floor with his back against the wall, in his pantaloons and his Irish coat, feeling like a lad just up from the country to the Cork butter market for the first time.

There was another promise to make and another debt to pay to Jamie and that would be his passage up the Hudson River and through the Erie Canal and on a ship again to Cleveland. There was a third promise to make and money to send back to Pat for the lodgings for Mary and Tim and Danny and little Ellen.

"And what if I took them with me?"

"No, no." Pat shook his head. "No, that wouldn't do. Not at all."

First, where was the passage money to come from, for Jamie had sent him the money only for the men. That was Dan and the two upstairs, young brothers with neither wife nor child and one more man he had yet to find out of one of the rooming houses that took in the men off the ships. Next, what would Dan do with the woman and the children when they got there, for he would be digging and moving on and digging and moving on with no settled place for a family at all.

"What you will do," Pat tapped Jamie's letter that he had laid down by the candle, tapping each word down to hold Dan fast to it, "is up in the mornin and with the two Sligo men upstairs to the river boat and away with you to the west, for the sooner you're off, the sooner you can send for your wife. Jamie's in need of you there and it's glad he'll be to see you."

Dan didn't like this stranger to be telling him what it was he would do Maybe he wouldn't go off to the west at all The Good God knows they had all had enough of the travelling. He stood up, to be feeling less like a young lad and more like the man he was, as much of a man as Patrick O'Connor, if he *was* new to the country.

"Sure there must be work to be had in a big city like New York. If there's no place for us all in the west, I'm thinkin maybe I can find a place for us all in this city. How will those two lads of mine learn to work and myself not there to bring them along under me? Tim's ten years old already and Danny only a year behind."

Pat got a bottle and a mug out from under the counter and poured a dram for Dan. "Ah, now, Mr. Griffen, maybe you'll find work in the city and maybe you won't, but sure, you'll never be makin wages like this." He tapped the letter again, this time for the promise that was in it. "Eight dollars a month—eight dollars, that's more than sixty shillins—*and* your board *and* your lodgin. Besides," he remembered the whip he had over Dan, "don't you owe Jamie for your passage over?"

"That's between me and Jamie." Dan emptied the mug and held out his hand for the letter. "Give us a look at what it is there in Jamie's words."

Pat filled the mug for himself, then handed the letter over, watching Dan closely over the mug's rim to see was this a bit of play-acting. Dan was bent over to bring the letter close to the candle, his eyes travelling slowly across the page, his lips moving. He was trying to get the business of it and the sight and sound of his old friend from the few short words on the paper.

At the same time, Pat was trying to get the weight of Dan himself. He had the reading, certainly, unlike most of his countrymen who came Pat's way. The weathered face bent toward the light topped a body that was strong and sinewy for all there was little height to it. There was stubborness to the mouth in that long face and a sharpness to the blue glance beneath the shaggy brows. It wasn't likely he was afraid to face the west alone. He needed his own reason to leave the family behind. Pat's reason was what there was in it for himself each time he sent a man to Jamie or another canal contractor. He did business, too, with the river boats.

"Let me tell you the way of it." Pat leaned forward confidentially. "There's a grand chance for a man like you out there in Ohio, but you got to be free to put your hands on it. You're young yet and you're a man that won't be pushin a barrow all your life. But for your own good and the good of your family you'll do better out there alone, without the worry of keepin a roof over their heads while you're makin your way."

Dan put the letter down. His eyes were on the candle now, but it wasn't the candle put the spark in them. Pat's words popped the lid off the box that had been shutting him in, close confined in the ship with nowhere to go and no way to move.

To walk off alone . .

"It's no place for a woman out there, take it from Pat O'Connor. Now is the time to tell her she stays here. She can lodge with us and no harm will come to her."

Walk off alone and I'll never see you again   . I know it.

Mary's voice was in Dan's head and her face with the look it had when he

came back with the cows from the high pasture after that worst of all summers in
'22. Mary had met him at the door with that look and the news that Maggie was
dead and the baby sick.

*Does Pat think I can walk off with my hands in my pockets, whistling like a
young lad? I'll have a power of things to do with my hands in this Ohio place
besides puttin them in my pockets. I can't shrug my shoulders and let little Ellen
slide off my back.*

So Dan listened and looked at the candle flame bending in the current of cool
air that crept in through the crack of the door.

Dan turned back to Pat. "Where's Jamie's family? In Ohio, is it?"

"But Jamie's a made man. You, now, just off the ship . . ."

Dan's mind was made up. "I'll be keepin Mary and the childer in Ohio the
way Jamie does."

Pat trotted out the hardship and the Indians and all the rest but he could see he
might as well save his breath to cool his porridge. He would have to send Mary
instead of a fourth man. Jamie wouldn't like it but there was many a mile between himself and Jamie. The boats would take the little ones for nothing or a
few pennies.

"Allright then, sir. Let me see can I fix the thing up to suit you."

When the closed door opened and the men came through, the children and the
old woman were stowed away for the night, and Mary was on a pallet on the floor
with Ellen between her and the wall.

Dan slid in with her and the two of them were close under the blanket, Mary
whispered, "What is it? What are we to do?"

"We're outa this tomorrow," Dan whispered back, "and off to Ohio. You'll
have to go on the water again, but not on the sea, only a river and such as that."

Mary let a long shuddering breath out of her and tucked Dan's hand under her
cheek. She touched his hard palm with her lips. "Yes, yes." She was content
now. They would all be together.

Chapter 3

THEY HADN'T BEEN in Cleveland long before Dan was cursing Pat O'Connor
for landing them here with almost empty pockets and altogether false hopes.
He had said the canal was here, but they found no sign of it. This was too
small a village to be lost in it, but no one seemed to know Jamie McCarthy. At last
Dan asked a young man from the ship's office.

"He's not here in Cleveland. What is he, a contractor on the canal? You know
the section number? No? They're workin on forty-fifty miles of canal. They say
that's near about a hundred sections. Ask the teamsters along the lakefront here
where at they're headed. Get one that's got a load for one of the contractors up

toward the Portage Summit. Akron, they call the village up that way. Start askin wherever you see canal construction goin on. You'll find him sooner or later Told you in New York you'd be on your job when you got off the Lake boat here, did they? City fellas is all alike. Everything in New York is a stone's throw from everything else and they think it's the same out here, but it ain't "

They found a teamster headed for Akron who agreed to put their baggage on top of his load if Dan and the two Brennigans—the Sligo men Pat had sent with them—would help push the wagon when it got stalled in the mud. Mary and Ellen could have a place in the wagon for a dollar which was all they could scrape together. Dan's face was grim when he handed over the money. The long-sought and ever-receding end to their journey had better be reached soon for they had nothing left to carry them further.

The wagon jolted past plowed fields where the green tips of new growth stood in rows that wavered around stumps and around weird shapes of burned and blackened trees. They passed log houses where the forest was hardly more than an arm's length from the cabin. Then they began to hear the thud and clash of tools against earth and rock, the tramp of horses and the voices of men. The first sight of the canal work soon followed.

The canal was a raw gash straight across the face of the country; the big trees felled, the stumps uprooted, smoke rising from the piles of slashings, the cover ripped off the earth to the mud and rock and seeping water below. Between here and the Ohio River two thousand men or more and hundreds of horses and oxen were laboring to make of it a shining highway, a ribbon of water tying Lake Erie and all north of it to the Ohio River and all south of it; all the wide land west that could be reached by lake and river to the newly completed Erie Canal and all the land east as far as the Atlantic Ocean.

All Dan saw was a confusion of activity, so many more men laboring together on the one job than he had ever seen before that the sight and sound of it beat against his head as if it would knock him off his feet. It was another strange piece of this strange new world. He would have to shoulder his way into it, shout at it to make himself heard, and what was he to say?

He went up to two men standing aside from the turmoil of swinging arms and moving bodies, heaving earth and creaking barrows. He took off his cap, for he could see these were not men to be shouting at. He waited patiently till the man holding a paper in his hand stopped talking. The other looked at him then and at John and Owen standing behind him. The Brennigans would have been almost foreigners to them back in County Cork but young as they were—not yet twenty— they were lost in this strange country and had fallen in behind Dan as if he were a man from their own parish

"Lookin for work? I've got as many hands as I need now but they might be able to use you farther up." He made the last words a question, looking at his companion

"Oh, yes, up around Peninsula and up to Akron They need hands on several of those jobs '

"Thank you, sir. I was lookin for Jamie McCarthy Would you know where his job is at all?"

"McCarthy   McCarthy? Let's see   " He pulled a small black book out of his pocket and leafed through it. "Oh, yes, he and Lordon are on the locks at Akron."

It was late the next day when the wagon creaked and jolted up the hill to Akron. The wagoner drove in front of the row of buildings that made the town and stopped at the store. Tim and Danny, exhausted from two days of walking, dropped to the ground. They looked like two peas from the same muddy pod The usually alert look on Tim's thin face was lost in one smudge; the ingratiating grin that usually widened Danny's round cheeks had disappeared beneath another. Mary handed a sleepy Ellen down from the wagon seat to Dan and climbed down herself while John and Owen unloaded their things.

"It's the end of the journey this time, I'm hopin," Mary said to Dan, "for sure, it's near the end of us."

It was just sundown Life at the canal was moving from its daytime center in and around the ditch to the uneven row of rough log and slab buildings at the edge of the right-of-way. Workers were turning in barrows and tools at the toolsheds. There was no pay coming in return, this being still early in the month, but men were standing in line to get their evening jigger of whiskey, week's-end weariness bowing their shoulders. As they downed the drink and moved away, they turned singly and by twos and threes toward the shanties where their evening meal was waiting. Some went off down the hill where another group of shanties clustered in the valley or over to the tavern that was nearby the store.

And out of the crowd of strangers, there was Jamie walking toward them with the familiar swing to his shoulders, the way he used to come walking up the hill from the McCarthy farm to the little Griffen place. As he came closer, the face on him under the American straw hat gave Dan a jolt. It was the face of a man he had never seen, not the lad he used to know. Then the old smile broke out on it and the old voice called Dan's name.

The gladness of the way they used to be boys together and the gladness of knowing Jamie meant the end of the journey mixed themselves up in Dan till he shouted out, "Jamie McCarthy, and is it yourself, man?"

Jamie had always been one to move fast, but he moved now with a decision and a habit of command that showed the kind of man the years had made of him.

When he found that Dan had brought his family he said, "Well now, I was thinkin you was comin alone. What was it with Pat O'Connor sending me them two from Sligo when I told him it was Cork men I wanted? Don't he have the sense to know when you put a Sligo man next to a Cork man, the devil will make a third?"

"Myself and the Brennigans, we got no devil between us. You can put me next to 'em in the work "

"I'll do that, and I'll put your Mary to the cookin. Nora's carryin again and wants to go home to Albany to her mother and the other children "

It was journey's end for Mary but the dark that swept in to cover her with sleep was not the friendly dark of home, where the little people might come down from the hillside to get a sup of milk from a saucer on the doorsill; where the small noises of the night were the cow on the other side of the wall and the call of the curlew blown in off the Irish Sea.

The sounds that came up out of the forest with the dark this night were strange hoots and howls. It was too gloomy by far under those trees for the likes of the Irish fairies and Mary had seen with her own eyes on the way from Cleveland that St. Patrick had never cleared the snakes from Ohio. If she and Dan got their hands on a piece of this earth for their own it would be a proud thing, a place they could rest their heads with no more journeying, but it would never be home. The spirits of their own people out of the past could never come back to its hearth.

Mary's sleep was restless. First dreaming she was in one of the many chimney corners that had sheltered her childhood when she was wandering the roads with her Gran, she woke to strange shapes looming in unaccustomed places. Closing her eyes, she sought to return to the security of childhood in sleep. Instead, the creaking of a loose door became the creaking of the ropes on shipboard. She thought they were crammed in the shelf that passed for a bed on the ship and Ellen was falling out. Half sleeping, she reached for Dan and he was not there . . . gone . . . gone . . . caught by the yeomen and dragged off . . . This time she woke in terror and it was near dawn before she slept again.

Ellen slept peacefully, untroubled by shadows of the past or fears for the future, secure in the curve of her mother's body. Irish echoes had rung in her ears with only a light, childish sound; they had fallen away from her and drowned in Atlantic waters.

Chapter 4

T HE MC CARTHY-LORDON CAMP was only one of many up and down the Cuyahoga Valley and across the Portage Summit. Some camps were like this one, with Irish workers, a few with Germans. Some were manned by local men and boys, farmers' sons and the farmers themselves who were anchored in their own farms, or laborers saving toward the farms in their future who found in canal wages some welcome cash but knew this work was not a lasting thing and wouldn't have had it any other way.

Whatever the differences among the camps and in spite of their unfinished and temporary nature, they had a shared purpose. While the human pieces that made up the canal world were constantly being moved about and fitted together in new ways, it was always to serve that purpose: The building of the canal that had brought this world into being and dominated its life.

Canal Commissioner Alfred Kelley had pushed the canal project through the legislature and was now a hard man to satisfy, with his own reputation at stake in the making of a good canal system. He let the contracts on the northern end of the canal and then rode up and down the line. Neatly dressed on the hottest July day, wrapped in his blanket coat on the coldest January day, he had developed a sharp eye for defects in construction and kept as wary a watch on the state's money as if it were his own. He appeared sometimes when least expected to make sure that every specification in the contracts was carried out to the letter.

As intently as he watched the progress of construction, he watched the Eastern and British financiers whose money was needed to keep the ditch pushing through stretches of wilderness and past frontier settlements. He kept all the reins in his hands and would hardly allow the engineers to make a decision without consulting him, for he thought *he* was building the canal. But confident leader that he was at thirty-six, vigorous, intelligent, and determined, the one thing he could not do was to *build* the canal, as any of his engineers could have told him.

Each resident engineer was in charge of twenty to thirty miles of line. Some had started as surveyors and learned their engineering on the job. A few had gained some experience in New York on the Erie. They learned from each other, from contractors with longer experience, from the very nature of the problems they faced and the fact that there was no one else to solve them. Although conscious of the canal as a whole, each was most deeply involved in his own piece of line. That was what *he* was building and he knew it.

To McCarthy and Lordon, the Commissioner was a source of money—not easily tapped; of future jobs—and therefore to be carefully cherished; and of orders—lordly, inconvenient, sometimes next to impossible to carry out. The engineer seemed sometimes an arrogant boy, sometimes a close co-worker, sometimes the eyes and ears of the Commissioner. In the opinion of the contractors, both Commissioner and engineer had exaggerated notions of their own importance, but it was an opinion as closely guarded as it was firmly held. And beyond a shadow of a doubt, when it came to their sections, Locks Seven, Sixteen and Seventeen in the Akron Cascade, *they*, McCarthy and Lordon, were the builders.

For the Commissioner the canal was a vision, part of a growing State and an expanding nation in which he had an increasingly proud part. For the engineer, each construction problem solved was part of the canal he was creating and the career he was building. For the contractors, each section finished was money in the pocket and the satisfaction of one job of work done, making a step to the next.

When Dan walked down into the ditch that first Monday morning, he became just one of the hands. They began work each day as soon as there was light enough to see to do it, before the sun was far enough up to touch the tops of the trees. The men shook off the dark and the sleep as they reached for their tools. It was too early for visions.

They slogged up out of it when there was no more light to see by, soaked to the knees and muddy to the eyebrows. Some could feel the day's work in their thighs and the calves of their legs. That was from the run to get the wheel of the barrow on the plank that led up out of the ditch and from holding the barrow back as it was guided down the slippery plank for another load. Some could feel it burning in the shoulders that had carried the weight of their bodies into driving the pick or pushing the shovel into the resistant earth. Sometimes the digging was done by a scraper, pulled by a horse. That went faster than anything a man with a shovel could do, but there was nothing easy about following the horse and guiding the scraper, as any man who had followed a plow would know.

Every man could feel the work all the way up and down his back from the jar of pick or barrow wheel or scraper against root and rock and from the bending and rising, the striking, pushing, lifting, hour after hour. The arms that had been in motion all day hung at their sides, the hands that had grasped pick or shovel, barrow or scraper handles, dangled from their strong wrists. They were too weary to give a thought to what they might have created.

It wasn't likely there would be much money in their pockets when the section was finished. Many of them, like Dan, were working off the debt they owed McCarthy and Lordon for bringing them from Ireland. They took what pay they had to have in money and left the rest with Jamie MCarthy, counting the months it would take these payments to kill the dead horse.

These were the men who were building the canal. Dan became one of them. Their bodies swung to the same rhythm, they worked together and ate together and drank together. They cursed the same summer heat that poured the sweat into their eyes, the same mosquitoes that could not be driven off without dropping a tool, the same wind that drove the winter cold down the river valley and into their bones. They cursed the same storekeepers for the pennies added to the price of every pair of boots and straw hat, every plug of tobacco and gallon of whiskey because there was no other place for them to buy.

For all Jamie was his old friend, when Dan was working, he worked for the same boss as the others. Jamie was one of their own, a shield of strength against a strange country. He put more meat on the table in a week than they had seen at home in a year. He handed out the blankets when it was cold and an extra jigger of whiskey at the end of a bad day with the rain or after a good job done. But it was his voice that drove them all day, giving them a word with a laugh in it to pull them along, pitting the strength of one against the strength of the other to get every man's full weight going into the work, taunting them with how much better the lads on Section Twenty could do it, or with the mighty feats of the Germans down the line, till it was all of McCarthy's men together against the rest of the canal world. This went on from sunrise to sunset, from Monday morning to Saturday night. It seemed they had been in that muck since the day they were born and would be there till the day they died.

These canal builders made no reports to the legislature, gave no speeches when the first boat was pulled triumphantly down the canal water, wrote no journals and few letters, issued no statements to the newspapers. They left their mark nevertheless, a long, long mark across the Ohio earth.

No one—Commissioner, engineer, contractors, hands, Dan, even Mary herself—thought of Mary as a canal builder. Although, like the men, Mary worked for the contractors, her place of work was the kitchen, not the canal.

It was beyond question that men must eat, whatever work they do, and beyond question that women must put food on the table. Working on the canal had not changed those certainties. The sun rose and lighted the work. The women rose with the sun and cooked the breakfast. Without their work no pick would have been lifted, no barrow would have rolled, no stone set in place. No plans would have moved from the halls of the Ohio legislature, no money from the Anglo-American banking houses. It was work that was done one day, only to be done over again the next. It left no word on the printed record and no mark on the Ohio earth.

Chapter 5

M ARY'S BODY KNEW when it was time to rise. Perhaps it was the pre-dawn hush when owl and fox had fallen silent and the birds of day had not yet wakened. She hardly needed the sound of the horn that woke the camp.

She rolled quietly out of bed each morning, the only sound the crackling of the straw in the tick. Pulling her dress on over her shift, she stepped over the children. With Nora gone, Jamie had taken his own bed into the cabin where he kept the tools. Now the Griffens were together in the nights. She blinked her eyes till she was able to see the shapes of things while Dan stumbled sleepily past her and out the door to the job.

Mary raked the ashes in the big stick-and-clay fireplace gently away from the hot coals underneath. Blowing on the seed of the fire till it began to glow, she added a few twigs at a time till a steady flame sprang into life. Although its life came from the coals of yesterday, each day it seemed new. The crackling sound of it and the pungent odor were pleasant in the cool morning, but it did not have the clear warm flame of the peat fires of home or the earthy odor of those fires, so freighted with meaning and memory. This fireplace would hold three of those where the peat fires burned and Mary needed the whole of it to cook breakfast for thirty men. Once the fire was burning well, she slipped out the door and around behind the cookhouse where she could lift her skirt and let her water out. That was all the morning toilet she had time for.

Susan Walsh came in with the growing light and Mary stopped a minute to straighten her back and fasten the braid around her head while she gave Susan a good-morning. Susan was the young daughter of a digger, the only crew Mary had except for Tim and Danny whose task it was to fetch wood and water.

Mary's day didn't end till she put the next morning's stirabout on to cook and smoored the fire for the night. Then she could fall into bed and into sleep but without spirit enough left to say so much as a word to Dan, without feeling enough left to know he was there beside her.

She watched Jamie to see did he like what she put before the men. When he ate well and reached for more she knew he was satisfied. Now and again he gave her a smile or a pat on the shoulder that told her he was more than satisfied. It was a long time since she had cared for the smile of any man but Dan but here things were different. Dan was seldom beside her and it was the boss she had to please.

She had a special place as one of the few women in a camp of men, as the cook in a camp of hungry men. She was also one who often sat down beside the boss to talk over feeding the camp in the way the engineer sat down with the boss to talk over the business of building the section.

In Carrignahown, in the time of the struggle, she had such a place beside Dan. Now again, it could be seen by all that she had the trust of the one who was chief among them. It gave her a great liking for Jamie.

Since Mary's work was to pay for her keep and that of the three children, there were no paydays for her. She and Dan counted the same pennies.

Dan was a name in Jamie's paybook like any other, with the same count kept of days worked and days missed, the same pay for a full month as any other digger got. At the end of July, he took a piece of charcoal from the fire and made a row of nineteen marks on the wall, each mark standing for one of the dollars they owed.

"Look at this, Mary," he said, and with his sleeve rubbed five of them out again. "We do that every month and by the winter we'll have the dead horse killed, as the lads say. Then we start savin for the farm."

The dream of a farm of their own in this new country had been shaped for Mary by her experience of County Cork farms. The longer she was in the Ohio of the canal camp, the less that picture would fit into this world.

She held on to the dream but it was an insubstantial dream that faded and disappeared when she tried to look at it. When the last mark on the wall was gone, what could she put in its place to save her pennies against?

Many months went by before they could again rub out five of the marks on payday. The canal fever had begun to appear in July. In August it struck Dan. On the hottest day, he sat shivering by the fire, shaking uncontrollably, wrapped in a blanket. Then he stumbled across the floor, dropping the blanket on the way and slumping down on his tick, groaning with the ache in his bones and the heat that was devouring his body.

There were ten, twelve, sometimes more other men sick at the same time. Some of them made it to the job every other day, some hardly at all. Some gave up entirely, wrapping their few things in a bundle and going off down the road, swearing they would never work on the canal again.

Mary sent the boys for water twice as often now. She kept a bucket beside the bed. When Dan burned with the fever, she gave him a drink and wiped his face with a rag dipped in cool water. Her first thoughts were for Dan but she didn't forget the other poor lads. When she could snatch the time from her work, she carried the bucket outside, where a few were stretched in the shade of the cookhouse.

When Mr. Higbee drove up in his wagon with a load of supplies, he saw Mary on her rounds. "They all got the shakes?"

"It's the canal fever."

"Well now, call it that if you want. We call it the ague or the shakes. Ain't hardly one of us in the valley didn't have it sometime or another before we ever heard of the canal. Best thing for it's the thoroughwort tea. We learnt that from the Indians."

The next time Higbee came he brought a jug of the tea, sent by his wife, and a sprig of the plant so Mary could see what it was and know how to pick it and brew her own tea.

It was the first hint of neighborliness from a woman beyond the camp's borders. The other women in the camp were no use to her in learning American ways. Bridget O'Scanlon was almost as new come from Ireland as Mary herself. Kate Dugan, indeed, liked to make much of her six years on this side of the water but her interminable stories were all of how sick she had been in this Erie canal camp or that.

The day after she got the thoroughwort, Mary took Ellen with her and went off as soon as the noon dinner was over, leaving the supper stew simmering over the fire. She kept the sprig of the plant in her hand and searched for another just like it along the river bank where Higbee said it might be found. When she came upon one of the stalks, taller than Ellen, with its long pointed leaves, when her eyes told her the tracery on the leaves was the same as on those she carried, when her fingers told her the feel of their hairy undersides was the same, then she felt for the first time a friendliness in this American wilderness. Just as she was seeking and finding, so her Gran used to seek and find the herbs with herself plucking the bright flowers. Just as Ellen trailed behind now while her mother sought the healing herbs, so she used to trail after her Gran.

The bit of comfort there was in the friendliness of the shady riverbank and the green stalk of the herb was just enough to blind her with tears for the Gran who was dead and the bogside she would never see again. She wiped the tears away impatiently with the back of her hand. One plant was only the beginning. She needed her eyes to find more.

It wasn't long before she had her apron full of thoroughwort leaves, but that wasn't the best of it. She had wandered all the way down the riverbank to the place where the Higbee pasture bordered the river and just as she was about to turn back, she spied the familiar yellow blossoms of St. John's wort with their edges of black dots. It was like a gift from Gran herself, who had taught her to know its sunny face and to use its blossoms and leaves.

"Look at that, now," she said to Ellen. Holding the small fingers, she helped Ellen rub the petals. "See how they make your hand red?" She held the leaves up to the light to make sure it was the Saint's plant. There were what looked like many tiny holes in each leaf, but really were little drops of precious oil. "That's it, indeed. If only we'd had the juice of that one to drink on St. John's Eve, your father might not have the heavy load of fever that's on him, poor man."

The fresh winds and cooler nights of September brought Dan back to work on the alternate days when he didn't have the shakes. His face looked older and yellower and he no longer set the pace as he had often done in July, but he was on the job.

A new spirit was now enlivening Saturday nights. There was a good Irish fiddler in a camp just a few miles up the line but the boss there was a local man with a mixed crew. Doherty and his fiddle and the rest of the Irish often came walking down the line soon after supper. There was always a big campfire at McCarthy and Lordon's camp on Saturday nights and Jamie was ready to fill a gallon jug from the whiskey barrel in his cabin for any man whose account could stand another twenty cents chalked up.

The jugs went the rounds and Doherty's fiddle began to sing. A dance started on the flat ground between the fire and the cookhouse while the flames shot high and danced with the night shadows. A few sups from one of the jugs and Mary forgot she was tired. The gay notes chased each other inside of her and began to shake her foot and toss her head.

Doherty played jigs and hornpipes so the men could dance alone. There were rarely enough women for an eight-hand reel. John or Owen Brennigan some-times got a dance with Susan, who had her pick of the men. One night, Owen bent down to Ellen, who was capering about in her own fashion, took her small hand in his big one and began teaching her to dance while Doherty played the "Silver Tip." There was a laugh in that for everyone except Ellen, who took the honor with the utmost seriousness.

Sometimes the visitors put Doherty's brother, Jake, up to sing against Paddy O'Scanlon, the best voice in this camp, or they all raised their voices together in one of the songs of home.

The Irish fiddler and all drew the Irish from miles up and down the line but the Irish welcome and the freely circulating jugs drew others, too, like Zeke Johnson who had a low tolerance for work and an unfailing nose for a free drink. He had put in a day or two now and then at canal work and had drunk with the canal workers in Hart's tavern enough to be able to spin his rhymes around any of the people or the happenings of the canal world. Even the Commissioner was not beyond his reach. He stood by the fire and shouted out his prophecy that the devil would take Mr. Kelley ". . . by the throat . . . and hold him in the brimstone fire . . . and singe his blanket coat."

As one jug after another was emptied, the gaiety got boisterous. Sometimes under cover of the dark, one of the men tried to make too free with Mary but she had a sharp elbow and a sharp tongue for such tricks as that and it seldom went so far as to call Dan's fist into action.

Donal Shelley was one of those who had an eye for a pretty woman and a gallant way with him that was hard to resist. His skill as a carpenter and his high wages gave him a privileged position, along with the masons like Thomas Noonan, who held themselves to be a cut above the diggers. Donal had been smart enough to take a hint when Mary let him know she was having none of his nonsense. All the same, when he no longer joined them around the fire she missed his merry, impudent looks and the sound of West Cork in his speech. He and Pat Flynn were the only ones in the camp who came from the parish next to their own. The rumor was that Donal was now courting an American widow woman.

In the late summer and early autumn days, Mary went out gathering herbs more than once. She now had many bundles of thoroughwort drying by the chimney. She had found garbhlus—the yellow dandelion—and the purple-flowered camal bui. Some others that looked like Irish herbs, yet not quite the same, she picked sparingly. She would try them before she would trust them.

There was no St. John's wort anywhere except in the Higbee pasture. The changing colors in the trees and the cooler nights told her there was little time left if she wanted some before it was gone, so one day in mid-September she and Ellen went back along the river and over the fence into the pasture. Both were busy picking when Mrs. Higbee, on her way from the root cellar back to the cabin, spied them and came walking down through the grass to see who they were and what they were about. She walked with such a purposeful stride and looked so grim, Mary was sure the herbs would be snatched from her and she would be sent packing.

"Why didn't you come up to the house?" Mrs. Higbee reproved her. "You could of ast me, couldn't you? I wouldn't deny nobody a few of my flowers but you could of ast me, could you pick in my pasture."

Mary took the bunch Ellen was holding and joining it with what she had, held the whole out to the other woman. "Askin your pardon, lady, but didn't I search for the blessed St. John's wort by the canal and by the riverside, by the meadow and by the hill, and not so much as a scrap of a shadow of a leaf could I find."

Mrs. Higbee wouldn't take the bunch of herbs. "Keep it, keep it. There wouldn't be none of it around here but for me bringin it from Connecticut. Now it's got away from my garden and gone wild."

She gave Mary a hard stare. "My but you do talk peculiar. You must be that Irish woman Higbee was tellin me cooks up to the canal. What language is that you talk? It ain't English, is it?"

What could Mary say then, with Mrs. Higbee staring at her mouth as if she could see each word that came out of it? She dropped a curtsy, Ellen did the same, and they turned away to go back to the camp.

"Don't run off." Mrs. Higbee was offended again. "You can come in and set a minute, can't you?"

"You're after askin us in to your house?" Mary was amazed.

"After what? Come in is what I said."

She led the way, lifting a rail in the fence to let them through into the barnyard. Mary could see now what was not visible from down near the river: the log house and barn and two other smaller log outbuildings. They were all so spread out and looked so much like the house that at first Mary thought she was walking into a village, rather than into one farm with its own haggard.

Mrs. Higbee picked up the pan of potatoes she had set down at the root cellar door when she had first seen them. They followed her into the house.

"Set down and make yourself to home." She settled herself with her pan of potatoes and a knife.

"God bless the work," Mary said faintly, realizing that she had stepped across the threshold without a word of greeting or blessing. She sat down and took Ellen on her lap. "If you'd like to give me a knife I could help you with the praties."

Mrs. Higbee stared again. "Praties?" She held up a potato. "That's no pratie. That's a potato. Po-ta-to. Can you say that?"

"Po-ta-to," Ellen said, thinking this bit of edification was intended for her.

"Well, you're a quick little parrot, you are. I believe I could teach you to talk proper English in no time."

She made no effort to continue the lesson, though, instead firing one question after another at Mary. Between guarding her tongue against another mistake and taking in everything her eyes could see, Mary was almost wordless.

The fireplace was almost as big as the one she had to cook on at the camp. It had a fine chimney to it and Mrs. Higbee's spinning wheel beside it. The big bed had a coverlet on it most likely woven by Mrs. Higbee on the loom that stood against the wall. Mr. Higbee's gun was over the top of the door and on either side was a window to let the light in through greased paper. The whole cabin had a wooden floor to it. Around the table were as many chairs as she had fingers on one hand. And that wasn't all that was in it. There was a ladder leading to another chamber above.

She could have stayed here all afternoon looking at this American house but the rest of her day's work was waiting for her. Reluctantly she got up and gave Mrs. Higbee her thanks.

"Well, my land, it's a pleasure to me to have someone to talk to besides Higbee and the children." She seemed really sorry to see Mary go. "It ain't so bad now, with all this canal work and more settlers comin in all the time but I tell *you* there was times in those first years we was here when I didn't see another woman from one month to the next. I was like to die out here in the woods with the nearest neighbor miles off and no road worth speakin of to get there by."

All the way back to the camp, Mary was telling over to Ellen all the wonders of that farm. "And some day we'll have one just like it," she finished. Just like it? Now that she had stopped the talking that had been as much to herself as to Ellen, she could hear the echo of Mrs. Higbee's last words, ". . . like to die out here in the woods with the nearest neighbor miles off . . . miles off . . ."

Chapter 6

THE EARTH had been firm and hard in the dry hot weeks of summer but an early autumn rain began to soften it. It made the digging easier. They finished the lockpit they had been hacking and scraping at for weeks. All that night the rain continued to fall.

In the morning, Dan paused at the door in the half-light. The air was still cool and damp, with a constant drip from the trees and the roofs of the shanties but no rain was falling.

Jamie came up behind Dan. "Let's go, let's go."

He shouldered Dan aside and led the way to the lock they had been working on, almost a mile down the line. Owen joined Dan.

"Hurry, hurry, hurry," Owen muttered, making a joke of it as they slogged along the muddy path behind Jamie. "A-gallop, a-gallop, a-gallop. For my part, I wouldn't be runnin for that hole with all the rain and mud there'll be in it. Wasn't that a right downpour last night? A jugful of it came through the roof and went down my neck."

"Jamie'll put hammers in our hands this day, maybe. We finished in the pit, didn't we? The next thing is, a pile driver to be made. The stonies can't build the lock walls till there's piles drove in all around the pit to hold up their stone. Puttin that machine together, that's dry work."

Donal Shelley had already made a sturdy platform for the pile driver. It took all nine of them, Jamie and Engineer Dent included, to get it moved into place at the edge of the pit, settle it level and firm and lay the long pieces of timber for the pile driver out across it. When he gave out the tools for helping the carpenter with the building, it was John Brennigan, Pat Flynn and the two Caseys who got them. Dan and Owen he sent down into the pit to swing their picks at a few remaining stubborn rocks.

"A proper lough, the rain made of the pit," Owen remarked as they made their way down the slippery plank and splashed into the pit, twenty feet below the surface. "It's a wonder Jamie wouldn't give us a boat for it."

They dug into the work, Dan complaining, "How can a man see what he's about, with all the water and mud there is in it?"

An hour later they were side by side facing the lock wall, prying at a loose rock with their picks. The platform was directly above them. They could hear the voices of the men up there and the clean dry strikes of their hammers.

Suddenly a great chunk of the dirt wall broke loose and came down on them, hitting Dan below the waist with such force it almost knocked him off his feet.

At the same moment they heard a shout, "Look out belo-o-o-ow!"

They dropped their picks and headed across the pit, rocks and clods of earth pursuing them. Above, the platform had begun to tip toward the pit. The men who had been working on it jumped clear, shouting new warnings. Tools and timbers slid off the platform and thundered down in a chaotic descent with the mass of wet earth and loosened rock.

The corner of a timber struck Dan a glancing blow on the shoulder. He staggered, his outstretched arm reaching the opposite wall, keeping him upright. He turned, his back against the wall, just in time to see Owen go down, hit by a flying hammer, and disappear under a heap of rubble.

Before he could move toward his mate there was another shout from above. The heavy platform was teetering on the edge. It seemed to be heading straight for him. A second later it had crashed down on the mass below, missing him, but splashing him with mud.

He wiped his arm across his face, then pulled up his shirttail to get the mud out of his eyes. Shaking his head in bewilderment, he tried to understand what had happened in the few minutes that had unsettled everything, filled the air with danger and himself with confusion and fear.

"Owen . . . Owen! . . Where are ye?"

A few last clods dropped on top of the platform and rolled down it, the sound small in the silence that followed the crash. The men above were staring down from the edge of the ragged break in the pit wall, seeing only one man where there should have been two.

"Owen!" John screamed, missing his brother. He leaped into the pit, followed by the others.

"Under there . . . there . . . " Dan pointed.

Together all of them grasped the platform and shifted it enough to dig for Owen.

"A pick . . . a spade . . ." Pat looked wildly around him for a tool.

"No tools," Jamie ordered. "We might strike him under all this."

Down on their knees, they scrabbled at the dirt and rocks with their hands till they reached Owen's body and dragged it out. John put his arm under Owen's shoulders and with his own shirttail wiped his brother's face. The head fell back under his hand.

There was no more breath in that body and no more beating of that heart.

Slowly, John laid the body down and stood up. He shuddered and his big mouth opened wide but no words came out, only a strange gasping sound. He looked unbelievingly at the muddy lump that had been Owen, lying there amid the other muddy lumps on the pit floor, then pleadingly into the faces of the silent men beside him. He wanted those last minutes back. Only a few minutes would give him his brother back. Dan put his hand on John's shoulder, the warm pressure giving the only answer possible.

Dan, Pat Flynn and Mick Casey bent down to lift Owen's body. Mick gave his younger brother, Kevin, a look that brought him into it. The four of them carried their dead comrade up the plank at the pit's end and slowly back along the path toward camp, with John walking behind.

"Pat," Jamie called after them. "You know what to do? And come back here when it's finished."

Pat gave him a grunt for an answer and continued walking. As the procession passed up the line, a wave of silence rippled ahead of them. The work paused as they came in sight and the men stood with their caps in their hands while they passed. As they moved on to the next section, with slow and rhythmic tread, the work paused there, while the clash of tools and grinding of rock on rock resumed behind them.

But when they reached camp, the work there stopped entirely. These men knew it was one of their own. They came running to see who was it and what happened. Tim and Danny, sensing some excitement, came running, too, halting abruptly as they saw Owen's body lowered onto the bench beside the cookhouse door.

Mary came out of the kitchen with Ellen at her heels. "Who is it? What happened?" She pushed her way through the crowd of men. "Owen . . . are you hurt bad then?" She dropped to her knees beside him, touching his cold hand, looking at the eyes that could not look back at her.

"O-o-o-och," her wail rose and passed over the heads of the men, bowing them like grass under a wind. The sorrow of all Ireland was in it, where death came too readily and too often. The sorrow of all mothers was in it, for she had seen two of her own go and had sorrow enough left for the son of a far-off mother.

"Owen Brennigan, why have they brought you from the work like this? What is it dropped on you, Owen? The fine lad you are, you wouldn't be leavin us, surely. Don't you know your own brother is here callin you?"

Mary looked up now at the frightened children and at the troubled men who were looking everywhere but at each other. Each lived with the knowledge that Death walked every mile of line and might point to any man to pay the price for that mile. This knowledge had crept up from the back of each mind now and looked out every man's eyes. If eyes met, it would leap out into terrifying reality and might never be forced back.

Mary's voice was warm against this cold fear and quick with what needed doing. She was speaking out of another thing they all knew, that death needs a ceremony, something to say that this human life was not lived without the care of its fellows and is not gone without due notice given to its end. Something to say that those who are left salute the life that was here and is now gone, rejoice that they still live and take comfort in knowing that when they go, they too will not pass unnoticed away.

"Tim," Mary said, "go now quickly and take Ellen to Bridget. Tell her what happened. Danny, you be fillin the buckets. Johnny, lad, let you get me the good clothes your brother has and we'll wash him and dress him. He can't go to meet his Maker the same as if he was goin down in the ditch. You, Dan, you wouldn't be leavin Owen here? You and some of the lads be puttin him on the bench inside where we can lay him out."

The children were glad to hurry away from the sight of that lifeless body and from its meaning, too cold and final for them to understand. Dan was not so quick to follow Mary's lead.

He asked Pat, "What was the word Jamie was givin you? What is it that's to be done and you knowin it?"

Pat lifted his bowed head and looked at Dan. He rubbed the stubbly chin on his broad, sun-reddened face with the long upper lip then turned and pointed south toward Lock One and the hill above Akron.

"That's the way there, to the buryin ground. What McCarthy was sayin, we should take Owen and put him away there."

"Tomorrow," Mary added her word. "Sure, he couldn't be meanin to put the poor lad in the ground now with the spirit hardly gone out of him, without a coffin, without a wake, without a prayer said." She moved toward the cookhouse. "Tomorrow," she said over her shoulder.

Jamie not being there, everyone looked at Simon Lordon. The mason shifted his considerable weight from one foot to the other and licked his lips. He had no more doubt than had Pat what Jamie had meant. Still, it did seem there needn't be quite such a hurry to huddle poor Owen into the ground. If it weren't for Jamie giving the order . . . and it not being endurable that a woman should be giving out with a different order altogether. . . and the unwelcome thought that the notion most of them had of a wake was that McCarthy and Lordon should knock the bung out of the barrel and let the whiskey flow all night . . . He could feel the silence of the men about to break and out of the corner of his eye could see Bridget and Kate coming across the clearing.

"What Jamie was meanin, I wouldn't doubt, was that Pat and Dan here should go to the buryin ground and make a place ready. Shelley will be makin the lad a coffin. Tomorrow mornin we'll sound the horn a bit early and whoever it is that wants to see Owen get a decent burial come and help us put him in his grave. Now, John, would you be wantin to give your brother a bit of a wake the night?"

"I would."

"Allright, then. The women have their work to do and the rest of us had best get back to the job."

Only John remained. Mary took him by the hand and pulled him away from his brother's body.

"There are things for you to do, Johnny, if it's tonight we'll be wakin him. Get Owen's clothes for me, that's the first thing. Then over to the store to get the pipes and tobacco for the wake."

When she had Owen's clothes and John was gone to the creek to clean himself, Mary returned to the cookhouse where Kate had begun to lay out the body. Bridget had never had such a task before. The shock of touching this cold thing that had been a living man, of cleaning the canal mud from the bruised and bloody face had been too much for her and she had run out.

Kate had done this many times before, she said, and talked without pause of those other times while they worked. The stream of talk which did not have to be answered made the task a little less hard. The shock of the death intruding into the regular rhythm of life had broken the day in two. Kate's talk turned the plain light of every day on this one more in a long succession of bodies, making their work with it an ordinary thing to do.

"Well," she said, as they finished. "There's a sup of the cup in every house and all must take it. I'll be goin now but I'll be back after they come from work and Larry with me. It's not much of a wake Owen will have in this god-forsaken place and him with no family but the one brother. It's well for him he had women like me and you to do the right thing by him or McCarthy and Lordon would shovel him under with a God-rest-your-soul-and-back-to-the-job-boys. That's what passes for a funeral on the canal."

Mary didn't know what the men got to eat that day. Kate's last words had brought it home to her that there was no priest here and no old woman who could be called on to keen at the wake.

Kate can maybe whine and cry a bit if someone else puts the words together but I never heard her claim to have the way of keening the dead . . . nor has she the obligation on her to Owen, him not being much more than a stranger to her. There's only myself. Can I do it?

There was a turmoil of feelings inside her. They could come out only in a sob or a wail but that was not enough. It was words that were needed. When she was handing out the noon dinner to the men who took it in unaccustomed silence, she managed to get a word with Dan.

"What kind of an end for Owen is this and no way to bury him among his own people at all? There's no priest to say a prayer over him. And where is his mother? Over the water, not knowin even the earth come down on him. No one but Johnny to grieve for him and no one to keen him at all."

Dan shrugged. "So . . . there's this in it—no priest, no wake offerin. We can say a few prayers, can't we? Johnny can keen his brother and couldn't you do it, too, as well as any of the old ones?"

Could I? I keened my Gran, I keened my babies, but then my words poured out of my grief. I don't have the full heart like that for Owen, sorry as I am for his goin. Without the heavy grief on me I can maybe think of the words easier . . . the best words to say for Owen.

She hadn't been long back in the cookhouse till she left Johnny to the sorrow and Susan to the work. The sun warmed her as she followed the path walked so many times to fetch water, away from the noise of the job.

Where the pool was, where they dipped the buckets, there was deep shade from the oaks on the high bank across the stream. It was green shade still, though red showed here and there on the sumac and the dogwood had already shed some red leaves on the pool. The bank was low on this side and covered with stones. She sat down, shifting her body about to avoid the sharp places.

Swift and smooth, the water slid over the rock that carried it into the pool. It sounded the pool's depths and ran shallowly on over the gravel beyond. The cool sound of the water flowed into her troubled thoughts, sounded their depths, murmured quietly on till she murmured to herself that a moment's rest would help. She stretched out her tired body and fell asleep.

The bumpy hardness of her bed soon woke her and she hardly knew she had been asleep, so easily she slipped into sounding the words.

Here far from home . . .

She sat up and dipped up some of the water to cool her face. Words echoed from keens recited around the hearths of Carrignahown or at other hearths when it was Gran doing the keening . . . words from the lament Gran had made for the son that was her own father . . . words she herself had recited from that lament many a time . . . words she had recited from Ellen O'Leary's famous lament for her husband.

Now it's young Owen I'm keenin . . . Owen so gay and strong. It's words I'm needin to shape his livin and his dyin . . . young Owen who made a gay fight of it, here far from home.

Homesickness Mary carried around with her always but hardly knew it was there under the ceaseless activity of the daily work. Now it swept over her and almost swept the words away but she held on to them.

She said them over to herself and began to add more, drawing them from her own grief and longing for home, from Johnny's grief, drawing them from the small last part of Owen's life that was all of it she knew, choosing the words with the right sound to them, fitting them to the rhythm.

Owen Brennigan's wake was talked of for months along the canal. As Pat and Dan walked back along the line after digging the grave, they had taken the news of it with them. That night more than two hundred came to walk around the bier in the cookhouse, to kneel and say a prayer for Owen's soul, to take a pinch of snuff or smoke a pipe and then to drift outside for a drink, leaving room inside for others.

Johnny had mortgaged his winter's work for the whiskey and the tobacco so it could be known here, as it had been known back in Sligo, that Owen was a fine lad and a brave fighter and so it could be seen that he had a brother who could wake him properly on his way from this world to the next. But try as he would, when it came to the keening, Johnny could only stammer incoherently over his brother's body.

Mary gave his grief expression. She began with the words she had found in the afternoon by the stream. She had gone on building on them as she hurriedly threw the evening meal together. Now Kate and Bridget sat with her at the head of the bier, rocking their bodies and clapping their hands in time with hers as they joined in intoning the words of woe that came in like a chorus.

> You were the one laughing,
> Always laughing, Owen,
> Young Owen of the merry eyes.
> You made a gay fight of it
> Here far from home.
>> Far from ho-o-ome, far from ho-o-ome,
>> Och-o-one o-o-oh, och-o-one o-oh.

They were all far from home and most were young. The shuffling of feet quieted till her voice could be heard in every corner of the cookhouse. Donal Shelley, standing in the open door, turned and hushed those outside.

> Too soon it is

To put down your pick
Owen of the strong arms.
Too soon to lie quiet
In the cold ground.

Her ringing tones brought more men from outside to the door, pushing those at the doorway in. Dan was standing near Johnny, resting his hand on the younger man's shoulder.

Mary's voice is hittin me like she's the clapper and I'm the bell. I've heard her like that sometimes tellin a story . . . No, nothin quite like this before . . . nothin like this . . .

Lift the pick again, Owen.
Strike hard on the stubborn earth
Where it came down on you.
Take back the years
It was taking from you,
Years to find a wife,
To come in from work
To your own hearth,
To hold sons and daughters
In your strong arms.

Had it been myself . . . I can still feel it in the shoulder where the timber hit, how close it was to bein me instead of Owen . . . or the both of us . . . What would have happened then to Mary and Ellen till the boys was old enough to work?

Mary's voice changed. It was the mother herself now, crying for her son.

My love and my babe,
I cried once
And you coming out of my body
Where I cradled you
For three seasons.
I cried twice
And you going away from me
To a man's work,
Bouchaleen of the bright hair.
I cried three times
And you going across the water.
Now I will cry once
And twice and three times
Each day and each night
For the pain under my heart
Where I cradled you,
For the space in my cabin
You will never fill.

The great numbers that had come to the wake bore Mary up. More and more words seemed to come from them to her and flow back to them. Owen was borne up on her words, his life given the dignity that belonged to it.

All in the room were hushed by the sound of Mary's voice and the rhythm of the keening. Johnny moved closer to Dan. The tears were running down his cheeks but he was catching his breath to keep from sobbing so loud he couldn't hear Mary's words. Dan felt the tears in his own eyes.

What a power is in Mary. More than ten years we been man and wife and I never knew . . .

She was giving Owen his due, so it should be known who he was, so he shouldn't be thought a bit of driftwood, tossed up on a foreign shore with none caring.

> Here is your brother John
> Who was with you in Sligo
> With you on the water,
> With you coming to Ohio.
> For every day he was laughing with you
> He'll have a day grieving for you.
> Here is Jamie McCarthy,
> Chief to you in the new country,
> You the good man to him
> With the spade and the scraper.

Here is Jamie, indeed, standing near the head of the bier as if this was all done by his orders and swellin up when his name comes in it. Is he hearin any of the words at all, the way his head turns from one side to the other? . . Mary still thinks Jamie the fine man entirely. She thinks the notion of puttin Owen away without a wake was nothin but a confusion in Pat's head but I doubt it was . . . I doubt it . . .

The look Dan gave Jamie was colder and more appraising than any he had ever cast on his old friend before. He moved closer to Johnny, listening with him, with the other diggers who had worked beside Owen. It was them Mary was speaking for.

> Here are your friends
> Coming to you in the hundreds,
> Tipping the jug with you
> At the end of the work.
> They know you for your hard strike
> On the stubborn earth,
> Men that dug with you.
> They will strike many blows for you
> With their iron picks
> On the earth that closed your laughing mouth,
> And you to lie under it,
> Under a strange stone, far from home.
> > Far from ho-ome, far from ho-ome
> > Och-one o-oh, och-one o-oh.

Chapter 7

W HEN THE MUD had been shoveled out of the lock pit and the pile driver put firmly in place above, they began to drive the piles. Then Owen's strong back and sturdy arms were badly missed. They got everything in place late one morning and began with a good heart to drive the first pile. There were only Johnny, Pat, Larry Dugan and Dan to grasp four of the five ropes dangling from the lead line to pull the heavy oak-butt hammer high on the leads. When the hammer was released, it descended on a pile and drove it with a satisfying *thunk* into the earth.

"Suas libh!" Pat called out and again they wound the rope up and raised the hammer.

"Sios libh!" and down it went again. It took the hammer only seconds to fall, driving the pile a few inches further in. Again they had to grasp the ropes, again they felt the lead line tighten, again they braced themselves against the weight of the mighty hammer. They had not been many times through the cycle when their feet began to slow and their chests to heave with their labored breath.

"They're slowing down," Jim Dent said to Jamie. "You've got to put another man there on that fifth rope, one at least, maybe two."

The need was so desperate, Jamie even offered Zeke Johnson a job, when he strolled up to see what was doing. Zeke shifted his plug to his other cheek and chewed in silence, casting the glance of an expert canal-watcher at the straining men, then gave his considered opinion.

"What you need there, McCarthy, is one or two as strong as Hobbs."

"I know what I need," Jamie said impatiently. "What I don't know is where to get 'em. Who's Hobbs?"

"Strongest feller in eastern Ohio. Black as a piece a iron and just as strong. You want him?"

"Can I get him?" Jamie was skeptical about Zeke's stories but it was clear Zeke wasn't going to work and he wasn't more than half a man, anyhow.

"Tell you what I'll do. I'll go over to his place—it's no more'n two miles north and I'll see if I can't get him over here for you. Or, no . ." Zeke squinted at the sun and shook his head regretfully. "It's most noon. I'll have to be gettin on home and get some victuals."

"Allright, allright. Stay here and have some victuals and then go after this Hobbs."

While they were eating, Zeke told them about Peter Hobbs. "He could pick up that log there under one arm and another log under the other and just walk off with 'em like they was a couple of twigs."

Dent finished his bread and meat and lay down, putting his hat over his eyes to keep out the October sun. "And I wouldn't be surprised if you weren't the biggest liar in the State of Ohio, Zeke."

"It's the God's truth." Zeke was all injured innocence. "Let me tell you about Hobbs and Godfrey. Drives a sharp bargain, Godfrey does. This time I'm tellin, he come along with a barrel of flour in his wagon, when he seen Hobbs. He figures he'll have a little fun with the black feller and see can he get double his price for the flour.

"So Godfrey says to Hobbs, 'What'll you give me for this barrel of flour?' Well, Hobbs he'd done his butcherin and he had him a smoke house full of good ham and bacon, so he offered Godfrey forty pounds in trade for the flour. First Godfrey held out for fifty, then he said he'd give Hobbs a real bargain. He could have the barrel of flour for forty pounds of ham if Hobbs would bring him the ham and then carry the barrel of flour off. And if he couldn't carry it, then Godfrey would keep the ham *and* the flour. You know how much a barrel of flour weighs?"

They were all gathered around Zeke now. Even Dent had got interested in the story in spite of himself, and answered, "Close to two hundred pounds."

"That's right, and Godfrey didn't think Hobbs could do it. Hobbs ain't all that big—not tall like Brennigan here—but he's got a pair of shoulders on him Godfrey shoulda looked at closer. He went back to his smokehouse and brung the meat like he was carryin nothin but a bag of sugar candy. Then he jumped in the wagon, dropped the ham, let down the tailgate and rolled the barrel off. Upended it and just picked it right up and damned if he didn't get it clear up on his shoulder and walk off home with it. I seen it myself. Fact is, if I hadn't, probably no one would have knowed. Hobbs don't talk much, kind of a close-mouthed feller. Just happened me and the old lady come along just then and seen the whole thing. Oh, I tell *you* . . ." Zeke slapped his leg and snickered. "Folks around here wouldn't let Godfrey forget that. 'Sold any flour to Hobbs lately?' they'd holler at him."

As the rest of them walked over to the pile-driver to maneuver it into place for the next pile, Johnny said to Dan, "You ever worked with one of them black fellers?" When Dan shook his head, Johnny went on, "You want to?"

"You want to wind up that capstan by yourself?" Dan asked him.

By the time Zeke came back with Hobbs, Dan was ready to drop and John was in no mood to refuse help. They all stared curiously at the man as he stood with Jamie and the engineer, listening as Jamie explained the work and the wages and responding with an occasional, "Yes, sir," or "Why, sure."

His broad shoulders, thick neck, deep chest and muscular arms confirmed Zeke's opinion of his strength. His skin was very black. To the Irish that gave him a strange, almost an exotic look.

When Dent asked him for his free papers, he looked squarely at the engineer and said, "I was born free."

"Yes, that's allright," Dent didn't know why he should be flustered. "But you see, it's the law. We can't give you work unless we see your free papers."

"I don't think you're givin me nothin. I'm gon do some of your work and you're gon pay me some wages. I'm a free man and this here is a free state. I come from a free state—that's Pennyslvania. I was born free and that's all about it." He paused for a moment. "You want me to go to work or not?"

"*I* want you to go to work," Jamie didn't see why he should give a damn about the law and if Dent would keep his mouth shut about it, no one else would know or care either.

Hobbs walked over to the crew and grasped the last of the ropes.

Pat gave the word in English, knowing the black man wouldn't have the Irish.

"Up!" and the five men leaned into the task. The capstan began to move. It would have taken more than the addition of one man, however strong, to make the job easy but now at least it was possible.

The next day Mary left Susan to take care of the Lock Seven crew and brought the noon dinner down the line herself to see the black man, with Ellen tagging along.

Hobbs had brought his own dinner and sat a little apart from the others as Mary handed out the cold bread and meat. He was listening to the talk of the Irish workers. Their brogue and the frequent Gaelic words rang with a strange, almost an exotic sound to him.

Ellen stared at Hobbs with unabashed curiosity, gradually moving a little closer, At first he paid no attention to her. Except for an occasional questioning glance at Mary or the men, he seemed to giving his whole attention to his food.

When Ellen had come quite close, he said, "Howdy, little girl."

She moved still closer and slowly putting out one finger, touched his bare arm and then bringing her finger back, looked at it in surprise.

"It won't come off," he told her.

"Is it black you are all the way through?" she asked.

"No, just on the outside."

"Is there a girsha at home in your shanty?" Now it was the man who looked blank. Ellen repeated her question. "Do you be Daddy to a girsha like me?"

"Oh, a little girl? Yes, I got one about your size. Got a little bitty baby, too, and a big boy and a big girl."

"Would they be black, too?"

"Yes, they black, too."

"Why?"

"'Cause God made them and me black, just like he made you and your papa and mama white."

"Why?"

"You got more questions than my little Lucille. I don't know why. I reckon he just likes some of his folks white and some of 'em black."

As the days passed and Dan became accustomed to Hobbs, he began to see Peter as a man who had started with nothing and now had an Ohio farm. In the brief pauses in the work, Peter showed that when given the opportunity to talk he was far from being as close-mouthed as Zeke had described him.

He had left home in Philadelphia about twenty years before when he was sixteen and begun to work his way west. In Pittsburgh he had tied up with a white man by the name of Robinson, a single man travelling west with a team, a wagon and the basic tools of the frontier farmer. Robinson had been taken sick in Pittsburgh. Peter had driven the team from there while Robinson lay in the wagon.

They had squatted on Spring Creek, building a cabin there, with Robinson supplying the tools and the experience and Peter doing the work. Years went by, with Robinson always thinking he would be better the next week or the next month. Meanwhile, Peter cleared the land, put in the corn, bought the hogs and learned how to be a farmer. When Robinson had a bad spell, Peter was cook and nurse as well as farmer. When Robinson died, it was obviously Peter's place. He had stayed on, building on the start they had made together. He had gone east only once, to get a wife.

"The place ain't rightly all mine, yet," he explained to Dan. "Us bein squatters, we didn't pay nothin when we come. Turned out it belonged to one of these here rich men back east. He sold a thousand acres to Mr. Kirkham. When Kirkham come out here, I thought I'd have to go." He shook his head. "That woulda hurt, after all the work I put in. But he wanted to be down by the river, not up where I was. I helped him build his cabin and pretty well supplied him his first winter and he say I could buy my hundred and sixty acres off him. That's what I done but I still owe him some. Since this canal work started, I been sellin some of my truck to one or another a these canal folks. That helps. Never did sell nothin to your boss, though. Now I reckon I'll get a little of his cash money as long as the pile drivin lasts."

Ohio's October days followed each other, not with grey skies above and white mists curling up out of the glens, as October came to Ireland, but with a high blue in the sky and a warm dry golden fall of sunlight and autumn leaves. One Sunday afternoon, Dan took Ellen along and let the sun and the breeze carry them past Kirkham's farm and up Spring Creek to Hobbs's place. The bare ground was covered now with drifts of color. Ellen ran ahead, kicking the leaves and tossing them in the air by the handsful till she tired and had to be lifted to Dan's shoulders.

Lucille Hobbs ran out of the cabin behind her father as they approached but she was not content to look at Ellen from below and had to be swung up to her father's shoulders. While the fathers walked barnyard and field, the two girls, lofty and secure, peeped sidewise at each other with solemn faces. Then Lucille, a teasing glint in her dark eyes, the red ribbons on her tight braids bobbing, leaned over and gave Ellen a little push. Ellen pushed back. The fathers set them down.

They chased each other through the sunshine, buried each other in the rustling leaves and rocked Lucille's baby brother in his cradle. Late in the afternoon they sat side by side in the cabin doorway while Lucille's mother gave them each a cup of buttermilk. Ellen called it 'skimmagig' which made Lucille giggle till Ellen caught the infection. The two of them were soon pointing at each other, yelling 'skimmagig' and breaking into new fits of giggling.

Dan's dream of a farm, like Mary's, had been sketched in lines borrowed from the farms of Cork, lines he had been trying without success to connect with Ohio woods and hills. There would be a whole new farm to make here, in one of the places where there had been no farm. He had never put his hand to that kind of task.

Jamie, who had been so quick with an answer to every question about the new country and its ways, so full of stories about his own success in mastering its difficulties, had been no help. He had no interest in the farms and the farming here and Dan began to believe he had no knowledge of them, either.

Now, as Dan walked back to camp, he was picturing to himself a solid log barn and cabin, neatly enclosed in rail fence, with fields and orchards mellow in harvest abundance. He was sketching his dream anew, fitting it snugly into the Ohio country. The cost of horses and harness, of wagon and plow, of cows and hogs, of seeds and fruit trees, was forgotten; so were the years of clearing and planting, of good harvest and bad that would have to come between dream and reality.

It was a dream so bathed in October sun that it warmed Dan even in November and December when the cold wind from the lake came tearing down the valley, when his bones ached with the wet cold and his ears got frostbitten.

As much as they wanted to make up for lost time, Jamie and Simon didn't keep the whole force working through the winter. There were too many days when work was impossible. Masonry couldn't be done in the cold weather at all. The diggers who still owed passage money were kept on and a few others. When the weather was good and more hands were needed, Hobbs and other local farmers or farmers' sons were hired by the day.

There was grumbling among the Irish when the local men appeared on the job. Why couldn't Jamie and Simon have kept on Falvey or Regan instead of bringing in these foreigners with their strange speech and unfamiliar ways who seemed to think themselves better than the Irish. Most of the men had a grudging respect for Hobbs's strength; still, his dark skin made him the strangest of all the strange men with whom they had to work. At least they themselves were white like the other local men, not black like Hobbs.

Garrett Riley was the worst at such talk. He had come up from Cincinnati in early fall and was full of stories about what a big man he was in that city, ever ready to give the rest of them lessons in American ways. When resentment rose against the local farmers, he turned it against Hobbs. Others might have to be tolerated, Riley suggested, but the black man was fair game.

"In Cincinnati," he said, "we know the difference between a white man and a nigger. We don't give white men's jobs to niggers."

Hobbs became the butt of one nasty little trick after another. When he opened his noon dinner one day, the meat had been taken out from between the two pieces of bread and replaced by a dead frog. He fell in the mud at the edge of the lockpit on a wet morning and might have gone over if Pat hadn't caught his legs. He rose up, dripping and angry, looking for the man who had tripped him but no one was ready to point a finger.

Mary had a dislike for Riley who gave orders at the table as if he were the lord and she the servant and who took every chance he could get to put his hands on Susan. She was blossoming out with the first signs of womanhood and several of the young men, Johnny Brennigan among them, were looking her way.

"You watch your step with all of 'em," Mary told her. "A girl likes a kiss and a cuddle with a good lad, but you be ready to slap and run if they try goin further. These canal men is here today and gone tomorrow and you're young yet. Riley, now, don't you let him get in arm's reach. He's one of them kind thinks God put women on earth for their pleasure. Rotten on the inside, that one is."

On one of the bad days when all the men were in the cookhouse, Riley was standing in front of the fire when Mary came with a heavy pot to hang over the flame.

"Get yourself out of the way of the work, will you?"

He went on talking to the men nearby without moving an inch or giving her a word in answer.

"Now then, *Mister* Riley, *sir*! Do you hear what I was after sayin? I can't hang the pot and tend the fire and cook the dinner with you standin in the way." She had raised her voice. The men standing around stopped talking to listen.

"Go along, woman, go along." He flapped his hand at her. "Don't you see I'm talking here to Kevin and Martin?"

She gave him a bump with her hip, shoving him a step away and reached around him to get the pot on the hook. "If it's a piece of your fat rump the men wants for dinner, you can go on roastin it. I'm thinkin they'd like a bit of somethin tastier."

That brought a laugh. Martin Daly moved farther from the fire himself, saying, "Come on, come on, Riley."

"Get out of Mary's way or she'll be puttin *you* on the fire," Jamie called from across the room.

"That moved him," Mary said to Dan later. "It's a wonder to me Jamie kept that one when he let men go that was with him longer than you and me. 'Go along, woman,' he says to me. Thinks he's king of America."

"And not worth a tinker's dam on the job," Dan added.

"He'll catch Susan by herself one day and her not much more than a child. He's always pattin and pinchin and whisperin in her ear till he's makin her dizzy with it. Wouldn't you say a word on it in Jamie's ear?"

He looked at her in astonishment. "I don't wag my tongue against any man works beside me."

"You're talkin like Riley is one of Ours and Jamie one of Them."

Dan shut his mouth and shook his head. That seemed to be the end of it. Mary had to be satisfied to say her own word in Johnny's ear about walking Susan home when her day's work was done and behaving himself while he was about it.

A few days later, while they were having their noon dinner, Dan heard Riley telling Jamie he wanted to leave the job in the middle of the work.

"There's some business I have in the town, Mr. McCarthy, and it can't be done of a Sunday," he was saying.

"Go to town, then, damn you. Go," Jamie snapped. "There'll be no pay for you this day. What little you done in the morning don't half make up for the way you come draggin in here at the tail of the crew and leanin on your shovel like it was a walkin cane. If I don't start gettin a day's work out of you, you can go to town and stay there."

Kevin Casey was sitting next to Dan on one of the big stones that would be going into the lock walls. When Riley had gone off Kevin gave Dan a dig in the ribs with his elbow.

"McCarthy can cuss and blow all he wants. Riley don't care. He won't be here long anyhow. Did McCarthy know what his business was, he wouldn't a been so quick to let him go to town."

"What's Riley up to now?"

At first Kevin kept his mouth shut and looked smug but he couldn't resist letting the secret out. "It's them free papers Hobbs was supposed to have to get hired. He don't have 'em and the boss took him on anyway. Riley's goin to town to get the law on Hobbs *and* McCarthy. The boss, he'll have to pay a fine, and Riley gets half of it for turnin him in. Soon as he gets it in his pocket, he'll be off down the road."

They were on their way back to work by this time. Dan stopped and grabbed Kevin's arm to stop him, too. "This is the God's truth? That gommoch is goin to town to bring the law down on Jamie and put Peter out of a job?"

"Now don't you go tellin the boss. I swore to Riley I wouldn't tell nobody. Don't you go gettin me in trouble."

Dan pushed him away. "Och, go on to work and try keepin your own mouth shut for a change. Don't you know if we get the law down on us here, there's no knowin where it'll stop? They take Jamie away, and what happens to us and our jobs?"

He looked around for Jamie. This wasn't carrying tales on one of his mates. This was protecting his own against the law.

"I'll kill him, I'll kill him." Jamie hissed it out between his teeth when he heard what Riley was about. "We got to stop him before he gets to town. Come on, Dan, you and me . . ."

He left Pat in charge and the two of them were off up the path, their thoughts and their bodies in step. This was the way they used to be in it together. They weren't but a stone's throw away from the job before Pat came pounding after them.

"McCarthy! McCarthy!" he called out, "We just got the word from below, the Commissioner's been down on Section Twenty. He's comin this way."

"God damn it, he would come today."

"Let me take Pat with me then," Dan suggested, "if you have to go back. Or Hobbs—he's got reasons for stoppin Riley and he can keep his mouth shut."

"Take Hobbs," Jamie decided. "Just as well if Mr. Kelley don't see him on the job today."

"The both of us to get our pay the same as if we was here?"

"My word on it," Jamie threw over his shoulder as he hurried back to the job.

Garrett Riley strolled slowly up the road toward town, feeling quite pleased with himself. He had taken his time about shaving, putting on a clean shirt and brushing his good trousers and his city hat. It was important to look respectable when he went up in front of the Judge to swear against McCarthy.

The Judge would get Hobbs up before him and find out Riley's had been a true swearing. The only question was, how big a fine would they put on McCarthy? If the Judge had the right attitude about uppity blacks that broke white laws, the fine might be as much as fifty dollars. That would mean a nice fat twenty-five for himself. There was no telling what it would be, up here in this part of the state. Hobbs would be out of a job, anyway, and out of his farm, too, more than likely. That would teach him to act like he was white.

He heard a rustling in the bushes by the side of the road and had his knife out even before he saw who the men were who jumped to the road from behind the trees, but Dan was too quick for him, Peter too strong.

He was on his back in the dirt with the knife under Dan's foot. Dan was about to give Riley a kick but stopped himself. "Let's leave it till there's a word said while he can still hear it."

He looked down at the man in the road. "You're not wanted in the camp and you're leavin out of it when we're done with you. There's your things beside the road. Show your face around here again and that's the last time you show it anywhere. Open your gob about what has nothin to do with you and we'll find a way to shut it so it won't open again. Do you take my meanin?"

"I do, I do indeed." Riley cautiously got to his feet. "You'd be lettin me go now, wouldn't you now? I'll be out of here this very minute, now this very minute. You'll never see me again, I swear to God." He edged toward his bundle, but they were closing in on him again.

"Don't let the holy name of God cross your lips," Dan said contemptuously. "You do well to call for help but the likes of you has a right to call on your master in the other place."

"Why Dan Griffen." Riley backed away, holding out his hand to ward them off. "Why would you be angry with a Cork man like myself that has only the greatest respect for another good man from the old country?"

Talking like they were two Cork men together deserved only one answer. Dan gave it to him between the eyes. Riley staggered and would have run off but Peter blocked his way and he suffered for his sins in the next few minutes. He was bloody and reeling when Peter's fist, propelled by a lifetime of coming up against high walls and low insults, hit him one more blow on the side of his head. He collapsed in the road.

Dan cooled off at once. "You take him under the arms, there, Peter and I'll get the feet. Off the road with him. He's not fit to be seen. You come close to finishin him with that last tap."

As they dragged the unconscious Riley into the woods, Dan continued, "We're far enough away from the road, now. Just roll him under that bush while we give a thought to what we'll be doin with him."

He stood looking down at Riley's face, swollen and smeared with blood and dirt. "I'll tell you how it is, Peter. If we hadn't been so gentle we could drop him in the river. A little more gentle and he could have walked away on the two feet of him. The way it is, he's like a sack of spoiled oats. It's in need of a horse and wagon we are now to get him out of this."

"I'll fetch my team and wagon quick's I can," Peter offered. "I reckon you don't mind watchin over him? Don't look like he's gon wake up yet awhile."

He looked down at the inert Riley. "If we hadn't shut him up, I wouldn't get another day's work on the canal, but that ain't nothin. They claim black folks not supposed to settle here at all 'thout free papers and we supposed to get somebody to go our bond for five hundred dollars. Most folks round here don't care nothin bout that. I was here before they was, anyhow—give many of 'em a hand gettin started. They won't start no such foolishness. But if *he* bring in the *law* and the *court* no tellin what might happen. Reckon I could lose my place. When it get in the courts our folks don't have a chance. The white folks do all the preachin in court. We have to just set there and say amen."

"Wouldn't there be a way you could get free papers?"

"I had 'em." Hobbs struck the rough bark of an oak with his open hand for emphasis. "*I had 'em.* Leastways, my pa did. Him and my mama bought theirselves. Work out, you know, for wages, and the master, he let 'em keep part till they save enough to buy theirselves. Had a paper to prove it. Brung it all the way from North Carolina to Philadelphia. Then that little old place they live in got burnt out and the paper burnt up with everything else." He struck the tree again. "Why they have to tie us up with all this paper foolishness?"

When he came back, Riley was groaning and showing signs of returning consciousness. They heaved him into the wagon bed and covered him with an old horse blanket and a couple of sacks.

"If we have any sense in us at all," Dan said to Peter as he climbed in beside Riley, "we don't be leavin the likes of this behind the backs of both of us."

They rode on till dark, having agreed that Riley should be left far enough down the road toward Cleveland to keep going in that direction. When they deposited him a few yards off the road near the village of Boston he moaned that he was destroyed entirely. Dan took this for a sign that he would be well able to be on the move in the morning. They left him with some confidence they wouldn't be seeing him again.

On the ride back through the dark, free now of their burden, the two men sat side by side on the wagon seat while the horses clopped slowly up the cold, moon-lit road. Both were tired. The quiet between them was an easy quiet. The moon was round and full; before their journey was over it was high in the sky, its light everywhere, the shadows as scant as in the noonday sun. It wasn't a light to work or fight by. It was a quiet light.

When Peter halted the team near the camp, Dan jumped down without a word. Then he turned, gave Peter a grin and a little salute. Peter's smile was wide as he lifted his hand in return.

The work went more smoothly with Riley gone but when Jamie paid Hobbs at the end of the month, he told him not to come back. Dan got Jamie aside when he was through giving out the pay. "Don't you know it was Peter helped rid us of Riley?" he protested.

"Don't you know Riley wouldn't a had a handle against me if Hobbs hadn't been on the job?" Jamie retorted. "I got enough trouble. I won't be invitin no more."

Hobbs was climbing the hill behind the shanties. When he reached the road he looked back and saw the two white men standing together below. Then he turned and walked away.

Chapter 8

ONE MORNING when snow made it impossible to work, Dan spent the time in Hall's store, carefully turning over each of the few books that Hall laid before him. He came back with *The American Spelling Book* by Noah Webster. He and Mary had the thought since they first saw how Tim took to the books that he might make a priest someday. It would never do to let him lose the little learning he brought over the water with him and it would do Danny no harm to get the reading, either.

Each day thereafter when the weather interrupted the work, Dan took the boys into the cold end of the room where he could make himself heard and gave them a lesson in the reading and the spelling. With the blackened end of a stick from the fire they learned to write their letters on the rough slabs of the wall.

Ellen loved the lesson times. Sitting in Dan's lap, she could look at the pictures in the book and listen to the fables being read. Taking a stick like her brothers, she could make her own marks on the wall.

One day Dan opened the chest they had brought from Ireland and carefully took out the book he had from his father.

"You, Tim and Danny, you can read out of this book when you get more of the reading. You're not too young now to know that your grandfather was one of those called United Irishmen. It would be a shame to him were you to grow up too ignorant to read his book."

Both the boys could read out the name, *The Rights of Man*. Both could touch the worn cover with respect, where it bore the scars of much reading and much hiding when the finding of it could mean hanging. Then Dan gave them a bit of it here and there, the way it made sport of the English king and held up the better way things were done in America.

"This book come from the days when the people in America threw the English into the sea," Dan told them, "when the people in France cut off the head of their king. There was an uprising in Ireland itself and my father was in it. It wasn't against Them in the Big Houses only, it was to put the English out of the island of Erin altogether. It wasn't a fight to bring back the old days neither, but to do without kings and lords and give each man his own rights, the way it tells in this book."

Dan used the winter days too, to prod the men who were native to the country with questions on the way of the buying of land and the way of the working of it. It wasn't all good news he got in the answers.

Twenty acres was a mere dooryard in their thinking. Even a hundred and sixty such as Hobbs had was looked on as a small farm. Land along the canal route was going fast and the closer to the canal, the higher the price. Farther south there was said to be some Congress land still a man could get for a dollar and twenty-five cents an acre but you'd better be a good man with an axe with all the clearing there would be to do on it. At best, it would be several years before you could get a crop in. A man had to be more a hunter than a farmer in those first years if he wanted something to eat and something to trade for flour and salt and shoes.

A dollar and twenty-five cents an acre! For a hundred and sixty acres he would need two hundred dollars, fifty of it to start with. They gave you four years to pay but what was the good of that if it was three or four years before you could make a crop?

Dan asked Donal Shelley was he saving from his good carpenter's wages to buy a piece of land or was his American woman bringing him a farm.

"Would I be plantin my two feet in the ground when there's a whole world to see? All I need is my bag of tools to find me a job in another place. That's a ripe woman I've got and a kind one. I'll tell you what she gives me: A warm welcome whenever I come to her door, a plate of good food on the table, a jug at my elbow and kisses from her soft lips. A touch of Donal's hand only or a word from Donal's tongue and she's down on her back for me. The rest of these lads lay in a row in the shanty there, groanin and complainin they haven't got a woman this side of the water or they line up behind the tavern for their two-bits worth of a whore and all the time, Donal Shelley is pickin the sweetest fruit that grows in Ohio."

"But there's no farm in it?" Dan persisted.

"She's got a farm itself that I could get for the askin but I'll be off over the hill before she can hitch me to that nag."

Dan didn't half believe it. If Donal could get the American farm with her, he'd be a fool to go off unless the woman was an old hag altogether and not the pretty piece Donal made her out.

Mary was entranced with the idea of a farm like the Higbees' with a barn for the cows and a pen for the pigs and a cellar dug into the ground to keep the potatoes in. She told Bridget about it one afternoon when she came in with her two little ones, Kathleen and Terry, playmates to Ellen.

Bridget came often to get a bit of the warmth from the big fire. She turned to and helped with whatever task Mary had in hand and they talked along with it, their heads close together to get each other's words under the noise. Or if the weather was open enough for the men to work outside, they had the cookhouse to themselves.

They could have spun away whole days telling the way it was in the childhood and youth of each and how they found their men and what had happened to them since marriage. When Bridget knew she would be having another baby come summer, it was Mary had the first tidings of it and it would be Mary who would be at her side to help her with the birth.

Sometimes on a work day, Jamie left the men at it and popped into the cookhouse in the middle of the morning or the afternoon for a hot cup of tea, a quick warm-up by the fire and a little friendly talk with Mary—a pinch of salt that took the sameness out of the day's work. He teased Susan about how the young fellows were all after her, making her giggle and toss her head. He gave Mary's hand a quick squeeze when he handed back the cup, patted Susan's cheek and was off to the job.

Mary had to rise as early as in summer while the rest of the camp still slept and cook the breakfast while it was like midnight outside. Every moment of light was precious, none must be wasted in eating, except at noon. The men had breakfast in the dark of the morning and were out on the job before the sun rose at seven. They worked till the dark of the evening and had supper by firelight. Still, the workdays were short for the men and there was some ease to Mary's work, too, from the cut in the work force.

Mary was out in the clearing one late afternoon, having come out to call the boys and send them for water before dark. She stood there after they had run off with the buckets, watching the color fade out of the clouds in the western sky. It was a pleasure to her eyes, not a fear clutching her heart as it had once been. It was no matter if Dan were not safe inside, there was no curfew here. There was no danger the constables would come searching the house and find him absent. In those times, the very cows were supposed to calve only between sunrise and sunset.

The night itself had lost its terrors. When the river of men flowed out of the cookhouse at the end of the day, the Griffens were left to themselves. Quiet settled over them. The children fell asleep. Mary and Dan lingered a little at the hearth. The dark that was all around the pool of firelight was peaceful. There was no fear in the shadows around the sleeping children. The dark and the quiet stretched away from the camp as far as the ocean, so far there was cold and loneliness in it but it was peaceful still even in those far reaches.

They could talk a little about their own place they would have some day. That was the one thing that was for themselves only in this crowded camp. The hope was peaceful, like these moments by the fire, but it was lonely, too, to think of going off alone. They had gone off already from their own place and their own people. What would it be like out in the woods with only foreigners for neighbors, or maybe no neighbors at all?

When Mary had smoored the fire for the night, banking the ashes over the burning logs, she and Dan could move into the cold at the other end of the room, get in under the blankets and huddle close till their bodies warmed each other.

"Maire," Dan whispered then in the old way, bringing back her Irish self, while the dark hid all that was new and strange.

Sometimes the dark brought drowsy comfort, a few words said between them and a long night of sleep. Sometimes the warmth grew more intense, began to glow in breast and limbs, fused their bodies together. That was a pleasure no one could live without. There would be no more children for the two of them; they had known that since soon after Mary's bout with childbed fever. It had been a sadness to her then. She had said to herself that her woman's life was over and she still young. Yet there is something in being a woman and a man together that goes on whether there's another child to be making out of it or not.

Jim Dent rode into camp one rare sunny morning and came into the cookhouse where Mary was kneading the bread. He had a sheaf of papers in his hand and nailed one up on the inside of the door. All that day, Mary was wondering what was that paper, nailed up like an order from Cork Castle. It worried her but there was no one to read it to her, with the boys making the most of the good day to go after wood for the fire and all the men working.

When they came in at dusk, Jamie held up a candle and he and Donal read it to themselves while the men watched and waited.

"What is it sayin, then?" Pat asked as Jamie turned away.

"Why would Dent be puttin that bit of paper up here?" Jamie gave him a question for an answer. "It's not for us it has a thing in it at all. It's after hittin the contractors like Simpson who left out of here without payin his hands."

The men drifted uneasily away, looking over their shoulders at the white paper with its black, mysterious message. Dan, though, held out his hand to Jamie. "Give me the loan of that candle, will you, Jamie? Let me see can the boys read this for a lesson."

Tim ran over, eager to show off his learning. Danny followed and Mary left the stew to take care of itself on the fire and came, too.

"Notice to Laborers on the Canal." Tim's clear, boyish soprano brought the men around in an instant. He pointed at the words as he read them, with Danny trying to see under or over his arm.

He managed to get through the first paragraph of Mr. Kelley's notice with Danny chiming in on the easy words. Their father helped with 'character' and 'absconded,' mouthsful even for himself.

"Didn't I tell you what was in it?" Jamie was impatient. "There's not been a payday missed on this job."

"There was more than one payday missed down on Section Twenty-Nine where I was workin before," Martin Daly spoke up. "Your boys give us a nice bit of readin, Dan, but there's such a boilin of the big words there, I wouldn't know do I take its meanin or don't I."

"A boilin of the big words it is, indeed," Dan agreed. "Leave me study on it a little."

"Them big words don't mean a thing," Kevin Casey said contemptuously to hide his inability to read even the small ones.

No one minded him. They were eating now, keeping an eye on Dan who was silently reading the notice to the end and then going back to the beginning, going over it slowly, thinking and nodding to himself. He was closing his mouth more and more firmly, stretching his lips into a thin, straight line. When he joined them, heads turned toward him with questioning looks.

"Stew first and talk after," he said, picking up his spoon.

When supper was over he lit the candle again and went back to the paper. The rest stayed on the benches by the table, listening. Dan felt like a teacher with a big class of overgrown scholars.

"This bit of paper, here, it's like a letter from Mr. Kelley. He's after tellin us we should watch the bosses so they give us our pay. Like Jamie was sayin, we do get our pay on this job but some of the lads that left here when the winter started may hire on with a boss that wouldn't be keepin payday like a priest keeps Sunday. It could be that would happen to us one day."

"And what'll we be doin then?" Martin wanted to know.

"He's got four rules wrote out for us here." Dan held up one finger. "The first is, not to go to work for a boss with a . . ." There was a pause while he looked for the words, "a doubtful or bad character."

Dan's scholars became unruly at this point, their previous attention breaking up into a babble of talk.

Finally, Pat's voice dominated the rest. "Come on, now, Dan Griffen, were you a boss and myself askin you for the work, what would you be sayin if I asked into your character?"

"Myself bein a gentleman, I'm thinkin I'd say to you, 'Shut your gob, Pat Flynn, before I shut it for ye, or I'll be throwin ye into the canal.'"

The second rule told laborers working for a subcontractor to get a written order on the original contractor for their wages. This made no more sense than the first. If one of them did get something that was said to be such an order, he couldn't read it and wouldn't have the least idea what it really said.

The men were losing patience with Mr. Kelley's letter when Dan called out. "Now here's sense at last, lads. Let one month go by without pay but no more. If the boss won't pay you on the second payday, tell it to the Commissioner or the engineer."

"And what will they be doin at all?" Martin was skeptical.

"I'm thinkin they *could* make the boss pay, if they *would*," was the best answer Dan could give. "Mr. Kelley's not makin a promise, though, to any canal hand that comes askin. The last thing he says here . . ." Dan held up the candle and read it out: "Laborers who are unfaithful, idle or insolent, or who refuse to obey the direction of their employers, need not expect any assistance from the Commissioner in obtaining their wages."

Jamie had filled his pipe and walked over to the fire for a hot coal to light it, thinking that if Kelley were here he would put the name of 'insolent' on Dan for the way he was wagging his chin when silence would serve better.

Chapter 9

ARCH CAME to Ohio drenched in rain and melting snow that year of
1827. The canal camp was a sea of mud. Neither children nor adults
were ever dry and there was more coughing than there was talking in
the morning. Halfway through April there was a burst of sunshine. The leafless
forest that had been a gray-brown mass, the tops of its trees etching sharp lines
against the sky, began to soften its hard outlines with a hint of misty green. Finally, even the oldest oaks put out new leaves, tipped at first by a youthful pink.
Patches of grass came up beside the path to the Run. The sun shone on the green
blades that moved a little in a small wind.

Walking to the Run with a bundle of dirty clothes to wash, Mary felt the warmth
on her skin, breathed the smell of things growing, saw the green of the new leaves
and the way the sun shone through the trees to make moving patterns of brightness and shadow on the water.

The warmth went to her heart but there was a twist there with it from the
reminder it was of the way the sun shone through the trees on the water when she
carried her clothes to the stream in Carrignahown.

Ellen popped out of the cookhouse like a new bud bursting from a dark branch
and began to run about with Terry and Kathleen. Tim had real work to do now,
on a level below the locks, picking up rocks in the ditch for eleven cents a day.
That left Danny with all the fetching of wood and water to do. Being left behind
was hardly compensated by having the axe for himself.

For the men, spring brought a new drive to get the line finished from the
Summit south of Akron to Lake Erie. Mr. Kelley had the word that paper promises would sell no more canal bonds. There would have to be water in the canal
this summer to float real boats, bringing New York salt and merchandise from the
Lake and carrying Ohio wheat and corn, potash and whiskey back. If the boats
didn't float, the bonds wouldn't float either and there would be no funds for the
years of construction still ahead.

So Kelley was driven by the financiers in Philadelphia, New York and London.
He drove the engineers, the engineers drove the contractors and the contractors
drove the men.

Sometimes, when spring flooding damaged the canal banks, the work went on
even after sundown and supper. Fires burned at the canalside and torches lit up
the spring night. On McCarthy and Lordon's jobs, Lock Seven was finished and
paid off and the whole force concentrated below on Sixteen and Seventeen.

New men, just off the ships from Ireland, found their way to the canal as the
spring went on. Many were hired before they got as far as Akron. Nevertheless,
the force on the locks built up again. Cork bosses and Cork men in the crew were
magnets for men from that county. McCarthy and Lordon's reputation for good
food and regular pay helped, too.

With the longer days and the competition among contractors for hands, wages went up to ten dollars a month for the new men. It galled Dan that he was tied to eight dollars till his debt was paid off. Still, at the end of April there were only five marks left on the wall. There was a good hope that May or June would see the dead horse killed.

Tim's work would bring in a few pennies and Danny wanted to do what Tim did. He showed his father what strong arms he had. At ten, Danny was big enough, surely, to work. Back home he would already have been out of his mother's management and learning a man's work in field and haggard under Dan himself. There was no job for him under Dan's eye here but Dan had a word with Jamie as they walked back to their supper one evening, about a bit of pay for what Danny was doing.

"Come on, now," Jamie laughed. "You wouldn't be callin that work. It keeps the boy out of mischief and pays for his keep."

"Pays for his keep, is it?" Dan straightened his tired shoulders and threw Jamie a quick look. "And what is it that Mary's work pays for, if it wouldn't be for her keep and the childers?"

Jamie turned away with a question for Donal but Dan was not to be so easily shaken off. He kept pace with the two of them. At the first pause in their talk he said, "You have a right to know, Jamie, I'll be lookin for a place for Danny the way I found it for Tim."

Jamie went on talking to Donal, Dan dropped back to walk with Pat and Johnny and a moment later was laughing with them but there was a sore place inside him. It had something to do with Jamie keeping him tied to eight dollars when he paid new men ten and something to do with did the boy get paid for his work or didn't he and something to do with walking beside his old friend and getting Jamie's silence and Jamie's head turned away as if there were no Dan there at all.

After supper that night, Jamie called Danny over and making much of him for growing so big and strong, promised he should have two bits a week from there out. Mary was pleased. That night as they lay in bed she and Dan counted over all they would have coming in. "Sure we'll make it in May," Mary was exultant.

"I'm thinkin it will be a good day when we pay Jamie the last shillin we owe him," Dan said bitterly. "He's after becomin too grand a man entirely. Look you at the way the squireen of the Ohio Canal do be handin out a penny or two to Danny like a free gift from his kind heart."

When the May payday came around, Dan was in a holiday mood. This was the day he would kill the dead horse. It seemed only part of the holiday that Jamie was full of jokes and handing out a double jigger of whiskey when they came off the job. But when it was time to hand out the pay, Dan could see that there was something else entirely on Jamie's mind. The drinks had been just to grease the wheels before he took them over a bump in the road.

Usually he sat down at the table in the cabin with his paybook open in front of him and a stack of money at his hand. Today, he and Lordon and Dent, the engineer, all came out where the men were in front of the cabin. The paybook was in Jamie's hand but there was no money in sight.

"What we have to tell you," Jamie said, "We can't pay you today. We're out of money. There's a big payment due from the State but the Commissioner's check hasn't come yet. You have the promise of both Simon and me the minute the money comes from the State you'll get yours. You're after knowing the two of us never went back on a promise. The Commissioner don't go back on his promises neither but he's sometimes late. You didn't know it but it happened before. The other times we could put our hands on enough cash to pay wages but this time it will be a bit of a wait for all."

There was a stunned silence. The men looked at each other and back at the bosses.

Dent spoke up then and made his promises. "I certified a big piece of work finished and sent the word to the Commissioner. There's no doubt the money will come . . . certainly by the June payday, if not before."

The two bosses and the engineer went back into the cabin and closed the door. The silence of the men broke apart in angry muttering.

"That's a fine word to be givin a man at the end of a month's hard work," Martin Daly said bitterly to the closed door. "It don't just suit me to be payin you this day, but work another month and I'll see does it suit me better on the payday after."

"And what if it don't suit on the payday after?" someone called out from the edge of the crowd.

"That's the day I'll give out another handful of promises," Martin answered. He snatched off his hat and holding it upside down in the crook of his arm, threw out one handful of nothing after another. "Come one, come all, promises aplenty. Eat 'em, drink 'em, send 'em home to bring out your wife and your old parents. More where these come from!"

Pat Flynn turned to Dan. "You read it off that paper months back. If your boss don't pay, tell the engineer. If the engineer don't pay, tell the Commissioner. And what are we to do when the Commissioner don't pay?"

"You'll eat, whether or no," Larry Dugan threw in. "What about me and O'Scanlon here and the rest that boards ourselves? What do we eat? Canal mud?"

The words were hardly out of his mouth before Johnny picked up a chunk of wet dirt and slung it against the door. The door was jerked open and Jamie stood there, glaring out.

"Who threw that mud?" he demanded, knowing well he would get no answer. "Don't be a bunch of bloody fools. Do you think this is sport for me? There's material and tools and food that me and Simon has to buy and how the b'jesus I'm to do that without money, maybe y' can tell me." He looked challengingly from one to another, then added more calmly, "Go on, get your suppers now. There's nothin else to do."

"Mr. McCarthy, sir," Larry spoke up. "How are we to do that boards our-selves?"

"If you've been payin regular, Hall will be like to give you credit," Jamie answered impatiently. "It's only a few weeks. Go on, now, there's no use hangin around here. If I could pay you, I would. When I can pay you, I will."

Slowly, the men turned and began to walk toward the cookhouse, all but Dan. He had been turning the thing over in his mind, and it came to him that money or not, this was still his day. When the others were gone, he turned to Jamie.

"You can pay *me*."

"What?" Jamie was outraged.

"There's no money you'll be needin. Give over that paper I signed, where it says I was owin you five dollars. Then you can write in your book that you paid ıne five dollars."

"Why not?"

They went inside the cabin and it was done in a minute. Dan crushed the paper in his hand. A year's work it had taken, and now it was done. He wanted to let out a yell that would take the roof right off the cabin but there was another thing to be said. "And now, Jamie, it's ten dollars a month for me, like the other lads?"

"It's ten dollars."

Dan walked jauntily across to the cookhouse, whistling as he went. When he came through the door, his exuberance dashed against a wall of glum silence.

Pat looked at him suspiciously. "You look like a man that just got paid."

Dan wasn't listening. He waved the crumpled paper at Mary. "I killed the dead horse!"

That was all Pat needed. His ruddy face turned dark. Everybody knew Dan was a friend to the boss, but for him to get paid when no one else had a penny and then come in and throw it in their faces was too much. Before Dan could get a word said, Pat's fist was in his face. Johnny jumped to Dan's side. Kevin Casey, who had been cherishing a grudge against Johnny, was after him in a minute with his brother Mick close behind.

Soon all the men who were waiting their turns at the table were wading in on one side or the other, it didn't much matter which. All the resentment they couldn't take out on Jamie or the engineer or the absent Commissioner or the abstract State, they took out on each other. Those who were eating dropped their spoons and got to their feet. Only the Old Man, at fifty the oldest on the job, went on calmly eating his stew.

The cookhouse rocked under clumping boots as the battle raged in the cramped space between the table and the door. Trenchers and food began to fly. Ellen screamed.

"Get under the table," Mary commanded, pushing her down to safety with one hand while she grabbed her big spoon with the other. Ellen found it at least as terrifying under the table where she could hear the thunder above but could not see the storm. She hadn't been there a minute when the round red face of the Old Man on the round red bald head of him, with its fringe of gray hair, bobbed down.

"There now, there now, why you're bawlin like a new calf and nothin to bawl about at all, at all. Do you want your supper? Sure and why wouldn't you? Stay where you are now. Wipe the tears from your pretty eyes. Me and you, we'll have our suppers together."

Down he came under the table, with a trencher full of stew and two spoons. The two of them sat there and ate with the Old Man making such a joke of what was going on above that Ellen's fear was soon gone.

It seemed to Mary that everyone was against Dan. She began to lay about her with the spoon at whoever was near. She caught sight of Johnny reaching for the pot of hot stew. Down came the spoon across his hand. "Leave that. I didn't cook it to have some gommoch throw it."

Danny, determined to help his father, climbed up on the table and jumped on Pat's back while Tim dove for his legs. Pat shook himself free of the boys and sent them skidding into the corner but Dan was ready for him, rushed him and sent him sailing out the door. Jamie, Simon, and Dent were just coming in. They went down like ninepins with Pat on top. Johnny and Kevin, slugging at each other and seeking more room to do it in, came stumbling out the door and fell on Pat before he could get up.

Quite unaware of who was on the bottom, Mary ran to the door with a bucket of water and emptied it on the lot. "That'll cool you off a bit."

As the men struggled to their feet, she caught sight of the bottom layer and retreated inside, expecting retribution. But Jamie and the others wanted no more of the battle. They went off to the tavern to eat in peace.

That part of the fighting that had spilled out the door was about to resume when Pat stopped it with a word. "Look at that, now. There they go, with the keys in the pocket and there won't be a drop of whiskey taken in the camp the night."

As the bad news came in and circled the room, peace followed in its wake. The men crowded through the door and stared across the clearing in the gathering dark at the locked door of the cabin. What was behind it was in every man's mind: The round, full contours of the barrel of whiskey. A mighty thirst united the warring factions.

"A shoulder or two against that door?" Pat suggested.

Dan, rubbing his sore jaw with one hand, pointed to an oak timber with the other. Left from the building of Lock Seven, discarded because it was cracked, it was nevertheless a powerful piece of wood, a foot square and twenty feet long. "How do you like that bit of wood there for a battering ram?"

With ten of them on each side, they had it up in a minute. It could have destroyed the cabin entirely. It made short work of the door.

The whiskey flowed till every jug was full and the barrel was empty. Then they returned to the cookhouse and the long-delayed supper became a feast of triumph. With the bosses absent there was no one to dampen their spirits, no need to watch their tongues. Mary recklessly brought out the ginger cake she had baked for the Sunday dinner.

While they were still packing in the food and before the drink had made them all uproarious, Dan told how he had killed the dead horse so his mates shouldn't go on thinking him a suckhole. Those who still owed Jamie passage money could do for themselves what he had done, whether the cash was there on the payday or not.

Pat set his spoon down and gave Dan a long look. "Now there's a man with a head on him that he uses for another thing than keepin his shoulders apart." He took another bite, chewed it thoughtfully. "And all that goes on behind the ugly face on him—a face that's no prettier since I made it a bit fat on the one side of the jaw."

Dan touched the swelling tenderly. "That's no fist you've got on the end of your arm, Pat. Would it be a pile driver, maybe?"

Danny and Tim, having taken part in their first adult brawl, got their first taste of whiskey, liberally watered by their father. Danny came back for more when big Dan wasn't looking. He was soon very sick, but managed to crawl outside to empty his stomach where no one could see. There wasn't a doubt in the mind of either boy but that he was a man now.

When Jamie surveyed the damage the next morning, he put a charge against every man in camp for a gallon of whiskey. That gave him enough to pay for the whiskey and the broken door and something over to warn them against such adventures in the future.

"Now we start down the road to a farm with a debt against us," Mary complained to Dan.

"A small debt surely. Not too much to pay for the wake of the dead horse."

Chapter 10

GREAT NEWS came to the camp and went running on north along the line: The Bishop himself, from Cincinnati, would say a mass especially for canal workers at McCarthy and Lordon's camp. His Reverence was traveling the whole state. Because there was no church closer than Canton, he would make a station at the camp by Lock Seven and the word should be spread to all the Catholic canal workers that the second Sunday in June would be The Day.

A big fire was built outside each night to light the work of preparing an altar and a leafy scalan to shelter altar and Bishop. The debris between the cookhouse and the Lock was cleared away, too, to make a place for the people to sit.

Ellen and the O'Scanlon children made their own scalan in the daytime, at the edge of the woods. When they had laid a few broken branches between two bushes, they were quite pleased with the shelter but at a loss how to play in it. Kathleen, as the oldest, said she would be the Bishop but Terry said a girl couldn't be a bishop.

"I'm playin like I'm a man," Kathleen explained, "and I have to come a far journey from Cincinnati—that's in Ireland. No, I know what I'll be. The Bishop is bringing Holymarymotherofgod with him from Ireland, so I'll be her and you can be the Bishop, Terry."

"He's not either bringin Holymarymotherofgod," Ellen objected. "She lives in heaven. I think he'll bring some of the Little People that stayed in their lisses when we came over the water."

So Kathleen was the Bishop and Terry and Ellen were the Little People and they all rode stick-horses from a far distance up to the scalan. There they got off the horses and Kathleen made them get down on their knees and say their prayers. That was a poor ending, saying their prayers being an everyday kind of thing, but a better way would have to wait the great day when the real Bishop came and they could see what he would do.

Mary swept the cookhouse again and again, scrubbed the table and set all things in order, so the place would not shame her, should His Reverence step in the door. She spent their last pennies for soap. All heads in the Griffen family were washed and combed, bodies and clothes scrubbed, till the dirt was banished and the lice destroyed entirely. The angels themselves couldn't have been cleaner.

The people began coming early on the Sunday morning. By the time mass was to be said, the whole hillside from the Lock up to the road was covered with men, men everywhere with their dark clothes and here and there a small feminine island giving a touch of color. There was a knot of Germans near the front, straining to catch every word and make what they could of the English. This was a day of the peace that passeth understanding, surely, for the bad blood between the Irish and the Germans was forgotten and not a finger lifted nor a bad word spoken on either side.

Mary sat in the door of the cookhouse with Dan beside her, Ellen on her lap and the boys at her feet, feasting her eyes on the grand sight. There stood the Bishop in his vestments, with a priest on either side, a Dominican in his white robe, an Irish priest in his black.

It was a precious thing the Bishop had brought them: The knowledge that the Church had not forgotten her children, even far out here in the American wilderness.

Sunday after Sunday had gone by without a mass said. Men had died and been laid away without the last rites. Babes had been born and grown without a christening. Men had sinned and sinned again with no priest to hear their confessions. Man and woman had wed without a wedding. But now His Reverence was reaching out his hand to them to care for their souls' salvation. The same heaven was above Ohio as above Cork. The same Church was in Ohio as in Ireland . . . and yet . . . and yet . . . it was the same church and it wasn't.

When the Bishop began to preach, he had the sound more of the English vicar than of the priest at home. Not a word of Irish said, for the one thing, and for the other . . . Mary didn't know exactly, the Bishop being an American was all the difference there was in it, she supposed. She was too far away to catch every word.

Mary was very tired. Anticipation had kept her strength up through the week but now that the day was here, it ebbed away. The voice from the altar was calm and soothing; she couldn't make the effort to put the words together. She leaned against the doorway in the warm June sun, her attention wandering over the congregation.

There isn't another family the like of mine on the hill, nor a finer lookin man than himself . . . but the truth is, it's past the time he should sit under a priest again, that careless he's gettin with the prayers and takin the Holy Name in vain every time he opens his mouth, like all the rest of these sinners . . . And the boys, too, proper heathens they'll be if we don't get out of this soon.

Bridget's baby will be soon comin, anyone can see that with half an eye. Well for her that my own Gran brought all the babes in the parish into the world, the way I can help Bridget when her time comes . . . Kate Dugan, God help her, can't take care of her own babes. Little Tommy there, looks like he hasn't had a taste of the soap and water since the day he was born.

Doesn't Susan have the fine new dress on her and the American bonnet on top of it, and the men around her till you couldn't count them on your two hands—Johnny, Kevin, that lad that's always comin up from below on Saturdays . . . That bonnet didn't come from Susan's bit of a wage and most of that goin to help at home with the five younger ones . . .

Where would Johnny be gettin the money for it and no payday since April? It's better for Susan, she should have one young lad the like of Johnny or surely the men would be at her, one after the other, that starved for a woman they are in this place and nowhere to go but to those hussies behind the tavern.

How could Susan and Johnny marry, when he doesn't have two shillins to rub against each other? And if it's presents she's takin from one of the others—who would it be, now? I'd be knowin it surely, would it be any of the men in our camp.

Look at the outlandish clothes those Germans have on them. It's a great wonder how they can make their way in America and them not havin a word of the English. God knows it's not an easy thing for any of us.

Mary closed her eyes and prayed for the intercession of the Blessed Virgin on the hard way they had to go and wouldn't they be brought soon to the farm America surely had for them. Her body sagged against the doorframe and she slept.

Ellen wriggled and Mary opened her eyes, looking in wonder at how she could be here among all these people . . . slept again . . . woke just in time for the benediction.

The others could stand about and talk but not she. It would be a miracle if the meat she had left roasting over the fire wasn't burnt and she had the rest of the dinner to get ready.

Jamie came in as she was turning the meat on the spit to tell her there was something better for her to do on this day. Simon would bring the Bishop and the two priests in to rest themselves while their horses were being saddled and brought to the door. They wouldn't be having their dinner here but Mary should have tea ready and there would be a bit of something to offer, surely?

Mary was proud to say she had cakes baked on the Saturday. Susan could turn the meat and put the potatoes to boil for dinner would she come in as she'd been told. As if she'd heard her name spoken, Susan came in, untying her bonnet strings as she came, meeting Jamie as he went out. Stepping toward Susan with the orders about the dinner on her tongue, Mary caught the look that passed between the two.

Later, when the great men had finished their tea and cake and gone away,

when the dinner was over and the washing up done, Mary sat down in the doorway again with her own cup of tea.

She thought with satisfaction how His Reverence had taken the cup from her
own hand and given her his blessing. The men of the camp and some of the
others from up and down the line had followed in after the priests. Standing
respectfully crowded around the edge of the room, all had seen how the Fathers
gave her a word of thanks and a word of praise for the cake.

"It's like a taste of my own mother's baking," the Irish one said.

The words gave a sweet taste to her tea and she should have been content, but
there was something sour about the day, too. How could that be? Then it came
back to her, the look between Susan and Jamie.

*Susan's grown from the scrawny girl she was a year ago and lookin her pretti-
est in her new dress and bonnet. Wouldn't any man want to look at her? . . That's
all that's in it . . . No, no, it was more than that. New dress, indeed. Jamie's head
bent toward her and her lookin up at him . . . That was the look of a man and a
woman that's been together with no dress and no shirt between the two of them.
Jamie, Jamie, and you with a wife and three childer in Albany. That was a look
shouldn't pass even between husband and wife on a Sunday like this, near under
the very eyes of the Bishop.*

*It should be no surprise to me, the things I've learned since I came to this
godforsaken camp. Half the men married, but if I didn't know them like my own
brothers I wouldn't know from the way they carry on which half that was. The
Blessed Virgin must have been guidin me, the way I wouldn't let himself come to
the canal without me.*

*Poor Johnny, lost his brother and now like to lose his girl. Lost her already, if
he only knew. Jamie gave her that bonnet or the money to buy it. . . Och, it's that
makes Susan so saucy lately, I could have slapped her. She'll be saucy from this
out and let me lift a hand to her and she'll run to the boss—"Jamie, darlin,
Mary's that hard on me, you wouldn't be lettin her hit your own sweetheart,
would your now?"—Och, what a brutheen that will be makin of the work.*

There was shame under her anger. Shame for Jamie that he couldn't let a child
like Susan alone. Shame for herself that she had smiled at the swagger Jamie had
on him and listened to the sweet words and let him pat her shoulder and squeeze
her hand as if she knew no more of men than Susan did. What was it Dan had
said of Jamie?—"He's after becomin too grand a man entirely the way he thinks
he's the squire of the Ohio Canal."

*The Squire at the Big House it was who thought every pretty girl should be his
for the takin . . . and wouldn't he have taken me when I was a girsha of twelve
summers only and no more idea what was in his head than if I'd been a goose
swimmin in the pond.*

*Gran knew, indeed, the time we were in the kitchen of the Big House and Gran
curin the ache in the back of Patsy Daly, the Squire's cook . . . Patsy was a pretty
girl in her time, they say, and that's how she came to the Big House. Walkin the
road of a mornin when the young Squire sees her and just picks her up and throws*

her over his saddle. Many a year was after passin between that and the old woman with the ache in her back.

Gran was that busy with the bundle of herbs in her lap, separatin the one from the other, seekin the cure for the ache, she didn't hear the Squire come into the kitchen that time till he was behind her.

Up she jumps so quick to make her curtsy, the herbs all fall on the floor. The Squire calls Gran 'Old Witch' and me 'Little Fairy,' his fat red face shakin the way he was laughin. He pinches my cheek and gives me a shillin and tells Patsy to send Gran off and keep me there.

Wouldn't I be in hell now—alive or dead—in hell, surely, if Gran didn't whisk me out of there. Even then, it was takin a new fancy to Brigid Crowley made the Squire forget about me.

So that's Jamie, now, is it? The Squire of the Ohio Canal that pays the wages and takes the women.

Ellen came running around the corner and threw herself on Mary. "Can I have a bit of the cake was for dinner? And a bit for Terry and a bit for Kathleen? We played the Bishop says the mass and now we want to play the tea and cake that comes after."

Mary looked down at the tangled curly head, the same brown as her own with reddish lights in it and smiled at the eager pleading look on Ellen's face. Whatever the child was talking about, she didn't know, but she gave her the few crumbs that were left.

As Ellen ran off again, Mary said under her breath, "We'll be well out of this before you're grown, alannah. There's no two ways about that."

Chapter 11

B Y MID-JUNE Simon, with the stoneworkers and their tools, was off with the team and wagon to the new camp where clearing of the line had already begun and there was stone to be quarried for the aqueduct. The rest of the crew stayed behind with Jamie to finish the lock gates and mend the places in the bank that a heavy summer rain had washed out.

When the day came for the letting in of the water, the men gathered near their own handiwork, watching as the first water slipped along the bottom of the ditch and the lockpits. Then it came with a rush, rising in the pits, splashing down to the next level through the open lockgates, sweeping past them to number 18 and below. The men roared in answer to the water; from hundreds of throats the cheer swept along the line as the canal began to fill.

The June payday brought two month's pay. Almost everybody got drunk that payday night. Jamie gave up trying to get any work out of them the next day though work was still to be done on the canal banks. It was the first of July and they were already talking of starting for Cleveland and the big celebration of the canal opening.

Johnny and the Old Man lay about in the shanty all morning. When they came to the table at noon they pushed their food away and held their heads.

"I never had such a head as this since my first taste of the jug," Johnny groaned. "The devil himself must have brewed that whiskey, the way the poison was in it."

The Old Man agreed. "Or one of the Little People was up to mischief. It wouldn't be the first time. I mind once . . ." His voice trailed off before he got his story started. He had breath only for complaining. "If it was only the headache, that might be the poteen itself, but if I'm no burnin, I'm shiverin."

Mary came over and looked closely at their flushed faces and heavy eyes. "Och, you and your bottles and your poison," she said. "The devil of a hangover you've got, the two of you. It's not you will be jauntin."

Greatly to the disappointment of the children, the Griffens were not jaunting, either. Dan and Mary agreed that none of the little hoard put away in the chest after the June payday would be taken out for such merry-making. On the Monday they would see the first boat start down the canal. That would be their celebration. Not content with this, Tim and Danny hatched a plan to sneak away on Sunday night and be well down the road before mother or father would miss them.

Sunday night came but the road to Cleveland had no attraction for Tim. Mary was sitting in the doorway to get a breath of air after the supper was cleared away when Tim sat down on the ground beside her and leaned against her leg, dropping his head to her knee.

"I'm hurtin all over."

Mary's hand was cool and comforting on his throbbing forehead. He couldn't see the fear in her eyes. "Timmy, lad," her voice shook a little. "You've got the fever. Go lie on your bed."

Tim moved listlessly away and Mary closed her eyes, praying against her fear. She dragged Danny's tick and Ellen's far over to the side of the room away from the sick boy. She sat beside him in the dark, giving him a sip now and then of thoroughwort tea, stroking his hot head till he fell asleep.

Early the next morning, Simon came driving down the line with a wagonload of men. "We're off to the big doins in Cleveland," he called out, "and there's room for a few more."

Jamie was waiting for him. Susan came hurrying up in her best dress and her new bonnet. All the rest of those going to Cleveland were already gone.

Simon had something on his mind besides the Cleveland excitement. He jumped down from the wagon, got Jamie by the arm and walked him aside. His serious face was a contrast to his jovial greeting.

Dan walked over to the wagon to get the news of the new camp from Martin Daly.

Martin had a question for him first. "Are any sick here?"

"Why would you be askin that?"

"Comin up along the Tuscarawas we heard there's a terrible fever breakin out. Between you and me, Dan, it's well for all of us if we stay away from the Tuscarawas country as long as we can. I'm to drive this wagon back here after the celebration so we can load up what's left of the camp when the work is done. Are all well here?"

Dan shook his head. "What kind of a fever?"

"They say it's the swamp fever from the big swamp around the Summit Lakes. There's none sick in our camp but there's men dyin in the other camps. Who's sick here?"

"Johnny and the Old Man and now Tim . . . a touch of the canal fever."

Jamie disappeared into his cabin with Simon. Their voices could be heard in heated argument. When the partners emerged, Jamie threw a bundle of his clothes into the wagon and came over to Dan with the paybook in his hand.

"Well, Dan, it's you will be in charge of finishin up and five dollars a month on your pay while you do it. You to be foreman. I'm off to the celebration and I won't be back after. There's business in Albany for me to attend to." He gave Dan the paybook and showed him where to mark the days each man worked.

"By this month's payday, you should have all finished here and be at the new camp. Do a good job of it and it could be we'll have somethin else besides diggin for you to do there. If you need any more supplies, our credit is good with Higbee and at Hall's store. That's for necessaries, you understand? Anything beyond necessaries we won't be payin. That would be comin out of your own pay."

Dan took the paybook in one hand and tapped it casually against the other as he talked over with Jamie what there was to do. It was a proud thing to him to have the big wages and this sign that Jamie and Simon knew his worth. This was the first token of leadership that had been in his hand since he had greased his gun, wrapped it in straw and buried it along with his hopes for the success of the uprising.

Just as the wagon drove off, Mary came out of the cookhouse with a bit of breakfast she was carrying to the sick men. The long night of wakefulness with Tim was still in her head, filling it with shadows and giving the bright July morning a look of unreality. She watched them go, Susan sitting beside Jamie on the seat, her head in its fine store bonnet turned toward him. The wagon wheels raised the dust from the road; it went smoking upward in the hot sun, a grey curtain between those in the wagon and those left behind. As the rattle of the wagon and the clomp of the horses' hooves faded, the camp grew very quiet.

Dan showed Mary the paybook. "That says I'm the boss."

"Are you, now? What would they say back home if they knew?"

"And it's fifteen dollars I'll be gettin at month's end."

"A big rise in the wages and yourself a boss already!"

On any other day she would have made a celebration of it. On this day her eyes remained troubled. She didn't linger but disappeared into the shanty to see to the sick men. It was a men's place that she had never been in before but it was Johnny sick in there and the Old Man who was another of the lone ones. She was out again in a few minutes.

"Dan, Johnny and the Old Man are too weak to get out of the blankets. Not a mouthful of stirabout could I get into either of them. If that's the canal fever, it's not the way you had it last summer." Her voice dropped very low. "Do you remember the fever that laid us both low the year after Danny was born?"

They looked at each other, remembering. That summer had been the first of the bad times. When the typhus had struck Carrignahown, Mary was the first to fall sick. Dan had made a bed of clean straw outside where the house would be between it and the wind and built a shelter of branches over it. Then he had carried Mary out and laid her there so the sickness couldn't creep from her into the rest of them.

He had gone questing through the parish till he found Mary's Gran. The old woman was going from one to another of those with the fever but she came to Mary at once. For weeks she continued her rounds, always coming back to Mary and to Dan, who was soon stricken, too. Gran was a real cullough of the old times, with the cures made of the herbs and with the holy water and the charms to make them firm and good. She was the only one who would touch the fever victims. The other well ones would put food and water where they could reach it but would come no closer.

That nightmare was behind them. Dan wouldn't have it that it might be coming again, not just when he had a job of work to manage and a crew to boss and his pay almost doubled. "You're dreamin too much of the bad days we run from. Tim looks better the day and the other two will have their days up and their days down the way it is with canal fever." The word he had from Martin, he kept to himself. Mary's thoughts were dark enough as it was.

She turned away from the spoonful of cheer he was offering and went on remembering. "Gran cared for us all and the sickness never touched her. The Good God never takes us to death's door twice over the same road, she said. God willin, you and I are safe, Dan, but Timmy . . . and Danny and Ellen . . . Johnny, too . . . Lost his brother, lost his girl and now like to lose his life. We'll have to put Johnny and the Old Man outside before Jamie and the rest come back."

"Jamie wouldn't be comin back. It's Dan Griffen that's the boss, now, or didn't you hear that news?"

"Jamie . . . wouldn't be comin back? Just when the trouble is on us?"

The third of July was a great day in Akron. The boat, *State of Ohio*, was bright with new paint, its tow-horses gay with colored ribbons. It was loaded with gentlemen in the restrained and uniform opulence of black coats, tall hats, and snowy linen, their importance set off by the vivacious blossoming of color and variety in the ladies' dresses, bonnets and parasols. The boat was ceremoniously locked through the Akron Cascade. As it passed the camp and disappeared down the locks below, the troop of cavalry that accompanied it pranced through the camp, sending spectators scurrying out of the way. People streamed along the towpath behind the boat, waving and cheering.

Danny and Ellen were wild with excitement. Mary stood beside Dan and the children for a few minutes, too preoccupied to be swept up in the furor. Yet it was not until many years and hundreds of canal boats had blurred the image that she could see a packet move down the canal without that picture flashing into her mind: The people with the bright colors and the glossy shine of money on them standing out against her own grey web of sickness and fear.

The Fourth of July was an even greater day in Cleveland, the sun bright, the crowd gay, the speeches exuberant, the food plentiful, the taverns riotous. It was an Ohio celebration of Ohio plans coming to fruition, Ohio work accomplished. It announced that Ohio was no longer a collection of frontier outposts scattered in the woods. It was an expanding agricultural state, ready to pour canal boat loads of corn, wheat, pork, wool, lumber and who knows what other products into the cotton-growing South and into the seaboard cities of the East with their overseas trade. Ohio was a growing section of a growing nation. True, it had mortgaged its future to Eastern and English investors but it would have a growing population whose taxes could pay off the debt.

The celebration went up like a rocket and burst into dozens of starry signals to Ohio farmers and bankers and merchants, to land speculators and prospective westward migrants in all the states to the east, to statesmen and politicians in the nation's capital, to financiers in the money markets of Philadelphia, New York and London.

But while the rocket was being launched and the speeches applauded, in the back of the Cleveland crowd the dark rumors of the fever were circulating. Not a word of these rumors was allowed on the platform. The men who sat there would not admit that the fever was anything but the usual summer shakes, and if it was, didn't want the news to put any obstacles in the way of the money flowing into the canal fund or the labor flowing into the work crews to build new miles of canal.

But when the celebration was over, long before the good news, untainted by the rumors, reached the distant investors who had gambled on the success of the Ohio canal venture, the stream of workers had begun to flow away from the pestilence.

Some of those from McCarthy and Lordon's crew sought work along the wharves or—those with a few dollars left from the double payday —took passage to Buffalo to look for jobs along the Erie. Some headed into Pennsylvania where new canal building was said to be starting. Susan met Garrett Riley again and he helped her to a job in the ladies' cabin of a Lake steamer.

When the time came, there were only two men in the wagon going back to the camp, Pat Flynn driving and Martin lying sick in the wagonbed, rolling back and forth on the hard boards as the wagon jounced over the rough road. The few others who went back chose to walk rather than to share the wagon with the sick man.

Chapter 12

ONE BY ONE the tenuous bonds between the canal camps and the larger community stretched thin or snapped altogether. It was indeed the typhus that struck all along the line that summer, from the Tuscarawas north to Cleveland, spreading into the nearby villages and farms.

Commissioner and engineers were seen no more in the camps, contractors and local workers disappeared. On many sections, the tools lay idle all through July and August and well into September while the workers struggled to survive.

In the McCarthy and Lordon camp, when Martin had been put to bed alongside Johnny and the Old Man and a rough lean-to built against the sleep shanty wall to shelter them, Mary brought Tim over where he would be away from the other children and she could watch over all four of the sick.

Dan sat down to count over his little force. There were eleven with himself. But Mary couldn't care for the sick and cook, too. Johnny alone was about all a man like himself could handle, as he had found out this last day and night. In his delirium, Johnny thought Susan was waiting on the road for him to go to Cleveland and he kept getting out of bed and staggering off. There were two other women in camp but Bridget would be birthing her baby any day now. Kate would have to help. He went across the clearing for a word with Kate but she was having none of it.

"The fever hasn't come in our door yet and Kate Dugan wouldn't be the woman to go out and make it welcome."

There would have been little breakfast for anyone if it hadn't been for Hugh Cadigan who had been a cabin boy and then a ship's cook before he jumped ship in New York and fell in with a gang headed for the canal. He put a meal on the table and carried some stirabout to Mary and the sick lads.

"Will you cook while Mary's nursin?" Dan asked him after breakfast.

Hugh squinted at him. "Will you see that McCarthy pays me the same as I get workin in the ditch?"

"I will," Dan said with more confidence than he felt.

"I'll cook then," Hugh announced in his bass rumble. He spoke little but when he did speak, his voice rolled through the cookhouse and could be heard all the way to the canal.

They left Hugh in the cookhouse and the rest started for the work but there were only nine. Where was Paddy? Dan yelled for him and he came out of his shanty with a bundle in his arms—little Kathleen wrapped in a blanket. Dan sent the others on ahead and walked across the clearing with him.

Mary straightened up from where the Old Man was lying to take the whimpering child from her father. "Don't cry, darlin, you'll sleep a little the way Timmy's sleepin, won't you, now?"

"Is Bridget ailin?" she asked Paddy.

"Bridget is fine, barrin the worry over the little one, there. Kathleen's been cryin all night with the hurt that's on her. Will you take good care of her, Mary?"

"Like my own. Tell Bridget I'll do for her like my own."

When Paddy left, Mary looked a question at Dan. He knew what it was she was asking.

"Ellen's as cool and lively as a young salmon, and Danny the same. Tim?"

"He's sleepin yet, but he's so hot I'm afraid for him. Pray for him, Dan." She leaned against his shoulder and he held her tight. "We've given up two. Wouldn't that be enough?" She pulled away in answer to a feeble call from Martin. "Wait a minute till I see to Martin. There's a thing I'm wantin from you."

Dan stood in the sunshine where a morning breeze brought a little touch of the world of the living into this place of strangling coughs and tortured bodies with the strange spots on them. Only Mary was upright and whole, pitting her slight, quick-moving body against the dark shadows that hung over the beds. He waited while Mary brought Martin a bucket to relieve himself. She was beside Dan again in a minute, taking a breath of the sweet, fresh air.

"Now that it's yourself is the boss, would you see to one of the lads diggin a pit in the back, there, where I can empty the slop bucket? God knows it would be easier here if it didn't smell like the devil's own backhouse. And tell Danny he's to come over there where I set the bench often and often through the day. If he finds the water bucket there, empty, he's to fill it . . . Would Jamie be callin a washtub a necessary, think you? Mr. Hall has some in his store. I can't keep Timmy clean if I have to run to the canal or the stream to wash for him, let alone the rest of them."

"Jamie took care not to be here where he could say yes, and the best of that is, he's not here where he can say no. You'll have the tub."

She stood in the sun a moment when Dan was gone off toward the canal and the work. Warm though it was, it couldn't reach inside here, the way she felt as cold and alone as when they were in the midst of the ocean. Since coming to the camp there had always been Jamie, knowing the way of things in the new world. She had found her own place under his protection. She turned away from the canal and looked up the empty road. It's a grand McCarthy Jamie is, she thought, full of the proud talk when things is easy, quick to run when things is hard. Off in the wagon behind the grey curtain of dust, letting the sound of the wheels and the horses' hooves tell them to live or die as best they could.

In less than a week, there were eight with the fever in Mary's house. Except to go to the washtub and the slop pit, she was out of it only once in the next two months. It was a long narrow room she had to work in. It reminded Mary of the ship, although it was open at both ends. That let in the air—and the flies and mosquitoes. It let out the spirits of those who died.

The night was like the day, if not worse. What with the pain and the thirst from the fever and the coughing and the dirtying themselves like babies and the going out of their heads altogether, Mary was going from one to another all day and all night. Her back was so tired that sometimes she got down on her knees and crawled from this one to that one rather than stand and bend over.

It was her one bit of luck that she had a good supply of herbs. Hugh made the hot tea of them for her and she gave it to the sick ones to sweat out their fever. There wasn't a drop of holy water in this place at all and there were other Irish herbs she should have had, but she comforted herself with words remembered from Gran's wisdom, that God never sent any disorder into a country without a cure for it planted in the fields.

She had to keep the brave words and sweet words ready, too. Kathleen was always crying for her mother and the men grew lonesome and afraid with none of their own closer than Ireland.

The door stayed shut on the Dugan cabin. No one there was yet sick but they were staying inside with no company but each other and their fear. As few men as Dan had, he had to spare a helper for Mary. One man got in a great huff at being asked to do women's work. Another feared he was growing feverish himself and a third would give him no answer at all. The first and last of it was, the men would take Dan's orders on the job but none would step inside that lean-to. All had the fear that once in it they wouldn't come out alive.

Dan had to keep the work going as well as he could and give Mary a hand himself. He hoped Mary was right and the two of them were safe from it but he wasn't without a fear of the fever for himself and for her. He covertly watched Mary to see was she sick when she sighed with weariness. When she touched him he could tell she was feeling was he fever hot.

The first breath of hope came when Tim's head began to feel cooler to Mary's hand. Soon he was sleeping easier and asking for something to eat. His recovery gave her more heart to fight for the rest of them. That night she slept as she hadn't slept for almost two weeks. The next day, Johnny was better, too.

But when Danny brought next day's first bucket of water, he sat down beside it till his mother came to him. Looking down at his feet, he muttered, "I can't carry no more water. It hurts my back."

Mary looked at him to see was he maybe just getting lazy on her but she didn't like the look of him. "Are you hot?" He nodded. "Go get your blanket and tell Hugh he'll have to carry his own water for the cookin. Then come here to me. Your brother's better, thank God. I don't think I could stand it for the both of you to have the fever on you at the same time."

When Mary had first disappeared from the cookhouse, Ellen had cried to go with her. There were no words and no blows that could make her understand that she couldn't be where her mother was. Several times she was almost into Mary's house before Danny was told he would have to be father and mother to his little sister. This new responsibiity filled the awful vacuum that was in Danny's life with Tim gone and mother only an anxious face giving him a quick look out from among the sick now and then.

It was a day or two before Ellen became convinced that the brother who had scorned her as a nuisance was now hers to follow, hers to run to, hers to hold on to at night in the big room that was so empty without mother, father, and Tim. Once convinced, she was again ready to run and play with Terry at the wonderful new place they had discovered.

The hot summer days had led them to a little stream that trickled down the hill, fell over the rocks in a miniature waterfall, widened into a shallow pool and a few yards farther on disappeared into Wilcox Run. They paddled with their bare feet in the cool water and played with the tiny fish that darted away and then came back to bump soft noses against their ankles and their toes.

They reached for the swift little swimmers, trying to catch them, slipping and falling into the shallow water, screaming and laughing, splashing each other until both were wet and cool all over. They urged each other on to more daring adventures, sat under the waterfall and let it pour over their heads and down their backs, walked on their hands in the pool, bodies wiggling in imitation of the fish.

It was far from the lonesome nights, far from the loud-voiced, impatient Hugh who had her mother's place among the pots and pans, far from the dark well of shadows that was Mary's house. Then Danny disappeared into the well of shadows and Terry's mother took Ellen into the O'Scanlon shanty.

Two days later, as Ellen and Terry were trotting across the road toward their stream, intent on playing fishes, they heard the rumble of a wheel over the hard earth and saw Dan pushing a wheelbarrow toward them. Well knowing that children must be out of the way when tools and barrows are in operation, they skipped out of the road and behind the bushes.

As Dan passed them, they could see his load. The Old Man lay in the barrow, his face no longer red and cheerful, but now a dreadful clay color. His legs hung limply over the edge of the barrow. Beside him were a shovel and a pick.

When Dan and his load were out of sight, curiosity overcame their fear. Holding hands, they walked up the road in the path of the barrow.

Dan didn't much care for this job but the fear that kept the men away from Mary's house kept them away from the dead as well. There could be no wake for the Old Man and there was no one but Dan to bury him. When he had dug a shallow grave in the dry earth, he laid the Old Man in it, picked up the shovel again and covered the body with the loose dirt. As he straightened up he found himself looking into the wide eyes of Ellen and Terry.

"Oh, God in heaven," he said under his breath. He was about to shout at them and send them scampering, but thought better of it.

"Come," he said gently. "Don't be afraid. The Old Man died. He'll be goin away from us now. He's takin his soul with him but he left his body behind. That was nothin but the body of him I put in the ground.

"Come," he repeated. Slowly they came toward him. "Now the both of you stand over there and you'll be helpin me say good-bye to the Old Man." He made the sign of the cross and the children did the same. "Now say, 'God rest your soul, Old Man.'"

"God rest your soul, Old Man," they repeated.

"Now go away and play and don't be comin here any more. You hear me? I don't want to catch you anywhere near this."

They turned without a word and went back to the road, at first slowly and then faster and faster, then off the road and up the hill, till they could no longer hear the empty wheelbarrow rumbling over the road behind them.

There was a thunderstorm that night. The thunder rumbled into Ellen's sleep and she saw a whole file of men pushing barrows, the wheels rumbling, the barrows going down over the edge into the canal. In every barrow was a body. Her father was in one and her mother and Tim and Danny and Terry. She was in one herself.

She woke up screaming in terror. Bridget took her into her own bed. Bridget's round soft arm and big soft body surrounded her. Bridget's murmured words of endearment and reassurance comforted her and at last she sobbed herself into a dreamless sleep.

Chapter 13

B RIDGET WAS AWAKE long after Ellen slept, too much alone to sleep in spite of the small warm body curled up against her. Her lodger had moved out to sleep with the other men and eat in the cookhouse when Paddy had been taken with the fever. There were only Terry and Ellen with her now.

She lay there praying for her Kathleen and her man to be getting well and for help to come to her when she needed it. Where were the women who should be around her as they had been when she bore Kathleen and Terry? Where were her mother and her elder sister and Paddy's mother and Old Peg who had helped more than a hundred women bring their babies? There was no woman here but Mary and she nursing the sick . . . and that Kate Dugan.

She could feel the new life stirring in her womb and willed it to stay quiet and safe where it was till it could come into a world without the fever. But the new life was ready to emerge and knew nothing of the readiness of the world to receive it. Early Monday morning, Bridget send Ellen and Terry next door to tell Kate she was in need of her.

Kate opened the door just enough to call out, "Get away with you. Get away. We don't want nobody in here."

Terry yelled at the crack in the door, "My mother says she's in need of you."

"I wouldn't be no help to her, tell her. I'm took terrible with the shakes." Kate's sallow face disappeared and the door slammed.

Hugh heard the yelling and came to the door of the cookhouse. "You, Terry," his voice rolled across the clearing. "Tell Bridget I'll get Mary."

He strode toward Mary's house, roaring her name.

"Och, that good-for-nothin of a Kate Dugan," Mary said when she heard what it was. "There's nothin for it but I'm the one to help Bridget."

It had been a bad night, with Pat taking sick and Kathleen and Danny both coughing till she thought the insides would come out of them.

How can I do for Bridget and this the first time I've had the call come to myself alone? I've given the help to the old ones them other times. I promised

Bridget as if I was a midwife these many years without givin a thought to it how it would be when the day came. I should be walkin across to her now . . .

She sat down on the bench to gather her strength, feeling like the sickness from those inside was thick all over her, wondering would it wash off.

She would have smiled at the notion had there been a smile left in her. She looked down at her soiled dress, torn where Martin had grabbed at it when he was raving with the fever. A picture of her Gran rose up before her, setting out for a birth with a clean apron on and her little bag in her hand, the bag that was tucked away now in their chest.

"Dan," she called over her shoulder, knowing he was lying in the far corner, trying to get a few winks of sleep after the bad night. "Dan, I'm leavin the sick to you and goin to Bridget. Johnny can maybe get up out of his bed a bit if you need him."

She walked quickly across to the O'Scanlon shanty and put her head in the door. "Bridget, acushla, how is it with you?"

"Oh, Mary, I'm that glad to see you, you don't know." She had been pacing back and forth across the hard-packed earth floor, away from the door and then back to it, hoping for Mary to come through it. "I wouldn't believe it when Terry said you was comin and I feared if you come at all you might be too late. Can the sick ones get on without you?"

"Dan can take care of the fever but there's no man can help you bring your baby into the world." Mary was feeling better herself, just getting away from the sickness. "Are the pains comin down on you hard? No? Hold on, then. I want to wash myself and fetch my things."

When she came back she had changed her dress. It was the only one she had and might get birth-stained in spite of the apron tied around her waist but she needed to drop the torn and dirty garment that belonged to the sickness and death she had lived with these past weeks. For Bridget's sake and her own she needed the presence a dress that was clean and whole would give her.

She carried a bucket of fresh water in one hand and the little bag that had been Gran's in the other. She walked through the door saying the charm for a safe birth: ". . . Woman, bear your child as Anne bore Mary, as Mary bore God."

She left the door ajar behind her to bring some light into the dark shanty. The few men still working would not be passing here and there was no other camp life to shut out. Hugh had promised to keep the children out of the way and give them a bite when the men had their dinner.

The scapular came out of Mary's bag first of all and went over Bridget's bowed head, the strings across her shoulders, the two woolen pieces tucked under her dress, front and back. The familiar words of the charm, the reassuring touch of Mary's hands, the scapular's holy protection in place—these things gave Bridget the feeling that all would be well. The hard work of it was still ahead of her but she would be having a new baby, fine and healthy like her other two.

Mary settled Bridget on the bench where she could lean back against the wall, the pad Terry slept on under her to soften the hard seat, a blanket rolled up and stuffed in behind her back. Then Mary moved quickly about the room, getting all ready, hearing from Bridget all she had to tell of when the labor started and how it was going. She began to sense the rhythm of Bridget's body, drew near when a pain came on.

"I'm here with you for the help of it," she said, wiping the sweat from her friend's face, "but it's only you can do the work of it and the hard work it is, don't I know it? The hardest work a woman has to do in her life."

Mary soon had everything arranged to her satisfaction: Gran's scissors and thread to cut the cord and tie it laid on the bench on one side of Bridget; next to them, the things Bridget had prepared—a pile of clean rags and a warm shawl to wrap the baby in. She set a stool in front of Bridget for herself and a pail beside it to catch all that had to come out with the baby, leaving Bridget clean inside. She built a small fire to purify the air and warm a pot of water, opened the door a little wider to let the smoke out.

She talked as she worked, telling how it was with her when she bore Tim, her first. She listened as Bridget told of Kathleen's birth—what a long labor that had been.

"With Terry, it wasn't so long. I sent Paddy for Old Peg in the middle of the night and by the time the sun was high in the sky I was resting from it with my son at my breast. Maybe this third one will be still quicker?"

"It could be," Mary agreed, "but that's yet to be seen. The first is always the hardest to bring into the world. It was so with me but after the second the other four weren't any quicker."

She sat down—not on the stool, that would come later—on the bench beside Bridget, putting an arm around her, letting Bridget's shoulder rest against her own. As long as she was busy there had been no fears. Now the weight of Bridget's need pressed against her with her friend's heavy body. She felt hollow inside where she should have been firm and sure.

It should not be the two of us alone here. There should be someone like Gran who liked to say she had helped more babies into the world than a tree has apples. It isn't a Gran only that's missing. There should be a woman to tend the fire and do the Gran's bidding and one on each side of Bridget to help her and hold her. Here I am like a single finger when Bridget needs a whole hand . . . Holy St. Brigid guide me and help me . . .

As she sat there, her body began to respond to what was happening in Bridget's body, so close against her. She could feel each time it pulled up hard and let go again. It was like a tide coming in, each wave bringing the baby closer. Once that tide began, a woman's body was in it and there was no getting out of it.

I'm in it myself with Brigid. It will carry us both as we bring the baby ashore. This isn't the first time I've seen it and felt it. I can give Bridget some of those other times . . .

"The first time I went to a neighbor woman in childbirth, that was a different thing entirely from bearing one myself. What a sight it was to see for the first time a new life come thrusting out of another woman's body into the world! That was one of my people, a woman of the O'Sullivans, her seventh child. I was with her again for her next one and when we left Carrignahown she still had every one of them alive and growin up to her."

"She was rare lucky, then. My own mother had ten but there's only six of us now livin and the ocean between me and the rest of 'em . . . Och, Mary, I want my mother by me. . . I want her by me." Bridget's body began to shake.

Mary braced herself against the wall and got both arms around Bridget, holding her firmly on each side of the swollen belly. "It's not your mother you should be cryin after. Yourself a mother twice over and the third one to be cryin after you before the day's out." She went on talking, recalling each of her own five births and the three where she had been a helper ". . . all the same and every one different."

Gradually, Bridget's body stopped shaking and she had a few words in answer to a question, then the memory to recount of how Paddy had been wanting to run for Old Peg a dozen times that last month she was carrying Kathleen . . . what a pretty baby Kathleen was when she came at last . . . how it was with her sister . . .

The talk moved gently back and forth between them, filling the room with the supporting presence of other women who had experienced the recurring miracle of producing a new life. It ceased with each wave that carried Bridget up, began again when she had expelled a wordless sound and sagged back against Mary.

The July heat grew more intense as the morning advanced. Bridget's dress was drenched with sweat and Mary could feel her own sticking to her. She eased away, letting Bridget lean against the wall; wiped her face again with a cool wet rag, fastened up the hair that had tumbled down so it would not be hot on her neck, fetched her a drink of water.

"The heat of the summer's no time to choose for this work," she said, dipping the rag again and cooling herself off. "What were you and Paddy thinkin of at all? In Carrignahown, the marriages was always in the winter and the most babies would come in the fall, after the harvest."

"With us, too. But what's the difference when the work isn't by the seasons any more? I'll tell you . . ." Bridget reached for Mary's hand, held tight to it, groaning . . . let go again . . . leaned back panting from the effort. After a few minutes she looked up at Mary with a half smile. "I'll tell you how it is. There's no thinkin to it with Paddy. Isn't that the way with your man? The wonder is I didn't have another one before now, the way he won't hear me when I tell him to take it out of me before he starts another baby. Wipe my face again, will you, Mary? I'm that hot and tired."

"You're not gettin on with it very fast, are you? That last pain was a long time comin. Let me see do I see any signs is it gettin closer. Turn a little toward the door. Nobody can see in here and I need the light."

She was on the stool in front of Bridget, pushing her skirt up and gently separating her legs.

What a strange thing it is, that a woman can walk about through her life with her legs so close together they would be touchin, leavin no room there for any-

thing else at all, and when her labor begins, there she is, all spread out, soft and red and wide with room for the child with its big head to come pushin out . . . Bridget will have to be wider open than this, though . . .

"You're not ready for it yet. You have to open up more and you know your water's not broke yet. Do you want to lie down and rest a bit? Get your strength together, like, for the hard work of it?"

She helped Bridget get her feet up on the bench and put the rolled up bed cover under her head but Bridget shifted uneasily from side to side.

"How can I rest and my back hurtin me?"

"That's it, is it? Roll over away from me and I'll rub on it."

Mary could feel Bridget's body easing under her hand, could see her eyelids drooping. The baby would let her sleep only a few minutes at a time but that was something. The tension went out of Mary's own body, her hand moved more slowly.

"Press on it, Mary. It feels so good when you press on it."

She pressed firmly against Bridget's back with each new wave, let go in between . . . wiped Bridget's face often, held the cool cloth to her hot forehead.

An hour passed, an hour with the two of them together in the center of the world. Things were going on as usual out there but they were trivial compared to this. It was almost a surprise to hear a man's voice in the distance now and then, from the direction of the canal, or Terry and Ellen in some childish dispute or Hugh booming out a call from the cookhouse. Reality was in this small space and every sight and sound and feel of it was intensely and immediately present to Mary: Bridget's flushed face, the little tendrils of hair that usually curled around it, wet now and clinging to it, a small shadow across her cheek from the coat hanging on the wall behind her, her slightly swollen, parted lips.

Bridget shifted and pushed Mary's hand away. She sat up. When Mary put the cloth against her face, she complained fretfully that it was too wet, the water was trickling down her neck.

Mary could feel the rhythm changing, the waves coming closer together and lasting longer. She got Bridget's feet planted firmly against the floor with the pail between them just in time. The bag of water broke and the water gushed out. Mary dried her off, then got a candle, putting it on the floor where it would give her a little more light. Although it must be getting on for noon, it was too dark here for her to see the baby when it came out.

"O-o-och . . . Jesus, God and Mary . . . Och, Blessed Virgin . . . och," Bridget groaned.

"Now you're getting about it," Mary encouraged her. "Bring it down now. Push on it."

Waves of pain were coming one close behind the other, giving Bridget no respite. Her face was different now. She was all turned inward.

"You're wide open now, acushla. It won't be long. Cry out with it if you want to and why shouldn't you?" Mary let her words trail off. They were hardly reaching her friend, alone now at the center of the world.

It went on . . . and on . . . and on.

Bridget's hand came down between her legs. "It hurts there, it hurts. It's burnin me."

Mary pushed her hands aside. "I'll hold you here so you won't tear with it. . . There! There!" She almost cried out herself in the excitement of it. "I can see its head!"

There it was, showing hard and blue-gray against the soft redness of its mother's body, with little wet hairs plastered all over it. Just as expected, but incredible all the same. Her hands were there, holding it. It disappeared . . . reappeared.

"Come then, o-o-och, come then," Bridget groaned. "O-o-och . . . come . . . come."

She gathered up her whole body in one intense effort and bore down, pressing it out.

The head was out on Mary's hand, warm, with the soft wrinkled scalp over the hard skull, the dark purple face. A piece of the night. The spirit wasn't in it yet . . . Now, now the change was coming. It was turning rosy as the sunrise. The life was in it. It cried. Everything was happening at once. She pulled it gently toward her, felt it turning itself, one shoulder out, then the other. She had the head in one hand and the whole body in the other. She got it in her lap and was wiping the face. Was it choking? She held the head downward, patted the back. A sneeze. Another cry.

Bridget was peering down over the curve of her belly, the change in her face as great as the change in the baby's. Beautiful she was, indeed.

"Ah, a girl," Bridget said softly. "Ah, the darlin." She sank back, exhausted.

"A little beauty she is, Bridget. See now?" Mary held the baby up, the cord that still fastened it to its mother dangling from the small stomach.

"Ma ghrianach . . . my sunshine . . . I wish Paddy could see her."

"I'll take Paddy the good word. It will put the heart back into him. He'll be seein his daughter soon now." It was the first thought she had for any of the sick ones since she walked in Bridget's door and she had no time to hold on to it. The baby had all her attention.

She reached for the scissors, then pulled her hand back. Was it too soon? What was it Gran had said when Timmy was born? . . Patience, patience Wait till the life is out of the cord and into the child.

When the cord stopped throbbing, she tied it firmly a broad thumb's breadth from the child and again two thumbs breadths away, then cut it. A bit of bright blood spurted out. She fastened a cloth around the baby's belly and gave her to Bridget.

The mother's arms went around her, holding her to the breast. Midwife and mother looked at each other, glad to rest, to absorb what had been so long in coming and had happened so fast at the end. They let the feeling of it flood through them, pass from one to the other and back again, smiling to each other, understanding what couldn't be said.

But the cord still hung from Bridget's body. The afterbirth hadn't come out. Mary tugged on it gently but it was still fastened inside. "You've got some more push in you yet," she said, "Where is it, then?"

That was the last wait. Like the others it seemed too long, though it was only minutes, not hours this time. Mary rubbed down on Bridget's belly, pulling down, encouraging Bridget to push it out. At last Bridget began her last labor. Mary could feel that the cord was loose. One final grunt and the afterbirth plopped into the pail.

Mary knew she should get back to the sick but she couldn't help lingering. She got the baby wiped off and wrapped in the shawl, Bridget clean and comfortable and both of them lying on the bed. Gran always stayed after, saying this was a danger time, when the woman might be wounded inside and begin to bleed. All seemed well with Bridget, though a little anxiety was creeping in between her happy thoughts of the baby.

"Paddy will get well of the fever, won't he, Mary? And Kathleen?"

"Why would you think a thing else? I haven't lost but one and that was the Old Man. Johnny and Timmy are up out of their beds already and Paddy and Kathleen will soon follow." God willing, she added to herself, not liking the way the cough seemed to be destroying Kathleen.

"I'll have to be gettin back to them soon and won't I be carryin the best news was after comin to this camp these many weeks?"

She took the pail and Paddy's shovel outside to bury the afterbirth. Then she found a bite for the two of them, but Bridget had fallen asleep. So she ate by herself, looking proudly and fondly at mother and child. All was well. Gran herself couldn't have done better.

She laid one of Paddy's shirts over them. When a husband is away, something of his is needed lest They come, seeking a mortal nurse for a fairy child. Then she gathered up the birth-soiled rags that would have to be washed and reluctantly moved to the door. As she stood there, her eye fell on the Dugan shanty.

Now then, before I go back, I'll do myself the favor of givin Kate a piece of my mind.

"Kate! Kate Dugan! Come to your door!"

The door opened a crack. "Now Mary Griffen, don't come in here."

"Are you out of your mind, woman? I wouldn't cross your doorsill again as long as I live, not if you paid me a hundred pounds. I have the news for you that Bridget gave birth to a fine girl, no thanks to you."

"I'm sure I'm glad of it and you have no call to be throwin the hard words on me. I've been taken with the canal fever every year since we was first on the Erie and here it is back on me again or I'd have been that glad to help Bridget. Don't you remember how it was with me last summer?"

The door opened a little wider and Mary could see Kate's long thin face pushing out at the end of her scrawny neck, the way she was always pushing her troubles at you as if they were the only troubles in the wide world.

"What I remember, we could every one of us die before you would so much as open your door to let a kind thought slip out."

Kate's whining voice began again, protesting and resentful but Mary was in no mood to listen. "Take the ugly face of you back in the cabin and may I never see it again."

She was about to go on, for it was a hard thought she had in her against Kate and she wanted to fling it out on her, wrapped in fiery words. Kate was quiet, so quiet Mary heard her own voice echoing in the stillness . . . May I never see it again . . . never see it again . . .

She picked up her bundle and turned back toward the sick that were waiting for her.

It's not like I have the power from Them to put a curse on the woman. God forgive me, I wouldn't put a death wish even on the likes of Kate Dugan . . .

She heard Kate's voice now, crying to her husband, "Larry, Larry. Do you hear how she put the curse on me?"

Larry jerked the door full open and bellowed out, "Shut your dirty mouth, Mary Griffen."

Mary felt better at once. "Would you look at who's givin me the name of a dirty mouth," she mocked, "and him with a wife that's greasy dirt from the hair of her head to the last toe of her foot and not one of her seed, breed or generation that ever knew what it meant to be clean. And you, Larry, hidin behind her skirt the way you're in such a fright over the fever."

She was back in her house before either Larry or Kate could return the abuse. She soon forgot them but the thought of Bridget and the baby, so sweet and healthy, helped her bear it when Martin died and like the Old Man, had to be put in the ground without being waked.

Chapter 14

TIM WAS STILL WEAK and darkly flushed around his eyes but Mary sent him away from the sick and the dying. Johnny was out of his bed, too, but he stayed to help with the others. He had clung to Mary like she was his own mother all through the sickness and now he would do whatever she asked of him. She needed him, for Dan now had to deal with what had become the camp's most pressing problem—food. Zeke and Higbee had stopped coming to the camp and Hall's store was boarded up. Dan had driven the wagon to Higbee's farm but Higbee wouldn't so much as let him into the barnyard.

Canal work was forgotten now and those who were well went out foraging. They shot some squirrels and once were lucky enough to get a deer. That supplied meat for the well ones and broth for the sick ones for days. The venison gone, they killed one of the hogs that ranged through the forest, feeding on acorns and other wild things. It doubtless belonged to one of the farmers. Dan hoped it was Higbee's.

"He could have sold it to us, bad 'cess to him. Serves him right if we take it."

Danny began to improve toward the end of July, and soon after Pat Flynn and Paddy O'Scanlon were up out of it. Two more of the men took the fever the next week, though, and Sean Murphy died. Dan trundled his body to the cemetery as he had the others.

"If Jamie wasn't after goin off and leavin us, he might have got someone to care for the dead while we care for the livin," Mary said to him, "but what does Jamie care for any of us? Wasn't he ready to bury poor Owen almost before he was cold? I didn't see it then but he has two thoughts only in his head: one for himself and one for the job. Not half of a quarter of a thought for those that look to him as their chief."

One hot August afternoon the Dugan's door opened and across the clearing came Larry carrying young Larry in his arms. Kevin and Mick Casey followed, holding a blanket by its two ends with Kate on it. Tommy, the younger boy, made the tail of the sad procession. Their faces were gaunt and their feet dragged slowly through the dust. It was clear they had been worse off for food than the rest of the camp.

They laid the two down in front of Mary's house.

Five days later, Kathleen died. Mary watched Paddy carry her away to the burying ground with Bridget walking behind, both of them keening and crying. Then she went in and lay down on her own bed.

Every time someone walked out of there on his own feet, it was a battle won. Every time someone had to be carried out, it was a battle lost. This was the worst defeat of all. She still had five to care for, but she couldn't move.

She turned her back on them and lay there, tears running weakly out of her eyes, till she fell asleep. She slept all night so heavily she didn't hear Thomas and young Larry coughing, or Jimmy groaning, or Johnny moving about, helping one or the other.

Johnny woke her when Hugh brought the breakfast stirabout.

"You're not sick, are you Mary?" he asked anxiously.

"Tired, Johnny, just tired."

She helped him get some breakfast into those who could eat and then fell back into bed. She slept all that day and that night and woke the next morning to see Dan on his knees bending over her with such a look on his face that she started up.

"What is it, then? Is it Thomas died on me while I was sleepin?"

"Thank God, you're yourself, Mary. I feared you would never wake. Did you know you slept a day and a night away?"

Mary struggled to her feet, pushing her hair out of her eyes. "How could I? And who took care of the poor sick ones?"

"Johnny did his best, but they're callin for you."

She clapped her hand to her stomach. "I'm that hungry, I could eat a cow."

"Well, now that I see you're as brisk as ever, I'll look for a cow or a pig or some creature we can eat on. There's a little bread and tea to take the edge off that big hunger you've got in you and if the luck's with me, there'll be more before the day's out. I'll try some of the other farmers about here. They may not all have the hard hearts of Higbee."

Dan drove up the Spring Creek Road to Peter Hobbs's farm. As he got out of the wagon and tied the horses to the fencepost, he could hear a distressful mooing from the barn, as if the cows needed milking. He walked up to the door, fearing what would be behind it. It opened and Peter's ten-year-old daughter, Sally, looked out with a face so full of misery Dan hardly needed to ask the question that was on his tongue.

"You got the fever here?"

She nodded, trying to sniff back the tears so she could talk.

"Where's your father?"

Sally came out and pointed. Peter was near a big oak, digging. Dan walked slowly over to him. As he got closer he could see a small mound covered with fresh earth. Peter was digging a larger grave next to it.

He stopped, leaned on his shovel, and without looking at Dan asked, "What do *you* want?"

Dan took off his cap and pointed at the grave. "Sarah?"

Peter looked at him now, with feverish eyes, then sat down heavily on the edge of the hole he was digging. "Sarah."

He wiped the sweat from his face as Dan sat down beside him. Then he began to talk, his slow, deliberate tones almost expressionless. "The doctor drove his buggy up here, it's weeks ago now and said to my wife, 'We need you, Miz Hobbs, to help care for the sick.' She's a great hand to care for the sick, Sarah is—Sarah was. I didn't want her to go, knowin how bad this sickness was gettin. . ."

Peter turned his head away from Dan. When he resumed, all warmth was gone out of his voice. The words were coming from some bleak place where a cold wind had stripped them to the bone. "The doctor, he said, 'You folks won't get this here fever. In all my days as a doctor,' he said, 'I never hearn of a black man or woman gettin this fever.' No, he never hearn tell of a black man or woman gettin the fever. Nobody knows our life and our death."

He was silent for a moment and then began again, slowly. "So Sarah took care of the sick and I buried the dead and we brought the fever back home and ever one of the children got it 'cept Sally. Sarah took sick and there was nobody to take care of her but me and Sally and then I took sick. The baby died day fore yesterday and this mornin about sunup, Sarah died."

Again the silence fell over the two men.

A chill rose from the bleak, half-finished grave and again Peter's words grew cold and bone-hard. "We needed someone to care for the sick in this house and nobody came. We needed someone to bury the dead here and nobody came."

Dan could find no words to say till Peter looked at him as if seeing him for the first time and asked, "Why did *you* come?"

Dan stood up and picked up the shovel. "I was thinkin it was to ask for a bit of milk and a bushel of potatoes, but more like it was to help bury your dead. Sit there while I finish this." He threw out a shovelful of dirt. "It wouldn't be the first grave I'd be diggin, but I haven't had to lay away one of my own, thank God. The two boys had the fever but Mary made them well again."

"Yes," Peter's voice was deep and warm again. "You had your troubles, too. I see that."

When the grave was dug, they walked slowly back to the cabin. Together they wrapped the body of Sarah Hobbs in a quilt and laid it in the box Peter had hammered together early that morning. Together they carried it to the grave, with Sally following after, and knelt beside it while Peter prayed.

That was praying such as Dan had never heard. It seemed to take the place of a wake for Sarah but Dan didn't know was this the way here in America or was the wake missing here as it was on the canal because the fever made things different.

Peter was growing weaker as the sun got higher in the sky and the day hotter. He let Dan cover the coffin with the fresh earth and help him back to the house where he dropped into bed, his powerful body at the end of its strength.

When Dan drove away from the Hobbs farm that afternoon, his wagon was loaded. On a bed of straw lay the two sick children, Lucille and Sam. Beside them were bushels of apples and potatoes, a heap of cabbages, a basket of eggs and two jugs of milk. He had offered to take Peter with him, too, but Peter said no.

"Me and Sally will get along allright now, if your missis can make Lucille and Sam well like she done your boys."

It was agreed that Pat Flynn would come and stay at the farm to do the chores till Peter was well enough to work again. Dan could come for milk and eggs and garden stuff for the camp.

"I'll *be* well," Peter said. "That's all about it. I has to be well."

When Dan got back to camp, Mary looked in amazement at the two Hobbs children, lying in the wagon. She had never had more than a brief look at their father, not enough to take away the strangeness.

"Can they understand our talk?" she asked dubiously.

"They don't know the Irish, but they know the English, the way it's spoke here. Haven't they lived in this country all their lives and their father before them?"

He climbed into the back of the wagon and handed Lucille down to her. The little girl opened her dark eyes, full of pain, and began to cry. Her tears washed away the strangeness.

"Och, the poor baby, she's no bigger than Ellen. There now, darlin, Mary's takin care of you. There now, acushla, don't cry."

The next day there were two more beds occupied. When the fever struck the Dugan shanty, it struck hard. Kevin Casey and Tommy Dugan had it now. But that was the fever's last strike.

Michael Kieran was up out of it. The fever had been milder for him than for any of them but to hear him tell it, Mary had snatched him from the edge of the grave. He was a young stoneworker, so quiet a lad that Mary had scarcely known him. She knew him well now and felt a special gladness when he walked out on his own feet.

She lost the battle, though, for the Dugans' Larry. All the next week she fought for the other three children and tried to keep her patience with Kate who was crying and complaining all day and half the night. Tommy lay almost motionless on his tick. Lucille and Sam both had the same terrible cough that had racked Kathleen. Then, the day Jimmy Grogan died, all three of the children seemed to turn the corner together.

"God forgive me, I can't mourn for Jimmy," Mary said to Johnny. "I'm that happy about the little ones."

She turned to Kate. "Kate, do you see your Tommy eatin his bit of bread and milk? He'll get well, or I'm not Mary Griffen."

"The poor baby. What will he do when his poor mother's dead? It's near the end for Kate Dugan, sure."

"Och, go along with you," Mary said in exasperation. "Johnny's bringin me a kettle of hot water and I'll make you a cup of tea with a drop of whiskey in it. You'll go to sleep and wake up feelin better like Tommy. I'll sit in the door and have a cup of tea, myself."

As she sipped her tea, she said in a low voice to Johnny, "If I have that woman on my back much longer, a cup of tea won't be enough. I'll be takin to the drink, that I will."

She thought Kate would surely live to go on complaining forever but the next day Kate was unnaturally quiet. That night she slipped into unconsciousness and never wakened. A few days later she was dead.

It was September now and suddenly the whole thing was over. Larry silently carried Tommy home and the next day the two of them as silently disappeared from camp. Kevin was almost well. Peter Hobbs was out of bed and doing his own chores. He brought Pat back to camp and took his children home. He thanked Mary again and again and laid a bundle in her arms. It was Sarah's Sunday dress and bonnet, real American clothes.

Dan had enough of a work force to top off the bits of the job that had been done between the sickness and the hunting. He tore a piece out of the back of the paybook and wrote a letter to Jamie at the new camp. The work was almost finished now, the letter said and all would soon be ready for Dent to inspect. Those who were left were all well but there was no money for food and Hall's store was still closed.

"We have missed two paydays and will have to sell the team and wagon if you don't come with money soon," he wrote. "If that don't fetch him, nothin will," he said to Mary.

What it fetched was a message back, carried by Mr. Dent when he came to look over the job. He gave the directions they were to load up and come south and west to the new camp. There was a small piece of money, too, to feed them till they got there.

Chapter 15

MARY SAT ALONE at the long table in the cookhouse, feeling like a piece of linen laid on a stone in the stream, beaten and beaten with a wooden beetle and then every drop rung out of it. She wished she could lay herself out in the sun as she used to do with the clean cloth till she got some fullness back in her limp body.

She looked at the few people scattered around the big room that used to be so full of men. It seemed to her that nearly everyone had died.

What was the use of comin all the way across the water, leavin behind everyone we knew, everyone we loved, the place where we belonged, only to find death waitin for us here? Death used to be a stranger who came and went . . . now, now he's been too close, too long . . . He'll never be farther from me than that shadow.

The men who had recovered from the fever wanted to forget it, forget the deaths of the others because that same death had come so close to them. They wanted to forget they had shown Mary their weakness and depended on her strength.

Kevin, the last to get back on his feet, was hardly up before he was claiming he was as good as ever. It was the strength of his own body beat the fever off, was his claim. Mary hadn't been in it at all.

Before the sickness, Mary had scarcely noticed the Caseys. They were two sandy-haired brothers with freckled faces, looking much alike to her, no knowing which was Kevin and which was Mick. She wondered at that now, so different they were. Mick was the older, slow of speech and thought, ungainly of movement and plain of face. He watched over the younger Kevin, proud of his good looks and his quick tongue. It was Mick gave Mary the thanks for keeping his brother alive.

Mary moved slowly and listlessly about the cookhouse. She should have been getting things ready for the journey to the new camp but she hardly knew what she was doing. Once asleep, no need of husband or children or campmates for food or comfort could rouse her. Once awake, she remained indifferent, responding only out of habit, often with irritation.

Dan tried to cheer her with talk of the new camp they would be going to, with the fever forgotten and himself likely getting the wages of a foreman. Jamie was there now, he reminded her, making all ready.

"Jamie," she pushed the name out of a puckered mouth to get rid of its taste.

"What is it that's in your head about Jamie?" Dan was surprised at her tone. He had forgotten the awkward gap between himself as a hand and Jamie as a boss. When Jamie left him in charge, the old accustomed friendly feelings, like an incoming tide, had washed over the resentment. And Mary had always thought Jamie the grand chief of the camp.

"Don't talk to me about that one and him off to Albany the minute he smelled the fever, leavin us to it."

Mary felt vaguely surprised on the morning of their leaving to find herself on the wagon seat next to Dan, Bridget on her other side with the baby on her lap.

The wagon was heavily laden with tools and all till there was hardly room for people. Their own things were packed into a two-wheeled cart that Jamie hadn't thought it worthwhile to move. Paddy and Johnny pushed the cart. It had one solid wood wheel, sawed off a big log and trimmed down to match the cart's one good wheel. Now it limped along like a drunken sailor with a wooden leg.

Pat had gone off ahead, for he had a longer journey all the way to New Orleans, where his family should be after coming across the water. Hugh had gone with him as far as Coshocton where the new camp was. Now there were only the Griffens and the O'Scanlons, Johnny Brennigan, Michael Kieran and the Casey brothers to go the road together from Akron to Coshocton.

As the little caravan made its way slowly across the summit and down the Tuscarawas River, Mary was still lost from what was going on around her. She didn't see the summit lakes as they passed around them, or the canal camps, where work was beginning to get under way again. She was hardly conscious of the talk going on among the men. The children's voices barely reached her as they ran ahead at first and then lagged behind till Dan threatened to knock smoke out of them with his stick if they didn't stay in sight. Even Bridget might as well have been off somewhere in another wagon entirely.

The white tiredness in Mary's face told them all how hard it would be for her to put one foot in front of the other and she was never asked to walk. It wasn't her look of fatigue, only. It was a feeling all had though no one put a word to it. There was something new even in the turn of Dan's head toward her. His look didn't pass over her, picking up the familiar reassurance that she was his Mary and was there as always. It saw her fully, the woman who had stood between them and the plague that had almost wiped them from the face of the earth. It was right that Mary was the one who should ride.

The rest of them kept on their feet. Even Bridget walked a mile now and then and let one of the young ones ride. There was no quick march about their going. It was more a slow wandering. When Mary asked Dan for a halt to the journey in mid-afternoon, there wasn't a word said about pushing on.

They camped beside the road like tinkers, making their beds under the wagon in case of rain. When the horses had been fed and watered and staked out for the night, when the supper was over, there was no work to do. The September night was warm and the sun not down yet, so they let the fire die out. They sat on around the glowing coals in a companionable quiet.

Mary and Dan had their backs against one of the wagon wheels, Ellen between them and the boys sprawled on either side. Mary was resting now in the warmth of Dan and the children. Tim begged Mary for a story but it was too much of an effort to fetch one up out of her memory.

"Maybe Paddy would be givin us a song?" she suggested.

So Paddy sang. Then Bridget had something to tell of what happened to her own grandmother through the Little People and one of their pishrogues. After that, Michael began a tale, the shy quiet Michael who had hardly opened his mouth among the loud talkers in the Akron camp.

"A story-teller the like of Michael was with us all those times in Akron and none of us knowing it," Dan said in wonder.

"It's from my grandfather I have the stories," Michael said, "God grant him a bed in heaven."

The second night, it was Johnny who had a request for Mary. "The way we're gone out of the old camp where I left Owen buried," he said, "It's beyond my knowin whether I'll ever see his grave again. Would you remember how it went, the way you was keenin Owen? And maybe you could say over the words, till I could get them in my head, like?"

The wake for Owen seemed so long ago. Could she bring the words back from that past time? Johnny and the others were all looking at her, waiting.

In the quiet, the words began to come back. "This is the Lament for Owen Brennigan," she said. "made by me, Mary Griffen, to wake him when he died and keep his memory after." She drew a deep breath and began:

"You were the one laughing,
Always laughing, Owen,
Young Owen of the merry eyes.
You made a gay fight of it,
Here, far from home."

As she went on, the timbre came back into her voice. The words rang out as they had done at the wake.

"Here you lie by a strange hearth
Far from home,
Owen Brennigan,
In a strange land,
But not alone, not alone."

Nothing was said for a few minutes. It was Michael who first spoke. "I wouldn't be takin a thing away from your brother," he said to Johnny. "What I would be sayin, this seems like it's for the rest of them, too, that we left behind."

"It is . . . that it is . . ." The murmur came from all around the campfire.

The next morning, Johnny gave over his pushing of the cart to Mick and walked beside the wagon, close by Mary, saying over the lament for his brother, with Mary giving him the right word when he needed it. When he had it all firmly in mind, he was satisfied.

Mary too, felt that the dead were buried at last and she was riding in the midst of the living. She was sitting in the place she had earned.

Bridget's Kathleen is gone, but without myself, would Bridget be sittin here with plump baby Nora on her lap and her man walkin the road, almost as well and strong as ever? . . There's my own Tim and Danny . . . There's Johnny and Michael and Kevin. Off ahead somewhere there's Pat Flynn. What a sad comin to America it would have been for his wife if there was no Pat livin to greet her . . . Somewhere too, there's Larry's Tommy and the two little motherless black ones. Maybe they wouldn't be growin up to their father now did I not bring them through it . . .

She could talk with Bridget now. It made the time and miles pass. There were things to see on either side of the road. Sometimes they were following close to the canal line; sometimes it was out of sight behind trees or across fields, but they were never far from it.

On the journey from Cleveland to Akron it had been all a foreign country, too new and strange to see anything clearly. Now they were coming from an Ohio workplace, an Ohio living place they had learned to know well. They were going to a new Ohio place that would be like it in the nature of the work and the living.

Now they had travelling companions with whom they had shared the work of the past year and the suffering of the past months.

Some of the canal sections they passed were already completed, some just being cleared, some only marked out. But whatever the state of the work, it was not the mere noise and confusion it had been to them when they caught their first glimpse of it. They looked with practiced eyes at what the men were doing.

They stopped to watch the monstrous big stump-puller on one section. "Look at that, now," Dan said. "The two wheels on it are higher than a house." It had a smaller wheel in the middle with horses hitched to it and it was pulling huge stumps out of the ground with hardly more effort than it takes a man to pull a potato out of the dirt. As they stood there, the boss on that job came over and asked them did they want to go to work.

That wasn't the only time they had the offer of a job. Once Kevin almost said yes for himself and his brother. Dan asked them were they ready to forget there was pay owing from McCarthy and Lordon at the end of the journey. As they talked over the jobs offered, they all stored it in their heads that twelve dollars a month and keep could be had now by a digger and eighteen or twenty by a skilled stoneworker like Michael.

The stream of labor that had been diverted from the canal by fear of the sickness had barely begun to trickle toward it. The bosses were desperate to use the good fall weather to make a dent in the work they had contracted to do, so the workers could choose their bosses by the pay offered. If Jamie and Simon were paying like the other bosses and had it in mind to keep Dan in a foreman's place, he would likely be getting more even than the fifteen that was in Jamie's last promise.

The good news about wages put more distance between them and the gloom of the past months than did the miles travelled. The farther they went along the line, the more Dan's spirits rose. He began to see, not just each job, each section, but the whole immense project. For all the weight that was on him to get the twelve of them and their heavy wagon load and their creaking, rickety cart to the new camp, he was swinging free now between jobs. His feet, so long rooted in Irish earth, were no longer held to a piece of land, nor—for the moment, at least—were they forced into the daily rut back and forth to the job. They were carrying him south along the line of the canal that was itself moving south as the earth was dug and heaved and the stones laid and the bridges and aqueducts built.

"Was there ever a thing built in the world that pulled so many men together for the one job?" Johnny asked Dan.

"Likely it's a thing they do in this country without hardly a thought," Dan answered. "There was the Erie Canal we was on comin from New York and they say there's another canal buildin in Pennsylvania and a road that goes right over the mountains that's between here and the sea. Such jobs bring men from every corner of the country and across the water, too."

They passed houses and fields and villages and places where there were no settlements and the canal work was not underway. They could plod through the forest for the better part of a day without seeing another wagon or anyone on foot or on horseback. They moved slowly there for there was hardly a road at all. It was no more than a narrow opening between the trees with their leafy branches meeting above it.

It was not a new road. For at least a hundred years and no one knew how much longer, it had been an Indian foot trail. Now it was wider. Men on horseback had ridden here. Oxen and horses had pulled heavily laden wagons, wearing the path down, churning it up into dust or mud till the roots of the huge oaks and chestnuts were bared.

They had never been closed in like this. Even where the fields are small in Ireland and enclosed by rocky hills, the bend in the road is visible and around it there is another house and another field. On the cloudiest day there is more light and more space than this

They emerged from the woods late one afternoon and found themselves near a canal camp. There seemed to be no Irish among the men who came out of the shanties and watched them make camp. No word of either welcome or warning was spoken till Dan led the horses over to the small stream that ran down the hill toward the Tuscarawas River. First one man and then another strolled over and they were soon in conversation about the merits of the team.

"Reckon you better stake 'em out pretty close to where you sleep," Dan was advised. "Been a coupla horses stole around here lately."

When they had some supper inside them, Dan got to talking about the farm the Griffens would surely have before long, now that the wages were up. Paddy and Bridget had the same dream. As they talked of it, it began to seem real to Mary again.

"Why wouldn't we be gettin our farms in the one place, with the fields of one next to the fields of the other?" she asked. She hadn't forgotten those words of Mrs. Higbee ". . . out here in the woods with the nearest neighbor miles off."

"Why wouldn't we indeed?" Paddy liked that notion. "We'd be the friends to each other so there could be the coorin back and forth when either had need of the help."

"Poor coorin with only two of you," Johnny said. "When I get the old folks over from Sligo and maybe a wife to work beside me, it's a farmer I'll be on the other side of Dan."

Michael was not to be left out. That would make four of them to buy the land together. Dan took a stick and drew a square in the ashes with the American name of a section.

"Not a canal section," he explained, drawing a line across the middle of it one way and another line the other way. "See there now? That's a farm for Paddy and Bridget and a farm for me and Mary and a farm for Johnny and his father and mother and a farm for Mikeen here when he finds a girl can maybe bring a cow or a horse for her dowry."

"Draw one there for us, too," Kevin said, after a look at his brother. "If it's good land, I'm for it. I've had my eyes open for a farm ever since I come across the water. A few more months work and we'll be bringin our wives over."

"How big would such a farm be?" Paddy asked.

"A hundred and sixty acres." Dan tossed it off as if it were nothing.

"No, what I'm askin," Paddy persisted, "what is it for each farm inside the hundred and sixty acres?"

"A hundred and sixty for each farm," Dan told it as it had been told to him by Peter Hobbs and other Akron farmers.

Paddy shook his head over a farm with such a size. "Might be Jamie would buy one of them big pieces and us that don't have the price could rent," he suggested.

Dan laughed. "When Jamie can raise potatoes in the canal and geese in the lockpits, that's the day he'll go to farmin. You can buy your own land. You don't have to pay it all at the one time, neither. One part of the price this year, another part next year. Look here, now . . ."

He pointed with his stick to each of the small squares inside the big square and then to each of the men. "They call that a quarter section. Mine and yours and his and his together makes a section and a farm for the Caseys makes another quarter section."

"Mick and me, we'll take a hundred and sixty each," Kevin said grandly.

Staring at the marks in the ashes, how could they make a farm out of such as that? But when Dan pointed to each with his stick, it was as if each man indeed had something of his own. They began to outdo each other in the potatoes and corn they would raise and the cows and pigs and sheep and geese and chickens they would have and the horses and wagons and plows.

"Listen to them," Mary said to Bridget. "Isn't it the big landowners they are? And them comin in from their fields to the dinners cooked on a fire like this with no hearth to it and the wives and children sleepin under the trees, is it?"

But neither she nor Bridget could resist the contagion. Before sleep that night, there were five snug houses built out of Irish memories and Ohio experience. Though they were as insubstantial as the smoke, the thought of them was as warm as the fire itself.

Their American farms filled so much of their talk it seemed that the farms, instead of another canal camp, should be at the end of this road. Five farms together made such a wide open place in Mary's thinking, the shadows were pushed back. She and Bridget talked of where they could find good Irish wives for Johnny and Michael and wondered what would the Casey women be like. For all of them, though the fields might not be theirs yet, nor cleared yet, nor plowed, already they had begun to produce the first green shoots of returning hope.

They had been on the way almost a week when the sky cleared toward sunset. The journey next day ended in the sunshine of an autumn afternoon, just above the Forks of the Muskingum River. As they plodded across the flat valley, the new job loomed ahead, overwhelming the dreamed future.

The work itself was known. They would be digging a new piece of the same canal. But the work would be in an unknown place. Beside the accustomed bosses would be an unknown boss with the American handle of "Judge" to his name.

When the old job was still going on in the spring, Jamie and and Simon had been absent down the line somewhere about business. Even Dan had paid little heed afterward to Jamie's bragging about the new contract they brought back and the new partner.

Now, they were walking into a sea of uncertainties.

Part Two

To the
Forks
of the
Muskingum

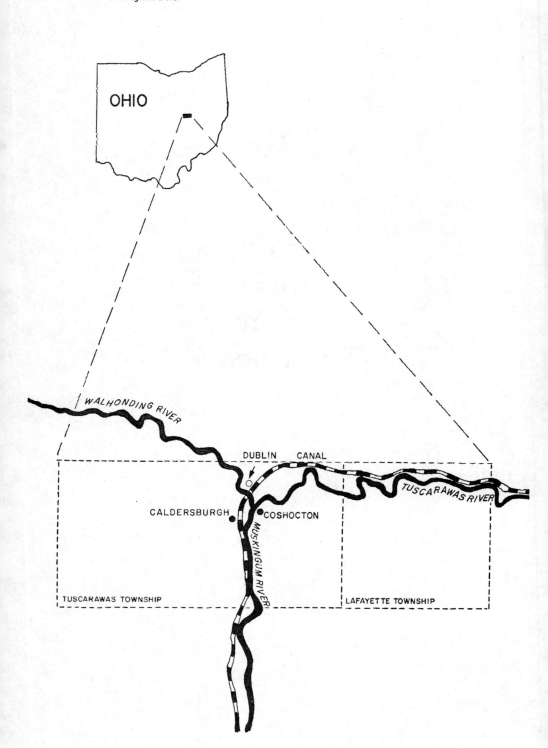

OHIO

WALHONDING RIVER

DUBLIN   CANAL

TUSCARAWAS RIVER

CALDERSBURGH   COSHOCTON

MUSKINGUM RIVER

TUSCARAWAS TOWNSHIP   LAFAYETTE TOWNSHIP

The Forks

THE HEADWATERS of the Muskingum flow south out of the hills that divide the Lake Erie plains from the Ohio River Valley. Collecting the water of many smaller streams on their southward journey, the Tuscarawas curves westward and the Walhonding eastward to meet at the Forks. There the Muskingum begins. Below the confluence, the Muskingum flows south to the Ohio.

For hundreds of years, early summer saw the rain cascading from the crowns of tall spreading trees down over green leaves, falling on small shrubs and grasses, washing over the rocks that thrust bare weathered faces out of the soil on the steeper slopes, soaking into the earth, restoring the diminished rivers.

After the autumn fall of the leaves, the rain ran down the bare branches and trunks of oak and hickory, sycamore and locust and dripped from the ends of millions of twigs. Winter halted the flow, then the snow melted and the frozen earth became marshy. The snow fields put out fingers of water in mild imitation of the glaciers that once covered the land where the Tuscarawas and Walhonding begin.

Every year the rivers were replenished, yet the days of the seasons were infinitely various. No winter repeated the winter before; each spring came in its own time and in its own way.

As the rivers changed from day to day, from season to season, they slowly changed the land, tunneling under their banks, scouring their channels with gravel carried down from the hills, wearing away limestone and sandstone, shifting their courses, deepening and broadening their valleys.

Infinitely various, constantly renewed and slowly changing was the life that drew sustenance from the rivers. The dams of the beaver interrupted the flow of the small streams, the heavy tread of the buffalo beat trails along the water. People followed these trails, moved up and down the river in their canoes, hunted the animals for food and skins, drew fish from the rivers, burned trees to make way for planting corn. The Forks of the Muskingum became a crossroads.

The life of the people flowed out of the past toward the expected future. Renewed from season to season, from year to year, from generation to generation, this life was slowly changed by encounters with the water and the land, with other creatures that shared these hills and valleys, with other people whose lives flowed out of another past in another place.

Erie people had named these rivers, built their long houses from the bark of these trees, planted the three sisters—corn, beans and squash—in these open places, fished these rivers and hunted these forests. At night, as the wind moved the branches of the great trees, as wolves howled and night birds called, they heard echoes of gods and ancestors assuring them of their own place in the flow of time.

The Erie were gone now, defeated by the Iroquois, killed or absorbed into the Iroquois nations. After the Erie, the Wyandot had come this way from their northeastern home, having learned the bitter lesson of what happens when swift silent arrows meet the swifter and less silent death of foreign guns. After the Wyandot, the Lenape. The Muskingum Valley was Wyandot country when the Lenape came, but both Wyandot and Lenape knew that the land belonged in common to all. Only special rights to its use could be given away by those who lived on it. These rights—to plant in it, to hunt the animals in its woods and the fish in its rivers, to put cabins and wigwams and council houses on it—were hospitably extended by the Wyandot to the Lenape.

In the same spirit, a hundred and fifty years before, the Lenape had welcomed the people of the ships to the shore of the ocean bay and to the valley of the Lenapewihittuck River far to the east. But the newcomers had accepted the hospitality in a different spirit, out of a different understanding of the relationship of people and land. They had crossed the sea on missions of trade, on errands of empire. They had alien notions of conquering the land and denying it forever to those whose mothers had tended the crops given by its soil, whose fathers had brought in the meat and the skins given by the animals in its woods.

The ships came more and more often, bringing people who remained on the land. To these people, the Manitowuk who lived in sun and wind, in tree and animal, were as nothing and the Lenape as less than nothing. They took from the Lenape everything, even the names of their places and their own names. The Bay, the River, and the Lenape themselves came to be called by the name Delaware, the name of an English lord who never saw bay or river or Lenape people.

Generation after generation of Lenape were pushed west from the Lenapewihittuck to the Susquehanna, from the Susquehanna to the Allegheny, and then to the Tuscarawas and the Muskingum. Their former towns and hunting grounds were sold and resold, cleared and fenced in, with all but those who were called owners fenced out.

But here on the Muskingum, the land had not yet been completely estranged from the ancient sharing of it among all the people and all living things. New generations could live here in the old way, for this valley, though different, was also generous. There was food enough if every man and woman worked to make their common living. They could raise their children, govern themselves, and choose their leaders as they had always done.

Yet they did not live quite in the old way, for long before the Lenape had reached the Muskingum they had ceased the ancient sharing with the beaver, the deer, the buffalo, and the bear. They had been drawn into the rivers of trade that had brought the people of the ships. These rivers bore away the pelts the Lenape harvested in the forest and brought back blankets, ironware, rum. The Lenape had become professional hunters and dressers of skins, their lives affected by the price of beaver hats in Amsterdam, deerskin breeches in London, fur coats in Paris, wool cloth in Bristol, guns in Philadelphia. They were paid for their work as were the weavers and hat makers and gunsmiths. Their work enriched traders, merchants and manufacturers in both near and distant places.

The wisdom of peacemaking had once made the Lenape the grandfathers of other Wabanaki—other people of the sunrise country. As they were forced farther and farther from that country, they were no longer called on to make peace. Their young war captains took part in the councils along with the elders. Lenape warriors made swift raids against the invaders and trod precarious warpaths when the armies of hostile empires fought each other.

The Lenape town at the Forks they named after the black bear, for Cushog still lived in the nearby hills and came down to the river to drink and scoop a fish for his dinner from its plentiful waters. In Cushogwenk, they built a Big House in which men and women could speak their visions and give thanks to the Great Manito, the creator of all, to Thunders that brought the rain, to the mother, Earth, who carried them and gave them everything they needed and to all the other Manitowuk, great and small, who were present in the sky over the Muskingum as in the sky over the Lenapewihittuck, in the earth beneath, in the sun, the wind, the stars, the trees and the animals. They put up bark wigwams and log houses and cleared many acres of land for their corn and for pasture for their cattle. From Cushogwenk they followed the rivers and the creeks up into the forest where the hunting was still good.

Out of the long past in the sunrise country, out of the troubled past of the movement westward, out of the Ohio earth and sky and waters the Lenape life was shaped, moved toward convergence with other native Americans, toward new encounters with the alien people.

Neolin, a Lenape from the valley of the Cuyahoga, had a vision of a trail for the Lenape to follow. It was a trail that went peacefully among all living things, marked by the almost forgotten signs of their ancestors:

Take the flesh of animals for food and their skins for clothing, but do not sell what has been placed on earth as food; then the animals that have been removed from the depths of the forest will return. You need neither guns nor rum nor any of the other alien objects that came with the evil spirit who transforms men into horses and dogs to be ridden by him and to follow him in his hunts.

It was a trail that led toward meetings with brother Indians, where each would take the other by the left hand, the hand of the heart. Yet it was a trail that led to war, for in Neolin's vision the message from the Creator of All to Lenape and Wyandot, to Shawnee and Mingo, to Ottawa and Chippewa, to Potawatomi and Seneca was:

This is the land I have made for all the Indians. Drive the
people who are strangers to this land back to their own lands
that I have made for them.

The wars pushed the invaders back, but never all the way to the shore of the sea. Always the strangers returned, crossing the Alleghenies that solemn promises had set as a barrier to westward settlement, crossing the Ohio, coming up the Mississippi and down from the Lakes.

Coquetackeghton was chosen by his people as a chief. He was not a prophet like Neolin, but he too had a vision. It grew slowly out of many councils among the Lenape, much listening to a different sound in the talk of the people who now called themselves Americans, much thought of its meaning for the Lenape. There was no need for British king and British governors and British soldiers, it was now said. They could be driven out of this land, leaving it to the people who lived in it and who could live in peace with each other. If the Lenape would help to drive the British out, the new Americans would live with them in peace.

There were journeys to Fort Pitt, words spoken by Coquetackeghton to the Continental Congress. Finally, the vision of Coquetackeghton became a treaty, an alliance against the British and a promise that the Lenape should head a four-teenth state, open to other Indian nations who would join the alliance, sending their own representatives to Congress. No settlements except Indian settlements would be allowed north or west of the Ohio.

Colonel Coquetackeghton marched with the Continental Army. His life was taken, not by the enemy but by those with whom he marched. When he was gone the alliance eroded, the treaty was forgotten.

Three years later Cushogwenk died, too. Attacked in the absence of most of its warriors, its standing corn was burned, its cattle slaughtered, its storehouses plun-dered, its log houses and bark wigwams, its Big House with the carved pillars reduced to ashes. One of its chiefs was shot during a peace parley, fifteen men of fighting age captured, bound, tomahawked and scalped, all of its women, chil-dren and old men taken prisoner. Colonel Brodhead, the conqueror of Cushogwenk, who had once called Coquetackeghton "Brother" had other words, now: "I conceive that much confidence ought never to be placed in any of the colour, for I believe it is much easier for the most civilized Indian to turn Savage than for any Indian to be civilized."

A year later, the villages farther up the Tuscarawas were destroyed and their people slaughtered by militiamen from Pennsylvania. These were Moravian vil-lages, peopled by Christian Lenape, but even Christian infants of "the colour" might grow up to become so savage as to claim the land on which they lived.

There were already four hundred settlers on the Muskingum when the peace with Britain was signed. Eleven years later, the Ohio peoples made their last stand at the Battle of Fallen Timbers. The years of the Lenape in the Muskingum Valley were ended and they were confined to a small reservation.

Small groups came down from the northwest now and again to their old hunt-ing grounds, into the 1820s and even later. They found the fur-bearing animals decimated by the intense hunting demanded by the selling of pelts, their haunts disappearing in the pall of smoke that hung over every advancing clearing. The ashes that had once been trees were dumped in the ash hopper with fat scraps to make soap or sent down the river to market as barrels of potash.

Now when Lenape hunters stood on the bluffs above the Forks or roamed the country drained by the Muskingum and its headwaters, they saw surveyors mark-ing off the swelling hills and curving rivers into square townships. As the farms spread, as Cushogwenk was reborn as Coshocton and grew into a town, as the building of road and canal cut through the old trails and muddied the familiar fishing grounds, the Lenape came less and less often to the Muskingum Valley.

Finally, the line around their reservation was eroded by settlement, altered by purchase, wiped out by treaty. The Lenape were driven still farther west by the settlements and the soldiers of the United States as the Irish had been driven "to hell or Connaught" by the English. Remaining to the conquerors was the land that had nourished native Americans for centuries and with it a legend of their passing to be told and mistold by the invader till it drew heroic borders around his own deeds to the land and fenced his farms with righteousness.

The new life that was taking shape in the land the Lenape left behind moved slowly at first, then more and more rapidly, liberated from bonds of old empires and chains of tradition by a revolution. It was a constantly changing life, part of a rapidly expanding nation.

The hills and valleys drained by the Muskingum were no longer used in common, with work for all and a living for all. They were valued because their land could be bought and sold and because it could raise crops that could be sold and bought, because there were salt deposits, building rock, mortar limestone in the hills and coal deep underground that could be dug, quarried, worked, marketed. Fortunes were made by some who had thousands of its acres to sell. Ordinary people drew a living from working their own small piece.

The people came out of many different pasts, pasts that were sometimes quickly forgotten, sometimes proudly remembered. They clashed and mingled, sometimes were swept away in the swift current that was changing the face of the Valley. The Valley's past might be ignored, the bitter legacy of its conquest might be misunderstood; nevertheless, from beneath layers of neglect and denial, the underground stream of this heritage fed into the life of the Valley's new people as it flowed toward an unknown future.

Chapter 16

JUDGE JOSHUA LAURENCE and his wife, Eliza, stood on the front porch of their home above the Walhonding River on a bright early morning in the spring of 1827, watching Joshua's new partners ride off down the hill.

Simon Lordon's square figure jogged up and down with his horse but looked otherwise immobile. James McCarthy was constantly moving in his saddle, his head turning toward Simon, one hand holding the reins, the other pointing now this way, now that. These men would be part of their lives for the next year or more.

When they had disappeared around the curve of the hill, Eliza sighed. "Where did you find those Irishmen? Can't our own folks do this work?"

"Those that can are contracting their own sections. Maybe I could have got the contract for digging the section across our own place but the embankment all the way from there to the river and the aqueduct across the river, especially the aqueduct—that's one of the biggest jobs on the whole canal. Mr. Kelley told me I'd have to have experienced canal men in with me and when I saw what the job was, I wouldn't have wanted to tackle it alone. McCarthy and Lordon were going to bid on it anyway. It was only good common sense to get together on it."

"I suppose," Eliza agreed without enthusiasm.

On the whole Joshua was well pleased. All the previous day he had walked with his new partners over what would be the canal line; late into the night they had talked business. The canal would do wonders for the value of his own place and he had been buying up other land in and around Caldersburg which was bound to grow as a canal port. Plans for getting construction started had been worked out. He took a deep breath, stretched up on his toes and came down again to a firmly satisfied stance, just as he did when things were going well for him in the courtroom.

"We'll hire as many local men as we can," he reassured Eliza, "but you know the trouble we had finding stone masons to do the work on the house. There just aren't enough men in Ohio without bringing more in from somewhere. We'll put most of them yonder . . ." He waved in the direction the men had taken, "Closer to the canal line and well away from the house. Some up by the quarry to get the stone out. We'll just have McCarthy and Lordon and a few of the skilled men here. It won't be for long. When the job is finished they'll all move on."

"I certainly hope so. We wouldn't want a nest of papists in Coshocton County, just when it's beginning to get a mite civilized."

"Indeed not," Joshua agreed, "though McCarthy and Lordon seem decent men—a little hard to understand sometimes. Mr. Kelley says they know their business and have a reputation for fair dealing. I'll keep a sharp eye on them, though. Don't worry about that. They won't get the better of *me*."

That anyone was likely to get the better of Joshua had never crossed Eliza's mind. Her thoughts were elsewhere. "Joshua, don't you think it's time we sent Betsy to Lavinia in Cincinnati before all this commotion starts? We've talked about it and talked about it and keep putting it off. Now that we're going to have a regular army of men around, I'd rather she was in Cincinnati where she can get a little proper schooling and be with other young ladies."

"She's got more sense and more education and more manners than most young ladies I see in Columbus or Cincinnati. I don't know what more you want or who could teach her anything you couldn't."

"It will be bad enough for Robert. It's just not right and proper for Betsy."

Eliza's mind was made up. Joshua gave an abrupt nod which she could interpret as she pleased and ran down the steps and off to look over the old tenant cabin and see what had to be done to make it usable.

Eliza went inside, turning over in her mind the coming changes in their life. Instead of going directly to the kitchen where she could hear the clatter of dishes as Tessa cleaned up after breakfast, she lingered in the wide central hall.

The kitchen was the heart of the house, the center of her work; the parlor was her particular pride, finer than the parlor of her girlhood in New Jersey, almost the equal of her sister Lavinia's in Cincinnati. Yet it was the hall that in some ways meant the most. It gave her a sense of space, of distance from the years in the tiny house where she had given birth to the three babies who had died and the daughter and son who were almost grown. The gracious curve of the ascending stairway reassured her that the log house in Coshocton with its steep stairs—little better than a ladder—was a thing of the past. The wide front door and the fanlight above it confirmed the present in which they were now Judge and Mrs. Laurence, not merely of Coshocton County but of the State of Ohio.

Eliza stood for a moment where she could see in the oval mirror the reflection of the opposite wall and the tall clock that stood against it. Somehow, seeing it this way made it appear like a room in some other house, serene, perfect . . . but she couldn't linger.

She must get Betsy properly fitted out for the city. There would be a great deal of sewing to do. She would have to get Mrs. Weaver in. Joshua's mother had not taught more than the plainest sewing to Tessa.

Throughout the two years since Joshua's brother had brought Tessa and her two children to them from Virginia, Eliza had never lost the uncomfortable feeling that she was countenancing sin by taking them in. Joshua had called it their Christian duty to make a place for these three slaves of Paul's on their farm. Had they not long recognized slavery as an abomination? Could they send Tessa and her children back into it? What had never been discussed between husband and wife was that Tessa's two boys were almost certainly Paul's sons. Her black skin and the lighter skins of the boys were an ever present reminder of the unacknowledged relationship.

Eliza walked into the kitchen and began to put away the dishes Tessa had washed and dried.

"We'll have those men and more to cook for when the Judge's canal work gets started," she told Tessa.

Eliza looked at her big kitchen table and pictured it entirely surrounded by men in dirty sweaty work clothes. Swarms of foreigners would be invading their place if not actually coming into their house. She imagined the invasion as something like the day of the annual militia muster in Coshocton when the town square was full of men marching most of the day, drinking, yelling and fighting most of the night.

The canal workers were slow in coming, in spite of Eliza's fears and Joshua's hopes. The sickness that swept the line and much of the country round, although it touched this area only lightly, made workers scarce and disrupted the well-laid plans of Joshua and his partners.

Joshua got much of the clearing done in the spring and early summer with local men but it was autumn before the quarry work was well in hand under Simon Lordon. About the same time, McCarthy returned from Albany with a blacksmith and two carpenters and began to get a crew of diggers together. They were still waiting for what was left of the old force from Akron, expected daily under Dan Griffen who was to be foreman of the diggers.

"We'll get as much done in the winter as weather allows," McCarthy said. "By spring, the fever will be forgot and the ships will be coming over again from Ireland."

The camp at the quarry was two miles off, the one at the canal line was well out of the way, as Joshua had promised. The strangeness began to wear off the whole project for Eliza. The men who came into the kitchen at meal time ate enormously but there were no problems beyond the expected dirty boots and uncouth manners. She could put up with it all for a year or two.

Laurence got his first look at Dan Griffen on the evening of his arrival, when he came into the cabin that was now the office, for a reckoning with McCarthy over the weeks he had been in charge in Akron. This was no affair of Laurence's. So much the better. He could stand with his back to the fire, exchanging a word with Lordon now and then, listening to the way the fellow handled his business with McCarthy.

At first Griffen seemed ill at ease, looking over at Laurence from under his shaggy brows, then quickly away again. Gradually, he seemed to realize that Laurence was taking no part. As the tempo of the talk increased, it grew difficult for Joshua to follow. He had congratulated himself that he had mastered McCarthy's brogue but they were talking too fast for him and Griffen sprinkled his sentences with Irish words.

He didn't need to understand their words to see that these two were old cronies and were hardly talking business at all. After a bit, though, Griffen got out the paybook and a dirty piece of paper with what was apparently a list of expenses. Then Laurence was glad to see that McCarthy put the man through his paces. As they sat at the table going over the names in the paybook one by one, he could get at least the sense of what passed between them.

There were arguments over what Hugh Cadigan was to be paid for the cooking and what was owing to Griffen himself. When those had been settled to McCarthy's satisfaction, Griffen turned over a bundle of raggedy odds and ends belonging to men who had died.

"There's a letter there Martin got from the old country and some other things might tell where it is you'll be sendin to the families what's owin to the men, along with the sad news you'll be givin them."

McCarthy took the bundle and set it aside, reaching for the account of Akron expenses.

Griffen's eyes stayed on the bundle. "You would know where the men's pay goes?"

McCarthy shrugged. "Some I know, some I don't."

"I could maybe put a name or a place to the things, or Mary could. Some of the lads talked about home when they knew they weren't long for this world."

"When I need help from you, I'll ask for it," McCarthy said brusquely, taking up the list of purchases. He read it slowly, checking each item as he accepted it. Suddenly he exploded.

"A washtub! Did you have men up there or fine Dublin ladies? They had to scrub their lily-white arses in a washtub? Where's your lace petticoats and your bottle of perfume? Wouldn't you be askin me to pay for them things, too?"

Griffen got up from his stool looking so fierce Laurence thought he was going to strike McCarthy but McCarthy seemed quite unconcerned and Lordon was smiling as he listened.

Griffen leaned across the table, bringing his face down close to McCarthy's, pouring out a flood of words. The name "Mary" recurred from time to time but that was about all Laurence could catch. McCarthy moved back uneasily and dropped his eyes to the paper in front of him, pushing it back and forth on the table. The smile faded from Lordon's face.

At last Griffen straightened up. "Martin Daly!" he called out as if summoning someone. Laurence involuntarily looked toward the door but Griffen responded to his own call.

"Dead!" He lowered his voice and rolled out the word, striking the table with his hand.

"Old Man Hennessey!" he trumpeted. "Dead!" and again struck the table. "John Murphy! Dead! . . Thomas Sweeney! Dead! . . Jimmy Grogan! Dead! . . Kate Dugan! Dead! . . Larry's Larry! Dead!"

Jamie cleared his throat but before he could speak Griffen forestalled him. He was speaking so slowly and distinctly now that Laurence got every word though it was the other two he was addressing.

"You, Jamie McCarthy, and you, too, Simon Lordon. I wouldn't say another word of this hereafter. They're dead and gone and whatever we say won't bring 'em from Akron or return 'em to Ireland. But it was Mary kept 'em from dyin a dirty death in their own shit and that's the meanin"—he pointed at the list—"of the washtub."

Jamie got up without a word, collected the noggins and filled them with whiskey again. They drank to those who were dead and nothing further was said about the list of expenses.

After a decent interval, during which Griffen's pipe was filled from Lordon's pouch and all smoked, they began to talk again. At last they got down to the business of the new job and now Laurence could join in the discussion.

Griffen listened respectfully enough to the orders he was given. He seemed to be satisfied with the eighteen dollars a month pay he was promised with three dollars more as long as he boarded himself. Laurence wondered if they really had to put it that high, which reminded McCarthy to make it clear the high pay was promised only for the fall months. It would be coming down in the winter.

Still, Laurence shook his head over it. For all McCarthy seemed so tough, there was a tendency for him to think of himself as the father of all the Irish hands and Griffen would take advantage of that. It wasn't going to be as easy as he had first thought to turn a profit on it. However, McCarthy and Lordon had done it on their last contract and were as eager as he to do it on this one. No need to borrow trouble.

Chapter 17

W ASN'T IT almost a piece of County Cork, Mary said to Dan about the new camp. There were men from Skibbereen and Cork City and from townlands between the harbor and their own Carrignahown. There were more families than in Akron, so it was less like an army and more like a village.

Judge Laurence called the cluster of shanties on the edge of the hill "Dublin." That was because, like most Americans, he could name but the one Irish city. There were "Dublins" scattered the length of the canal but Dennis and his family were the only ones here from Dublin City.

Some of the men in this camp had worked elsewhere on the canal or before that on the Erie. Others, like Tom Quinlan and Dennis were just over from Ireland. Dennis and Michael Kieran were the only stonecutters here, the rest being at the quarry camp. Dennis was here because there was no place for his family at the quarry, Michael because it was a matter of course to him that he would be where Dan and Mary were. Jamie couldn't budge him. The rest of the men were diggers.

Donal Shelley and some of the other men of the skilled trades slept in a lean-to attached to Jamie and Simon's cabin. They ate with the bosses in the Laurence kitchen but when they were lonesome for Irish ways and Irish speech they found their way to Dublin.

There had not been so much as a roof to crawl under when they came. The first job was to put up the shanties. They went up quickly, simple boxes without floors or windows. Walls were of wood instead of earth or stone as at home, so they could not back a hearth. A few stones in the center of each shanty marked its fireplace. The smoke would have to find its way out the door or the cracks in the wall. Some kind of rough division was contrived inside to separate the lodgers' sleeping quarters from the kitchen where the cooking and eating was done and where the family slept. Dirt was pushed up against the slabs outside to keep out wind and weather.

"The house building that goes on in this country," Tom Quinlan said, putting his head on one side and giving the O'Scanlon shanty a critical look. "Pieces of wood that don't come near enough each other to say 'good mornin.' Why wouldn't they be makin the walls good and solid out of clay? Is it maybe always warm in this country, so they wouldn't care does the wind come in?"

"You'll wish for a snug Irish cabin and a turf fire to warm your bones many a cold day when winter comes," Dan promised him. "Push up the mud a little higher there. That's a gap big enough to lose a man through. It wouldn't do for Paddy, but a man the size of yourself could be out through it in a wink, was the law after you."

Tom took joking about his small size in good part but when Kevin called him 'little man' in a condescending tone, Kevin found himself looking up at Tom from below. He stayed away from Tom after that and stayed away from the work, too, leaving the rest of them to put the roof boards across. They cut a few sods to hold the boards down and make the shanties tighter but these were poor scraws, the best that could be found in a country that seemed to have no proper turf.

Mary was not satisfied with this. For all her hopeful talk about the farm, the shadows had not been dissipated, they had only been pushed back.

"What's around the next bend in the road, no one knows," she said to Dan, "or will we get there at all. This being our own home and not the corner of the cookhouse, we have a right to our own hearth."

She wanted an American fireplace made out of sticks and plastered over with clay, with a chimney to it, like the fireplace she had cooked on in Akron. She wanted the roof raised up high enough so there could be a half-loft, a sleeping place for the boys and the lodgers.

"All that work for the one winter or maybe two?" Dan was reluctant and Jamie was harrying him to make an end to the building and get to work on the line.

"It's well I'm knowin' we're here today and gone tomorrow," Mary said, "but it's not the tinkers we are or the beggars. It's not the poor cotters, neither, with such a bit of a patch we have to squeeze ourselves into the corner of it to make room to plant the praties. Look at that, now." She swept her arm wide to take in all they could see. "Why would the good God put down all the sticks and stones for us if he didn't mean us to use them when they're needful? If you have to go to work on the line, go then. We can sleep under the sky a while longer if we must and you can finish the cabin little by little on the Sundays. Johnny and Michael and the boys will all help."

So Mary got her fireplace with a stone hearth laid by Michael and was the envy of the other women. There were a few hard things said about her by Maggie Flynn but Bridget told Maggie to keep her tongue inside her mouth till she knew the woman she was lashing with it.

Michael, Hugh and Johnny lodged with the Griffens, Tom Quinlan and two other new men with the O'Scanlons, the Casey brothers with the Flynns.

Maggie Flynn was a fine big woman. In spite of her jealousy of Mary's hearth, the two of them soon got in the habit of standing in their own doorways after the men had gone off to work of a morning and exchanging a few words before starting the rest of the day's work. Mary was now the veteran who could tell Maggie the way of things in the new country. When she listened to Maggie's tales of the seven years at home without Pat and the way Pat was a stranger to his children she was pleased with herself anew that all the Griffens had come over the water together.

Maggie's sixteen-year-old son, Egan, was now working beside Pat but having been the man of his mother's house, he was resentful of Pat and quick to go roaming on a Saturday night with Kevin and Mick.

The Griffen, Flynn and O'Scanlon households were the strong beams in the framework of the Dublin loom. The bonds that had begun to tie these people together in Akron formed the warp through which the shuttle of Dublin's daily life went back and forth and a fabric of community was woven.

To newcomers like Rose Farrell and Eileen Dawley, this camp was life in the new country. They had nothing with which to compare it except a townland in the Irish countryside or a slum in Dublin. Mary and Bridget, though, could see how different it was from Akron. There was no cookhouse to be the center of this camp and the bosses were off by themselves. There was something like a Big House here, too, and that was more like Cork than Akron. It was a fine house on the side of a hill, made out of boards lapped over each other to keep out the wind. There were two great stone chimneys to it and glass windows downstairs and upstairs.

After Jamie and Simon had left Akron, Dan had been the chief. New men took that view of him from the old. All Dublin heard stories of those days. Mary's role in that time took on an almost legendary character; sickness in any shanty always brought a call for Mary's help.

There was another thing too, that was crucial to people who had slipped their mooring in the old country and were rudderless in these waters. The plan that had its beginning on the journey from Akron grew to mean moving the Dublin community into the countryside nearby when the canal work here was done, with every Irish family having its own acres and its own hearth, with countrymen for neighbors. This plan was not for everyone. There were some who had anchors in the Dublin that was beginning to grow in Cincinnati. Some men who were here without wife or child had drifted too long to come about and head for any port. The rest seized the dream. The confidence Dan and Mary showed in talking of it gave it substance. The hope gave the laborious days a new meaning, the common goal drew them together.

They hadn't been long in their new homes before Dublin had its first new life. Eileen Dawley had been pregnant when she left Ireland with her young husband and was near her time when they came into camp.

"How could she do it?" Bridget said to Mary. "Them ships, they was made by the devil to destroy a woman even without she's carryin a child. I know there was many days I thought there was no land left in the world or if there was, Bridget O'Scanlon wouldn't live to see it."

"Would any of us have set foot on the ship if we knew what was in store for us? But once you're in it, there's one thing only you can do and that's get through it. It's like the birth itself. Once started, no matter what the pain of it, gettin through it is all a woman can do."

This time there were women enough to help Eileen, though some were still in their childbearing years and properly should not have been called to a birth. Rose Farrell watched over the children. Maggie Flynn, her sister Kate, and Bridget took turns on helping and Mary was there through it all, more confident now since the birth of Bridget's Nora. This time, too, things went well. It was natural Eileen should labor harder, this being her first, but she had a fine boy in her arms when it was all over. Joe's round young face beamed with pride and delight when he saw his son.

Mary was proud of Dan for becoming a foreman. The bigger pay made the importance of it unmistakable and brought the farm closer. It did not sweeten her tongue when she spoke of Jamie, though. Hadn't he known the man Dan was from the way he was the leader when the troubles came down on them in Carrignahown? No thanks to him now that he got it in his head at last to bring Dan to the fore.

Jamie was the boss of the job still but when they left the canal they would leave him behind with no regrets. That was Mary's thinking. Jamie had been a smart lad and he was a smart man who knew how to count his own shillings but what care did he have for a friend or neighbor? They had no need of him in the life of Dublin outside the job and it was Dan would be the chief in the Dublin of tomorrow when they had the farms.

"Look at the way Jamie and Simon was after dumpin us down here like a pile of stones," she said to Bridget when they talked of finding no place ready for them when they arrived, "with hardly a word said about the ones we left behind under the sod. One man is like another to them, the way one barrow is like another. Did you and me drown in one of them rivers we was crossin on the way from Akron, would they know we was gone? Not them. So I'm not to do the cookin here, neither. Maybe Jamie will be pickin me up again in the spring like he says and maybe he won't. It's will I fit into the work the way a stone fits into a wall. Maybe he'll be leavin me without the way to earn a penny, not wantin me at all."

When she said such things to Dan, he paid little attention. She wasn't working on the job and didn't see how it was now, with himself leading the diggers while Jamie and Judge Laurence were down by the river with their own crew, getting ready to start the aqueduct. Dan and his men were digging into the hill where it had been cleared, wheeling barrowloads of the hillside to its edge and dumping them into the valley where the embankment would begin. Ahead of the diggers where the axemen had finished clearing, the Judge's son Robert, a tall lad but not yet a man, was in charge of cleaning up the debris of branches and brush.

Tim and Danny had left barefoot childhood behind. They were workers now, rising from their ticks on the floor of the loft in the dark before the dawn, pulling on their heavy boots and following Johnny and Michael and Hugh down the ladder. They no longer had to wait till all the men were fed before there was a bite of breakfast for them. Mary served them as soon and treated them as well---if not a bit better---than their father and the other men. They were so sleepy, though, she had to prod them awake to keep them eating.

When they walked out of the shanty with the men, the cold morning air blew the last rags of sleep out of their heads and shivered them full awake. They were part of Robert's clean-up crew along with Padeen Flynn, Pat's youngest, and two black boys, the sons of Tessa, who worked at the Big House. The big white oaks the axemen had downed had been dragged to the river by the oxen to float to the sawmill, stumps and lesser trees dragged off the line to be burned later for potash. The tangle that was left was for the boys to clean up. They pulled the limbs and brush into a heap and fired it, flinging more and more debris into the blaze till it soared high above their heads. Sometimes they had to chop at the tangle of branches to free them for handling. Then they vied with each other for the use of an axe. Robert had his own but they were seldom allotted more than two others. Tim, who had learned to use an axe in the Akron camp and Willie, the bigger of the two black boys, most often got their hands on the axes. Padeen was too new come from Ireland to have the heft of that frontier tool. Robert, who said every Ohio boy was born with an axe in his hand, showed Danny the way of it. Sometimes Danny and Arden, Willie's younger brother, would race for an axe. They came to blows over it once but to Danny's amazement, Willie yanked Arden away and gave Danny the prize.

"Don't you know better than to hit a white boy?" Willie hissed at his brother.

Dan appeared unexpectedly now and then. He never came down hard on "Mr. Robert" but if one of the others were caught idling, the guilty one was likely to get a stinging blow with the flat of Dan's hard hand. But he had a word of praise for all when they had a new piece of the line well cleaned up for the diggers.

Ellen had some new playmates in Dublin and new places to explore but her life would never again be all play. It was time for her to learn a little of women's work. Though Mary had work enough to keep her busy through the day, it was in her own small kitchen, not in the big cookhouse with all its hurry and bustle. She had time now to teach Ellen.

The little girl followed her mother to the well behind the Big House every morning for water. While Mary cleaned the pot the stirabout was cooked in, Ellen washed the spoons and tin plates Mary had bought from a peddler. Ellen learned to sweep the hearth, too, and to put the smallest pieces of wood on the fire without burning herself. She could watch when the potatoes had been put to boil and keep the white horses galloping on top of the water. When ash cakes were in the making, she couldn't yet stir the batter but after Mary's stirring, she could pat it into firm cakes.

This was usually on a Sunday when there was more time for the men to taste what went into their mouths. Mary made the cakes with buttermilk and eggs bought from a farmer who drove a wagon load of produce to Dublin once a week. Such cakes she had seldom made since the days of her girlhood when she and Gran were taken in by their kin on the big farm near Inchigeela. Their own butter and eggs in Carrignahown had been mostly for the market, not for their own bellies. Even now, the cakes were not quite right, for the meal here was made from Indian corn.

Mary showed Ellen how to get the fire burning hot all across the fireplace to heat the stone hearth. While the wood was burning down to hot ashes, they would make the ash cakes. Then, they would carefully brush the ashes away from one spot on the hearth after another with the bundle of twigs Mary had tied together for a broom. Ellen would lay down a cabbage leaf, put a cake on it, cover it with another wet leaf and then with ashes. As she raked the ashes over the cakes, Ellen told herself what Mary had told her, "ashes over all, fire over none."

The proudest thing came at the end of the day, when Mary was smooring the fire. If Ellen was not already asleep, she helped to cover the seed of the fire with ashes, repeating after her mother:

"I save this fire, as noble Christ saves;
Mary on the top of the house and Brigid in its center;
The eight strongest angels in Heaven
Preserving this house and keeping its people safe."

Chapter 18

ONE MONDAY morning when she and Ellen went to fetch water, Mary met Tessa at the well behind the farmhouse. She had often glimpsed her before, moving across the yard from her small cabin to the kitchen of the Big House, but they had never come face to face. Now she could see that Tessa was as black of skin as Peter Hobbs and his children. It was a smooth skin under the bright kerchief that concealed her hair and was knotted above her forehead.

So, she's a young woman . . . or anyway not an old one . . . one that can do a day's work, no mistake about that.

She was drawing water to fill the big pot she had hanging over a crackling fire. Near the fire was a bench with a great heap of dirty clothes on it and a washtub like the one Mary had used in Akron.

Mary wished her a good morning. She got a questioning look and a "Good mornin, ma'am," in reply but spoken as if to the rope that was lowering her bucket, not to another woman at all.

"God bless the work."

"Thank you ma'am."

Mary set down her bucket and waited for Tessa to finish. Ellen ran around to Tessa's side of the well and came back asking, "Where's Lucille?"

"What would Lucille be doin here? And her way back in Akron?"

"Isn't that Lucille's mama?"

"No, darlin."

Tessa was about to move to the fire but when Mary spoke across to her she paused, resting her full bucket on the curb of the well, though she was still turned toward her work.

"I thought the little one had forgot Lucille long ago, and here she's after thinkin it's you would be the child's mother. Poor Lucille, well for her if you was her mother."

"Lucille . . ?" It was barely a question but it was enough to start Mary on the whole story of the Hobbs family and the sickness, ending with Peter's gift of the American clothes that Mary cherished but had never worn. By the time she had finished, Tessa was looking full at her, her face alive with interest.

"Well, ain't that somethin? These black folks you talkin about, they had their own farm?"

Before Mary could answer, Eliza Laurence came out of the house with another armload of clothes. Tessa lifted her bucket down and moved away. Mary looked curiously at Mrs. Laurence who nodded to her, dropped her clothes on the pile and said a few words to Tessa. As soon as she had returned to the house, Mary came over where she could see the clothes Tessa was sorting but this made Tessa uneasy.

"She mighty particular about her clothes. Be back any minute to see am I doin right. You go on and get your water, please, Missus."

On her way back to Dublin, Mary thought about the washtub Dan had got for her in Akron. Where was it now? The river was a long way off and would soon be too cold for washing.

That night she asked Dan, "Where did they go, all the things was part of my work in the old camp?"

"Likely still in the corner of Jamie's cabin waitin for the spring when this camp will be so big the old one would be lost in it, the way Jamie tells it."

"And no woman usin them at all?"

"There's a bit of a cookhouse up at the quarry. Maybe some of it's up there."

Mary looked at Jamie's cabin as she passed it next morning on her way to get water.

A lock on the door, so how am I to get a peep inside? . . When Jamie comes to sit by the fire of an evening I could ask him for the tub . . . but goin beggin to him doesn't please me. Why was it I didn't put the washtub with my own things? It's no use to Jamie.

Passing from Dublin to the well and back, Mary always looked at the closed and locked door. One morning when Bridget was with her and the two of them talking, they were almost past it before she gave it a glance. The door was unlocked and standing slightly ajar. She set down her bucket.

"Wait now," she said to Bridget.

A knock on the door brought no answer, a peep in and she saw only dark inside. She stepped in and after a moment spied the familiar chest where she used to keep the provisions and there, beside it on the floor was the washtub with the handle of her big spoon sticking out from among all the other kitchen things they had packed into the tub. Ellen had followed her in and was poking about.

"Come out of that," she said, with a spank on the girl's behind to hurry her through the door. She stopped at the door herself and beckoned to Bridget.

"Come in here and help me. I'll take the washtub back with us. You and Eileen can have the use of it, too, to wash your baby's cloutheens."

Bridget drew back. "What's in your head, walkin into Jamie's house and out again with his own things?"

"What does Jamie want with a washtub? I'll just be borrowin the loan of it. Come on, now, Jamie has his mind on the big derricks he's buildin by the river. There's no room in his head for kitchen things."

Jamie wouldn't like it, Bridget said. Jamie was Paddy's boss and Paddy wouldn't like it. Maybe when they came from work, Dan and Paddy would get it.

"The door wouldn't stay open while we dither around. Don't you know it?" Mary was annoyed. "The men was quick enough to pick up the big stick and knock down the door when it was the whiskey was behind it but would they do it for the sake of a washtub? Not them."

Mary couldn't carry the washtub by herself and the bucket of water, too, but Bridget couldn't be persuaded. So Mary came out and picked up the water, marching off as fast as she could with Ellen running after. Bridget trailed, still talking.

Mary threw a word back over her shoulder. "I didn't think it of you, Bridget, you to be a woman can't put your spoon in your mouth till you have the word from himself will he allow it."

As they approached Dublin, their voices brought some of the other women to their doors.

"There'll be one here won't be afraid to help me," Mary said and indeed it was only a few minutes till she was on her way back to Jamie's cabin with Maggie Flynn and her sister Kate Toohey on one side of her and Peg O'Malley on the other. Ellen danced along, full of the excitement.

Peg was a girl yet, though she was the woman of her father's house with the care of three younger ones. It was the adventure of it that brought her along and put the light in her eye and the skip in her step. Kate was a little round woman with a turned up nose. Her husband had come from Cincinnati to take the job Pat Doyle held out. She had left her children with their grandmother and come, too, to be with her sister and to make a few more pennies by keeping lodgers. She had six of them in her shanty.

When Mary began to empty the tub, Kate picked up one of the pots.

"Isn't that the fine big pot I could use with all the mouths there is to feed in my kitchen?"

"Take it, then," Mary said. "I'll have this one and my big spoon. Why would I be cookin in the one pot that came over with us from Cork when there's more than one here with nothin in it but dust and mouse dirt?"

Maggie liked a frying pan with a long handle. That was allright, too.

"Jamie wouldn't be wantin these things till the cookhouse gets started up in the spring. We can have the loan of 'em till then," she told the others. "Now they're forgot, with the scraps of things thrown on top." She turned over a couple of broken tools with her foot. "Look at that . . ." Her voice trailed off as she saw what was under the tools. It was the bundle of things from the lads that died in Akron, exactly as she had tied them up.

She didn't need to open the bundle to know what was inside: The letter Martin had from his people at home, the Old Man's red neckcloth, the knife belonged to Jimmy, John Murphy's new Sunday shirt, the brass buttons Thomas saved off a coat that wore out and a newspaper showed he maybe had people in the city of Boston. Their faces came back to her. It wasn't a minute before she looked up but she felt she had been long gone.

The attention of the others had wandered to the rest of the cabin.

"It's easy to see there's no woman lives here," Maggie remarked. "Look at the dreadful brutheen."

"I wonder would Mr. McCarthy want a girl like me to tidy up for him now and again," Peg wondered.

Mary had an answer. "You stay away from Jamie McCarthy. What he wants from a pretty girl like you is somethin else besides tidyin up. Come on, now, let's get out of this."

Ellen had her hands on the big spoon and they put the two pots and the frying pan back in the tub. Mary added the bundle.

"What's in that?" Kate asked.

"That's a bundle shouldn't have been put here at all when we brought it from Akron."

Mary didn't want to say more then but she told Dan about it that night after they went to bed.

"Why would you be takin it out of there?" Dan asked. "Jamie was puttin it aside till the winter when he would have a bit of time in the bad weather to take care of it, I wouldn't doubt. Now how can he write the letters to the families would he be wantin to?"

"So the wives wouldn't know till the winter, or maybe not then, what happened to their men?"

"You'll have to put it where you got it some time when Jamie's back is turned or he'll know you was in there where you had no business."

"I wouldn't be puttin it back there in the dirt for Jamie to leave till he's forgot altogether what it is."

"What good is it in the corner of our cabin?"

She had hard words at the end of her tongue but such words belonged to the day, not to the night.

"What I was thinkin," she said softly. "You have the writin. Not bein the boss, you couldn't send the wages but you could write the news what happened to the men and the families could cry their tears and say their prayers to get the poor lads into heaven."

"Was I the boss, the letters would have been writ long ago and the wages sent. I wouldn't be waitin for the winter for it. Jamie's a bit careless, but he wouldn't be leavin it undone neither."

"Would you be here on the canal and myself in Carrignahown and no word come the year through was you alive or dead, it's likely I wouldn't be alive myself by the year's end."

"Five letters she wants me to write. Where's the paper and the ink and the pen? And the day long it'll take me to write? I'll stay from the job to do it, maybe. Is that what you want?"

Those were questions she didn't have to answer. Once Dan began throwing up the ditches he wouldn't rest till he was after climbing over them all. He knew there was a Sunday at the end of every week and a store like Mr. Hall's in the town where a man like himself with a piece of money in his pocket could buy almost anything, even paper and ink. Now that she was confident the letters would be written, she could lie awake awhile, savoring the sweet taste of the success of the raid on Jamie's cabin.

Chapter 19

DAN HAD never seen such a plow, with such a sharp blade to dig deep in the ground and cut off the roots. The plow was used each morning to turn over the earth so the diggers could shovel it into the barrows. One morning Dan followed along behind Buck McKendrie who was driving the two horses and guiding the plow around rocks and pushing it through roots. It was a marvel the way the plow cut them like a knife.

"Whatcha lookin at?" Buck yelled back over his shoulder. "Never seen a plow before?"

"Sure I saw my first plow before I was up to my Da's knee. Just want to see what class of plow you've got there."

Buck whoa'd the horses and leaned on the plow handles, not unwilling to take a few minutes rest. "This here ain't a farm plow, it's a canal plow. I've seen times I could use one like this on the farm. Cuts into that mess pretty, don't it?"

"You got yourself a farm?"

"I'm rentin from the Judge here but I reckon on a place of my own when this canal work's done."

"The same as myself."

"You a farmer?"

"And why wouldn't I be?"

"I dunno. Never thought about you farmin. Thinkin of settlin round here, Paddy?"

"Why wouldn't I settle around here . . . Yankee?"

Buck straightened up and narrowed his eyes. "Who you callin Yankee?"

"The man that called me Paddy."

They measured each other for a moment and then Buck let out a big "Haw,

haw!" He mimicked the exchange. "'Who you callin Yankee?' 'The man that called me Paddy.' But I ain't no tight-fisted skinflinty Yankee and don't you forget it. I lived here most all my life."

Dan was confused. In Akron, the native-born workers had sometimes referred to themselves as Yankees, though whether they were willing to accept the name from the Irish depended on the tone of voice. "Yankees don't belong here?"

"Oh, there's some settled around here," Buck conceded, "and more comin in from Boston and Vermont and them places, but my folks come a long time back, from Pennsylvania."

"When the farms is in it, do you come from . . . from 'them places' or from across the water, you can buy a farm in this part of the world?"

"Oh yeah, yeah, all it takes is money. Yankee or Irish or the devil out of hell—they'll sell you a place if you got the money."

When he had finished the plowing, Buck unhitched the team and leaving the plow behind for the next day's stint, swung himself up on one of the horses and rode off across the valley where both he and the horses were needed on the preparations for the aqueduct. The soil he had turned over was already being thrown into the barrows.

Dan had Pat leading the group that pushed the barrows. Pat was a good worker and his son Egan was so eager to prove himself a man that he did his best to keep up with his father. Egan was quicker, more nimble than Pat but Pat knew how to make every movement count. Johnny and three other veteran canal workers—Fergus, Tim Sullivan, and a man who went by the name of Tyrone, after his home county—Dan mixed in with the rest to pace the work of getting the barrows filled. Their strong steady thrust and heave gave a thrust and a heave to those who would have lifted one shovelfull to the other's three. When the mattocks were called for, to move the stones, Dan headed that work, with Joe Dawley a good second to him.

Sometimes Dan put himself by a new man who was used to a one-eared Irish spade and didn't yet have the feel of the American shovel. These new men found everything upside down. The trench they were digging was called a ditch when it wasn't called a canal and what would have been a ditch in Ireland was called an embankment. Old hands and new, though, soon fitted together. Dan was proud of his crew.

Each Saturday, when the week's work was finished, Dan went to Jamie's cabin to give him the record out of his paybook. He had to report, too, such things as the nature of the earth they were dealing with, since the Commissioner paid more for digging out rock than for digging out dirt, but only if the rocks were big enough.

"You were short four hands on Monday," Jamie said one Saturday night, looking at the paybook. "Where were Brennigan and the Caseys and young Flynn?"

"Who would know better than yourself it's a rare Monday you get a whole crew out?"

Those four had gone off with some young fellows from the section to the north of them on Saturday night and hadn't got back to Dublin till late Monday.

"It was a rare Monday morning in Akron when there wasn't a bit of trouble to get the hands all on the job," Jamie admitted, "but did you ever know me to leave 'em lie in bed nursin their sore heads? It's you that's foreman and the Monday mornin troubles is yours now. I want every man on the job Monday like every other day."

On some Saturday nights, Lordon and Laurence were there with Jamie, all of them chewing over the work that had been done and laying out what was ahead. Dan sat quietly in the corner and listened till Jamie was ready for him and sometimes lingered when his business was done for the pleasure he had in being with these men. He liked hearing their talk for the way the many parts of the job wound together in it and for the way it made him feel he was no longer just a hand, but not far from being a boss such as they. They were not down in the muck like the diggers. They were up on a hill where they could see where the canal was going and what had to be done to make it go.

He glanced at what was left of the kitchen things in the corner once in awhile and got a smile out of the way Jamie had never waked up to what the women had done.

Jamie never missed the things from the dead lads, neither. That was no way to do men that had worked beside you. If Jamie couldn't be a friend to them he should remember he was marching at the head of all and should take notice when they fell. It was his job they died on, as it was his job Owen died on . . . No thanks to Jamie there's letters wanderin the world now, carryin the news to Cincinnati and Boston and three townlands in Cork . . . Jamie's head is full of this job here till he forgets everything else, that's all that's in it.

On these Saturdays, Jamie did most of the talking except when Simon began about the stonework. Dan had seen in Akron that the one time Jamie would let Simon hold the reins was when the stonework was before them. Judge Laurence, too, though he might be standing with his back to the fire, looking pleased with himself the way Dan had first seen him, opened his mouth only to ask Simon a question.

Dan had been surprised when he first saw the Judge driving a team of oxen, bringing a load of stone down from the quarry. A man with a fine big house like his and him a magistrate, or anyway something more than a plain mister, Dan had thought he would be giving out the orders, not doing any of the work. Whatever work he did, it wasn't likely he'd get his hands around a shovel, nor around the plug and feathers the stonies used to pry the stone out of the quarry, nor around a cutter's chisel or a mason's trowel.

When the talk was of money instead of stone, then the Judge came away from the fire and sat down at the table with his bottle of ink and his quill. He knew these tools better than Simon or Jamie.

Most often, the talk was about the aqueduct and though Jamie was quick enough to get his words in then, neither he nor either of his partners spoke with the ease that comes from doing the same kind of job many times over. Jamie and Simon had worked on an aqueduct and a bridge on the Erie, but they had worked under someone else there, they hadn't managed the job. Jim Dent, the engineer, was spending a lot of time on their sections. He was still there one Saturday night, preaching away about how it was to be done while all three partners listened. He had supervised the building of four aqueducts on the part of the line between Akron and Cleveland, but three of those were across small creeks and even the one across the Cuyahoga couldn't compare with what they had to build here. The one time Dan saw the chief engineer, Mr. Bates, he got a feeling this was the master aqueduct builder, the way Simon was a master stonemason.

For all the talk he heard, Dan couldn't see the aqueduct in his head. Was it to be like a bridge, but a bridge over a river and a canal over the bridge? One Saturday when Dent had been there and the aqueduct plans were still lying on the table, Jamie let him take a look. There were lines and circles and strange shapes all over the paper but across the top was a picture of the way it would look when it was done.

Jamie explained how the hundreds of piles would be driven into the riverbed. Men wouldn't be doing it here the way they had done it in Akron. They would have horses for that piece of the job. When the piles were in, timbers would be laid on top. That would all be under the water to hold up the stone part. The stone piers would rise up above the river. Timbers would go across from the stone abutment against the river bank to the first pier and from one pier to another and would hold up the canal part which would be made out of wood and filled with water.

Dan was awed. "That's a monstrous big job you've got there."

"It is indeed," Jamie agreed. "I tell you it's too big to get it done by next September. If we could have got a proper start on it at the beginnin of summer we might have made it, but now . . ." He shook his head. "Once the Commissioner gets your name on a contract, though, he wants you to live by that piece of paper and if you have to die by it, you finish the job on time. We'll be bringin you and the others down off the diggin before long as soon as we're ready to put in the cofferdam."

Dan looked at the plans again. "Which part is that?"

"It's not on the paper, there. It's a wall, like, right in the river, to keep the water out of our way so we can get the abutment foundations in. We'll need every man we got on that piece of work. Two coffers we'll be buildin, one on each side of the river and more later out in the middle of the river for the piers."

"We're a long way from finishin the diggin," Dan reminded him.

"I know, I know." Jamie waved that away as if digging a mile of canal was nothing. "We can work on that anytime. This has to be done while we've got low water."

He rolled up the plans and laid them aside so he could pour out drinks. "Health and life to you." He raised his cup.

"Long life to yourself," Dan pledged in return, wondering what was coming.

"If we had enough men, I'd leave the diggin to you and let you get on with it. That was the way I had it laid out to do, but if we don't get the foundations for the one abutment, at least, in before the water rises, Simon won't be able to lay so much as a single stone all next spring and summer. We'll be waitin again for the low water. Now the way it is, you'll go on diggin till I give you the word and when the river rises, you'll go back to it."

"So I'll put my crew to the other job for a bit in between," Dan agreed. Did Jamie think they had such a liking for the digging they didn't want to do anything else?

"This will be new work to you and to most of the hands. It will be myself will have to show you what's to do. It'll be me that's foreman on that part of the work. When you pass the word to the others you can give a bit of good news along with it. The days are gettin short now but we won't put the pay down for the winter but just a bit as long as we're on the aqueduct. All of you will be gettin summer wages right into the winter."

"Good news you call that?" Dan could see now where Jamie had been heading. "I'm to come down from the foreman's job and the foreman's pay and you callin it good news?"

"Could I pay you foreman's wages when it's myself doin the superintendin? Have some sense, man. Don't you remember me tellin you the high wages was promised for the fall only? You'll be back to it as soon as you go back to the diggin. And I'll tell you another thing." Jamie spoke deliberately and impressively. "By the time we're done with this aqueduct you'll be a good all-around canal man. You'll be able to get the foreman's job and the good pay as long as this canal's in the buildin and after that on the next canal."

Dan finished his drink and set the cup down on the table. "You gave me more than a drink to put inside myself tonight. I'll be thinkin on your words, indeed I will."

"You do that." Jamie followed him to the door and put a hand on his shoulder. "We've got a lot of years behind us, you and me, and a lot ahead of us."

Dan walked slowly back to Dublin.

Was there ever a man like Jamie for pushin you down in the ditch with one hand and pullin you out with the other? That was a nasty clip in the jaw to knock me down to the same pay as the others is gettin. Bad weather will be comin, too, days with no work and no pay at all and food to buy to fill the stomachs that will be just as empty, pay or no. It won't be like last winter when we all ate at the cookhouse even on days without work. There'll be little left out of the pay to put away for the farm.

What will the men think that just got used to takin the orders from me? Some will be glad to see me get cut down. They won't have long to enjoy it though before I'll be back up again. So why should they know at all?

Mary will have to know. A good thing Jamie won't hear when I give her the news . . . What will she have to say about the good years ahead Jamie is holdin out? She'll like that no better. It's the farm is in her thinkin, not more years on the canal. And it's the farm is in my thinkin, isn't it? . . Isn't it? . . Well, it's maybe only Jamie's talk, anyhow.

Chapter 20

Y OU WANT Christy to be a spalpeen all his life with no way of livelihood but his day's pay?" Mary asked Kate Toohey.

It was that time in the afternoon when most of the day's work was done, it was too early to be getting the suppers ready, and there was no need for each woman to be off by herself in her own kitchen. One after another would emerge from her shanty onto the road that passed in front of Dublin on the way to the Laurence farmhouse.

This road was Dublin's common. They danced here sometimes of a Saturday night. The children played here. On Sundays, the young men had trials of strength here. In the early afternoon, unless the weather was bad, it belonged to the Dublin women.

They were sitting now on the dry leaves at the road's edge where the Toohey's shanty sheltered them from the wind, their hands busy with knitting or mending. The wind stirred little dust smokes up in the road and sent showers of leaves down from the trees to skitter across the ground. The children had been sent to pick up sticks for the fires, except Ellen and Rose Farrell's smallest girl who were playing nearby. Mary was coaxing Kate to say she and Christy would buy a farm along with the rest of them.

"There's no way you can lie down at night and go to sleep easy, except it's your own place you're sleepin in and your own place you'll wake up in, to the food your own land puts on the table."

"The food is on the table when the harvest is good and the bellies is empty when the harvest is bad," Kate answered, "but the wages gets paid when the work is done and that puts the food on the table whatever the harvest. It's beyond me why you choose to stay out here in the woods. In Cincinnati there's so many of our own people in the one place you can be as much at home as if you was in Cork itself and there's the fine church there and the priest you'll never see from one year's end to the next if you go to farmin."

"We had the bishop himself and two priests come to the camp in Akron," Bridget remembered.

"And time they came again." Mary looked at Peg O'Malley and her sister Molly, knowing how they looked to the eyes of a man, with their rosy cheeks and inviting lips, newly swelling breasts and rounded hips showing under their dresses.

"If there's one man with his eyes on these girls, there's a dozen. You wonder sometimes, do the men know there's such a thing as a weddin, it's that long since they've seen a priest. Some of them forgets they had a weddin once and left a wife behind when they come to the canal."

"Don't be lookin at me like that," Peg objected. "If one of those old fellows puts a hand on me, I'll rap his knuckles for him."

"And what about one of those fellows that's not so old, like Kevin? He left his wife and a baby in Clonakilty and his brother Mick the same. Bridget and me can give you the word on some we know from the Akron camp, but them that's new to us, we wouldn't know was they married or no, and are they meanin a girl good or no. It's best you keep yourself to yourself till a man's ready to ask your father."

"My father, my father." Peg lifted her shoulders and then let them droop. "I've been takin care of the young ones since my mother died and my father throws the cross looks and the hard words at any lad that so much as gives me a good mornin. Even the baby's big enough to take care of himself now but my father will be scarin off the lads till I'm an old woman and now if you aren't doin the same."

"It's yourself she's thinkin of." Bridget went on to tell about Susan.

"It was a mortal sin," Mary said somberly, "and they're both like to burn in hell for it. I wouldn't want that for you, nor for Molly neither."

Molly's face flushed and her lip trembled.

Her sister put an arm around her and looked angrily at Mary. "Molly never done nothin wrong."

"You're good girls, I never said different. And you should have your pick of the lads here, the way there's only the two of you and men by the dozens. Keep your heads up and their hands off."

"Put a spade in the bed with you," Maggie advised. "'Twill bring a husband, sure."

"I'll tell you one to watch out for." Bet Sullivan began talking about the Blower. He worked up at the quarry, but would often be down at Dublin for the good company or off to the Forks where there were two taverns now and gaming and women to be had by those with money to spend. Bet knew him from the Deep Cut, where she had been with her husband when they were blowing out the rock there.

"He followed the canals in Ireland and in England, too, years past before he came over the water," she told them, "and it's the stories he's got would give you the cold prickles. The way he tells it, he's shaken hands with death more times than he has fingers. They say a blower has a right to die by the time he's been in the trade five years and this one's been in it these ten."

Molly's eyes were shining as she drank in Bet's words. It sounded like a story to Ellen who left off her play and came close.

"Listen to his tales but stay out of his way," Bet warned, "for he'd stick his thing in every woman he meets—maid, wife, or widow, the way he sticks his black powder in the rock. She's no more to him than the rock itself when he's had his will of her. It's more than one he's left behind on his road, cryin after a daddy for the baby he gave her."

"True for you," Bridget agreed. "Didn't he come to our shanty for a game of cards with Paddy and right under Paddy's nose, he reaches for me under the table. I jump off my stool like the devil is after me and himself looks up from the cards as innocent as a babe. 'What is it, acushla,' he says, 'a spark out of the fire on you?' 'Yes, Paddy, I'll sit over where the fire can't touch me,' I says."

Molly stared at Bridget and Bridget answered her look.

"Oh, yes, he'd like to gobble you up, little girl, but hasn't he got the appetite even for an old married woman like me. Not that I'm so old when it comes to that."

Ellen's eyes were bigger than Molly's. So it wasn't only the old hag with the terrible long teeth that gobbled up little girls when they were bad. She had never seen that one and Danny had whispered to her that there was no such an old hag at all. She was only a made-up story to scare babies. Maybe Danny had the right of it and maybe he didn't but here was another thing entirely. A real man she had seen sitting at their own table, chomping his beans with his strong teeth. Could he chomp a little girl like her that way, or even a woman grown, like Molly?

"He thinks he's the cock of the haggard, indeed, and he's got the young roosters struttin around after him, walkin like he walks and talkin like he talks. I doubt there's enough sense among the lot of them to make one man worth a woman's second look."

The contempt in Mary's voice took the edge off the terror. Her mother wasn't afraid of anybody. If the Blower came after Ellen, Mary would hit him right on his sharp teeth with her big spoon.

"Look at the long faces." Maggie was laughing at the girls. "Don't cry. Your time will come. You'll have a good man in your bed to cuddle you and comfort you and give you babies. Just don't be too hasty and try to eat the puddin before the sauce is cooked."

They all laughed and the girls went off, blushing and looking more than ever like they were ready to cry.

"That was too bad of you," Eileen said. "You're like to scare them away from the men entirely."

"Small danger," Mary disagreed. "But couldn't we find them husbands before they come to grief like Susan?"

They went to work on that task with relish. Mary favored Johnny for Peg. Johnny being a Sligo man like Peg's father, he was more welcome in O'Malley's shanty than the others. Kate Toohey was for the youngest of her lodgers, the son of people well known to her in Cincinnati. Eileen had a kind word for Toby Weaver, a curly-headed Ohio boy who came down from the quarry now and then with Dennis and the Blower. Toby was promptly rejected on the grounds there were plenty of their own men to choose from.

It wasn't long before Peg made her own choice and when it proved to be Michael Kieran, the older women all approved. They conspired to keep the father in the dark and give the two of them a moment together now and again. Not that there was much chance of it and less after the men made sport of Michael about his girl in the father's hearing. Both girls were then shut up in their shanty as soon as the men came from work. Peg couldn't so much as creep out on a Sunday afternoon for a ramble by the river.

Michael brought his troubles to Mary, maundering on about the lovely girl Peg was and complaining about the father.

"Have you asked her father will he give her to you?"

"How would I be doin that when the man won't let me in the house or give me a good-day on the way to the job? And myself without the one I could send to him to speak for me . . . Unless you'd be helpin me with the match?"

"When you've left your old people on the other side of the water it's yourself must do it. Haven't you a squig of spirits about you at all? Have you asked Peg will she have you?"

"How can I get the one word with her, the way the old man barks around her like a watchdog?"

"You can get the one word with her. No reason to be standin by the brook the way you are now, afraid to lep across for fear you might be gettin your feet wet. Any father should be proud to have the likes of you for a daughter's husband, the steady lad you are with a stonecutter's wages and her without a halfpenny for a dowry."

"Tell me how to get the word with Peg, then, and if I get a yes from her own lips I won't take a no from the old man."

The next morning when the men began to leave the table after breakfast, Mary held Michael back. "Wait here now. You've got legs can carry you to the job fast enough and if you're late, it's well worth it once in your life."

She looked out the door. "There goes O'Malley with the other diggers. Now off with you to Peg."

She was still watching when he came out of the O'Malley shanty and ran for the job. He gave her a joyful wave, so she knew he had it settled with Peg but she had her doubts about his courage when it came to the father.

He had his own doubts, she could see that evening, with the worried look on him while he cleaned up, shaved off his whiskers and tied on a white neckcloth. He was taking sips of courage in between.

"You'll see I can bellow like a bull when the drink's in me," he answered her questioning look. "I promised herself I'd be goin to her father the night. See if I don't now."

Mary took the jug from him. "Here, give us a sip. Wasn't it myself helped you to the drink you got from her lips in the mornin? It's a fine brave man you look now and bull enough without any more drink." She passed the jug to Johnny.

"Here's luck to you." Johnny drank and passed it to Dan.

"The woman of your choice to you," Dan said, taking his turn and passing it to Hugh.

"Here's to your lass," Hugh boomed out. "May she warm your blood in your youth and your bones in your old age."

Michael was at the door, but he turned with panic in his eyes. "How well it would be for me if someone would give me the proper words a man would be sayin to the father of a girl like Pegeen."

"Go on with you now, while you've got your courage up," Mary said. "Don't you know what it is you want of him?"

Michael shook the jug and listened to how much of the whiskey there was to slosh against the sides of it. "You didn't leave me much of it, did you? How can I make a match without enough in it to wet the back of the old man's throat at all?"

Dan took it from him and gave him the full jug he had for his own drinking, leaving him no more excuse to hide behind. One more gulp for himself and Michael tucked the jug under his arm, picked up his sturdy oak cudgel and walked out.

They all followed out the door, laughing at the swagger the shy Michael was putting on him as he strode down the row of shanties. And then if he didn't lift up his cudgel and thunder on the O'Malley's door so loud it brought everyone in Dublin that wasn't abed out of their doors to see was the law down on them or what was it.

O'Malley opened the door and thrust his head out. Michael stepped back and for a moment Mary thought he would run for it.

"What is it you think you're doin here, knockin the house down with that stick of yours?" O'Malley shouted. "Behave yourself decent or get outta this."

Michael looked uneasily over his shoulder at all the people.

"Wouldn't you be askin me in along with the jug I brought has a drink for you and a drink for me while we're talkin together instead of flappin our business out here under the noses of the neighbors?"

Peg's face appeared over her father's shoulder. "Come in then, Michael Kieran, and welcome."

O'Malley tried to shove her back but her welcome was enough for Michael. He pushed in and closed the door behind him. The rest of them couldn't see the end of the story but there wasn't much doubt what it would be.

"The two of them's got the old man between them now," Mary said. "He can twist and he can yelp but he might as well give it up. There'll be a wedding soon in Dublin. Now that Michael's got his courage up, he can tell Simon and Jamie there'll be a priest needed."

Chapter 21

O N A COLD November dusk, Dan and his crew stood on the riverbank between piles of lumber, looking at the two derricks rearing up above them like hangman's scaffolds. They had trundled the barrows down from the line where they had been digging, Jamie having given the word the job would be at the river beginning on the morrow. There was a row of sticks Dent had driven into the bank and out into the water, showing where the abutment would go, and a line of sticks marching across the river, showing where the aqueduct would go.

Tom Quinlan walked down to the water's edge and put his hand in. He pulled it out again, quickly. "There's no colder water than that in the world, barrin the ocean we come across. It's in there we'll be workin?"

"That's what I'm thinkin," Tyrone said.

"Is that it, Dan?"

If that was it, Jamie should have told him. What could he tell the men but "That's for Jamie to say."

"Err, aye," Fergus agreed. Dan didn't know was he agreeing it was into the water they would have to go, or was he agreeing it was for Jamie to say. Fergus had worked with Jamie on the Erie and had come back from Albany with him. A little rumbling in the back of his throat did for 'aye' or for 'no', for a 'God bless' or a 'good night.'

As they walked back toward Dublin, the talk turned to the wages and the better pay some contractors were giving for work in water. Sixty-five cents a day and keep, that was the rumor. They were getting less than that and keep not included. Jamie said their pay would stay where it was, in the water or out.

It turned out they were in up to their knees or up to their hips enough of the time to turn their feet blue with cold and splash their bodies till they might as well have been in it up to their armpits.

A man's first thought when he came in from work was to peel off his soaking clothes and wrap himself in a dry blanket. The woman of the house stepped out the door of the shanty to wring the water out of the clothes. She draped them over a stool or a bench and soon the smell of drying river mud and drying sweat mingled with the smell of wood smoke. The clothes were often still damp in the morning, and the boots always. The dampness and the smell hung in the air of the shanties after the men had gone back to another day of it.

In the evenings the men huddled over the fire, soggy and sullen, giving off the resentment that had soaked into them. It hung in the air as persistently as the smell of the clothes. The children ran outside to escape it. The women breathed it all day and into the night when they got out of bed to throw more wood on the fire and turn the wet side of the trousers toward the flame.

There had been some excitement the first few days as the riverbank swarmed with men, oxen and horses. There was a quieter eddy around Dent in the midst of the big confusion, as he bent to his three-legged surveyor's instrument, looking through its little eye-piece and steering the operation like the captain of a ship. Jamie ran hither and yon, getting the men into place, his voice and the Judge's mingling with the voices of the teamsters. Mostly, the Ohio men were driving teams and hewing timbers with their broadaxes, but there were times when all had to leave those jobs and go into the water with the Irish to get the coffer dam walls in place.

One long part of the coffer dam was going up at the river's edge, but one part had to be put up out in the river, with sides joining them together. Once the coffer dam was in, the water that had been enclosed in it would have to be pumped out, making way for the piles to hold up the abutment. Those would be positioned by Mr. Dent and driven into the river bed, then sawed off and the timbers laid across on top of them, making a floor on which to raise course after course of stone.

As day followed cold grey day, each brought greater familiarity with the work and greater reluctance to wade into it. But the work in the water had to be done. Therefore it had to be endured. What the immensity of the job imparted after those first days was not a thrill but a threat: This kind of work would go on and on for more days than a man could count.

Dan cursed the cold and the wet along with the rest of them. All he wanted of each day now was to get through it. All he wanted of each night was to get his feet warm and his skin dry. His thoughts went no further into the future than the next Sunday. The brunt of his ill humor was borne by Tim and Danny and by Michael, who had the luck to be working in the dry quarry and to be getting the good wages besides.

It would have driven another man to anger but Michael, always peaceable, was now wrapped in unshakable good humor. Simon had promised to see about getting a priest for the wedding.

The bosses worked with one eye on the weather, thanking God as it continued relatively dry through November and into December. The clouds hung low in the sky, making the short days even shorter but they brought little rain and that in the shape of a fine drizzle or an occasional shower, not enough to halt the work nor to raise the level of the water significantly.

They were also fortunate in being able to keep their force together. They lost only three hands. One of the local men lost his footing on the slippery bottom and went under. This wasn't the first time it had happened and this time, too, the other men got him up and out of it quickly but he was missing from the work from that time.

The other two they lost were Kevin and Mick who took their bundles under their arms after payday and went off up the line in search of drier work or better pay.

Jamie had a bad moment on the next Monday, for more than the Caseys were missing from the job. He grabbed Dan by the arm. "Where are they? Did you let the Caseys pull three more off the job? Couldn't you talk some sense in them?"

Dan shook his hand off. "So you're jumpin on me with both boots and I was the one did talk some sense in Johnny and Hugh and Tyrone. Those three— they're three of your best. Why I should keep them here workin for you in your cold water I don't know myself."

"So where are they?"

"They'll be on the job tomorrow or sooner, maybe. I wouldn't be knowin."

Jamie slapped one fist into the palm of his other hand. "Wasn't I tellin you I want every man on the job Monday like any other day?"

"You were tellin me that, surely. You were tellin me the Monday mornin troubles was my troubles, myself bein foreman. Now I'm tellin you the Monday mornin troubles is yours again."

"Don't be a fool, man. You're not like these other louts, can't see past their noses. Wasn't it myself brought you over and give you your start on the canal? Can't you see you'll be back on your foreman's job the sooner do you help me get this piece of the job behind us?"

"Didn't I talk away the better part of a Sunday, keepin the lads on your job when they could be up the Tuscarawas gettin the good pay for the days in the water?"

The talk that Sunday had begun with Mary complaining about the loss of Kevin and Mick. They were two that been with them in Akron, she had nursed Kevin through the fever and he and Mick had been in the plans for buying the farms together since that night on the road when it had first come into their heads. Kevin had said they might be back in the spring but Mary had no faith in that.

"There's too much of this country to wander about in. Kevin is one to blow with the wind whichever way it blows and Mick will go where Kevin goes, to take care of him, like."

"If I go off to another job, you know I'll be comin back, don't you, Mary?" Johnny had said then. It was the first Mary knew he and Hugh and Tyrone had pledged each other they would be off up the road like the Caseys.

"*You* wouldn't be leavin us?" She walked to the door and put her head out, then back to the fire, shivering. A little rain had been falling off and on all day, a cold rain with a bit of snow mixed into it here and there. "Why would you want to go out in that weather? Don't you know these canal jobs is all alike? Haven't you been in the wet enough, without goin up the road in it, with no knowin where there's a job for you or a place to lay your head or if you'll find one at all?"

When Tyrone came in with his bundle in his hand, he found them all sitting by the fire, talking of their farms again, the first time for weeks they'd opened their mouths enough to get such talk beyond the teeth that had been gritted to bear the next day's work. First he scoffed at them for skulking by the fire in fear of a few drops out of the sky. Next he put down his bundle to accept a sup from the jug they were passing from hand to hand. Then he sat down to talk over would they wait till the morning to start a journey, it being the middle of the day already or maybe wait for a better day. Soon he was giving them a loving description of the twenty acres he had to leave behind in County Tyrone when the gaugers found his still and he had to run. He had left his family behind, too, but had saved enough on the Erie to bring them over. His wife and daughter were working in Cincinnati now and soon the younger children would be doing their bit. As with Dan and Mary, the dream of an American farm had been in his head ever since coming over and he was strong for buying it side by side with his countrymen.

"The winter's the bad time to change jobs," Dan told them. "That's when there's the least work goin and the contractors more likely to cut the force down than to build it up. If we're all together in the spring we can look over what land is about here we might buy and what would we have to pay for it."

The end of the day came with all of them drinking to life on an American farm—Land without rent! Johnny and Hugh went back to the O'Scanlon shanty with Tyrone to tell Bridget she still had a lodger. They started the talk and the drink all over again with Paddy and by the time they stumbled to bed it was as sure they wouldn't be up in time for work in the morning as it was that they wouldn't be leaving Dublin.

Next Sunday there was another thing brewing. Tom Quinlan and Pat Flynn brought it into the Griffen shanty along with a jug of whiskey Asa McKendrie had sold them. Asa was an old settler who had been around the Forks since Indian times. He was working on the job along with his grown son, Buck. Another son, Ike, worked in the quarry and Ike's wife, Emma, was cook there. Asa had made this whiskey himself and swore it was the best in Coshocton County.

It wasn't just a taste of it Tom and Pat were offering Dan. They were making him a present of it along with asking him to use his influence with Jamie to put the wages for the work in water up to sixty-five cents.

"When Jamie has his mind made up, six horses couldn't move him," Dan warned them.

"I couldn't move him," Pat said, "and Tom here couldn't move him but you're the friend to him and the grand opinion he's got of you—he'll be after listenin to you."

"Jamie McCarthy should be told, surely, you'll all catch your deaths in the cold and wet if this goes on through the winter," Mary put in. "The devil wouldn't send his dog out on some of these days he sends you to the job."

Dan tasted Asa's whiskey but he couldn't get the others to more than wet their lips with it. "It's not from ourselves only," Tom told him. "There was a few pennies from this one and a few pennies from that one all put together to get the whiskey that's worthy of a man like yourself."

"It's a bad taste the drink would leave on my tongue if I go to Jamie with the plea and come back empty-handed."

"You wouldn't come back empty-handed," Pat said confidently, "not you."

What with the warm words and the good whiskey, it began to seem to Dan, too, that he could find a way to put it to Jamie that would bring at least a small rise in the pay for the work in the water. When they saw he was coming around, they began giving him the way he could put one thing or the other so Jamie couldn't say them nay. He could see what they wanted was for him to give the words they were offering to Jamie as his own thoughts.

"If he knows it come from me that's only been on his job this short time," was Tom's excuse, "he's like to tell me to take my bundle and go off, but not you. He has the need of you to boss the diggin."

"The thoughts of one man means little to Jamie," Dan answered, "unless it's the Commissioner himself. And the fine words won't do it, neither. It's like one man could tell old Barry, the bunbailiff, 'I'll pay this much rent and no more,' and he'd have no rent at all to pay and no land to live on, neither. It was when he knew the one man speakin to him had us all at that one's back, that was when there was some changes happened in our parish and in all the mountainy parishes beyond Macroom. Don't fear I'd be sayin it's Tom Quinlan behind me or Pat Flynn. Isn't it every man of us thinks the extra bad work in the water ought to bring the extra good pay? If I can't go to Jamie with that thought, I might as well stick my head out the door and talk to the wind."

When they agreed to that, Dan stood up.

"I'm off then," he said. "You wait here to see what it is I'll be bringin back."

Mary's voice stopped him. "You wouldn't be goin empty-handed like a beggar?"

"But what . . ?" His eyes roamed the shanty, finding nothing till he saw that Mary's eyes were on the jug. "Ah, that's it, that's it."

As he walked toward Jamie's cabin, swinging the jug, he tried out what he would say. That way he could get the sound of it while there was none but himself to hear.

He was glad to find Jamie alone. If he got a hard 'no' at the beginning, getting Jamie to change it to 'yes' would be easier if there were no one watching or listening.

He got a warm welcome.

"Here I was without the cheer of a friend's talk," Jamie said. "Simon is up to the quarry, worryin over the stone that won't come out like he wants it and over there at the house, they're kindly enough but the talk doesn't have the home sound on it."

Dan set the jug down on the table. "Here I brought you what they tell me is the best whiskey in the Muskingum Valley. A good judge of whiskey like yourself now, roll a drop of that over on your tongue and tell me does it compare with the poteen we used to make in the hills around Carrignahown."

They drank and talked like there was nothing in their heads but to make a merry night of it, with Jamie knowing there was something in the back of Dan's head and Dan looking for the best time to let it pop out. When Jamie reached for the jug again, saying a good word for the whiskey, that was it.

"The truth of it is," Dan told him, "all the lads sent that jug over to you, wishin you the good health while you're drinkin it. There's few Irish bosses on the canal, nobody knows that better than yourself and none they'd rather be under than you and Simon, but I wouldn't be a friend to you if I didn't tell you there's been a bit of grumblin since we started workin in the water."

Jamie was about to speak but Dan held up his hand.

"Don't put the wrong meanin on it. We know the work has to be done, wet and cold though it be, and we're the lads that can do it. And your wages is good, too—for the diggin and the dry work. The one thing they're askin, wouldn't you give it another thought, what pay you'll have for us on the next payday for the days we work in the water?"

Jamie got up and began walking back and forth, his eyes on the floor. He stopped in front of Dan.

"You didn't like it when your wages was put down and I'm not blamin you. I didn't like it myself. I told the Judge that. I told him you were worth any two of the others, but he couldn't see payin foreman's wages except for foreman's work. Now that you've been down there at the river where he can see how you give the others the lead and help me keep the work movin, I think maybe I could get him to agree to bring it back up, not all the way, likely, but a dollar or two on the month, maybe."

Dan hadn't expected this. "Well, I . . . well . . . what can I say but my thanks to you. I know I can depend on you to say the good word for me and if you bring my pay up that would be . . . that would be grand . . . but what am I to say to the other lads?"

Jamie sat down again and leaned toward Dan like he would give him his heart's secrets.

"Here's the way of it, Dan. We was about to put the pay down to nine dollars for the winter and twelve for them that boards themselves. But I worked in the water on the Erie enough to know what it's like. I told Simon and the Judge we had to give the hands somethin for the cold and the wet. We talked about puttin the pay up for the days in the water like some contractors do it. But that don't seem fair. One man would be grumblin because he gets less than the other and the other would be grumblin because he's wet and the other man's dry. Besides, there's days a man's in the water half the time and out the rest. It would be nothin but trouble workin out what was owin each hand that way. So we agreed to keep the pay up for both the wet work and the dry work. That way the men's gettin *more* pay than they would did we just put the pay up for work in the water. You explain this to them like I explained it to you and you'll find them seein it the right way after a bit."

"You got me as dizzy with the fast talk as if I drained the jug . . . You always could put your own twist on a story. It got us out of more than one scrape but I doubt I could make this one go down with . . . with the other men. Let me see do I get what it is you're tellin me. If it wasn't for the work in the water, the wages would be nine dollars instead of eleven like we're gettin now. Is that it? So it's two dollars each month for the work in the water?"

"Two dollars on top of the regular pay. And don't tell it to 'em with a long face like you're bringin the news of a bad harvest. Show 'em what a good thing it is we're givin."

I don't think you're givin me nothin . . . That was what Peter Hobbs had said . . . I do some of your work and you pay me some wages.

"I doubt I could put the right twist on it. There's not a thing I could bring back would look good to them, barrin the promise of a rise for the work in water. The word is, it brings sixty-five cents a day and keep on some sections. I could say, 'Look at your pay with one eye closed and see if it don't look prettier than way,' but . . ."

Jamie interrupted. "Don't tell me I'm twistin the truth, Dan Griffen. I give you the plain facts and that's all that's in it. Except . . ." He looked hard at Dan. "Except I think you're lettin some talker up there in Dublin twist *you* around. Who was it sent you down here whinin and complainin? Don't tell me it was 'all the lads.' I know those men. They'll do what they're told and take what they're paid. They know the wages is for the bosses to decide. Unless some babbler comes around stirrin up trouble. Who was it? Or maybe it all come out of your own head?"

Dan got up and slapped the table, angrier than he had been when he argued with Jamie over the washtub. He had won that argument, though he had to call men from the grave to back him.

"I'm my own man, Jamie McCarthy. Do you know that, or don't you? Nobody twists me around. Nobody. And nobody makes a tongue out of Dan Griffen neither to say this one spoke first and that one spoke loudest. If you don't know that, you've been gone from Carrignahown too long. *All* the lads is wet and cold. *All* the lads is askin will you put the wages up for work in that goddam water."

"Sit down, blast you," Jamie yelled, "and listen while I give you the straight of it. Maybe you're not gone from Carrignahown long enough. There's nobody here wants a tongue to give the word which man should be hauled off for a gun under the bed or a still behind the rocks."

He clearly wasn't through but he stopped. Dan waited for him to go on. The silence lengthened. When Jamie spoke again his voice was low and cold.

"Sit down, Dan Griffen . . . Did you hear me tell you? Sit down."

Slowly, Dan sat down.

"So you're your own man, are you? Let me tell you about bein your own man in this country. You'll have enough sense to know what's your own business and what isn't. You'll always be hearin from some stupid digger that don't want to work here or don't want to work there or don't want to work hard or wants a pocketful of money instead of a day's pay. You just keep their shovels drivin into the dirt and let their words drain out with the water. I've give you your chance to *be* your own man. I thought you were smart enough to take it."

Jamie stood up, showing that he was through talking and that Dan was through talking, too.

When Dan got back, not only were Pat and Tom still there but several others had drifted in, waiting for him. Kevin and Michael were there, too, looking bedraggled and sheepish.

"What's this?" he asked them. "You come to see us on the Sunday and tell us about the good job and the high pay you got now?"

"Nobody's puttin on new men, this time of year," Kevin admitted. "Can you get us our jobs back?"

"Get you your jobs back? Me? I'm just a stupid digger. I don't hire nobody." His glance swept over the men. "The place is full of stupid diggers. Go ask the boss for your jobs. I'm not takin him any more messages."

They all knew what he meant but that wasn't enough for Tom.

"What did he say, Dan? Was the other bosses there, too, or was it McCarthy done it to us?"

"He said 'no'" Dan roared. "If that isn't enough for you, you can ask Lordon and Laurence and Dent and the Commissioner and they'll all tell you 'no' . . . No, no, no, no!"

Chapter 22

KEVIN AND MICK were back on the job, tied to it by the marks they put on a paper that was Jamie's promise to send the passage money to Clonakilty to bring over their wives and their own promises to work off the debt.

Dan felt that he now had another dead horse to kill, too.

Didn't I come up from a digger once, takin my place to the fore? Didn't I come up from under Jamie to bein near beside him? And now Jamie has me pushed under again, makin it plain before all in Dublin I got no more influence than the last man wandered in off the road. How am I to come up again to where I was before? Do I have it all to do over again like I was just off the boat?

The questions whined around him like the mosquitoes of summer. He grabbed at them but he could never get a hold on one to crush the life out of it.

As bad as the troubles was in Carrignahown, I knew the way of things. Here it's a different world every time I wake up in it. The men who work beside me here, even those I know best, are half-strangers. Those who were with me in the Brotherhood were tried and trusted. When we moved in them days, we moved together. Here I'm on a strange road with no landmarks to show where it's leadin and no comrades to go the way with me.

When the weather kept them inside, Dan was so restless there was little peace in the shanty. Hugh, Johnny, and Michael sat down to the cards, but though Dan took a hand once in awhile, he hadn't the patience to stay with it. He threw the cards down and slouched back and forth, pushing the children roughly aside if they got in his way, bumping into Mary as she went about getting the meals and tidying up. He even picked a quarrel with Hugh one day, a thing that was so much against his nature that Mary was quite taken by surprise.

The only quiet came when he sat down on his stool before the fire. Then he was gone from the place altogether, without a word to say, without hearing a word said to him. Mary sat an arm's length way, knitting the stockings that would keep his feet warm when work was cold and wet but she might have been still in Carrignahown for all he knew. He finally let a word out of him that told her he was sick for home.

That was a sickness she had no charm to ward off, no herb to cure, no comfort to heal. Were Carrignahown just over the hill, Dan would be on his way back to the old home before she could catch on to the tail of his coat. It was always his way to go from the thought to the deed with the leap of a hare. She had known that since their first dance together seemed to have no stop to it till the wedding.

With the notion that what he needed was the new home in this country, she began about how they'd be in God's pocket when they had their own farm but he wouldn't so much as dip his spoon into that dish.

"You think when we get a farm, all will be fine and grand? For us it won't be the acres of corn and the pigs and cows and sheep you can't count like the Laurences have it. And not like the old home, neither, where all you had to do was lift up your voice to call to the neighbor. If we ever get a farm here, there's like to be three hills between you and the next place. You'll be happy with that, won't you? You that's always at one neighbor or another."

She turned away from him to ask Michael, "Did Simon get the letter from the priest yet, when will he come for the weddin day?"

"I was after askin him so many times, he gives me his back when he sees me comin."

"Simon must have forgot to put it in the letter we'll pass the plate around to make up the marriage money," Dan suggested. "Does the priest think you're askin him to come for the love of God only, you and Peg will have the gray hair before you have the weddin."

"I'm wonderin did he write the letter at all. The last of it I had from him was why wouldn't we wait till the spring."

"And you thinkin Simon the grand boss that would do the world and all for you stonies," Mary remarked. "Him and Jamie is cut out of the same cloth. They think of you but twice. The first time is on the job, how much work can they get out of you and the second time is on the payday, how little can they pay you."

"It won't cost them nothin to bring the priest and wasn't it them brought the priest to Akron?" Dan reminded them. "There's another thing in it somewhere."

Michael brought home the news the next day of what that something was. Simon had said to him that he and Peg should take the stagecoach to Zanesville. There was no church there, but there was a small congregation in that town and a priest came several times a year. Not that this same priest couldn't be asked to come to the canal, but Judge Laurence said he wouldn't have a priest on his place.

"The way he told it to Simon and Jamie," Michael explained, "it was the kings and the priests chased his people out of France. He says he got no more use for the one than the other. The weddin's no business of his he says, but if it's a priest in it, we can't have it on *his* land."

"There you have it!" Johnny made a fist of his right hand and struck the palm of his left. "Sooner or later the other crowd comes out with it. He's just coverin over what he's doin to us and our religion."

"Maybe there was good reason the king and priests had for gettin rid of the likes of him," Mary agreed.

Michael had his mind on the wedding. If Zanesville was the place for it, to Zanesville they would go. He was heading off for the O'Malley shanty to make the plans with Peg when Mary held him back.

"Wait a bit. If the priest came here, we could have the confessions and the Mass said and Bridget and Eileen wants their babies christened. Can't we have a station right here in Dublin and the weddin here, too?"

"Dublin is on the Judge's land," Dan pointed out.

"Don't I know he's the landlord and a Protestant like the rest of them," Mary admitted, "But not since our grandparents' times was the landlords after stoppin us from makin the stations in the Catholic houses. These is Catholic houses and if we want a station here or a weddin, why can't we have it?"

"We don't have no lease on the Dublin houses." Michael looked questioningly at Dan. "We don't pay no rent. The Judge could turn us out."

"True for you, we don't pay no rent." Dan spoke slowly. "But if he turned us out, who would dig his canal? Now you got me thinkin on it, it's part of the bargain we work for wages *and* for the place to stay in while we're workin. The way I see it, that makes these *our* houses as long as we're doin his work. Why wouldn't we get the priest here and if Judge Laurence don't like it . . ."

"If he don't like it, let him try to stop us," Johnny said. "I'm with you, Dan."

"And I'm with you," Hugh's deep voice seconded him.

Michael wasn't yet sure. "Him bein a judge, doesn't that mean he's the law? You know what they say, 'Don't take the devil to law if the court is in hell.'"

They talked into the night about it and the next day all Dublin, on the job and off, buzzed with it. Kate Toohey said there was no house in Dublin big enough and fine enough for a station. It would be a downright insult to the priest to carry him into one of these poor shanties. Bridget took the insult to herself and told Kate it wasn't everyone in Dublin had six lodgers lying on a heap of straw. Some knew how to keep a good house though the devil himself threw everything into a threenahaila.

Some of the young fellows were for organizing a group of Defenders, the way it was done in penal times when Mass had to be said out in the hills. Let anyone lift a finger against the Mass or the wedding and they would make a fight of it. The more cautious thought Michael and Peg should do the way Simon wanted and some asked anxiously what Jamie had to say. Dan refused to speak to the bosses about it.

"If you ask, they can easy say no. That's a mighty little word, 'no' but once said, it would be hard for us to go against it. Don't ask and they can't say no."

But all didn't have courage for that. Peg's father spoke to Jamie one noontime as they stood around the fire on the river bank, drying out and eating their dinner.

"I know if the gift was in your givin, there wouldn't be no need of askin, but couldn't you maybe explain to the Judge how it is? I won't send my daughter off to some far place with a man she ain't married to, so if you don't see nothin wrong in it, couldn't the priest come to Dublin? He don't need to set foot over to the Big House."

"Tell you what I'll do," Jamie said grandly. "I'll go to Zanesville with you and the young people myself. We'll take the team and the wagon and as many others as it can hold."

Joe was standing nearby and immediately put in for a place in the wagon for himself and Eileen and the baby. Paddy chimed in. He had a baby not yet christened though months older than Joe's. The words were hardly out of his mouth before there were more of them crowding around, raising their own pleas. O'Malley wanted to bring Molly, who was to stand up with her sister, "and they couldn't leave the three younger ones behind."

Johnny was to stand up with Michael so he must go, and there were a dozen plausible reasons for one or another to be included. Jamie caught the sardonic look in Dan's eye as he stood a little aside, sipping his tea and watching the scene.

"I suppose you want to go to Zanesville, too," Jamie said to him. "What is it you've got to say, why Michael can't get married without you?"

"Oh, I think I'll bide here," Dan said. "There's all the women yet that's been talkin of the priest's comin these many days. One and all, they'll be wantin to go, along of Peg and Bridget and Eileen. It's a pity the one priest couldn't come to Dublin instead of all Dublin goin to the priest."

"That's it," O'Malley was right up against Jamie with his urging. "'Twould be the easier way, wouldn't it now, Mr. McCarthy? But we can't have it the way we want it, can we? We know you don't have the whole say on things here. It's the grand boss you are to offer the wagon."

"Time to go back to work, lads," Jamie said abruptly.

Dan was laughing as he walked back to the job with O'Malley.

"Didn't you have Jamie between the devil and the deep blue sea! Now he's got to come round the Judge somehow, or everybody will be sayin it's the Judge is the big boss and Jamie takin the orders from him."

Jamie saw the chance to deal with the devil without falling into the sea when Saturday night brought a fight in Charlie Williams' tavern at the Forks. The tale came back that the Blower and a half dozen other Irish were called dirty names by some of the local men. When it came to blows, "King Charlie" let the local men alone but put the Irish out. They came roaring back in. In the ensuing melee a lantern was upset and before it could be doused, the whole place was up in flames. King Charlie swore no Irish would ever set foot in his place again. He came out to talk to Judge Laurence, threatening to sue everyone in sight and send the sheriff to arrest the culprits. It was all the Judge could do to get the matter quieted down and keep it from interfering with the work. He was thoroughly angry with the men who caused the trouble and seemed to think Jamie and Simon were somehow at fault.

Jamie outdid him in accusations against the bad actors among the men till there was nothing left for the Judge to say, except how could they avoid another such thing.

"I'll tell you how it is," was Jamie's answer. "We'll give out the warnin to one and all but we can never find out who was at the bottom of it. They're all alibi'n each other. Runnin wild over here with no church and no priest to keep 'em in order. A good sermon, now . . ."

"Get them together, then and I'll read them a sermon, or you can do it yourself in your own language."

"I'm afraid that wouldn't do. I can't promise they would listen to a priest, but I can promise they won't listen to nobody else."

The end of it was, Laurence agreed the priest could come to Dublin. Jamie came to tell it to Michael and sat by the Griffens' hearth for the first time since his falling out with Dan over the pay. He was in the best of humors, recalling the old days in Carrignahown and giving them the grand tale of how he got a tight hold on Judge Laurence and wouldn't let go till he got the promise that the priest could come.

When he left, Dan and Mary looked at each other, the same question in the eyes of each. Mary put her answer into words.

"There goes Jamie McCarthy, defender of the faith and grand champion of all the Irish."

"He's a smart man, though, Jamie is. I wonder what really happened between him and the Judge. Seems like he's not smart enough to get the Judge to raise up my pay . . . if he ever tried."

Chapter 23

AS MARY STOOD in front of the Dublin shanties with Rose Farrell and Peg she felt that she was not herself at all but some other woman. For the first time she was wearing the dress and bonnet Peter Hobbs had given her. Around her shoulders was a big warm shawl. Maggie had given her the loan of it, her own being thin and small and her cloak beyond wearing on such an occasion. She had Bridget's white stockings on under the shoes Dan had bought her in the cold of the last winter. The final touch was the little bag that hung from her wrist.

"Look at the darlin American lady," Maggie had exulted when she was all dressed, "as if she was born to it."

Rose looked grand, too. She had sewed for the fine ladies in the real Irish Dublin and was the undisputed authority on dress in Little Dublin. She had helped Mary cut a piece off the bottom of the American dress which was too long for her and had showed her how to make a little bag out of the left-over piece. A reticule, she called it. It had money in it now and a piece of linen. She was to wipe her nose on that and not on her hand, Rose said.

Peg was the shabbiest of the three, but the whole expedition was on her account. They were off to the store in Coshocton to buy cloth so she could have a proper dress to be married in. Mrs. Laurence and her son Robert were going on one of their regular trips to buy supplies and would let them ride in the wagon.

Mary had dared to go to the back door of the Laurence house and ask the favor. She had first said to Dan, "The Judge's wife wouldn't be a ladyship, would she?"

"No, there's no lordships and ladyships in this country," Dan assured her. "She's Mrs. Laurence just like you're Mrs. Griffen."

"So I wrapped up my courage in my fist and gave a knock on the door with it," Mary told the other women afterward as they sat around the candle in the Farrell shanty with their needles going in and out. "She opened the door herself and I give her my best curtsy and says I, 'Knowin you're the kindness itself, ma'am, would you maybe be givin three of us the leave to sit behind the horses and you goin to the town?' 'Step in, Mrs. Griffen' says she. 'You are Mrs. Griffen, are you not?' says she. So I thank her kindly and I step in and then I was after askin the question all over again one time and then another time before she got the sense of it. When she did, 'Yes, indeed,' says she. 'Certainly. We'll be goin of a Thursday.'"

Mary described every detail she could remember of the Laurence kitchen and then Maggie asked, "How did you come by the American clothes?"

So Mary gave them the story to pass the time while they worked but she left out of it that the Hobbses were black people. Bridget kept her tongue in her head about it, too. It would have taken some of the shine off the clothes if it were known, it being the way in this country to think nothing good can come from black people.

When the wagon came rattling up, Robert gave the reins to his mother and jumped down. He handed Mary up to the seat beside his mother as if she were a lady and Mrs. Laurence gave her a polite good morning. The others had to sit in the wagon bed. Mary was conscious that they were listening as she returned the greeting.

"Good mornin to yourself, Mrs. Laurence, and may God bless you for takin us off to the town with you this fine mornin."

Eliza cast overt glances at the Irish woman. The hands that were pulling the shawl closer around the slight figure were red with cold and workworn but they were clean and the clothes were neat. There was a cold wind in their faces, bringing tears to their eyes and making them both sniff. Eliza took off one of her warm mittens and opened her reticule. Taking out a dainty handkerchief, she wiped her nose.

Mary opened her reticule and taking out her handkerchief, wiped her nose. That done, she began to be impatient. Didn't the woman have a word to say?

"Have you been long in this country?" Eliza finally asked.

"We have, then. Almost two long years its been since we came over the water."

"Do you like it here?"

"Why wouldn't we like such a grand country with the fine farms that's in it?"

"Would your husband like to work on a farm instead of on the canal?"

"Are the farms only for the Americans, then? Couldn't a man from County Cork buy one for himself?"

"Certainly, if he has the money. Anyone can buy land."

"That's what we were told this long time back, that in this country there is land for all."

"Quite right. Of course, improved land—land that is already made into a farm, you know—costs more than wilderness land. When we first came here, there was little improved land in this country."

"You bought wilderness land, then? And it wasn't costin you a bagful of dollars?"

"It didn't cost us anything. My father was a chaplain in the American Revolution. He had a warrant for land here in Ohio because of that."

"Your father was in it, then, when they threw the English king and the English soldiers out of America? And the land was a reward, like, for bein in the uprisin?"

"Why yes, you could put it like that."

"We'd be proud to meet such a man as your father. Is he yet livin?"

"No, he died shortly after we came to Ohio."

"Well, death is ahead of all of us, but it's a sad thing all the same." Mary crossed herself. "God between us and all harm."

Eliza drew in her breath sharply at this foreign gesture and closed her mouth tight. She stared straight ahead without a word. Poor woman, Mary thought to herself, she's grieving for her father.

"You're that proud of your father, I wouldn't wonder, and him the brave man that helped throw the English into the sea and take the land out of the hands of the English lords. I daresay it's to him and his like we owe it that there's a place for the likes of us that's been driven out of our own country. And there's no more lords and ladies here since that time?"

"What? Oh, since the Revolution, you mean? That's right. This is a republic. There's no aristocracy here."

Mary's next question was silent, accompanied by a quick glance at the expressionless face beside her.

What is it, then, keeps your neck so stiff you can't turn your head to give me a look what's in back of your eyes?

Eliza was forming questions of her own. It had never occurred to her that some of the Irish workers might stay when the canal work was over. It disturbed her particularly because Robert had shown a disposition lately to hang about with the Irish workers in the blacksmith shop during the day or even to disappear in the direction of Dublin in the evening. He said he just went to sit by the fire and listen to their songs and stories but she had visions of her son poisoned with popish superstitions or becoming innocently involved in some dreadful brawl.

"You and your husband are thinking of settling somewhere in Ohio when the canal is finished?"

"We are." Mary held up one hand and told off the fingers with the index finger of the other. "From Carrignahown to Cork we went, from Cork across the water to New York. From New York up the river and down the canal and across the lake to Cleveland. From Cleveland to Akron. From Akron to here. It's time we stopped and had our own place at last."

"Mr. McCarthy tells me that you did the cooking in his camp at Akron."

"I did and I don't need to tell yourself the hard work that's in it."

To Eliza, it was one thing to help her husband in this great canal project that meant so much to him, cooking for the bosses and a few of the craftsmen. It was quite another to be the hired cook for the laborers like this Irish woman.

"Had you ever done work like that before you came to Ohio?"

"Wouldn't I be after cookin from the time I could help my granny put the potatoes in the pot? But it's another thing entirely, isn't it, to cook for the one family and to cook for an army of hungry men?"

"Yes, of course. And how do you find it, to live in the camps with all the men. I mean, there seems to be a great deal of drinking and fighting and you don't seem to be the kind of woman who would like that kind of life."

"Like it? It's not a matter of the likin, is it at all? A woman does what she has to do and there's not much 'shall I, shan't I' about it. As for the drinkin and fightin, poor lads, it's the hard work they do and little of the 'shall I, shan't I' for them neither. It's not the life God meant men to live, far from their mothers and their wives and their own firesides but they're good lads, most of 'em."

When they came to the town there was so much to see, Mary couldn't put her mind to any more talk. There were buildings all around the town square and the store they went into was such as she had been in only once in her life. That was in Cobh when they were getting ready to go on the ship.

Mr. Campbell took care of Mrs. Laurence and his clerk helped the Dublin women. Rose took the lead now but Mary felt proud to be standing in this store with all the things in the world that could be bought here. There was Mrs. Laurence on the one side of the store and here were they on the other side, each giving out the orders to the men behind the counter.

All the way home she was thinking about it.

There'll come a time when we'll have our own farm and our own team and wagon. Tim will drive me to the store and when I walk in it will be "Good mornin, Mrs. Griffen," myself bein known there. I'll be the wife of a known farmer and the mother of the young Mr. Griffen, that will be Tim. Robert is a grand lad but when it comes to the heads on them, Tim is the better of the two. All he needs is a piece of land where he can plant his two feet.

Eliza told her husband that night that she felt a little easier about Robert's association with the Irish.

"Mrs. Griffen is a nice clean little woman. I think it will be allright for Robert to go to their cabin, though I must say, I don't understand why he wants to. I do hope when they are through here they will move on. Did you know some of them want to buy farms and settle down?"

"Do they? H'mm. I never thought of that. I wonder if they'll be able to save enough out of their wages. There's that piece of land up the Walhonding."

"Joshua! You're not thinking of selling to them?"

"Why not, if they have the money?"

"Well . . . they're *Irish* and *papists* . . . and I don't know, they just don't seem to belong here."

Chapter 24

ALL THE WHILE they were preparing for the priest's visit, Mary was fearful that the winter weather would keep him away.

"Now that all is ready it isn't in nature for the two of them to wait for the spring, whether the priest comes or no," Mary said to Dan.

"So?" Dan shrugged. "They wouldn't be the first to be bedded before wedded. It's promised the priest will come sooner or later."

"So it's a sin," she answered sharply.

There's no certainty to anything in this country. Only the priest can tie up the marriage tight against the death that walks the canal bringing the danger to the work and the sudden coming of the fever. Peg can be left with a babe, maybe, and no husband. Even if there's no babe in her arms, once she lies with a man without the church's blessing on it, no other man will have her to wife, only to pleasure.

But the priest did come. It was the Irish one who had been with the Bishop in Akron, so he was no stranger. He was there the whole of a Saturday, hearing confessions in the new shanty Michael had built for himself and Peg. The men he heard in the dark of the morning before work and in the dark of the night when work was done. The women he heard in the day.

There was rivalry among the women over who should prepare his meals. There were some high words before it was settled and some hard feelings left over afterward but there was nothing to give the Reverend Mister a hint of it except the air of triumph with which Maggie Flynn carried him his breakfast.

Mary took him his noon dinner. "How grand it would be, could we have such a parish priest as yourself when we're settled on the farm."

"I'm greatly interested to hear of your plans," he said. "But perhaps you should find a place closer to Cincinnati. There are so few priests in Ohio, and the faithful are so scattered, it is more than we can do to reach them all, besides the need to carry God's word to the savages."

In his sermon next day, he told them it had been part of God's great purpose to carry them safely across the water and bring them to this new land. It was their duty now to give thanks. They were to live pious and upright lives, as His children should, in peace with each other and obedient to their masters. Thus, each little Catholic community could become a beacon of truth in this wilderness of error.

Mary felt quite elevated by his words and by the cleansing they had all had, inside and out. There was the pleasure, too, of seeing Michael and Peg happily wed and the two babies she had helped into the world christened, Bridget's Nora and Eileen's Thomas. When that was all done, the priest said he must be off down the line to another Irish camp. No amount of urging could convince him to stay, though the wedding was only well begun. There was the eating and drinking in the Laurences' barn still to come.

The barn had a festive look, with the people streaming in and the long boards propped up to serve as a table, laden with good food. Peg having no mother, Mary and Bridget had seen to it that O'Malley bought the elements of a feast, though he had to borrow from Jamie against his wages to do it. They had done the cooking with some help from other Dublin women, this one and that one throwing in something extra of her own making. Simon Lordon, being the boss over the stoneworkers, had a right to do something for Michael. He had bought two geese and got Ike McKendrie's wife, Emma, who cooked at the quarry camp, to roast them. It was understood by one and all that it was the part of the bosses to supply the drink, but there had been much speculation about whether there would be anything from Mrs. Laurence's kitchen, or would she and the Judge come at all.

Every man, woman and child from Dublin was there and some of the Coshocton canal workers too, with their wives and children. All the stonemasons and quarriers came, Coshocton men as well as Irish, those who lived close e ,ough bringing their families. Yet at first things were altogether too stiff and subdued to be much like a wedding. The men had worked on the same jobs, rubbing off some of the strangeness, but the women had scarcely seen each other and could not so much as give another woman a name.

Coshocton men and women stood around, uncomfortable in their best clothes, looking furtively at each other for a lead as to how to act at this Irish wedding. The Irish would have been glad for a hint of what was expected in this American place, not wanting to put the wrong foot forward under all those judging eyes. The hands of all the men hung uselessly at their sides.

Jamie was here, there, and all over the barn with words of good fellowship. Soon each man had his hand around a noggin of whiskey and tongues were loosened. The children were all intoxicated with the excitement of the crowd and the prospect of the feast.

The food began to bring the women together. It had been a matter of course to the Coshocton women to bring a piece of boiled venison or pork, a dish of succotash or cabbage, a pumpkin or fruit pie. The natural thing was to hand the food to the bride's mother. Mary found herself thrust into this role again. It was a help to have Emma McKendrie and Toby Weaver's mother at her side, Emma standing proudly behind the two geese she had roasted. Mrs. Weaver assumed that Mary knew how things were to be done. It was in a kindly spirit that she nudged Mary forward when she was slow to fulfill her proper role. Between them, these women knew all the Coshocton people and the quarry workers besides. They were quick with the greetings and ready to peep under the lid of every offering. They would then tell Mary who the woman was that brought it.

The rising buzz of talk was stilled when the Laurences walked in, bringing a big turkey and a whole row of pound cakes. Mary was lavish with her thanks till Eliza Laurence, unaccustomed to such extravagance of speech, turned away in embarrassment.

"I dunno as its any more'n she should do, seeing as it's her place an all, and the Judge is the top man on this canal work," Emma said when Eliza was out of earshot. "It is a mighty pretty bird though, ain't it? Browned as even all over. I wisht I had her kitchen to cook in. You ever seed it?"

"I did. A grand place entirely," Mary agreed. They watched the Laurences giving Michael and Peg their good wishes. Peg looked quite overcome with shyness.

"Let's get these folks started goin after the eats," Emma suggested. "I'm ready to work up to a taste of that cake, myself."

Mary was hesitant. "Wouldn't it be Mrs. Laurence has the right to begin?"

"Oh, she won't stay," Emma answered. "Her and the Judge, they hardly ever show up to the frolics around here. She'll send over some of her cookin and onct in awhile she'll come to a quiltin or somethin but I don't look for them to stay."

Mrs. Weaver agreed. "Eliza Laurence is a real lady and a good neighbor but she don't want nobody to forget the lady part."

As they expected, the Judge and Mrs. Laurence soon went out, leaving Robert behind. With their disappearance, the lid popped off the simmering gathering. Eating began and the stiffness evaporated.

The wedding never became as merry as it should have been though, nor as rowdy as it might have been. Partly it was that the strangeness was still there, partly it was that Jamie and Simon were mindful of a promise they had made to the Judge, that there would be no disorder.

It was after it was all over that it had its greatest success with the women of Dublin. There had been no such social occasion for any of them since their arrival in the new country. It was the widest open window they had ever had on this new world. The strange food was well talked over. Even more interesting were the looks and behavior of more women than they could well keep track of. Young ones like Millicent Maddox who had drawn the young Irishmen around her and what would come of that? Old ones like Sarah McKendrie, gaunt and silent, sitting in the corner with scarcely a word to say to anyone, while her husband Asa stopped talking only long enough to eat. Friendly ones like Buck's wife, Patsy, who had a baby the exact age of Eileen's. Haughty ones, who kept their names to themselves and looked at the Irish only to find something to whisper to each other.

Although she had as much to say as any of the Dubliners, Mary couldn't put into words what was most important to her. It was the feeling of satisfaction, almost of content, that had begun to come to her with the coming of the priest. She took the feeling away with her from the barn when the wedding was over and it stayed with her for days.

The winds of chance that gave us such a buffetin are dyin down. The Dublin we'll build in the Ohio countryside will have the blessin of God on it. It won't be ourselves on an island in the midst of a sea of strangers. It will be a place of our own. Goin out from it, we can deal with the people that isn't all strangers nor enemies neither the way it seemed sometimes they might be.

Chapter 25

T HE HARD WHITE Ohio cold stripped the last leaves from the trees, buried the brown earth and all things that grew in it, turned the little puddles and the edges of the river to ice. Thin fingers of wind and snow reached through the cracks and into the shanties. Winter was driven into their bodies till their bones were as cold as the bare branches of the trees and they were aching for the soft weather and green grasses of home.

This was the second Ohio winter for the children and there were two summers of forgetfulness between them and Ireland. The cold did not slow their growing and their days were full of color. Tim and Danny liked the blacksmith shop, the warmest spot in the camp, where the diggers gathered when the snow drove them from the job. Cornelius Murphy presided there, shoeing the horses and sharpening the stonecutters' tools at his forge. The ring of his hammer punctuated the talk of the men.

Tim liked the long shed of the stoneworkers too. There he fetched drinks for the dry mouths and parched throats brought on by the stone dust and carried the stonies' tools back and forth to Corny. In exchange, he was granted the privilege of watching those tools in skilled hands shape the stones that would be the facing on the aqueduct. The rough, square-cut stones, just as they came down from the quarry, would do for the part that would be dug into the riverbank, Dennis told Tim, but the face the aqueduct and the piers turned to the water must have a smooth curve so the river would slip easily around them.

Danny liked to slide across the ice on the shallow pond at the foot of the hill. When he ran down the slope and skimmed across the ice, the wind couldn't better the speed of his feet. He even ventured daringly out on the ice at the river's edge but he would not let Ellen follow. When Padeen Flynn knocked her over on the hard pond, Danny pushed him into the snow and buried him in it till Padeen's brother hit Danny from behind. Then Tim got into it and then all of them. That was the snow fight of the world!

On a day Ellen was not allowed out in the cold, she discovered where the book was kept on a small shelf. By climbing on the bed and stretching as high as she could on her toes, she could just reach it down. She sat on her own stool Dan had made for her out of a smoothed off piece of a log. With the book on her lap, she looked at the pictures in the back where the fables were.

Dan had resumed the boys' lessons, though the thought of making a priest out of Tim was fading. The road to the priesthood at home was a hard one but it was a known road, leading through years as a poor scholar under a Cork schoolmaster to Maynooth, the Catholic Seminary in County Kildare. Here in Ohio there was no learning but what Dan could give him and there was no Maynooth to be found.

All the more reason for both boys to learn the reading and writing of English and arithmetic too. Dan knew what it meant to have more learning than his mates. Who else could keep the paybook and read in the contract for himself what the Commissioner's specifications were for the digging and the building of the embankment? Who else could be thinking of being a foreman again in the spring and maybe someday even a contractor like Jamie?

Tim was quick at the reading but whatever Danny had learned last winter seemed to be gone. The slower he was in plodding through the words, the more exasperated his father became; the farther Tim got ahead of him, the less Danny worked at his lessons.

One day when Danny could not spell a single word right, Dan gave him a beating and told him he would not go out the door till he got his lesson. Tim ran out and Danny could hear him and the others shouting and playing. He sat on the hearth, looking sullenly at the book in the light of the fire. He was wishing his father would go out too, so he could slip away himself.

Ellen crept up beside him and looked longingly at the book. "Danny, will you tell me a word?"

Danny sighed. His father was sitting on the bench by the table with his head in his hands. He was clearly not going to move.

"What word?"

Ellen reached for the book and turned the pages till she came to her favorite picture of two men and a bear. She pointed to the first word under the picture.

"Two," Danny told her. She repeated it.

"What's that word?" pointing to the next.

"Friends." Her finger moved from one word to another till she had them fitted together from the beginning to the end of the line. Then she jumped to her feet and flung herself against her father.

"I can read the book!" She beat on his leg with her two fists. "Don't you know it? I can read in Tim and Danny's book!" Dan came slowly back from his far thoughts.

"It's the readin you've got, is it? Don't bother your brother while he's at his book. God knows he needs the help of the Holy Patrick and all the rest of the saints even without you botherin him."

Ellen danced back to the hearth. "I don't bother, do I, Danny? I have the mouth on me shut tight and I'm just watchin."

She sat down by her brother again and looked where his finger was pointing at a word without any picture to it. "A-m-a-z-e, amaze," he spelled it out.

"A-m-a-z-e, amaze," she whispered after him.

So it went on under Dan's nose that day and many days after and he never knew what it was began to make a better scholar out of Danny.

Ellen chattered about her reading but no one believed her. One day when the boys had finished their lesson, instead of rushing out the door, leaving his book wherever it might fall, Danny handed it to Ellen.

"Listen to this, now. It's Ellen herself is going to read out of the book."

Dan laughed and Mary came over to see what kind of a trick the boys were up to.

"A dog growls and barks," Ellen read, "a cat mews and purrs." Only once did she have to look at Danny for him to whisper a word to her. When she got to the end of her piece of reading she looked up into the faces turned toward her. Her father had his pipe out of his mouth and the mouth a bit open without a word coming out of it. Her mother's eyes were open so wide they pushed her brows up till they wrinkled her forehead all the way up to her hair. If she had been any more astonished the top of her head would have come off with the feeling that was on her she had a changeling in the house and not her own daughter at all.

"That's the girsha-scholar we've got." Danny was proud. "Now would you believe her when she tells you she can read?"

"She just has it off parrot-like from hearin us read it," Tim scoffed.

"I don't then," Ellen insisted. " It's myself reads the book."

Dan took the book. "We'll soon see is that what's in it." Turning the pages, he asked her a word on this page and another on that. Enough times she had the words on the tip of her tongue, there could be no more doubt.

There was nothing for it now but Ellen must have her lessons along with her brothers. There was little either Dan or Mary had been able to deny her since she came to them after the death of the other two. That was the way of it more than ever now that they knew she would be the last of their children, the scrapings of the pot. She wouldn't have the same need of the book knowledge as the boys, but mother and father took pride in it that she would have the learning of a lady, need or no.

Better even than the stories in the book for Ellen were the stories and the songs of the grownup people around the fire at night.

The Griffen shanty was becoming the warm center of Dublin's life. It was a rare evening when there weren't four or five around the fire besides those who lived in the Griffen shanty and often it was a dozen.

Mason Thomas Noonan and Blacksmith Corny Murphy were not above joining the group. On a Saturday, there might be a man from another camp up or down the line, lonesome for the sound of home. Here was the nearest thing to their own neighborhood gathering they had found since crossing the water. Here the language of the new country, the English that belonged to work and authority, was spoken less than the Irish that belonged to the songs and the stories.

Tim and Danny, with such other boys as followed in after the older people, climbed up to the loft where they could scramble about as they pleased in the half-light, or lie on their bellies and hang their heads over the loft's edge to listen to what went on below.

Dan and Mary, being the man and woman of the house, had their places on either side of the fire. Ellen's little stool was always just next to Mary. There she could hear everything while the talk gleamed and crackled. When it grew gray and wispy, in the way grownup talk was prone to do, she could let it drift up the chimney while she went to sleep against Mary's knee.

Mary had always liked the story-telling, but it was one thing at home where everyone around the fire knew the bend in the road where it came around the stony hill and dropped down to the river. It was there Patsy Kerrigan met the three men with the coffin. When that story was told, the scene was there before the eyes of everyone listening. But hardly one of the people around the fire here knew that parish, much less their own townland, and some had never been in County Cork at all.

So Mary got into the way of giving them the place of the story, looking into the glowing coals, her voice dropping so low everyone would lean forward to her. When all could see as she did the way the big rock rising out of the brook shone when the moon was on it, or smelled as she did the road's dust when the cattle were being driven to market, then she would turn her head back toward them, giving them the story in the old words and the old rhythm just as she had learned them from her grandmother.

When she told the tales of the great fights of long ago, it was another Ireland she had to bring them. The Ireland they knew was one of farm fields and bare hills, with the trees just edging the rivers or growing here and there on some lord's demesne. The country they were in now was covered with trees, but it was not the only country with mighty forests. Ireland too, in that past time . . .

"The land you're born in," she was saying one night, "gives you the food to keep you alive and the shelter against your enemies that comes from foreign lands. That was the way of it in Cork in the uprisin in the olden time, when the trees was still on the hills below the high crags and all up and down the valleys. In them days a squirrel could make his way from a great oak to a tall birch and on to the next all the way from Killarney to Cork without the need of droppin to the ground.

"That's what the old people told us as it was told to them by their old people. The English could never reach with their crooked laws but a bit of a way beyond Cork. Let them take as much as a cock's step outside the city and they found a man of the old clans behind every tree. They could come in their ships where Ireland touches the sea, from Cobh to Leap, but that was the end of it. 'Beyond the Leap, beyond the law,' that was the sayin then. Even when the soldiers came by the thousands in Cromwell's time they couldn't go safely till they burned the woods or cut them to the ground."

Michael, who was always there with Peg beside him, picked up Mary's thought and gave them the *Kilcash* poem:
> "What shall we do for timber?
> The last of the woods is down . . ."

Sometimes Ellen fell asleep to the rhythm of Michael's poems, sometimes to the songs of Rose or of Paddy when Paddy could be got away from his cards.

Ellen liked the stories too, where each would be telling that certain past time only he or she knew. Ellen was in one of those stories herself, Mary telling it how they almost came to the new country without her and how she rode on her father's shoulders the long way from Carrignahown to Cobh.

Hugh had stories of the ships and Dennis told about the great city of Dublin, quite a different place from their own Dublin.

He liked to talk of the fine buildings in that city and how he was a man who had cut stone for this one or that one. That would rouse Michael again. Though he was young himself and could boast little of his own building, a Dublin man couldn't be left to such talk when it was well known the world over the beauty of the white limestone of Cork and the skill of the men who cut it.

There was nothing alike between Michael and Dennis but their stone cutters' hands. There was a softness to Michael's cheeks that gave him still the unfinished look of a boy and a roundness to his big shoulders and arms. He was a journeyman stonecutter but he was still an apprentice in the world of men and women. There was a touch of wonder in his voice even when he told the old stories he knew so well.

Dennis had worked all the softness out of his sinewy body. His shrewd eyes looked behind the words that tumbled out of a person's mouth. His own words were short and quick with a cutting edge to them.

Both had strong hands, sanded white from the work with the stone. These hands moved in the firelight and together with the words, built again the great buildings of Dublin and Cork till the walls rose up glittering in the bright flames.

Then Dan's voice whipped out. "It's proud you'd be, isn't it, to build the courts where they condemn the Irish and the courtyards where they hang them by the neck till they're dead and the barracks where they march out on the rest of us with their guns."

Michael put his hands in his pockets, looking at Dan out of hurt and sorrowful eyes. He would talk no more that night, but Dennis lashed back at Dan. Ellen hung on tight to Mary's dress while the battle of words raged, turning her head first to one, then to the other. Each time her father spoke she looked for his words to destroy Dennis entirely.

Dennis threw a big piece of talk at Dan, snapping out at the end, " . . so it was the Dublin men from the trades was behind Robert Emmet and it was them was hung by the English from every lamppost in the Liberties of Dublin." He folded his arms, his chin in the air.

For a few minutes no word was said, then Dennis spoke again in a solemn voice. "One of them was my own uncle. My father often told us no stonie ever handled a chisel better or struck a truer blow with the mallet. And no man struck a truer blow for Ireland neither."

"All honor to him." Now Dan was on the same side with Dennis in that long-ago fight, telling his own story "My father was such a man, too. He had his cattle taken and his house burned in '98. That was for not givin up the pikes and the guns to the redcoats. It was a grand farm he had then, on the other side of Macroom—the Cork side, where the good black earth is in the fields, not like Carrignahown, where we had to dig three rocks out of it before we could plant one potato."

"They put him out of his good farm, did they?" Tom Quinlan asked.

"There wasn't so much as the squeal of a pig left him. He slipped out of there in the night while the house was burnin. I was hardly out of dresses myself. I hung on to my Da's leg and screamed the head off me when they put torch to the thatch."

Ellen didn't like that story. She climbed up in her mother's lap for comfort.

She didn't want her Da to tell that story. It wasn't himself he was talking about. He wasn't a small scared boy. That was some other boy. It was better when he went on to the Keimaneigh story. That one was really about her big Da who could never be scared.

That story made even Tim and Danny remember back beyond the new things that happened since they came across the water. Back to the night their mother had wakened them and pulled them out of the house into the dark night to see the signal fires that carried the news of victory from Doughill Mountain to Sheehy Mountain and all along the ridge above Inchigeela to where even the people in Macroom could see. The fires told them it was not just a few cattle rescued from the pound, or one family saved from eviction, it was the gentry and the soldiers on the run. It was time to rise up and chase them into the sea. That was what the fires said.

The next day after Dan told that story, Tim and Danny told it again to each other, remembering how they had heard it told before by their father and by the other men from Carrignahown who had been in it, remembering their own waking and how they had seen the fire that seemed to leap from one high hill to light a signal on the next hill.

"And I got up out of my bed and took a big log and put it on that fire," Ellen said.

How they laughed at her then. "You weren't even born yet," they told her.

So she had to be content to tell it to Terry who was quite willing to believe her when she said, "And I was borned then and got up out of my bed and made a big big fire for all the people to come and hear the story, how my Da chased the bad people down the mountain."

Chapter 26

UNEXPECTED WARMTH brought an easier swing into the work one January day and made it go faster till a sprinkle of rain lifted heads for a look at the dark clouds rolling up. That warning sprinkle was soon followed by a downpour that drove them off the job. They made a run for Dublin, through snow underfoot that was turning soft and wet.

Johnny slipped in it and fell. Egan Flynn gave him a push that sent him rolling. He was up and after Egan with a handfull of slushy snow but it was no weather for horseplay. The promise of a dry seat by the fire beckoned in the smoke rising from chimneys and seeping through shanty cracks.

The best place turned out to be in their beds. Although the women had the fires built up to fight the damp, rain and melting snow had begun to trickle down the hill behind the camp and seep in under the walls.

In the middle of the night Jamie came hammering at the doors and calling them back into the storm. "Come on, lads," he shouted. "The river's risin on us. Quick now, or it'll be drownin our work and carryin off our tools."

As they stumbled reluctantly out of the shanties, he held up his lantern and kept up his shouting to draw the men around him. He didn't look himself at all in the feeble and flickering light but the very devil out of hell, all black and glistening wet with strange shadows playing over his face below his dripping hat.

The whole night was a hell of roaring wet dark. Familiar landmarks were lost in it. Known voices had a strange sound as they bellowed to make themselves heard above the thundering torrent of the river. Each man got a grip on the one next to him when he could, to get the feel of a friend in it with him. A man beyond arm's length was an alien hulk of darker solidity against the night without a known face on it.

The smooth-flowing river they knew had been transformed into a powerful flood sweeping down on them with the force to knock a man off his feet. It was carrying trees it had ripped from its banks, their branches tossed into weird shapes suddenly emerging out of the dark and as suddenly whirled out of sight. It was tumbling gravel and rocks across its bottom and flinging them, with the trees and all kinds of other debris, against the cofferdam they had just completed.

The dam had stood tall above the river, two firm walls of sheet-piling with gravel and clay between them, enclosing a pit they kept pumped out so they could work in it. Now the top of the dam was barely visible as a darker shadow against the dark water. The two scows that had derricks mounted on them were rocking dangerously in the current. They had been close to shore, their mooring ropes lashed to stumps, but the shore was no longer where it belonged and the stumps were almost submerged. The raft used to ferry men and material across the river was nowhere to be seen.

They gathered away from the water, near the tool shed that had been far up the bank when they left the job earlier in the day. They made a circle around Jamie, their shoulders hunched against the rain, heads pushed forward to hear his voice shouting at them hoarsely what they were to do. In the minutes they stood there, the water reached their feet and rose to their ankles.

The rest of the night was a race against the rising water, a struggle against the current. Judge Laurence and Si Maddox drove the oxen up to the tool shed, hitched to the two sledges that had been hauling stone down from the quarry over the snow. Some of the men loaded the sledges with pumps, barrows and hand tools. Jamie took Dan and the others with him, trying to save the scows with the big derricks on them before the river could carry them off.

They got one scow out of the torrent and through shallower water till it went aground. They lashed it to a tree and went back for the second.

Half a dozen of them were up to their hips in the roiling river, pulling on the scow's two ropes. It was a tug-of-war with the current. They had barely enough men on their side. Suddenly Tom Quinlan slipped on the treacherous bottom and fell in. Dan and Buck McKendrie both dropped their holds on the rope to grab at him.

"Are you drowned entirely?" Dan yelled as they helped him flounder out of the water, blinded and choking with it.

"He ain't drowned." Buck was thumping Tom on the back to knock the water out of him, "But he's sure as hell wet. Spit it out, man." He gave Tom a thump that almost sent him under again.

"Out of this with him," Dan said. They got his arms up over their shoulders and made for the shore.

"The rope! The rope!" Jamie was hollering. "Get on it, damn you or we can't hold."

They dropped Tom against a pile of hewn timbers, the only stable haven in the watery dark and splashed back toward Jamie's voice. The loss of their strength and Tom's on the ropes meant that the arms of those who were left were being dragged out of their sockets by the pull of the current on the scow. The broad clumsy body of it with its top-heavy machine pitched in the swift stream, threatening to go over when it was struck by a careening tree.

With Dan and Buck back they could hold. Inch by inch they gained on the river. By the time they had the second scow safe, the darkness had begun to recede before a dim vapory daylight. The rain was slackening, but the rough brown Walhonding was still pouring past them, wide and deep, down to meet the swollen Tuscarawas. The usually well-defined Forks were lost in spreading and conflicting currents. The valley between the river and Dublin was a marshy lake.

There was no work for three days after the storm. Bosses and workers often splashed through the slowly diminishing puddles in the valley to watch the flood recede and the old landmarks gradually reemerge.

The river ceased tearing at its banks and let its burden of soil settle. Though the water dropped almost as fast as it had risen, it did not get back to the low level of the autumn. In places it had carved out a new channel. As the water cleared, it revealed what was left of the work below the surface. They could see what had happened to the great structure that had grown under their hands through the past months. They would have to go back to the beginning and do much of the most difficult work over again. The main current had divided against the cofferdam. One stream had ripped into the bank, scooping out earth and rock. What was left of the coffer was now out in the midst of the river. The upriver side of it had caught the full force of the water and the load it carried. The load had built up behind it and pushed against it until it had been crushed. It was buried now beneath an island of gravel and rock, with trees and branches sticking out of it at crazy angles. The rest of the coffer looked like the mouth of an old man with big gaps between the surviving teeth. The only good thing was that what could be seen of the permanent piling driven into the pit inside the dam had held. There was scarcely anything left of the second cofferdam they had started on the other side of the river.

The other end of the job, farthest from the river, had been set back too. That part of the canal already dug had acted as a channel for the hill's runoff in the storm, pouring it down on the earth they had dumped into the valley, eroding its edges, loosening its footings, finally carrying it away entirely. The ditch itself was almost empty of water now, but it was sloppy with mud and full of debris.

The men walked the field of their battle, now strewn with wreckage, reliving the night's happenings. Tom Quinlan, who seemed to be as spry as ever, found the very place where he had gone down. He stood there, safe out of the water now. He measured on his body how high the water had been and described with relish every detail of the accident and the rescue.

There was one less fortunate casualty of the storm. After all the narrow escapes of the Blower's years of setting the black powder to blow out the rock, it was no explosion that brought him down. He and two others were lifting a box of heavy iron fittings onto one of the sledges when he slipped and fell in the mud. The box came down on top of him. They laid him gently on the sledge and carried him to the Griffen cabin, fearing the unconscious man was dead.

Mary could feel his heart beating but she could feel too, that something inside was broken. She made a poultice for the broken place and the Blower came to himself. She gave him whiskey for the pain he was in. He took it gratefully and tried to still his groans. She said over the charm for broken bones and the charm to stop bleeding, though he bled little. She prayed for his recovery. Neither poultice nor whiskey, neither charm nor prayer availed. On the fourth day after the storm, he died.

That same day they built a new raft and cleared some of the debris away from the workplace. At the end of that day, while they were swallowing the bad news of the Blower's death, the word came from Jamie that there would be no work the next day.

Tom asked Dan the why of it and Dan tried to get it out of Jamie. All he would say was that Jim Dent was coming the next day. That had never before been a reason for stopping the work. It was at just such a time the bosses drove them hardest, making a show for the engineer or the Commissioner.

The stonies that had worked with the Blower waked him that evening in the stone shed. Mary keened him briefly and hoarsely. The storm had left the colds and the fevers behind with its other wreckage. She felt her croaking was as sorry a keen as her nursing of the Blower had been and went sadly away to wrap her shivering body in a blanket by her own fire.

There was whiskey enough at the wake but it did little to take away the uneasy feeling rising from the Blower's death and the days without work. There was a fire in the center of the shed, inside a circle of the fragments that had been cut away from the big stones to shape them for the aqueduct but a fitful wind blew the smoke this way and that. The men moved constantly, seeking the warmth, trying to escape the smoke. The talk was as fitful as the wind.

Dan blinked his stinging eyes and bumped into Dennis in the half-light.

"Here's the man I want," Dennis exclaimed, grasping his arm. "See young Toby over there?"

Toby Weaver was standing by himself a few feet away with a mournful look on his usually cheerful face. The smoke was obviously not the sole cause of his red eyes and smudged cheeks.

Dennis spoke quietly for Dan's ear alone. "I could make a good mason out of that lad," he said. "Best of the lot, he is, out of all the spalpeens off the farms they've give us in the quarry, but I can't shake the farm out of him. He was with the Blower that night and near broke his back tryin to get the box off him. He's takin it hard, the Blower's gone. Will the two of us cheer him up a bit, hey, Dan?"

A few steps closed the distance between them and Dennis put a hand on Toby's shoulder.

"Here's the man I was after tellin you reads out of the same book as yourself," he said and turning to Dan, "Isn't it m'self is always tellin you we has a lad works with us, reads as good as Dan Griffen and out of the very same book? That's Toby."

He looked triumphantly from one to the other as if he had got two stones to fit together in a wall and went off to find a jug so they could have a proper drink over it.

"You have a book of the *Rights of Man*?" Dan asked. Toby nodded indifferently and Dan went on, "Where would you be gettin an Irish book the like of that on this side of the water?"

"That's no Irish book," Toby sounded resentful. "Thomas Paine was an American. He was in the Revolution like my own grandfather."

"In the revolution in America indeed, and in the revolution in France," Dan conceded, "but this book was writ to put down the king of England and his ministers and tell the people of Ireland the rights they had as much as the men of any country in God's world. I can show you the very book as I got it from my father, that had it hid in the straw when I wasn't big enough to tell a from b."

"I'd like to see that book." Toby was interested now, though skeptical. "Maybe he wrote two of 'em, one for the Irish and one for us. But I know this, Paine was an American, through and through."

Dan was shaking his head and Toby thought about it for a minute.

"Of course," he admitted, "I don't know where he come from in the beginnin. Maybe he was an Irishman, or his father was. Everybody in this country come from somewhere else or their fathers did or their grandfathers going back to Pilgrim times."

This was a new thought to Dan. "Everybody come from somewhere else?"

"Sure enough. My Pa's folks come from England and Ma's from Wales. The Judge, his folks come from France and Mrs. Laurence, some of hers was from Holland. Just like you and your folks come from Ireland."

"Them, too," Dan savored the thought. "The Judge and all . . . strangers to the land like us."

"Well, not exactly like you. The Judge claims his folks has been here more than a hundred years."

Dennis came back with the jug and filled all three cups. Dan lifted his.

"Here's to the rights of man and down with the kings and the lords and all such."

They drank to it.

"I'll bring my book over to your place some time and we'll see are they as like as two peas in a pod," Toby said.

"Come then," Dan urged him, "and soon or we may be out of it. Will they get this job pulled out of the river and started up again, think you?" He jerked a thumb toward Jamie and Simon who had just come in.

Everyone wanted to ask that or some question like it but the bosses took a drink, paid their duty to the absent Blower and went away again before the shift could be made from respect for the dead to the future of the living.

Chapter 27

EN CROWDED into the Griffen shanty with questions for Dan. When will there be work again? Will there be money at the end of the month for the work already done? What about us that's in debt to the bosses for our keep through the winter?

The engineer had come and gone and there was still no work. Rumors that the contractors were out of money swirled through Dublin. Judge Laurence ferried across the river one morning and rode off. It was said he was seeking out the Commissioner or trying to borrow money in Chilicothe or Columbus.

Dan didn't have answers but he got hope from somewhere, perhaps from the need of it the others had, their own hope having been washed away in the flood. When he finally got a word from Jamie he could pass on, it was, "No more work till the Commissioner himself has looked at the job. Jamie and Simon and the Judge, they want more time than the contract give 'em and a new agreement on the money."

That brought a hatful of new questions. What happens if the Commissioner says 'no'? How will we live till jobs on the other sections opens up in the spring? Will Jamie let us hang on here? Will we be out on the road in the cold of the winter?

"Such a thing won't be comin down on us while Jamie is the boss," Dan assured them. "Did you see how he come round Laurence over the priest? He'll come round the Commissioner too. You're cryin over a bad harvest before the potatoes is planted."

Mary didn't dispute him. She didn't want to think of the end of the job, the end of Dublin, the cold of the road. She had doubts but she kept them to herself. *It was a warm fire we had on this bit of a hearth for the short time we was here, but we was like children that don't know there's a tomorrow, thinkin this would keep us till we was ready to go to farmin. Dan's singin his tune about Jamie as if he was a friend still. And what makes Jamie think Mr. Kelley will come with a pocket full of money?*

When Mr. Kelley came, he stood with Jim Dent and the contractors around him, looking impassively at the muddy chaos where orderly construction should have been. He discouraged talk till he could absorb the dimensions of the problem.

Little clumps of workers stood at a respectful distance and straggled behind as he moved from place to place. He was barely conscious that they were there. He was reckoning the cost of the disaster, adding it to the setbacks suffered on other sections.

The men could see the Commissioner wasn't talking much. When he did speak, they were too far off to hear. One man would venture a guess out of his hope, another would contradict, out of his fear.

When Kelley had completed his inspection, he turned back toward the Judge's house, passing in front of the Dublin shanties. A woman stood in every door, brought there by the sound of tramping feet. The women watched the Commissioner and his entourage go by, watched their men following after. They were silent spectators of this march toward a parley in which they could have no part. Yet all knew it might keep them in possession of these frail shelters or turn them out on another journey in search of a home and a hearth.

The men exchanged glances that asked each other should they follow the Commissoner.

"What's to see?" Tom asked Dan. "And do we know aught from the seein we were after doin the day long?"

Dan looked at him briefly, then fixed his eyes again on Mr. Kelley's back and continued walking. "You got somethin else to do, go do it."

Jamie was talking. His hands were in motion as they always were when he talked. Mr. Kelley's head was bent toward Jamie but was he saying anything in answer? Their desire to hear was so intense it pulled them forward, closing the gap a little between masters and men. When the front door of the Laurence house opened and Mrs. Laurence stepped out, inviting the Commissioner in, they could hear his answer.

"Thank you, Mrs. Laurence, thank you, but Mrs. Kelley has made it clear to me that the back door is the proper entrance when I come home with canal mud on my boots. We'll just step around to the back and scrape some of that mud off before we come into your clean house."

Dan and Tom reached the back yard of the Laurence house just as the last of the bosses went through the kitchen door. It swung closed behind them. As the other men drifted into the yard, each glanced at the closed door, then attached himself to one of the little groups that were forming as if to talk, though they had little to say to each other.

Several of the Coshocton workers strolled in, looked at the closed door, turned their backs on it and seated themselves along the edge of the porch. Buck McKendrie nodded to Dan, then jerked his head back toward the door.

"Shet in, huh?"

Dan looked at him blankly for a moment then got his meaning and gestured at the yard full of men. "Shut out."

"Nary word outta the Commissioner yet?"

"One word. Scrape the mud off your boots before you go in the house."

Buck laughed. "Oh, yeah, yeah. We all heard that word, ain't we?"

He got up and retrieved a small piece of wood at the foot of the chopping block, settled back, took out his knife and began to whittle. The rest of the local men sat silently chewing. Occasionally one would send a stream of yellow-brown juice out of the corner of his mouth.

The Irish began to talk among themselves but whenever the talk became animated, someone would glance at the closed door and silence would settle again.

"Here comes your old man," Si Maddox said to Buck, as Asa appeared around the corner of the house. "I thought he didn't give a damn one way or the other about the job."

"He don't care nothin about workin," Buck answered, "but he ain't had such a good time in years. Ain't nobody in Coshocton County but what could tell his stories back to him. Since these here Irish come, he can drag out one a them moldy old tales of his anytime. It don't stink to them."

"What's that, son?" Asa was standing in front of Buck who acknowledged his presence with a grunt and kept on whittling.

"I see you're all here," Asa said, "bunch of workin fools, sittin up like a row of pigeons on the fence, waitin to say please to the judge, can I work on your job all day and all night. When I was your age I had better things to do than wait for some dressed-up eastern feller to hand me a pick and shovel."

Getting no response, he turned away, made himself comfortable on the chopping block and soon collected a group of Irish around him.

"See? What did I tell ya?" Buck mimicked his father: "Twenty notches on m'gun . . . scalped a hunnerd savages, killed a thousand bears, bullshitted all over the frontier." Then he added in his own voice, "while Ma and us boys worked the farm."

It was a long cold wait. The men tucked their hands under their arms and stamped their feet to keep themselves warm. Asa's stories helped to pass the time for some, desultory conversations sprang up among others, but what all wanted to hear was the talk going on behind that door.

Inside the warm kitchen, the men were seated at one end of the long table. There was another presence there, sensed only by Mr. Kelley. It was the 1828 canal bond issue which should be launched soon. It would have to be bigger than planned to cover the increasing costs. It would bring a greater flow of money into Ohio but the work would have to be done properly and on time, so it could begin bringing in the revenue to repay the debt.

"So you want another year beyond your contracted date," he said.

"We do and all," Simon backed up what Jamie had put before the Commissioner.

"That's it, sir," the Judge came in beside his partners. "We've talked it over most thoroughly, most thoroughly, I assure you and that seems to be the only realistic plan for the work."

"Mr. Laughry is well ahead of you on the Tuscarawas aqueduct. He expects to finish by the agreed date."

This touched Jamie on a sore point. "The Tuscarawas ain't the Walhonding, if you don't mind me sayin so, sir. It never was as big a job and Laughry got an earlier start by not havin two locks to finish up in Akron. Besides, you know yourself, sir, he was one of them responsible for puttin up wages as high as they went in the fall and keepin 'em up through the winter. I almost lost five men to him."

"Well, well . . . He's building a fine aqueduct. You think these men can do as well?" Kelley asked Dent.

"I'll see that they do."

Simon didn't like that way of putting it. "Mr. Laughry has some good masons on that job, but we'll do more than equal them. We'll better them."

The Judge pushed back from the table. It was time to sum up for the defense. He did it eloquently, laying out their needs both in time and in money. When he was through, he put a sheaf of papers down before Kelley.

The Commissioner leafed quickly through the papers and laid one aside. "We won't discuss the quarry. That's a separate contract. The quarry was not damaged by the flood and there is no reason for a change there."

"The only place we want a little consideration is on the stoneworkers' wages," Simon said. "If we had put in that bid in October instead of back in the spring we would have known those wages were going up and I don't see that we can bring them down again, with all the big stone jobs you have goin on the canal."

"I regret that you may have misjudged and bid a little low, but we in the Commission laid our plans on the basis of your estimates. Masons and stonecutters may be more plentiful in the coming season. Certainly laborers should be and you may be able to bring the pay down. In any case, you will have to bring that stone in under the figure you put your names to."

This was no more than they had expected. Simon and his experienced cutters had been making quarriers out of the farm boys for diggers' wages. They had put the quarry contract on the table to have something they could give in trade for what they really wanted.

When it came to the digging and the embankment, the Commissioner asked, "Didn't you say you foresaw no problems with this part of the job? Why can't you have it ready for acceptance by September next?"

"I'm not sayin we couldn't," Jamie answered, "but it's all part of the one contract and we can do better on the ditch end and on the aqueduct end both if we can move the gangs around acccordin to the weather and the needs of the two parts."

It took some doing, but at last Kelley was persuaded not to hold them to completion of the embankment by the following September, only to completion of the ditch. When that was settled, Kelley asked for pen and ink "so I can make a few notes as we agree on these matters."

Mrs. Laurence's back had been to the table as she worked with Tessa, preparing the dinner. She wiped her hands on her apron and moved toward the hall before Kelley had finished speaking. A moment later she set a bottle of ink, a quill, and a clean sheet of paper before the Commissioner. He thanked her with a smile that quite changed his looks from official to human.

"What about the aqueduct?" Jamie asked.

Kelley looked down at the paper, then into the faces of the others. "The quality of that job is of the first importance and I believe your request for an extension is not unreasonable. We will expect you to move forward as rapidly as you can, consistent with good workmanship. September of 1829 will be acceptable."

"Thank you, sir. Thank you. I was sure you would see it that way." The Judge was all but clapping his hands. "Every attention to the time, consistent with substantial building. That's the way we want to do it."

Jamie's eyebrows went up. The Judge was beaming and the Commissioner was writing it all down just as if something had been decided. But Laurence wasn't through.

"Now that the time is settled," he said, "we can settle the money." He looked at Kelley cheerfully as if the worst was behind them and only details remained.

"You were not able to show me anything today even approaching readiness for certification and payment," the Commissioner said coldly.

The discussion went back and forth between the two, all good humored insistence on Laurence's part, all icy resistance on Kelley's. Gradually, the Judge's insistence turned to pleading less and less hopefully.

Jamie bit his lips. Simon leaned forward, his face expressionless but his hands below the table twisting and clenching. The Commissioner picked up his pen again, signalling that further talk was useless.

It grew very quiet around the table, so quiet that Mrs. Laurence stopped slicing the bread and laid her knife down carefully without a sound. Tessa, who was halfway to the fireplace with a big fork in her hand, tiptoed the rest of the way. Through the open door into the hall, the ticking of the big clock could be heard. They became aware of what had been in the background all the time, the subdued rumble of voices and shuffling of feet in the yard.

They all glanced in that direction momentarily, then Mr. Kelley dipped his pen in the ink and began to write, the pen making a faint scratching on the paper, bringing all eyes back to him.

"It's no use for you to put nothin down on that paper," Jamie said, his hoarse voice loud after the quiet. He cleared his throat and got to his feet.

"We haven't agreed to nothin and we can't agree to nothin. If it's the way you say it is and we have to take the loss from the storm ourselves, we'll have to give up the contract. You'll have to get someone else to build your aqueduct and we can't handle the other sections, neither, not without you pay us for the work done in the river. Maybe Judge Laurence and Simon can get your stone out. I can't speak to that. As for the canal, we're done with it. You think we're just cryin with a poor mouth? Oh, no. Oh, no. It would break us entirely before the summer and we couldn't finish. We might as well give it up now."

Mr. Kelley put his pen down and leaned back in his chair. He had learned that contractors often came "crying with a poor mouth" as McCarthy put it and he had established with the very first contracts that the promises in those contracts were close to sacred. But he knew, also, that there were times when he had to give a little. The three years of work on the canal had shaken out the inept and the unable among Ohio contractors. The building that was going on in other states had shut off the source of new contractors from elsewhere. Wilder had made a mess of the Tuscarawas aqueduct and he had to relet it to Laughry but there was no one in view who could take over this one. Besides, McCarthy and Lordon were more competent than Wilder.

He turned to the engineer. "Mr. Dent, is it your opinion that the piles driven so far will be satisfactory for the abutment foundation?"

"Piles that would hold against that water will hold against anything."

"You had not inspected the cofferdam for the purpose of certification as yet, I know, but you had seen it when it was close to completion. What did you think of it?"

"I think I have to say that there wasn't much question but I would have certified it. Nobody could have predicted a storm like that. Even the Indians never saw anything like it. So against anything any of us could have expected, it looked sound."

"Very well. Judge Laurence has the calculations here on the cubic feet of timber and fill. If you will go over them, we will see that whatever you certify is paid. We will also not require that all the piling for the abutment be driven before a payment is made. Now, gentlemen, will that permit you to carry the work forward?"

There was almost another hour of talk before it was all settled. Mr. Kelley would not change the contract prices per cubic yard of excavation and so on. He did finally agree though, that if Dent found their costs exceeded contract prices because of higher wages, he would report that to the Commissioner who would consider an adjustment.

"But I count on you," he said emphatically, "to pay not one cent more in wages than you absolutely must. Is that understood?" There was ready agreement.

They all stood now, relieved to move, relaxing tense muscles. The Judge called to Tessa for glasses and brought a jug of whiskey out of the kitchen dresser. They drank to completion of the aqueduct.

"The men are waiting for the news," Jamie said when he put his glass down. "Will you speak to them, Mr. Kelley?"

All talk in the yard cut off sharply when the door opened and Mr. Kelley stepped out. The men on the porch stood up and turned around to face him. The rest moved forward to hear better what was coming. The contractors followed him out, the smiles on their faces promising good news.

Kelley gave it to them briefly and they answered with a cheer. He held up his hand. "Judge Laurence, Mr. McCarthy and Mr. Lordon have a very difficult job ahead, a great deal of hard work. They are counting on you and I am counting on you for good faithful workmanship and no idleness. A good hour's work done for each hour paid."

"You'll get that from us, sir," Pat shouted. "Won't he, lads?"

There was another cheer, then they streamed noisily out of the yard.

"Faithful workers, Mr. Kelley wants," Dan said to Pat as they walked back toward Dublin. "Where was he when the storm come down on us? There wasn't an idle man then, nor a dry one neither."

Chapter 28

A LETTER FROM Carrignahown came into the shanty one evening with Jamie. It was a letter from his mother, written by a woman who had the learning, her family being well-off and able to send daughters and sons to school. It was a beautiful letter, admired by all when Jamie read it out. It brought a packet of news to the Griffens.

Dan's mother still had her health; his brother Sean's wife had lost one child but had another on the way. Sean was falling behind in the rent and in the payments to the gombeen man on the loan that had helped them on their way to America. It would be a blessing could Dan send a bit of help.

"If you send him anything, send him passage money," Jamie advised. "Didn't I tell you a hundred times there's nothin left in County Cork but troubles? Send him the rent once and you'll be pourin money down that rat hole from this out. The rent comes due every gale day; passage money is paid but once."

Dan and Mary exchanged a look saying this would take much thought and much counting over of what they had and what they could spare. That was for later. Jamie was sitting now, as he always did when he came, across from Dan, in Mary's place and Mary back in the shadows.

You would think Jamie was the biggest man in the country, the way Dublin people come crowdin in to give him the greetin and listen to every word that drops from his lips.

There was no hint that he and Simon had been close to disaster. His talk was all of the great building there was to do in this country and how he would be one of those doing it. Not this canal only but more when this one was done, and not canals only but the National Road that was going across the state south of them. And the cities too, that were already going up along the canal and would be growing bigger like Buffalo and Albany along the Erie in New York.

The men gave sage nods and Kevin was quick with a 'true for you' after each of Jamie's pronouncements. Even Dennis, who often dropped a less respectful remark out of the corner of his mouth to the man next to him, was this night chiming in with Jamie. The word among the stonies, he said, was of the bridges there was to build over all the rivers on the National Road and stone churches and other buildings going up in Cincinnati, in Columbus where the state government was, and even in little Cleveland.

Jamie took it up again, saying Cleveland might grow to be the Buffalo of Ohio. Dan brought it back to the canals, asking Christy Toohey about the Miami Canal near Cincinnati he had worked on. Christy said the talk was that canal would some day go all the way north to the Lake, though there was nothing but wilderness up there now.

Mary hardly heard a word of this. The letter had brought home back so vividly, it was before her eyes. It was as if she were sitting at the old hearth with its peat fire and the old neighbors around it.

After all were gone that night, after evening prayers, after children and lodgers were in bed, Dan and Mary still sat by the fire and talked in low voices about the news from home. Carefully, they counted over the money. The pouch had been flat when they came from Akron. Every payday it fattened up nicely but by month's end it would be lean again. Whether February and March would be good paydays no one could know. They agreed to squeeze out twelve dollars to send to Sean with the word that Dan could get him a job on the canal would he come to America.

Just to think of a letter with the money and the promise in it coming to the old home and all of them sitting by the old hearth to read it and talk of it brought them all closer to Mary than at any time since she took her last look back at the old house and the neighbors in front to see the travelers on their way. If they could have some of their own people here with them . . .

Dan had been thinking of the same thing and putting the hope away again.

"Don't set your heart on them comin. Mother is too old to tear her out of the place where she's been her whole life and where she wants to lie beside my father when death takes her. And Sean would never move out of the old ways except I was there to push him. We won't be seein them on this side of the water."

"Put a little push in the letter then," Mary suggested. "Tell them its the farms here will be better than the ones they'll be leavin. The canal work will sound strange to them, the way it did to us when we were at home still but the farms now, that would be a known thing. Even your mother might think of comin with all of us on a farm of our own. Put that in the letter, that it's land without rent."

"There's a lot of canal work between now and a farm," was all Dan would say to that.

When a day came that was too cold and full of snow for work on the job, Dan sat down to write the letter. Mary had been carrying the thought of it around in her head all the days between. She poured out to him all the things she had been saying in her head to the folks at home.

"It's not like it was for us, tell them, knowin nobody but Jamie. Here's you and me and the childer ready to give them a hundred thousand welcomes. And tell them not to have too much sadness at leavin the neighbors. There's Bridget and Paddy is good neighbors to us and will be to them, and Dennis and Rose, and Johnny and Molly will be makin a match of it by the spring. There's Michael and Peg and Pat and Maggie. Tyrone will be bringin his family from Cincinnati and Tom Quinlan will be bringin his over the water. And Kevin and Mick's are on the ship already. It's a fine townland it will be when we have all our farms together."

Dan laughed at the stream of words she wanted him to put on the paper. "I'd be here the day long tryin to get all that wrote out. It's well you don't have the writin or you'd be sittin at the table day and night puttin the words on paper."

"I would then," Mary laughed at herself. She watched him dip the quill in the ink and begin to make the marks on the paper.

I would indeed. It's all in here, waitin to come out. If I could tell them at home the way of things here and what's happened since we come across the water, I doubt there would be enough paper in the store to take it from me through the quill and the ink.

"It's the one piece of paper and one only I've got here," Dan said. "Now leave me be till I think what it is I can put down here and it won't be a whole paper full of names of neighbors we have now and maybe we'll have next year and maybe we won't."

"But the farm—you can write that surely, the land without rent?"

"Leave me be."

When he read her the letter, it said all here were well and told the welcome there would be would the family in Ireland come over. It had the promise of more money for the passage and the job on the canal for Sean. Dan showed her that took up the whole paper that had to be folded up and have the place it would go written on the outside. The coins and pieces of paper money wouldn't go across the water, but he would give them to Jamie and next time Jamie went to the city he would change them into a different kind of money that would go all the way to Carrignahown.

"It's a grand letter." Mary looked at the way the words followed each other in lines across the page.

But after all, speech is best, the way the words can come from the heart and out from the lips still warm with the feelins inside, without the paper and ink to get in between. Couldn't Dan have squeezed the words a little smaller and put a word or two about the farm? All of it bein about the canal work, it's like we would be followin the canal the rest of our lives.

Jamie was there again that night and again the talk was all of canal work, this time the way it had been on the Erie. Mary had heard it before but the tales grew in the telling.

Now all could see that Jamie's prodigious feats as a digger and his bossing the best crews as a foreman were only what led up to the turning point: A piece of the canal was open but the completion of the whole hung in the balance. Had it not been that Governor Clinton of New York and the chief engineers could see that a man of experience was needed who had a head on him to manage the work, had not Jamie taken hold then as a contractor on the most important section of the Big Ditch, things might have gone differently. True, Jamie never got so much as a mention for it when it came to the celebration but it's well known how there's always many to step in front and take the credit for a good job done.

Hugh and Pat had a tale or two of their own about the Erie. They had been together with Jamie in that last push but listened to Jamie's tale of it with their mouths open like the rest. Old Fergus, who had been on the Erie longer than any of them and with Jamie from his first days as a foreman, never said anything except when Jamie turned to him with, "Fergus, here, can tell was it that way or no," and Fergus would give an affirmative rumble.

Jamie left early this night and Fergus followed but the rest weren't ready to pull themselves away from the fire, knowing there would be no work on the morrow, it being a Sunday and the snow coming down besides.

When the door had closed behind them, Dennis said in sarcastic imitation of Fergus, "Err, aye. Err-rr-rr, aye, Master. Err-rr-rr-rr, aye, aye, boss."

That brought a laugh and Dennis went on, taking the part of Jamie with the way he pushed his chest out and folded his lips together with his chin in the air.

"I dug my way through a mountain and come out the other end before break-fast, didn't I, Fergus?"

Then he became Fergus again and rumbled his agreement.

Mary was sitting by the fire knitting a stocking the next day near the children who were on their bellies where they could get the light of the fire on their book. Dan and Johnny were moving restlessly around the cabin, occasionally opening the door for a glimpse of the snow. Michael looked in to pass the time of day as he often did on a Sunday.

Last night's talk came back to Mary and brought a smile. "That Dennis, doesn't he have the sharp tongue on him? And he's not afraid of the boss neither, like some."

"Oh, it's easy for him to raise the laugh on Jamie," Johnny said. "You won't hear him raisin the laugh on Simon. It's Simon is the boss of the stonies."

"Maybe he don't laugh at Simon." Michael worked with Dennis on the stone and knew him better than Johnny did. "But Simon don't brag on himself like Jamie neither. Dennis is one to stand up to the boss all the same. I see him do it. He's a man knows his stone most as well as Simon. Dennis will be workin on all the stone jobs Simon is the master on and myself, I'll do the same."

Mary's needles stopped clicking. "What is it you're sayin? Simon has his house already off there in Columbus and it's there he says his stoneyard will be. God knows how far away that is from this place. You wouldn't go off there when this job is done? Then how could you and Peg be next neighbors to us when we have the farms?" Her fingers automatically resumed their work but her eyes were on Michael.

"How could we be neighbors? You see the way of it is, Mary, there's no work for a stonie in the countryside when the canal's done. Wouldn't you and Dan come to the town along of us?"

"We would not." Mary glanced at Dan. Couldn't he talk Michael around to staying with them on the road to the farms? Dan's attention seemed to be on his pipe. He packed it carefully with tobacco then stepped over the children to get a light at the fire.

"I wouldn't want to be far off from you and Dan," Michael said. "But Peg and me, we'll have a family and I can do better by them with the work I know. I'm no farmer, Mary. I'm a stonemason."

"Leavin us," Mary said bitterly, "Goin off and leavin us."

"Don't take it like we was goin across the water," Michael pleaded. "The way Simon has it, Columbus wouldn't be that far off. He was there after the Akron job and back here again before we came from the old camp. Four or five days journey, maybe. Me and Dennis has to go where the stone work is."

"Dennis and Rose, too." Mary looked at Dan again. "Were you knowin?"

"Didn't you hear Dennis talkin the night we got the letter? He was as full of the buildin he'll be doin as Jamie himself. Michael's in the right of it, there'll be little of that buildin hereabouts."

Michael looked sadly at Mary but she had nothing more to say to him and after a few minutes he went back to his Peg. Johnny moved toward the door after him. As much as O'Malley tried to keep Molly at home, she was always slipping away to her sister's shanty and Johnny would meet her there.

"Johnny," Mary halted him before he could get through the door. "You wouldn't be leavin us?"

"I would not."

"If you and Molly make a match of it, she might be wantin to go where her sister goes."

"Me and Molly is gettin married," Johnny announced proudly, "and Molly will be wantin to go where her husband goes."

When the door closed behind him, Dan got the children around him for a lesson. Mary's thoughts were still on the new Dublin they would have when they got the farm.

The people won't be all those that are in this Dublin, haven't I always known it? But Michael and Peg and Dennis and Rose . . . Well, that's only the two families . . . I'm not as sure as Johnny that Molly won't be pulled to the town with Peg. And isn't Jamie always tryin to keep Johnny and all behind him? When the men were fillin the cabin with bridges and all and I didn't listen for havin the letter and the old home stoppin up my ears, that time wasn't Dan buildin away like the rest? Look at him there, the head he's got on him with the learnin in it he's givin to the childers. Can't he see Jamie's no friend to him? Made him a foreman so he could run off and leave us with the sickness and took it away again when he wanted to push Dan out in the water with the rest of them. I'm his old friend from Carrignahown when he wants me for the cookin and I'm not there at all when he needs me no more . . . Dan, Dan, it's our own place we want and not the job Jamie has to throw us when it suits him.

Chapter 29

D AN WAS LOSING all patience with Jamie.
"He promises I'm to be foreman again soon, droppin the words one day like I knew it but might have forgot," he said to Mary. "Yet the days go by and now the weeks and he's always givin me a piece of work with two or three or a dozen men under me for the doin of it but do I have the name of a foreman? I do not. Do I have the pay of a foreman? I do not. Jamie McCarthy keeps the paybook and himself gives out the jiggers of whiskey at the day's end. Dan Griffen stands in line with the rest and gets the same drink and the same pay."

Other work had been laid aside while they built a row of shanties where new workers could sleep. Pitiful little pens they were, with no place to make a fire and not enough room to stand up. Even in the middle, a man couldn't get upright without cracking his head on the rooftree. They did have floors to them, to keep the ticks out of the wet when it rained, ten or twelve ticks lying side by side, filling the whole space. The rare family man that was hired got material to put up his own shanty. Some of the old friends from Akron days helped Kevin and Mick to build theirs before Kevin's Una and Mick's Aghna came with their children.

The other thing built was for their eating: Two long rows of tables with a fireplace at the end and a roof over the top. It would do for the summer, Jamie said, and the carpenters could put some walls around it before winter, whenever there was time.

"Tell Mary to come over to my cabin tomorrow to get the key to the chest and the orders."

Jamie told that to Dan the day they finished the cookhouse—if you could call it a 'house' with no walls to it at all. He held Dan back at the end of the work, while he looked it over to see was all ready.

Dan sat down on one of the benches, made out of the half of a log with legs to it. It had the good fresh smell of the inside of the tree. Even in the dusk at the day's end, it could be seen there was room at the tables for a big crew to be eating.

"What's the pay for the cookin?"

"The same as in Akron."

Jamie wouldn't sit down with him. That would be admitting there was a bargain to be made, as indeed there was. Mary had let Dan know she put a value on her work like neither of them did when they were new come to the canal. Dan would have her complaints buzzing around his head like a whole hive of bees if the terms of the bargain were not to her liking.

"She wasn't gettin no pay at all in Akron, just her own keep and the children's. Now the boys is workin for their own."

"So there's still herself and the girl and there'll be a piece of money in it too."

"What kind of a piece of money? It's to be dollars, surely?"

Jamie sat down and lowered his voice like he was giving a great secret into Dan's ear. "I wouldn't do this for no one but you. We'll give her five dollars."

"The cook up to the dam camp is gettin seven."

"She's gettin paid for more than cookin. Don't you know it?"

"Don't you drag nothin like that in when it's Mary we're talkin of. That's my wife." Dan sneered at Jamie's offer like it was another insult. "*Five dollars.*"

"If she don't want to work for five dollars, there's plenty of women that do."

Dan knew the Dublin women better than Jamie did. Peg and Molly were too young and inexperienced. Maggie was big with child. Bridget had been sick during the winter and wasn't ready for it yet. Rose was a needlewoman, not a cook. There were two or three others who were a slatternly sort of women whose lodgers were always grumbling about the food they put on the table. There was not one who could match Mary.

"The way you blow us out of bed by the horn and to the breakfast and the dinner by the horn and back on the job by the horn, you want a woman can have the food hot and ready when the horn blows, not some Biddy runnin around the cookhouse when we come in from the work like a chicken scratchin after a grain of barley here and a grain of barley there."

"Kate Toohey would be glad for it."

"Kate and Christy's leavin out of here. She's lonesome for her young ones and Christy says he can work on the riverfront if he can't get a canal job closer to Cincinnati."

"Christy's leavin? Why didn't you tell me?"

"That's between you and Christy. Mary's wages and my wages is between you and me. You're givin me foreman's work but I have yet to see any foreman's pay."

"Time enough for that when I turn the crew over to you. Till the water drops a bit more, I can't start work at the river and till then I'll superintend."

He got up to go but Dan said, "We haven't settled it yet what Mary's pay is to be."

"I'm not standin here all night higglin and hagglin over a woman's pay. Six dollars and she's to have breakfast ready on the Monday."

Dan triumphantly took the good news to Mary but the triumph didn't last long. New workers had begun coming south from Cleveland, west from Pittsburgh and north from other river ports. Now that the cookhouse and the shanties were up, more and more were being signed on for twelve dollars a month and keep. Jamie handed them over, two or three at a time, for Dan to show them the way of things.

While he did that, he picked up from them what was going on up and down the line. Twelve was the going pay this season for diggers, though some bosses tried to get by with ten or eleven as Jamie had before he found it hard to get men to take it. What foremen were getting was harder to find out. Some said it was twice what diggers made.

One of the new men told him about a section up near Newcomerstown where a contractor had run off with a pocketfull of money, leaving his partner with the job half done. The runaway had been superintending the job and his wife cooking. Now the partner, a farmer, was looking for a foreman and a cook.

What if I were to go off and leave Jamie looking for a foreman and a cook? Would that farmer take an Irishman like himself? Do I have the way of talking that could put myself into such a job and Mary with me?

The following Sunday Dan was up early. He shaved, put on a clean shirt and the American coat he had bought from one of the Ohio men to keep out the cold.

Mary was already at the cookhouse but he couldn't wait till she had the breakfast ready. He stopped there only long enough to get a couple of pieces of bread to put in his pocket.

"Where are you off to?" she wanted to know.

"Up the road. There's a thing wants lookin into."

"Whatever it is, you want to show yourself at your best, I can see that. Stand there a minute till I get the mud off you."

She rubbed the dirty edges of the coat together till the mud powdered and drifted to the floor. She was asking him questions at the same time but he would say only that he'd be back before nightfall.

No one had to know, not herself even. If I come back with nothing, that's as much as I go out with. If I find what I look for, time enough to tell it when I get back.

Not knowing what was at the end of the road was part of the great feeling of being off and away. Off and away from the job, from Jamie, from the Judge on top of Jamie, from the shanty, even from Mary and the children. Most of all from himself as a Monday-morning-to-Saturday-night digger.

He walked off into the early Sunday quiet, retracing some of the steps he had taken with his little band from Akron those many months ago. He cast an appraising eye over the progress of the canal since that time.

It was even better when he got a ride on a big Conestoga wagon that was returning to Cleveland after bringing a load of supplies to a canal contractor. He sat on the high seat of it, looking down on the canal works they passed with a knowing eye, talking with the teamster as only a man who had superintended some of that work could do.

He found the contractor he was looking for standing on the edge of a partly-dug section. He was a plain-looking man in muddy work clothes, more like Buck McKendrie or like Higbee in Akron than like the Judge. But digging anything out of the man proved to be like digging a stubborn rock out of a Carrignahown hillside.

"Good mornin, sir. I heard you was in need of a foreman."

"Yep." It was said with a look that was . . . hostile? . . . suspicious?

"This the section, here?"

A shake of the head, a jerk of the thumb northward, "Yonder."

Dan looked 'yonder' where a lock seemed to be well under way. He almost gave up then, not knowing the stonework. "On the lock, is it?"

Another shake of the head. Pumping hard, with one question after another, Dan finally learned that the man had two sections to dig, this one and one some distance past the lock. He was supervising this one and was wanting a foreman for the other.

Dan took a deep breath and launched into an account of his experience. He felt that he was talking to himself, the other man's attention seeming to be down in the ditch or off up the line.

". . . finished up the job in Akron and brought the crew down to Caldersburgh." He got the man's eyes then, but just for another quick suspicious look.

"That so?"

"Tis indeed. And foreman of the diggers on the Caldersburgh section."

"Kelley know ya?"

"Jim Dent knows me."

"Huh."

Does that mean he thinks little of Dent? And what would Dent say about me, if asked? That I should stay on McCarthy's job where I belong?

In the silence that followed, all the euphoria of the morning drained out of Dan into the ditch at their feet. He turned to go back to Dublin empty handed.

"Give ya a try. Twenty dollars."

Dan was so surprised it took him a moment to find his tongue. "Twenty and keep?"

"Yep. Got a woman t'cook?"

"My wife cooks."

"Six f'r her. Start tomorra?"

There it was suddenly, what he had been asking for. "I got two boys workin, not man-sized yet but they work good."

Another shake of the head. "Man's work."

"What about keep for the boys and my little girl?"

A long silence. Finally, "You and her do a good job, we'll settle that comes the end of the month."

He had the job. Did he want it? Wasn't that what he came for? He could go back and say to Jamie that he was a foreman and Jamie could find himself another man to do a foreman's work for a digger's pay. But did he want to leave Dublin and all? What would Mary say to it, with her heart set on staying with the Dublin folks the full of the time they were on the canal and after too, on the farm she was always dreaming about.

"It will take me more than a day to fetch the family from Caldersburgh."

"When c'n y' start?"

He hesitated over that till the man said, "You want the job or not?"

"It's a good offer you made me. It is indeed. But the thing is, I got me a job there, I'd be leavin . . . I'd like to think on it . . ."

"It ain't a thinker I want. It's a foreman."

They walked up the line and looked at the section he would have in his charge.

The end of it was, the man pointed a long forefinger at Dan's chest. "You be back here by the end of the week, you got a job. If you ain't here then, I'll git me another man."

It was after dark when he dragged his tired feet up the path. Mary was standing in the door of the shanty. When she caught sight of him, her anxious look turned to curiosity. She waited while he got his boots off and stretched his feet toward the fire, while he ate the dinner she had brought from the cookhouse for him. Then she could contain herself no longer. "So what is it? You were after lookin at a farm, maybe?"

Johnny and Hugh and the children were gathered round too, to hear the story of his day's journey.

"I was lookin over the canal from here to Newcomerstown." He gave them the bit about the Conestoga wagon and the man from the townland of Clonakilty he had met on the way back. "He's been in America a year longer than ourselves. He'll be comin some Sunday to get what news we've got from home."

That was enough to satisfy all but Mary. She well knew this had been no aimless wandering.

Dan hadn't wanted to tell her before, lest it come to nothing. Now that he had something, he was of two minds whether to take it. As he walked to the job on

Monday morning with Pat on one side and Johnny on the other, with Paddy and Hugh just behind, it came to him sharply that they would not be with him on the new job.

True, they were no kin to him, nor brothers to him in the fighting like some he had left behind but they were the nearest thing to it he had on this side of the water. And there was Jamie. Wasn't the devil he knew better than the devil he didn't? If he went up the line, that boss was a long string of silence with a few hard words to throw at a man like they were pebbles. Jamie was still one of his own, after all.

He let Monday and most of Tuesday go by without making a move.

Jamie and Simon always sat near the fire, close to one end of the tables. The spring evenings were still cool, making that a preferred place. As the men were leaving the cookhouse after the evening meal on Tuesday, Jamie beckoned to Dan to take the empty seat beside him. Dan threw one leg over the bench and sat as if on horseback and ready to ride off. It was now he must say his word or let it go up the chimney in the cookhouse smoke.

"I'm for Cleveland in the morning," Jamie said, "to the ironworks there. It's a big lot of ironwork we'll be needin for the aqueduct."

So Jamie was giving him the orders for the work to be done while he was gone? And the word at last he was to be foreman again? Maybe there would be no need to go off up the line. When Jamie had laid out for him what was to be done, Dan waited to hear if that's what was in it but Jamie was through talking.

All the men were gone now and the quiet was broken only by the chirp of crickets outside and the sounds made by Mary and Tessa: Wood against wood as they gathered up the trenchers, the lighter clatter of the tin cups, the familiar lilt of Mary's speech and Tessa's soft voice in answer. It was growing dark and Mary threw an armful of light stuff on the fire to make it flame up and give them some light to work by.

Jamie turned his face toward the fire. Dan moved away from him a little, gripping the bench with his knees. A shadow slipped between them, small and thin, like a knife.

"It's a foreman I'm to be, startin on the morrow," Dan said. There was no question in his voice.

Jamie's head swung around but his eyes were blinded from the firelight. He couldn't see across the shadow. "There's nothin to the work while I'm away but goin on what's well started. All the lads know what's to do."

"It's foreman I'll be. If not on your job, on another section north a few miles. If that's the way you want it, I'll be out of here by the week's end, startin the new job on Monday."

"That's not the way you want it surely?" Jamie was peering closely at him now. "You wouldn't be leavin me here in the midst of this big job, me that brought you all the way across the water? With the need of you I've got now and the miles of road we have yet to go together?"

Before Dan could answer, both of them became aware that the quick movements of Mary up and down the cookhouse had ceased. She was standing rigid on the other side of the table, staring at Dan.

So this is what was in it. This is what he was after on the Sunday and myself feelin like the times he was gone off to the fightin, not knowin would he come back. Back he came safe, but givin me the half of his day and keepin the other half to himself. It's not like there has to be secrets like it was in them days.

When she saw him talking to Jamie, the thought had come to her, maybe he had been off on Jamie's business on the Sunday. She had moved closer to hear was that it. The first words she heard were ". . . I'll be out of here by the week's end, startin the new job on Monday."

Out of here? A new job? And not a word to me on it?

Dan was not a man to knock his wife about like some, but this was a skelp from behind so unexpected she had to reach for the table to steady herself.

"What can we do with this man of yours?" Jamie was saying. He could see that Dan's words were a surprise to her too. His voice took on that caressing tone to it he had used to her in Akron. "Here he is talkin about goin off from us."

"I was after hearin nothin on himself goin off from me."

Dan whipped out some words quick before Mary could say more. "Nor Jamie didn't hear such a thing neither. It's two jobs is waitin. It's me for the foreman and Mary for the cook."

"Who is this contractor that's sittin on the edge of the ditch, kickin his heels, waitin for you till he gets his work goin? Waitin for Mary till his crew gets a mouthful?" Jamie had a smile on him like he knew Dan was tryin a trick on him.

"This contractor has the name of Andrew Mason. Two sections he has beyond the Tuscarawas aqueduct. We made the bargain on Sunday last. The jobs and the wages is all agreed. 'If you're here on the Monday, Mr. Griffen,' he says to me, 'the jobs's yours.'"

Jamie turned to Mary again with soft words in the Irish he mostly seemed to have forgot. "It's a cold fire when there's no friends around it. I'd be lonesome for the two of you if you went off and why would you be doin it at all?" Mary had no answer for him, nor for herself, either.

There's a job in this for me, too, is there? And why do I hear it for the first time under Jamie's nose?

Dan was leaning toward her with some kind of a signal fire in his eyes. She could see it but the anger in her was so high she couldn't read the meaning of it and didn't try. She turned her head, not to swallow the plamas still coming from Jamie in the Irish words, but to show Dan the back of her head.

Shuttin me out and makin me little in front of Jamie. Now Jamie thinks he can come round me with sweet words till he gets me in his hand to throw me against my own man.

She drew back from the table, back from both of them. "Och, Jamie, we wouldn't forget the many nights around the fire and you givin us the way of things in this country. God love you, wasn't it you put up the signpost we're followin has the dollars on it? So you hear what himself tells you. We go where the good jobs are."

"But the good jobs is right here," Jamie protested. "Here I was tellin Dan he's to start bossin the crew and before I hardly have the words out of my mouth he's throwin the job back in my face."

"I wouldn't throw no foreman's job back in your face. Is that what's in it?"

"It is. Wasn't I sayin I'm off to Cleveland and you're the man in charge of the diggers?"

"Till you come back, or from this out till the job is done?"

"From this out do I have your word you'll stay with it."

"The pay?"

"Twenty and whack, and it's good whack you get in this camp, don't you know it?"

He held out his hand and Dan took it. It wasn't a clasp of friendship, just both of them getting a grip on the bargain.

Dan and Mary walked slowly back to the shanty when her work was finished, Dan elated and talking all the way about how he got the foreman's pay out of Jamie, though he had to journey up the canal to do it.

"It's the fat pouch we'll have now, with the dollars we'll get on the payday. And not a word from you, Mary? It's all the same to you do we go or stay, do I bring in twelve dollars or twenty?"

"What word would you be wantin from me, Mister Griffen? You've got a bagful of your own words to tell it's a great thing you did for yourself."

Dan stopped in the path. "For myself? Don't you know if it was myself I was thinkin of only, I'd be after givin Jamie the back of my hand and off up the canal on the morrow? Mary wouldn't like that, I says to myself. Mary has the big likin for the neighbors she's got the small likin for leavin her own hearth."

Mary stopped too, facing him and pouring out the thoughts she had been storing up, hardly knowing they were there.

"Such kind thoughts for your wife, you're tellin me now. Where was the thought you might give me an answer to my question where were you off to? Where was the thought when you came back to tell me the new job you got for yourself and the new job you got for me? And the thought to tell me the new place we were to live? Or did Jamie have the right of it and it was all a trick to see could you get him to give you a 'yes' but if he give you another 'no' you was ready to take it like you took the 'nos' he was after throwin you by the dozen? And didn't I be standin there, not a word of it would I have from you yet. Like there's not a word I was after havin from you these many months, how you put your feet on the canal road to drag me and the children after you up and down the canal to this job and that job or follow Jamie through the wilderness wherever a canal's buildin. Not a word to me from month's end to month's end how Jamie McCarthy's wind blew the farm out of your thoughts entirely. Musha, my pity on your head that you thought you could keep it all from me."

That struck sparks out of Dan. "Enough from you and lavins of it. Any more and I'll raise my hand on you." He walked off.

"Och, was there a bit of straw about, where I could stretch myself," she said to his back, her voice shaking, "It wouldn't be beside you I'd be sleepin the night."

He came back to her, looking close into her face in the dark. Their eyes held, their hands touched. A cool wind came down the valley, blowing the scents of spring to them picked up from the soft moist earth, now full of living movement. The smell of spring in Cork was in it, of many past springs in Cork It was gone again, carrying the smell of Ohio's budding branches, its young grasses, its new-ploughed fields.

They stood together in the cool evening till all the anger was gone out of them.

Chapter 30

W HEN SEASONS CHANGE, work changes. That was the way in the Irish countryside, that was the way on the canal. When spring came there was work every day for Dan and his work days were longer. There was work for the boys, too. There were long days and hard work in the cookhouse for Mary. Ellen was the only one not big enough for the work. The changes for her were that Dan had no time for lessons and she followed her mother around the cookhouse instead of around the shanty.

Mary had the big pots and pans in her charge now, some of them relinquished reluctantly by the women who had been using them since the raid on Jamie's cabin. She had the key to the chest at her waist.

Mrs. Laurence wasn't cooking any more. Mary had to feed the men who had been eating in the Laurence kitchen but she had Tessa to help her cook and Bridget to come always at meal times. The long lines of men came pouring in from the job three times a day, looking to her to feed them.

Many she knew, but as the days passed, more and more were men just hired. They had not had the months together with the rest of them to know Dublin and the place each had in it. Sometimes a new man would wander in alone, often they came in little knots, some formed back in an Irish townland, some on the road or on shipboard. If the ties that bound them together had served only for company and mutual protection in the recent past, these small groups dissolved, the men fitting in with those who worked or slept on either side of them, learning from their fellows what was expected and how things were done in this camp. The groups that had been longer together remained hard knots for a time, looking to each other for comradeship and at all others as strangers.

When Jamie was in the cookhouse, it was understood by all that they were to eat and get back to the job with little commotion and scarcely any talk. But Jamie was not always there. Mary had some concern about keeping that many men in order with the boss out of sight.

In her second week at the work a fight broke out as the men were lining up for their noon dinner. Mary and Bridget were behind a table, each with a big pot of beans with chunks of pork in it, ready to ladle the food out as the men came along. Tessa was putting out the bread in piles where every man could reach it.

Mary couldn't see who started the trouble, Pat being first in line and his big shoulders hiding from her what went on behind them, but it was some dispute as to who was to be behind Pat.

She took her big spoon out of the pot without giving so much as one bean to Pat and began to beat on the pot with the spoon.

"Stop it now," she called out. "You might as well know first as last that the fightin and the dinner don't mix. You can have the one or the other."

The scuffling continued and Pat held out his trencher impatiently. "Here, Mary, give us the dinner. It's not myself that's fightin."

Mary gave Pat a look in the eye that reminded him she knew him when he was down on his back, hanging on to her hand like she was his mother and his Maggie and his very life.

"There's no dinner for nobody till that stops."

Pat handed her his trencher, turned, and grabbing the scrappers each by the neck of his shirt, yanked them apart. "Stow that, or I'll kick you back to the end of the line. Who are you to keep all of us from our dinners?"

Both of them would have turned on Pat but there was a rising mutter from those behind that told them they would have more than Pat to deal with, so they let it go with a little grumbling.

From that time out, the first sign of trouble would bring Mary's spoon clanging against the pot. If that didn't get results, the troublemakers would find themselves shoved out of line. They could take their choice of finishing the fight or following after the others in peace and order.

"You're the wonder of the world," Bridget said to Mary one day when the women were having their dinner after the men had gone back to the job. "Did you see those two that thinks they're the cocks has got the finest feathers in the camp, and them creepin in at the end of the line? I think they've all got their lesson now and we won't have no more trouble."

Mary accepted the tribute complacently. "We'll have peace enough till they get their bellies full," she agreed.

This was the time of day Mary liked best, noontime, when the men had gone back to the job. There was a little breathing space then between the work that started at dawn and the work that ended after dark. The other women of Dublin drifted down to the cookhouse when they had fed their own men. Mary wet the tea again and they had a comfortable colloguin.

Bridget took Baby Nora out of the cradle where she lay while her mother was working and gave her the breast. Sometimes other small children followed their mothers. Then Ellen had playmates. At other times she lingered nearby, listening to the talk of the women and playing her own games. She made a boat of her trencher, floating it across the table in front of her with beans for passengers. Or she carried on a small war against the flies that were always buzzing about.

The first day, Tessa took her food and started across to the other side of the cookhouse. Mary called out, "Where are you off to? Sit over, Tessa, sit over."

Tessa sat with them after that, quietly, with a little distance between her and the rest. Bet Sullivan, who had been longer in Ohio than any of them, was always giving newcomers Una and Aghna Casey lessons in how things were done in this country. She was glad of a chance to show that her knowledge of American manners was superior to Mary's. In the Laurence kitchen, she explained, Tessa would not have been eating with the white folks.

"Of course not." Mary did not take kindly to Bet's notion that the few years earlier she had come across the water endowed her with all the wisdom of the country. "Servants don't eat with the masters in Ireland neither."

When Bet opened her mouth to give another lesson, Mary added, "This is my kitchen. I told her to sit there. If you don't like it why don't you go over to Mrs. Laurence's house and sit at her table?"

The jibe had an added sting because Bet knew that Mary had once been in the Laurence kitchen and she had not. She was absent from the cookhouse for several days after that and made the rounds of the Dublin shanties with the word that "it was a pity Mary Griffen had no more respect for herself than to sit next to a nigger at table." She said it to her husband Tim, who, as usual, made no answer. She said it to Bridget who told it to Mary.

"I hope that throllop has respect for herself," was Mary's response, "the way no one else has any for a woman with her dirty tongue."

Bet reappeared at the noonday colloguin a few days later. She made it obvious that she was ignoring Tessa, and Mary made it obvious that she was ignoring Bet. But the group, though not too small for hostilities, was too small for separations and after a few days there were no more averted heads or drawing aside of skirts.

The talk often passed Tessa by, having to do with such Dublin concerns as would Maggie make it with the babe she was carrying. After the years without his woman, Pat hadn't wasted any time and Maggie was teased about that, but she wasn't carrying the babe well. She couldn't keep up her work and had to let Pat and her son Egan and her lodgers eat in the cookhouse. There were enough neighbors to see that the two youngest Flynns were fed and to look in on Maggie several times a day.

Kate and Christy Toohey's going off to Cincinnati was well talked over, in one way when Kate was present with more to say on it than anyone, in another when Kate was absent. It was Kate had started the talk about going but now Christy was impatient to leave and Kate was holding back for her sister Maggie's sake.

Sometimes Tessa became the center of the curiosity those new come from Ireland had about her different looks, her different speech, her other real or imagined differences. She had come from that land across the Ohio River called The South where black people were slaves. The women were curious about that, too. They resented her having been given a place in the cookhouse that belonged by rights to a Dublin woman. That gave a vindictive edge to some of the questions.

One day Kate started the prying. "Your boys aren't near as black as you. Will they turn blacker when they're grown?"

Bet snickered. She knew what Kate really wanted to ask was, did the boys have a white father. It had been the gossip among the men since they first saw her that she was the Judge's woman. It kept them at a distance but at the same time gave her an added attraction. More than one licked his lips at the thought of getting a piece of what belonged to their American gentleman boss.

"No, ma'am," Tessa answered Kate, keeping her eyes on the cup of tea she was holding in both hands. "They stay that color since they born."

"What color is their father?"

"He lighter than me."

"And where's himself?"

"He down south."

"You run off and left him?"

"No ma'am. I never run off."

There was a moment of silence.

Tessa looked at the row of white faces turned on her from across the table. She had Mary on one side of her and Bridget on the other, the two she worked with every day. For the first time she gave them an answer without waiting for a question. "Master, he brung me two years back. Give me a chance to raise my boys where they never be slaves."

"Why would he do that?"

"He the Judge's brother."

"Are you slave to the Judge?"

That brought Tessa's head up and her eyes to Bet's. "No ma'am. I works for the Judge and Mrs. Laurence but I ain't no slave. I belongs to nobody but my own self."

Kate and Bet both had their mouths open but before any more words could come out, Mary was on her feet. When she got up to resume work it was understood their bit of noonday ease was over. The other women went back to Dublin. Mary and Tessa cleared away the dinner and turned to the afternoon tasks.

The work went smoothly between them. Mary's judgment of Tessa when she had first seen her was confirmed. She indeed had the strength and the carriage of one who knows work and can do it. There were only a few things Mary had to show her. She had never heard of kale-canon, so how could she know how to mash the potatoes and the cabbage together? She learned how to make it but would never eat it and Mary laughed at her for missing a good mouthful. One time, she had to stop Tessa from throwing out the dirty water after dark.

"Don't you know They are out after dark? If you dirty Them with our leavins in the water, They are like to come down on us with some a their pishrogues. Leave it till mornin when you can see where it goes."

As they worked, Mary often talked of the home she had left and of the ship coming over. Tessa would give back a few words. Mary began to know a bit of what had made her the woman she was.

Slave she had been, but mistress of the kitchen on the Laurence farm in spite of it, after Paul Laurence's wife died. It was when there was to be a new Mrs. Paul that Tessa had come to Ohio.

Someday Tessa will take the lid off her pot and won't be clappin it back on before a woman can get more than a sniff of what's inside. Not a word do I get out of her now on the husband she left behind. She's not the Judge's woman, I can see that. My thought on it, Paul Laurence is the father of the boys.

Several times, Mary found herself talking about the Hobbs family, unaware that Tessa had started her on it.

"That place where Peter Hobbs and them live, it's far off?"

"Far off. Weren't we the devil's own time gettin here," and Mary went on to tell the story of that journey.

"And back yonder, where you come from, there was a pack of colored folks?"

"Not a one where I come from in Carrignahown. Oh, you mean where the old camp was? A pack of colored folks? Like the full of a townland? No, Peter and his childer, that's all I ever seen."

Tessa sighed. "Just like it is here. Pryor Foster, the smith, over crost the river in Coshocton, him and his wife and children. That's all they is of our folks. I heard tell about others but I never seed none."

Mary had to lay out for Jamie what was needful about the food. She stood across the table from him when the men were through eating, marking off on the fingers of one hand with the forefinger of the other the things she bought from the farmers who came with their wagons. What he had to buy elsewhere, she warned him about before the supply was gone.

This was a piece of her work and he listened without a thought for anything but the cost of supplies. She never sat beside him as she had done in Akron but made a space too wide for any pats on the shoulder or any sweet words.

Jamie's thoughts were on the high cost of supplies he had to put out to feed the growing work force. Mary knew from feeding her family and her lodgers through the winter that things were up from what they had been in Akron. In the spring they had taken another jump.

Jamie began getting downright miserly. He told her to stop buying bacon for the breakfast, and to put less pork in the beans. She no longer asked for sugar to bake a bit of sweet cake as she had done now and again in Akron—she and Tessa had all the baking they could do to keep these hungry men in bread.

The men grumbled. "Beans and stirabout, stirabout and beans. That's all you give us," Johnny complained. "Where's the potatoes? Where's the piece of pork like you put on the table in the old camp and on a Sunday through the winter?"

"Wasn't that a tasty stew last night?" she reminded him, "and you lickin up every drop of it?"

"Squirrel," Johnny snorted. "I wouldn't be callin that meat at all."

She told Jamie the next day and not for the first time, that there were no potatoes and none to be had from the farmers who brought cabbages and Indian meal and milk.

"There's no potatoes to be dug out of the ground here," Jamie said, "because there was none put in the ground at plantin time. Potatoes comes from far off and they want a pocketful of money for a hatful of potatoes."

"If there's no potatoes, there's pork surely. The farmers, they tell us how they were after drivin the pigs and cattle to market as far nearly as the big ocean we come across. Now they can sell their meat here. The lads is pickin at me for givin them no meat."

"How often do you think these boyos got a piece of meat in Ireland? At Christmas, maybe. Now every spalpeen never had so much as a bite of herring with his potatoes wants meat every time he comes to table. What do they think they are, gentry? Or priests? Cook up enough to fill their plates and don't be worryin if its no feast."

Mary folded her arms and let him wait a minute for her words. "Any swill is good enough for the pigs, is that what you're sayin?"

"Now Mary, you know me better than that. Did I ever call your cookin by such a name? I eat it myself, don't I?"

"You do. And it's yourself was tellin me this long time back how the men come to your camp for the good Irish food they get in it."

She could see she had sounded the right note on her fiddle that time. There was a rumor now that an experienced digger could get thirteen dollars on some sections. If Jamie were to hold this big force through the summer, he would have to treat them well or he might have to pay them better.

She watched him walk out of the cookhouse, swinging his shoulders the way he did always but looking different to her from when she first came to the canal. She walked out herself and stood there, with the tables behind her, watching Jamie take the road to the job.

When we first come, what a power he had then, with the keys to the new world in his hand! How simple I was when I got down from the wagon that brought us to Akron! He's only Jamie McCarthy from Carrignahown after all. The years in the new country, so many more than the rest of us and the climbin up to be a boss only put a hardness on the inside of him. He's Dan's old friend, isn't he now, and ready to use the friendship to squeeze the foreman's work out of Dan without the pay should go with it. Why does he look so different to me now? He's up in the world with the Commissioner and the Judge. Thinks he, that puts him high over other Carrignahown folks. And myself? Am I the same woman I was when a smile from the boss was like a bright shillin and every word out of his mouth the God's truth?

Standing now with her hand against one of the logs that held up the cookhouse roof, looking toward the river without seeing it, she was lost in the past, unconscious of Tessa and Bridget moving about the work, looking at her and then at each other, wondering what it was that kept her standing there.

The strange life it is here, a woman has to get her own hands on it to know how to deal with it and how to push it away to leave a little place in it for her ownself and her own people. The newness isn't yet gone out of the ways of livin here, but I'm beginnin to feel what it is that's the same and what's different. How could I do that when all was strange? After the long, long year in Akron and all the life and death in that camp, I didn't come to this place the stranger I was comin fresh and simple to the new country. Not that death was a new thing, God knows. There was death in the guns that was against Dan, death in the hunger that took my two babies and wasn't I after feelin the hot wind of sickness on me in Carrignahown that comes before the cold wind of death? We thought to leave it behind us, comin across the water but that same hot wind was blowin on all I had in my care those long weeks in Akron and no one but me to fight off the cold death.

Mary came back from the past slowly, its pictures fading, leaving her with the feeling of satisfaction from the victories she had won in that struggle. She began to see again what was in front of her eyes—the road to the river and Jamie walking it, made small by the distance.

A small man he is, for all his big talk. Dan, Dan do you see him like I see him? Don't let him pull us behind him down the canal to another camp when this job is done.

It's a small man you are indeed, Jamie McCarthy, for all the power you got to push men into the ditch or pull them out of it, feed 'em well or feed 'em scanty. They'll be fed well is my word on it. I gave him the warnin. It's a bit freer I'll be with gettin the meat from the farmers and puttin it on the table. A little more this week and give him the account of it like its another head of cabbage. If he swallows that, a little more next week. Time enough to quarrel with him if he makes it a plain order I'm not to do it. To a woman who knows the power of death like myself, who stood against it like myself, no livin man can have more than a wind's whisper of power.

Chapter 31

DAN WAS again leading the digging of a mile of canal. But this time he had twice the crew of the autumn. He had men bumping their hard edges against each other, pushing this way and that like a crowd on Fair Day and as likely to burst out in a faction fight.

All the young fellows who had been signed on this spring were beginning to gather around either Johnny or Conn Mor, Mor being the name of the big one partly to distinguish him from the smaller Connie O'Riordan, one of his friends. He had the size for it and the strength too. At first Dan tried to deal with the whole crew as one to keep the rivalry from disrupting the work. After a few days of that, he divided the men into two gangs, with Johnny leading one and Conn Mor the other. The older men and those who had not fallen in with either Johnny or Conn he put in one gang or the other to keep the two well matched. Instead of trying to damp down the rivalry, he spurred it on.

Johnny had the greater canal experience and a gay humor that sparked a liking for him and a willingness to follow where he led. Conn had the greater strength and the will to push himself and pull the others along. The competition put an edge on the shovels, drove them into the ground with a powerful thrust, and helped to push to barrows up the plank out of the ditch and empty them into a wagon.

Buck McKendrie's team was hitched up to the plow the day through, keeping ahead of the diggers. One local man was a seasoning to the crew, like a herring to the potatoes, especially the good-natured Buck. Si Maddox made the dish too salty. Si's job was to drive the wagons full of dirt down to the valley. There were two wagons; one was always being filled while the other was being driven off and emptied. Si wanted to leave the empty wagon wherever it suited him, hitch up his team to the full one and drive off. Dan told him to put the empty where the diggers could put their planks up to the wagon bed and run the wheelbarrows up.

Si gave him no answer except to turn his head away and shoot a stream of tobacco juice out of his mouth. On his next trip he left the empty in a provocatively awkward place, with two wheels off the outer edge of the wagon track that ran along the top of the ditch. Conn and his gang had to drop their tools and waste time maneuvering the wagon back where they could load it, cursing Si from Coshocton to Cork while they did it.

Dan walked away from the digging to meet Si on the return trip. He placed himself in the road, said 'whoa' to the team as it came up to him and got a grasp of the off horse by the cheek straps.

"I'm tellin you one more time," he said to Si. "It's your piece of the work to put the empty wagon where the diggers can load it before you take the full one off."

"Don't tell me how to drive my team."

"*Your* team?"

"It sure as hell ain't yours."

"This team belongs to the job and it's myself runnin this end of the job. You put the wagon where I told you to put it."

"I'll put it where I damn please. Take your hand off my horse. The Judge give me this team to drive and I'm drivin it."

"Are you now? Down out of that wagon with you and off to the River and maybe the Judge will give you another team to drive. I've got men know how to drive horses and put wagons where they belong."

"You won't take this team away from me."

"I will then. It's Dan Griffen tellin you, you got one more time to drive this team. You got some angry men waitin for you and if you don't put the wagon where it belongs, I wouldn't stop 'em from pullin you out of it. And it's myself will give your ass a good kick toward the river. You go cryin to the Judge and see will he give another team to a man that puts a rock in the way of the work for us to stumble over it."

He let go the horse and stepped back, waiting to see what Si would do. He didn't feel as firm on the inside as he sounded on the outside. Jamie would back him up, surely? Would the Judge be on Si's side?

He stood there, watching, till Si had the wagon where it belonged. The firmness on the outside had been enough. Si did his piece of the job right from that time on.

It was another problem to stay on top of the two gangs. Johnny thought Dan should be with him, old friend that he was. Conn expected him to side with the Cork men, being a Cork man himself. It was easier to be hard with Conn. There had never been a different way between them. Putting a distance between himself and Johnny was a harder thing. Little time as there was between work and sleep, Johnny would be using it to contrive some plot against Conn and his men. Living in the same house, Dan would know what was up and had to close his ears if Johnny's plot would help the work and open his mouth if it would harm.

Now that the sun rose early and set late, the job engulfed them all. There was seldom a day without work. They kept going through the spring rain except when a big storm opened the heavens on them. There was no time to sit around the fire, except on a Saturday night, no time to talk of buying a farm or even to think about it.

The Saturday night fires were most often outside, the crowd being too big for the inside of any shanty. Dan would be there late, if at all, having to make his report to the bosses about the week's work. Even on Sunday there was no rest for him. Dan was closer than Jamie and had the name of being able to bring some sense out of the way of things in the new country or to put down the words for those who wanted to write a letter home.

It was a Saturday night in Jamie's cabin when the talk began about the whiskey. The three bosses were sitting around the table and Dan was a few feet back, listening as usual. There was often something to learn out of their talk and it was not his place to open his mouth except to answer for his part of the job. The talk had been mostly of the cost of supplies for the job and supplies for the cookhouse. They were on to the cost of the whiskey before he understood the why of it. Then he could hardly believe what he was hearing. They were talking about cutting out the evening jiggers.

"What we're paying them now is enough for them to buy their own whiskey," the Judge was saying. "They drink too much of it, anyway. All we're doing is giving them a start on the night's drinking and that's bad for the work next day."

Dan looked at him, sitting there with a jug at his elbow and a glass like the gentry use for their drinking. When himself was out of it and the business finished, there would be drinks for Jamie and Simon and the Judge out of that jug. The drinking was one thing for the bosses and the people in the Big Houses and another for the men in the ditch.

He turned his eyes down, so the bad feeling wouldn't show out. He stared at his boots, calming himself so he could get the sense of the talk again.

"The way it was the first year on the canal," Jamie was saying, "We give out a jigger halfway between breakfast and dinner, another one at dinner and a third between dinner and supper, besides the one at the end of the day. Kelley put a stop to that. The men didn't like it but the work went better without it. Myself, I'm against drinkin on the job but that jigger at the end of the day, that's a bit different."

He looked at Simon.

"The stonies keep it," Simon said firmly. "They call our trade 'the dust' and it's that we have in our throats. If there's no beer goin, we'll take the whiskey. We won't take it neat while we got our hands on the chisel. At the end of the day, though . . . at the end of the day there has to be a proper jigger to wet down the day's dust."

Simon was standing by the stonies. Would Jamie stand by the diggers?

"There was a growling surely," Jaime said, "when we brought it down from four jiggers a day to one but the men had to take it, it bein the Commissioner's orders and the same on every section. This would be on our sections only. We might lose workers by it."

"No," the Judge said. "I have the agreement of the contractors on both sides of us and a few others, to cut it out if we give the lead."

When it looked like going against the men, Dan cleared his throat and scraped his feet on the floor to remind them he was there.

"What do you say, Dan?" Jamie asked. "Will you have trouble over this?"

"Trouble you'll have," Dan said. "I wouldn't know the shape it would be comin in but trouble you'll have."

"I'll take care of my crew," Jamie said confidently. "You handle yours."

"I don't . . . I wouldn't . . ." Dan found himself stumbling over the words. "We turn out the work, don't we? Then give us the drink at the end of the day like you're givin it to the stonies. There's dust on the dry days on our job too, and mud on the wet days. Why wouldn't there be a sup to wet the throat or warm the belly at the day's end?"

He could see he wasn't changing the Judge nor Jamie. "At least, don't knock the cup away from their lips altogether. Let me give out the drinks on the Saturday. That's only a few sixpences. There's no work on Sunday. The bitter draft you're givin, it might go down some easier, could they see the usual jigger comin at the week's end."

They agreed to that but Dan came away feeling it was a pitiful small thing he had pried out of them.

"Don't look so down in the mouth," Jamie said to him as he left. "We're not takin the drink from you. You'll still have the barrel in your shanty and we've never measured it on you."

No, you didn't take it away from me and let you not try. But I should have saved it for the others. I didn't give 'em the words right . . . Why should I have to give Jamie the words at all? Don't he know how it is? A man has somethin, he feels he's got a right to it. Then you take it away and the hurt's worse than if he never had it. Men that had nothin and would get out of the road for the gentry, bowin and grinnin as if they liked swallowin the dust from the carriage wheels, those same men, after the good years when they got a little somethin, hung on to it and wouldn't let go. They would even lie behind the ditch and shoot a bullet or heave a rock at that same carriage. And now it's myself has to do some of the dirty work of takin the evenin jiggers away. I won't take the blame for it, though. Let the blame land where it belongs.

It was from his hand the men were accustomed to getting the jiggers each evening, though, and now it was his hand that was withholding it. Some of the blame landed on him. The mood of the camp hadn't been so sullen since the worst days of working in the cold water back in the winter. Dan couldn't whip up the spirit at the work.

On Tuesday evening, Johnny went out after supper, looking for Molly no doubt, and came in just when Dan was filling a jug from the barrel.

"Look at that now," Johnny said to Hugh. "There's no whiskey in the barrel he tells us, except what's to be saved for the Saturday night. But when it's himself is dry there's a barrelfull to draw on."

Dan poured a noggin for Mary who had just come in from the cookhouse, weary from the day's work. He poured another and passed it to Johnny. "Did you ever know me to drink alone when a friend was by?" he asked. He gave Hugh a drink and took one for himself.

"It's many a good drink we had together," Johnny agreed. "There was one time we had to get it with a timber knockin down the door on the way to it."

He lifted his noggin to Dan, it seemed by way of apology. "May there always be whiskey in your barrel."

Johnny's good spirits seemed to revive after that and Dan didn't suspect anything till Johnny and his gang strraggled to work late after the noon dinner on Saturday, every man of them happy. When Dan got close, he smelled whiskey. They had been up to something but it wasn't till the day's end that he found out what it was.

The men lined up for their jiggers, the line starting in the corner of Dan's shanty, near the barrel and stretching through the door and down the path. Dan put the jug from which he would pour out each man's drink under the barrel's edge and began to ease the bung out of the barrel. It fell out in his hand and not a drop of whiskey followed. Dan stood there holding the empty jug in his hand, feeling like a fool. Johnny and his friends were laughing uproariously.

Conn Mor pressed forward angrily. "Where is it then? You give us promises to drink all the week and lead us to dry barrel at the end of it."

Dan was so furious he lost his English but not his tongue. He scorched Johnny in Irish for taking the whiskey when his back was turned and leaving his mates dry. That turned Conn's anger and he swung at Johnny. It was all Dan could do to push them outside. That just widened the battle. He left them to fight it out while he got his food.

"What's the row?" Jamie asked as Dan sat down beside him.

"It's the trouble I told you was comin over the whiskey," Dan said and gave him the story. "There's no lock on my barrel and no guard on my shanty when all are at the work. You'll have to be givin out the jiggers on the next Saturday."

Mary came over to them, saying, "The cookhouse is half empty and the pot's half full. I can hear a fight going on. What's in it? Would they rather fight than eat?"

When she heard what it was, she picked up her big spoon and an empty frying pan. "I'll see can I fetch them."

She walked out, beating the pan with the spoon. The sound that meant food to hungry men began to fray the battle at its edges and soon the men came pouring in, all but Johnny and Conn and a few who stayed on to urge them on, till Johnny clearly got the worst of it and Conn stalked off victoriuosly.

Johnny came in with a face scratched and dirty where Conn had knocked him to the ground and beginning to swell where Conn's fist had hit. Johnny's friends were telling him he'd made a good fight of it and look at the marks he'd put on Conn and there was another day coming.

"What that means," Jamie said to Dan, "is more of the same tomorrow and men that wouldn't be fit to work Monday. Johnny's your boy, wouldn't you talk the teeth out of that saw before it cuts wood?"

"It's yourself that has that gift and 'twas yourself took the drinks away and brought the devil into camp with it."

Jamie thought about that for a few minutes. "It's Johnny and Conn is in the front of it?"

Dan gave him no answer. Jamie could see for himself if he had eyes in his head and if he wanted a tongue he shouldn't be looking to Dan Griffen.

Jamie walked over to Johnny. "Murdered entirely, was you?"

"He got the better of me this time but I'll make him smell hell for it."

"And when would you be doin that?"

Johnny opened his mouth but Kevin gave him a dig in the ribs to remind him the less said to the boss, the better. Johnny shoved Kevin away. "Leave my sore bones to mend, can't you?" he snapped.

Jamie leaned across the table and swept his eyes over the whole group. "There's to be no fightin in the camp tomorrow and none on the job comes the week's work. I'm tellin you, Johnny Brennigan, and I'll tell Conn the same. The day the next fight breaks out, you'll have more than a shirt full of sore bones. You'll have your bundle in your hand and you'll be out on the road. And the same to any other man that's in it."

He crossed to the other side of the cookhouse and gave the same word to Conn and the men around him.

It was a strange Sunday. No one came asking Dan for this or that. Most were circling around Johnny or Conn. Jamie's threat might hold them off each other for awhile but sooner or later a taunt from Conn or one of his men would drop on the smoldering wish for revenge in the other gang. Dan said this to Dennis and Michael as they sat on a log near the Griffen door, smoking a peaceful Sunday pipe together and watching the life of Dublin drift in and out of the shanties and along the road in front of them. The stonies hadn't been in it at all and could size up the contenders judiciously.

"That Conn has a fist like a rock," Michael remarked. "It's my opinion Johnny better leave him alone."

Dennis was itching to see another good scrap and was ready with the way Johnny could overcome Conn's advantage.

"Now what I'm askin m'self," said a voice behind them, "is why would they be murderin each other over the whiskey when it's the bosses took it away?"

It was Tom who had stayed out of yesterday's fight, though he was in Johnny's gang on the job. "What I'm askin, why would the bosses be doin a thing like that? Is it right? Is there a thing in it but trouble? Couldn't you see it comin?"

"I could indeed, and I told them the dollar they were after savin would bring them more than a dollar's worth of trouble. But try to tell the Judge that, or Jamie either. Simon's the only one has the sense to see it."

"Simon knows he's got us stonies to deal with," Dennis said complacently. "He knows better than to take it from us."

"And what would you stonies be doin if the drink wasn't there at the end of the day?"

"Down tools till it was."

"No whiskey, no work?" Tom pursed his lips and thought that over.

"We could do it," Dennis explained, "because they damn well can't build their canal without us. Good stoneworkers is scarce in this country. In Dublin itself, for the matter of that, we got us a Friendly Society. It helps the sick and buries the dead and keeps the men together for the dealins with the master masons. One of the new men says the masons has one in Cincinnati these ten years. You hear him say it, Michael? That's Henry Sykes, the Cincinnati man come a few weeks back."

"He's a big talker, that lad," Michael said. "It's the Yankee way of talkin he's got but he's a good stone man all the same. There's a mason's society in Cork too, but it couldn't keep the wages up when the bad times come. That's why I come over the water."

"Did you ever hear of such a thing as a Diggers' Society?" Tom asked.

Dennis laughed. "Carpenters, printers, bakers, tailors, all the trades, but diggers? No."

"Why not?" Dan wasn't ready to let Dennis have the last word. "Diggin is a trade too."

"It's no trade," Dennis contradicted. "You can make a digger out of any man with a strong back. In the trades, we have our rules these many years, the time it takes to make an apprentice into a journeyman and them kinds of things. Do the stonies say, 'down tools' the builders can't get another man off the street, like they could a digger."

"To tell the God's truth," Dan said, taking his pipe out of his mouth and pointing the stem at Tom, "When you get in a fight with them that's on top of the world, it wouldn't matter is the journeymen fightin the master masons or the spalpeens fightin the big farmers and squireens or all us in the Cork hills fightin the gentry. Will you get somethin out of the fight or won't you comes mostly from do you stick together on what you want and keep fightin till you get it, or till you get as much of it as you think is worth the fight. Diggers wouldn't be no different."

Tom put his head on one side in that way he had, pursed his lips and finally nodded. "True for you. What's worth the fight? And do you stick together or do you go batterin each other?"

Soon after, Dan saw him in earnest talk with Johnny and then with Egan and the Caseys. Twice he approached Conn Mor but the big fellow had no patience for listening to talk. The next morning, Tom followed Connie O'Riordan out of the cookhouse and walked the way to the job with him. Connie listened and laughed. Being one of Conn Mor's gang, he got the word into Conn's ear.

As the week went on, the truce between the factions seemed to hold but clearly if it wasn't another scrap brewing, it was something else. Whenever Dan came up on two men talking, the talk would stop.

Wednesday night, Johnny and Hugh weren't in their beds. There was scurrying around outside but when Dan looked out, he could see nothing. He got the story at breakfast from Jamie. Someone had got into his cabin through the window when he was out of it and emptied a barrel that had been half full. They must have taken the jugs they had filled to the woods and had a merry time.

Dan could hardly keep the smile off his face while Jamie damned and blasted the men for scoundrels and robbers.

"Looks like to me the lads will have their jiggers one way or another."

"Damned if I don't get rid of Johnny or Conn. One of 'em's at the bottom of this," Jamie sputtered.

Dan shook his head. "Johnny couldn't go through that little window, nor Conn neither. Look around." He waved at the tables where there were men with obvious hangovers and empty places beside them. "You've got all of 'em in it now."

The bosses gave up the fight and restored the evening jiggers, though they took the price of a jug out of every man's pay that month to make up for the stolen whiskey, the way they had done it in Akron after the wake of the dead horse.

Dan was still sore from Johnny playing the trick on him that had made him look a fool in front of the men and now they had left him out of the merrymaking, though it was him tried to keep the whiskey for all.

"Why wouldn't you be tellin me what was up?" he asked Tom "Don't you know I'd be with you?"

"Would you? Would you indeed? I thought so myself but some of the lads says 'The man that gives the orders on the job is a boss and the bosses is the ones took the jiggers away.'" After a moment he added, "Well for you, you weren't in it, or even m'self might be thinkin it was you give me away to the boss."

"Someone blabbed?"

"Well," Tom's head was on one side, considering. "Jamie gave me and Conn and Johnny all the sharp warning to keep our noses clean if we want to stay on the job. It was like he was after knowin it was me come in through the window but who else is there of a size to do it? What I'm thinkin on, did he know I got the lads stirred up to it?"

Chapter 32

P AT CAME into the cookhouse late one morning when the others were nearly through eating. Mary dug her spoon into the stirabout pot to give him his breakfast quickly so he would not be lagging. As Pat took the trencher from her, she could see the trouble lines that creased his face.

"Maggie?" she guessed.

"She's taken bad."

"She wouldn't be left alone?"

"Kate's with her. I called out for Kate when I woke and seen something was amiss."

Pat went on standing there, holding his trencher in his two hands as if there were no hurry on him at all, though the others had started for the job already.

"If you could get out of this? Kate's a good sister to her but she needs . . . she needs . . ."

"I will then. I'll go to her as soon as these spalpeens get out to the job."

"Pat!" That was Jamie's voice. Pat began shoveling the food into him as he crossed the cookhouse, dropped the trencher and spoon on the table without finishing and quickened his stride to catch up with the rest.

Mary downed her own breakfast as if the devil were after her. "You'd put a lick into the clean-up for me this mornin, wouldn't you now?" she said to Bridget and Tessa, "while I see what it is that's come down on Maggie?"

She came back only to ask Bridget to stay through the day and to send Ellen after Peg. She had no good answer to Bridget's questions.

"Maggie's water's broke, the babe will be comin, so, and how can it live? The world will be too cold for it these two months yet. Say a prayer for her. And as for the dinner—you know what's to do, Tessa?"

"Yes, Ma'am."

"Let you be in my place this day," Mary told her, "and Bridget in your place and Peg in Bridget's."

When the men came in for dinner, Jamie looked at the three women dishing out the food. "Where's Mary?"

"Maggie's took bad, Pat says," Dan told him. "It's helpin her is where Mary is, likely."

"Her place is right here." Jamie pounded on the table. "Right here. That's what I hired her for and that's what I pay her for. A man's wages she's gettin, more than what a man's wages was when we started diggin. There's other women can nurse Maggie. Mary's not the only woman in the world. You tell her that from me."

Dan let Jamie pound away without giving him an argument. Mary would be back tomorrow and Jamie would forget it as long as no one pounded back on him. Mary might not be the only woman in the world but she was the only woman in

Dublin having the gift of healing and the knowing way of bringing babies into the world.

It was late at night when Mary came dragging into the shanty. Dan woke to find her sitting on the floor, her head against the bed, sobbing and crying. He had been so deep in sleep, he couldn't understand the first minute why she wasn't in the bed.

"Maire," he muttered, his own voice waking him to the sight and sound of her and the remembrance of her absence. Then it wasn't hard for him to see that Maggie's story had come to a sorrowful end.

"Get in the bed now and rest yourself," he said gently. "The night's half gone."

Her sobs broke out louder now that he was awake.

"Whisht, now, whisht, you'll wake the little one."

When she was lying beside him, he held her until her body stopped shaking.

"Lost . . . lost . . ." That was all she could say at first. "I lost the two of them. Poor Maggie, she put up a fight for it till the last and her lookin on me . . . lookin on me for the help."

"Death comes to us all. There's no help for that, is there now?"

"And that poor little scrap of a baby, no bigger than your hand, all blue and limp. One breath and that was the beginnin and the end of it."

"Sleep now, sleep now. It's gone and done with and you can't bring it back. Rest yourself, you're weary with it all."

Mary sighed deeply. "Yes, weary. Weary with it all."

In the morning, Mary asked Tessa if everything had gone well without her in the cookhouse. Tessa shook her head.

"Would a been allright, but that other woman you fetched, she no better than a child. Mister McCarthy, he got mad with her and scared her a'most out of a year's growth. Miz Bridget and me, we would a done better without her. You look tired this morning. A hard birth, was it?"

"A hard birth and a bitter end."

When Bridget came in, the tears on her face said she had the news. She ran to Mary and they cried together for Maggie and for Pat who would be alone again and for the two youngest children who were now motherless. Mary pulled away after a minute.

"Burned bacon and salt tears will make a poor breakfast."

Jamie never stood in line with the other men but often walked along the line slowly, having a word with this one or that one. This morning he fell in beside Pat who was shuffling along, following the man in front of him as if without knowing why. The trouble lines had disappeared from his face. The stunning blow of Maggie's death had knocked all expression out of it.

"Your wife is gone from you, Pat. " Jamie put his hand on Pat's arm.

"She's gone from me."

"She gave you a good family."

"Two big girls is in Ireland yet and three children I've got here but with herself gone, I don't know what I'll be doin with them at all."

"Egan, he's a man already and the two little ones, they'll be growin up to you before you know it."

"We'll be wakin her, tomorrow's the night. You'll be comin?"

"I will."

Jamie moved on up to the head of the line and took his breakfast from Mary's hand. "So." He looked at her as if in surprise. "You're here doin your own work? And where will you be off to on the morrow?"

Mary was truly surprised. What was in his head to say such a thing? There never was a day she wasn't here, doing her work, except when Maggie's need had to be answered.

The men were pushing forward, she spooned out the stirabout and the men passed on, getting between her and Jamie. He moved away to sit down to his food.

When all were seated and Mary coming along behind them, filling the cups, he said over his shoulder to her, "Dan give you my orders, did he? I pay you for the cookin, not for the nursin. You're to be here . . ." He tapped the table with the end of his finger, "each day and every day."

She poured his cup full and passed on to the next man.

"You hear me?"

"I got two ears on me. I hear you."

"Did you ever see the like of that?" Mary said to Bridget later. "When he's bringin Pat the sympathy, butter wouldn't melt in his mouth. The next thing, he's tappin on the table like he'd pound a nail on me to fasten me to it so I shouldn't go to help Maggie in her trouble. I declare to God, Jamie McCarthy cares for nothin in the world but his own four bones."

All that day and the next, the last hours of Maggie's life and the first and last moments of the baby's life stayed with Mary. Shadows spread out from the recollections of those sorrows to the way they would be losing Pat who had been with them from their first days on the canal. He was going to take his two youngest and go off to Cincinnati with Kate and Christy, leaving Egan here on the canal job.

The spreading shadows turned cold from the coldness there was between themselves and Johnny since he and Dan had the falling-out over the whiskey. Johnny was wed now and living with Molly in the O'Malley shanty.

It should have been Dan that stood to him. It should have been myself doing for Molly like I did for Peg, instead of the two of them goin off to Zanesville without a word to us.

The shadows darkened with the separation there would be between them and the families of the stoneworkers at the end of the job. The shadows crept into their own shanty with the fear that was still in her that Dan was forgetting the farm. All Dublin was under the shadows.

Something had been happening to Dublin since the spring but she had been inside the changes herself and working, working without a moment to give it a thought. Now it seemed she had known all along that the big changes in the work, the big new work force that had flowed into the camp, had flooded Dublin, undermining its shallow foundations, breaking the bonds that held it together, fragmenting its frail structure, submerging the hope that its people would have a future together. Now Maggie's death told her there would be some among them who would have no future at all.

Her sorrows broke out into wailing and crying while she watched by Maggie and the babe after her work was finished, where Kate and Aghna Casey had laid them out. Then she and Dan drank a noggin of whiskey to drive the shadows away and he went to take her place in the Flynn shanty. In her sleep, the sorrows sank deeper into her.

When they rose to the surface the next day, they were in the Irish words for keening Maggie at the wake that night. They were words to fit the rhythm of keening, rhythms that had carried the sorrow of so many Irish generations, bearing the dead away and carrying the living back into life.

It was broken words and phrases that came to her while she worked. The shadows were still choking her, the words could not spring up freely, ready to open the gates of grief and let the sorrow of all pour out in a healing release.

All the old friends out of Dublin gathered around Pat's shanty in the dusk. The new men were coming too. It was easy to see that the shanty would be too small for the wake. It would have to be in the cookhouse.

Pat took the shanty door off; Dan and Hugh and Johnny and Christy laid Maggie on it with the child beside her. Kate put a blanket over them. The crowd drew back to make room. As the four men moved toward the cookhouse, bearing their burden, Pat and Egan followed, sobs breaking out of them at every step. The women fell in behind and the keening began.

The voices of the women were flung impetuously into the night, the shrill edges of their abandoned cries knifing through the darkness, their more controlled and richer tones surging over the procession and dying away into moans.

The sounds of grief rose from a ritual so old and so well understood it gave the voices the freedom to rise as far as they could soar into the night, the right to break out of the confinement of daily work and daily discipline, roll over the imposition of new authorities and strange ways, and express the pain that comes with living in the world and the sorrow that comes with leaving it.

When the door with the bodies on it was set down on two benches in the cookhouse and candles placed at the top of it, things were as near the way they should be as was possible in this place. Maggie had husband and son, her one sister and the sister's husband by her. She had neighbors here as she would have at home. All were close around her.

Others, new in camp as they were, were not family, not yet neighbors, yet they belonged here too, from the working beside Pat and Egan. The strangeness was falling away from them as they took part in the familiar ceremony. They didn't have the right to the grief for Maggie but the grief each had carried since parting with home and family on the other side of the water came to the surface and spilled out. It shook some of the young men loose from their gang, drew them to the Flynns and the other families. Connie O'Riordan stayed close to Egan, mourning as if Maggie had been his mother, too.

All went down on their knees beside Maggie for a word of prayer. When it was time for the rosary to be said, they joined in. Then they gathered in the background, enjoying a blast of the pipe and a jar of the whiskey, talking among each other in the everyday voices of the life that would be going on, the way it does always.

Kate had a right to be the leading keener, for it was she knew Maggie's life from when they were girls together in their mother's house. The other women swept in at each pause with the "Och-o-o-no-ooo." Words were welling up in Mary freely now. When Kate broke down from the words to the tears, Mary stood and took up the keening.

> My friend and my neighbor,
> The day you came
> Here to this place
> That was the first time I saw you.

Tessa had lingered on the road between Dublin and her own small cabin behind the farmhouse, watching the procession that followed the bier. The mourning cries struck against the loneliness she carried inside her and brought forth a cry in response. The other cries drowned her own, leaving her empty and unfulfilled.

These people had watched beside the dead as she had done with her own; these Irish walked together behind the dead as she and her folks did. But pine torches should have lit up the night. Drums should have sounded deeply beneath the human voices. The voices should have had a different rhythm and a different tongue.

She was alone outside this singing. At this moment she forgot everything else she had left behind and was shaken with longing for mother and father, brother and sister and all, all with friendly color and warm voices whom she would never see again.

She could hear Mary's voice . . . Mary, mourning her friend, wrapped in the spirit of her own folks.

> You come across the water,
> Coming to your man
> He that was seven years gone from you
> Your fields with no plowman
> Your house with no husband
> Your bed lonely without him.
>   Och-ho-one o-o-oh, lonely without him.

The children who had been sent to bed had crept out to watch the procession to the cookhouse with its flickering candles. The sounds of woe shook their small bodies like leaves in a wind, filling them with a premonition that the mothers would not always be there. Only Padeen Flynn and his little sister stayed on the bed Kate had made for them in her shanty. They didn't want to hear it, the sounds saying their mother would not be there any more.

> Nine children you bore,

Maggie Flynn.
Three babies taken from you,
Two daughters looking for you
Across the water.
They can look forever
And never see you.
It will be a cold house
And you no longer in it.
The husband will speak
But the wife will not answer.
Children will call
But the mother will not come.
    She will come no more, no more, no more.

My friend and my neighbor,
Your tenth child was coming.
Hard you labored
To give it life.
It was too small
For this big world
Without a mother.

My friend and my neighbor,
We thought to be neighbors
Many months in this place,
Many years in this country.
Your door in the sound of my voice,
My door in the sound of your voice.
I heard you for the last time
When you cried out to me
In your hard birth
And myself with you . . .

Mary looked around for Jamie without missing a beat of the rhythm. There he was, over there on the bench, one leg thrown over the other, smoking his pipe, talking to Simon.

I would be there again
And you calling me
Whatever Jamie MCarthy says
That thinks he is king
Over men and women,
A king without ears
To hear the pain.

She sat down with the other women, all of them keening together. Jamie was half out of his seat, his face growing red with anger. He stepped over to the bier.

In an instant, the atmosphere changed. The keening of the women sank to a murmur. Everyone's eyes turned to Jamie and from him to Mary.

"A good woman you were, Maggie Flynn," Jamie called out, sounding like he was about to give an order on the job.

> Not like some that drips bad words
> Off a bitter tongue.
> Don't listen to her.
> I had ears for your pain
> And sorrow for your man.

He turned and stamped out. Mary was on her feet again, ready to fling a curse after him but Dan put his hand on her shoulder.

"You do be keenin Maggie, not makin a fight of it with Jamie and him gone now, anyhow."

There were a few more words spoken to Maggie but they were letting her go, now. Even her family were letting her go. There was a group gathered around Simon and a group around Michael, the stories being told and the jugs passing from hand to hand. There were many glances at Mary, followed she well knew, by the questions and answers from one to the other till all knew what was behind her words. There were judgments rendered on the rashness of her speaking and some admiration for her daring.

The curse itself that Dan had held back was still in her throat. When the company had dispersed and she was back at her own cabin door, she looked in the direction Jamie had gone. She let it roll out then, though no one but herself could hear.

> May the grass grow on your doorstep, Jamie McCarthy
> And no ears hear
> When your time comes to call out.

Chapter 33

I⸀T WASN'T ONLY the seasons that changed the work. Now another change was rumored. The quarry camp was to be closed, all the needed stone being down by the canal. The aqueduct stonework was beginning, all masons and stoneworkers were needed there and the quarriers were to be turned into diggers or mason's helpers.

"What will Jamie be doin with them others?" Mary wondered. "The Irish he's bringin to Dublin. But what about them that's not? Will I be feedin all?"

"He's puttin the others in the Judge's barn," Dan told her, "along with the new local men that's startin next week. The Judge's wife, she to be cookin again so you'll have a few more Irish only."

"A few more Irish! You talk like Jamie. 'Another man or two means nothin,' says he, 'a few more beans in the pot, that's all.' A dozen men or more on top of the too many I got already! Another woman in the kitchen, that's what it means and it's that I'll be tellin Jamie. Mrs. Laurence is cookin again, is she indeed? She'll surely be takin Tessa back in her kitchen. The likes of me can cook for the whole of Dublin with only two helpers and one of them for the servin only, but a lady like her, does she have naught but a dozen at table, she'll need a woman to carry the hard part of the work."

As soon as the word was out there might be another woman needed in the cookhouse, there was pushing and shoving among the Dublin women to get next to Mary for it. One day when the women were having their noontime colloguin, Peg asked Mary who was to have Tessa's place.

"The first word on it has yet to come out of Jamie's mouth," was all Mary would say.

Tessa said nothing at all till the other women were gone. "You and Mr. McCarthy fixin to move me outa here?" she asked when she and Mary were gathering up the dirty cups and trenchers.

"It's Mrs. Laurence would be doin that. Don't you know she to be cookin for some of the men the same as when we first come, the way you was helpin her? She needs you again surely?"

"No'm. She gon cook for them stays in the barn but Emma McKendrie done cooked up to the quarry, she gon help. She Mrs. Laurence's hired girl fore she married."

So there was to be no change after all but she would still need one more helper. Mary was thinking who it should be and scarcely heard the next thing Tessa said.

"Mrs. Laurence, she don't want me around, nohow."

The two women moved apart to opposite sides of the cookhouse. As they came together again with armloads of dirty utensils, Mary looked at Tessa and those last words came up in her mind through her own concerns.

"She don't want you around? Why, I thought you and her . . . You knowin her ways and the grand worker you are . . ."

"You don't mind me stayin with you?"

"I don't then." That was the truth. Not that she wouldn't rather have one of her own but no need to show Tessa what would be the bitter side of the truth, to her. "Why was Mrs. Laurence after sayin she don't want you around?"

"She don't say it but I knows it. She got her reasons."

What the meaning of that was, Mary had no way of knowing but she could sense the current of feeling that flowed from Tessa.

They moved apart again, their hands carrying out the monotonous thrice-daily chores. Ellen recognized their preoccupation and slid quietly out to play. When all the utensils were piled up, Tessa lifted a pot of water from the fire and set it on the table between them. Each took a rag, dipped it in water, wrung it out and began to wipe off the dirty trenchers and sticky spoons, stacking them neatly for the next meal.

"You like the cookhouse better than her kitchen?" Mary asked, finding it hard to believe.

"It ain't the place. All it is . . . I like it here with you." That was the truth, as much of it as she could trust to Mary.

Mary had to know what it was would make Tessa choose her over the fine lady and her grand kitchen.

"The Laurence place—it wouldn't be home to you?"

"Home?" A shake of the head, a repeat of the word, low and bitter. After a moment she said in a different voice, "Oh, I got a home here, for me and the boys. I goes in my cabin and shuts the door and don't nobody come in without my say so. Not even Mrs. Laurence. She wants to come in, she knocks on the door."

Mary was puzzled. What was it Tessa was saying? The bitterness said one thing and the pride another. Suddenly, Mary saw herself in her own cabin with Ellen and Tim and Danny only, no Dan, no Bridget and Paddy in the next cabin, no Dublin people to come in to the fireside and talk of home and make the home-sickness for all across the water bearable. What a loneliness Tessa must have.

"It's a lone woman you are, isn't it? Without your man, without your kin . . ."

Tessa tried to answer but her voice broke and her grief poured out in tears and lamentations.

Mary joined in, "Och, Ochone . . ." The work forgotten, they sobbed out the loneliness, each of her own exile, both lonelinesses eased a little in the mingling of their voices.

When they were quiet again and their hands busy, Tessa told her story. Once she began, it poured out with hardly a pause except what the work demanded.

Mary learned that exile was the price Tessa had to pay for her own freedom and that of her children but the sorrow of exile was only the edge of the wave that came from greater depths of distress. Though she was separated from her parents, her sisters and brothers and all the rest of her people, separated from the farm where she was born and where she had lived and worked all her life, her freedom was not secure. She didn't yet have those precious pieces of paper that would tell the world she and Willie and Arden were free.

Her parents had been the only slaves of the Judge's father. Tessa had grown up working in the fields along with her parents, her four brothers and sisters and the Laurence family, making a farm out of a piece of Virginia back country. When old Mrs. Laurence got sick, fifteen-year-old Tessa had been brought into the house to cook and clean and care for the sick woman. It wasn't long after the death of the mistress that Tessa's body began to swell with her first child by Paul, the oldest of the Laurence boys.

"Old Master give me a beatin," Tessa said, "and sent Master Paul away to his brother's place and I lost that child. Prettiest little girl you ever saw but Old Master done hit me too hard and she come too soon. I didn't have her but three days. Never had another daughter."

A few years later, the old man died. Tessa sighed, recalling that time of mourning.

Mary was astonished. "You talkin about that same old man beat you and killed your child? That was me, I'd say the devil came to get his own and good riddance. You cried?"

"We wasn't cryin for him. We was cryin for ourselves. We was scared our family be all broke up. Old Master already sold Sam, that my biggest brother. He so far off, he only get a pass to come home at Christmas."

Paul had come back to take over the farm and only her two sisters had been disposed of to Paul's two sisters, both married and living in the neighborhood. Paul built a lean-to behind the kitchen and installed Tessa there.

"We live along like that till Willie eight years old. Master, he that fond of the boys, he promise me when they big enough to be turn loose in the world, he gon set both on 'em free . . . I reckon we done here now, ain't we?"

"Yes, this water's too cold for any use. Is that pot on the fire boilin yet? We got to wet the turkeys."

Tessa threw out the cold dirty water while Mary fetched two headless turkeys, holding one in each hand by their legs. She plunged first one then the other in the boiling water and threw the hot birds down on the table. The two women sat down away from the fire, each holding a bird down firmly with her left hand wrapped in her apron to protect it from the heat while she plucked the feathers.

"What come down on you when Willie was eight years old?" Mary prompted.

What had happened then was that the master had decided to marry. The first Tessa knew of it was when her father and brother were told to build a cabin for her and the boys. She would have to be out of the farmhouse before the new mistress came. As soon as Tessa heard that, she took the boys and moved out of the house and in with her parents, not waiting for the new cabin.

"I never cooked Master one johnny cake or one piece a chicken for weeks," she said with grim satisfaction. "He reckon on a white wife bring him another parcel a land, live in his house, and me doin her work and him sleepin in whatever bed suit him. He order me and beg me but I tells him I prays to the Lord and the Lord tell me get outen his kitchen and get outen his bed. 'You master and I mus work for you,' I tol him, 'but I work in your field, not in your house no more. Too bad you done me like that,' I say, 'put your chillun and the mother of your chillun out, but since you done it, you done it.'"

"Weren't you afraid to talk to him like that?"

"Oh, I knows him inside and out. He be back, I knows that, but he leave me alone awhile. That something. This woman he want to marry, she start in on him and her pappy, too. They wasn't gon have me on the place. Ever'body round there know about Master and me. Them other white folks, they couldn't hardly stand it, the way I right in the house.

"Mr. Little, that's her pappy, you know what he say? I hearn it from one a his people at Meetin. Down home we have our own meetin of a Sunday, singin and prayin, and Brother Mose preachin and we get all the news from the other peoples comes from round about. Henry, he one a Mr. Little's people, he tells me Master done rode over to court his lady that Saturday night. Her pappy go out to the stable with him to get his horse when he ready to leave and Henry hear 'em talkin.

"Mr. Little tell Master he don't hold it agin him, havin me in his bed. He stand there braggin over all the nigger womens he done it to hisself. He the dirtiest, nastiest, meanest old man in Virginia, old Little. He say Master got me so uppity I think I his wife. That a downright disgrace, he say. That enough to make us think we owns ourselves and our chillun, too.

"Master swear he done moved me down back a the barn and don't have nothin to do with me no more but that ain't good enough for the old man. 'You ain't gon have nary daughter a mine,' he say, 'or nary piece a my farm, les'n you get rid of that gal. You hear?' He say I bring a good price and the old man gon let Susie bring Maria along of her when they get married. 'Maria know her place,' he say, 'I seen to that.'"

Tessa was looking at Mary but her eyes were wide, staring into the past. "Oh, Lord have mercy, I thought I die when I hear that. Master might sell me away from my chillun. I went cryin to my pappy and mammy. Brother, he come and we all sit round in that cabin cryin and prayin and askin each other what can we do?"

Mary had been making pictures for herself from Tessa's words, pictures more like Cork than Virginia. She could see an Irish stablehand standing quietly in the next stall listening to the squire and some other half-sir pawing over the bodies of the women they had. Then she knew the picture was wrong. The stable hand should look like Peter Hobbs. But what Tessa was saying now . . .

"He sell you, like you was a horse or a cow?" Forgetful of her task, she stared at Tessa, one hand full of turkey feathers. For all the talk of slaves in the south of this country, it had never come home to Mary before. After a few minutes she asked, "Wouldn't all your people be comin together in the night to hamstring his cattle or burn his barn or . . . or . . ."

"I just tol you. All my peoples on the place come. Mammy and Pappy and Brother and me, that's all we had left. Pappy say maybe I should run off but I didn't hardly know whichaway to go, me never bein more'n about five-six miles from the farm my whole life and Arden too big to carry and too little to walk over them mountains. . . This bird ain't got no more feathers to fly with. Whereat's the knife?"

"Here 'tis. So what did you do?"

Mary plunged another turkey in the boiling water and began to pluck it while Tessa dismembered the first two with practiced hands, the sounds punctuating her story.

"After I laid down that night I had it in mind to run off"—crack! as one wing was pressed away from the turkey's body till the joint gave—"but I didn't know nowhere or nobody to run to"—whack! as the knife severed skin and flesh and the wing dropped away.

"Then it come to me, what Master's brother Joshua, that the Judge, you know"—

crack!—"what I hear him say. I didn't hardly know him after he was growed"—whack!—"Gone off to school and lawin and leavin our part a the country"—crack—"He come home when his father die and Master say he give him one a the servants for his share of what his pappy left. What he say I hear with my own ears, he say 'We don't 'low no slaves in Ohio' and on top a that, he say"—whack!—"'Slavery wrong in the sight a God.'"

Tessa's strong hands were cutting and tearing the carcass apart.

"I said them words over to myself that night and seemed like there must be some kinda way I could get to Ohio and maybe Joshua Laurence would help me." —whack, whack, whack!

"Cut all of 'em smaller. We got three turkeys only to put in the stew and each man got to have his piece," Mary reminded her. She went over to the fireplace to get the big stewpot, calling back, "What way was it you got to Ohio at last?"

"I gets up outa my bed right then, in the middle of the night"—crack!—"and I walks and worries and walks all night"—whack!—"I see I been goin about it all wrong. The way I actin, I makin it easy for him to sell me"—crack!—"Fore light I was watchin the house and soon as I see Pappy and Master headin for the barn to do the chores I goes in the kitchen and cleans it up"—whack!—"Lordy! You shoulda seed it after Master done for hisself a few weeks. Dirty clothes where he drops 'em. Lumps a farmyard on the floor, lumps a food on the table"—crack! whack!—"Well, I makes it shine and I cooks up his piece a ham and his two eggs and his hot biscuits and his coffee all jus the way he likes 'em."

She paused, rapidly chopping the turkeys into smaller pieces. Mary picked them up and dropped them in the pot. Then Tessa resumed.

"He so happy when he come in, he lick it all up to the last crumb. 'You the stubbornest nigger in Virginia,' he tell me, 'but I knew you come round. Didn't, I whip you round. You knew that, didn't you, gal?' 'Oh Master,' I say, 'You know, ever you needs me, I come runnin.'" She looked over at Mary to see if she understood the words meant something else than what they said.

Mary nodded. "And he licked that up to the last crumb?"

Tessa dropped the knife and throwing her head back, let out a screech of laughter such as Mary had never heard from her. Again and again till Mary joined in, swept up in the joy of the way the master had gone down like a ninepin, hit by a little ball of deceit.

"Oh, Miss Mary, you a caution. 'Lick it up to the last crumb.' That's just what he done."

She broke out again in a rich joyous peal. The two of them rolled their laughter across the table, inciting each other to new bursts, applauding each other. The hard balls of their laughter caromed against each other, knocked the master down again and again, making him smaller and smaller till the laughter rolled over him altogether and the women stopped, gasping.

"Well," Tessa picked up the story when she had recovered her breath, "I goes on like that a few days, cookin what he like, doin what he want, cleanin up the house, sweet talkin him and he go on, lickin it up to the last crumb"—another snort of laughter—"Then I tells him," she paused, showing that it was all serious now.

"I tells him I cleanin like that for the new mistress and I say, 'Master, you know you can't have me roun here when she come. And these two little fellers, they gettin most big enough for them free papers you promise.' I beg him to take 'em to Master Joshua in Ohio and lemme stay with 'em till they big enough to work good. 'Won't be but a year or two,' I tol him. 'Willie can hoe his own row now and Pappy teachin him all bout the horses.' Willie, he love the horses. You ever see him ridin that horse, bringin it back from pasture? He sit up there bareback, most as tall and straight as a growed man."

"You come to Ohio, so you did. That you may never live through such a time again."

"Oh, it was a time, I tell you. I couldn't hardly eat from the day I went back in the kitchen till we got to Ohio. And sleep? Lordy, I didn't know what sleep was. Master wouldn't a brung us neither, hadn't been Mr. Little cotched me in the house one time when he come over unexpected. He give Master a week to get me outa there, or the weddin gon be off. Master so mad I thought I wouldn't live to see daylight, him yellin why couldn't I keep outa sight, tellin me what he gon do to knock some sense in me and all like that. He cool off after while and the next day he tell me get my things together, he gon take us to Ohio. When we cross the river, I so happy I want to bust out singin. What I done, I bust out cryin and what you think? Master lean over and pat me and say, 'Don't cry, honey. You won't be gone from home long. I gon find a way to bring you back.'"

"You wouldn't be goin back?"

"I ain't crazy. No, ma'am, I ain't goin back. But that man, he may be blind in one eye when it come to what any a God's chillun is thinkin, but he smart as the devil. He still holdin me on the end a the chain. No free papers yet."

The two women each put a hand on the handle of the stewpot. Swinging it down from the table, they carried it across to the fire and hung it on the hook at the end of the crane. Mary poured water in and put the lid on while Tessa got a few sticks to build up the fire. It was a warm June day. A few minutes by the fire was enough to bring drops of sweat out on their faces. They wiped faces and hands on their aprons and walked out the open side of the cookhouse to get a breath of air.

"Wasn't he after promisin you the boys' papers?"

"Oh, he promise me that many a time. And I think he mean it. I think he do. When he brung us, he say the boys still too little, he gon send the papers later. After we been here a year, I ast the Judge, would he write him a letter bout it. But I couldn't splain it right to the Judge or he don't listen. I want the boys' papers in my hand fore I ast Master can I have my freedom. Do he say no to me, maybe I just take the boys and light outa here. You think I can make it, iffen I takes a chance on myself? Get far enough away from Virginia?"

Mary returned her look helplessly. Tessa sighed.

"What's the use a talkin? I ain't got the boys' papers. The Judge, he the one writin the letter. Say he won't have no slaves on his place no more. Tell his brother set all us free right quick. You know Master not gon like that. Master write back, say he gon send the boys' papers, sure, or maybe he bring 'em hisself after harvest. He don't say nuthin bout me. And he don't send papers and don't bring 'em and we ain't heard nary word since. Judge done write again here a few Sundays back.

"Why the Judge won't help me get what I maybe could get outa him?" she sighed again and answered her own question. "Him and Mrs. Laurence, they never want us in the first place. They don't want no black nephews. They pretend like it ain't so. Master had to talk most all night to get 'em to let us stay here when we come. It still stickin in their craw. They thinks I's a bad woman. I ain't. I ain't. I's a Christian. I been washed in the blood of the Lamb. The Lord done take all my sin away."

She flung her defiance at Eliza Laurence's judgment and then looked a question. Was Mary with her all the way? The answer in Mary's eyes was satisfying. That was enough. There was another secret but it was not for the telling. When it came to that, Mary's judgment might be like Eliza's.

The women reluctantly returned to their work. There were still the turnips and carrots and onions and a few potatoes to prepare for the stew and the men had devoured so much bread at the noon meal, there would have to be bread made from Indian meal before supper time.

Tessa had given Mary a glimpse into a part of the life of her new country she had never seen. Struggling as she still was to understand the differences between Cork and Ohio, she could not bridge the distance between Cork and Virginia. Perhaps it was not such a great difference after all. She told Tessa the story of the Squire and old Patsy and her own twelve-year-old self.

"Ay-ah," Tessa said at the end of it. "Lucky for you, you had a granny could whisk you away." She rose from the bench where they were sitting and went over to the fire to drop some carrots in the stewpot. Then she asked, "How long you reckon you be round here?"

"Dan's been after tellin me the job will last another year. What he don't be sayin, what begins when the job ends."

Another year. It wasn't an unexpected answer but Tessa had never looked it in the face before. Another year in the cookhouse where she had made a place for herself with her work, then back to the Laurence house where she was unwanted, her work always done under Eliza Laurence's critical eye. Another year with someone to talk to and laugh with while they worked, then back to the too-quiet days when there was nothing for her to say but "yes, ma'am." Another year in which there would be someone who had seen trouble close enough to know its name. Then no one left but the Laurences.

She had been passionately grateful to the Judge at first for giving her this toehold in freedom. She wasn't fenced in here. How she had reveled in the feeling that she could stand straight and breathe deep without something always pressing down on her from above. She could stretch out her arms all the way without touching the walls that had always surrounded her. But what was the use to have the freedom to go if there were no place to go to, no free papers to protect the boys from the slave catchers? And the Judge was the Master's brother, after all, so if trouble came from that quarter, what help could she expect?

The Judge being another Laurence, she had feared that the price of a place under his protection might have to be paid with her body. She had been thankful that he had never touched her, never so much as crossed the threshold of her little cabin. He was a master of a different kind, one who hated slavery but despised slaves. When she understood that, she was less grateful but it did ensure that her cabin was her own, her bed was her own, her body was her own.

It was her own choice that she shared them now. On some deep nights, when the farmhouse was dark and the camp asleep, Donal Shelley knocked quietly on her door and she opened it.

When the canal work had first begun, when the Irish bosses and the Irish tradesmen had come to eat in the Laurence kitchen, Tessa had soon felt the eyes of the carpenter on her as she served the food. One night, she found him hanging around her cabin when she came from work. He stood in front of her door so she couldn't go in but he didn't grab at her, just smiled and said sweet things to her in that strange way the Irish had of talking, the sweetest things she had ever heard from a man. Then he touched her face gently and said goodnight and went away. She lay awake that night, telling herself not to be a fool but she couldn't tell herself not to be a woman, not after the lonely time of lying alone. The third time she found him at her door, she let him in.

In the bed that had been so lonely, there was now the warm presence of the man she had chosen to admit. The body that had known the pain of brutal taking, now knew the pleasure of freely giving, but at what a risk! If the Laurences discovered it, she would be scorned and driven out as a sinful woman. If the other men in the camp discovered it, they would all be knocking at her door. Whatever Donal might say, he didn't have the power to protect her as the Judge did. However friendly Mary might be, she too was among the powerless. Ah, well, she still had her children and her own cabin. She could still cling to her freedom with all her strength. And as long as the Irish were here, she had a friend and a lover.

Mary cornered Jamie about the kitchen help a few days later. He agreed to another woman at mealtimes, having seen for himself it was the only way to keep the breakfast and dinner from taking too much time away from the job. Another fulltime worker? He wouldn't hear of it but he did let Mary choose her own helper. She chose Aghna.

"Aghna and Mickey need another bit of a wage to pay off their dead horse," she said to Dan, "And Aghna's the one out of the new women that's come will be the most help to me."

There was another difference in the cookhouse besides having Aghna to help. Tessa was more talkative and sometimes sang at her work, songs that in all her three years in Ohio she had sung only in her own cabin.

Chapter 34

IN THE MIDST of the dirty utensils, broken crusts, spilled food, shreds of tobacco, and flakes of dried canal mud that littered the table as usual, the paper with all the printing on it seemed to announce a message from another world. Ellen ran with it to her mother who was lingering over her dinner, talking to the other women.

"It belongs to Jamie," Mary said. "Or Mr. Dent was with Jamie today. It's his, maybe. Leave it here, ma griannach."

"That's one of them Coshocton newspapers. Mr. Laurence gets 'em all the time," Tessa remarked.

"Can you read it?" Bridget asked Ellen.

Ellen laid the paper on the table and knelt on the bench, looking for familiar words. It was a poor piece of reading with no pictures to it.

"There!" she put her finger on two big black words at the top of the page. "I can read that. 'Land Sale' it says. See, Bridget, 'land sale.'"

Mary leaned over, her eyes following Ellen's finger. "Is there more to it?"

Ellen looked at the next line but the big words were beyond her. "Danny can read it. Tim can read it. Will I bring Danny to read it to you?"

"This is one of them days the boys has no work? Go, then," Mary agreed.

Ellen had seen her brothers saunter out of the cookhouse and wished she could follow but like her mother she ate her dinner after the men and boys were through and after that she had the task of helping with the clean-up. Liberated now, she ran out into the hot July afternoon. In front of the cookhouse, she stopped to look out over the valley. There were masses of men at work there now, bare to the waist, their bodies blackened by sun and dust.

It was the same every day since the digging of the mile-long ditch had been completed. Now they were scooping the earth out of the valley in one place and building it up in another. Her father and his men were at this end, every day making the embankment reach farther out toward the river. Jamie and his men were building in from the river. One day they would meet. Ellen barely glanced at the accustomed scene; she was unlikely to find the boys there. On the days when they were told they were not to work, they stayed as far from the job as they could get.

Ellen scanned the immense pile of stone that had been hauled down from the quarry. That was a favorite haunt but there was no sign of life there. The big blocks of sandstone were full in the sun; the glare on them made her blink her eyes and feel how hot they would be to the touch. The boys had more likely headed for the river but they were not in sight in that direction either. It would be a long hot walk to the river bank and no knowing whether she would find them there at all. She would wander around Dublin first and get Rosy Farrell or Terry to go with her. She was in no hurry. If she got back to the cookhouse too soon, she would be put back to work.

Rosy and Terry were busy in a shady spot behind the O'Scanlon shanty. Terry had taken advantage of his mother's absence to drag the bucket of water out of the shanty. He and Rosy were making nice cool mud which could be scooped up and shaped into all kinds of things. Ellen dropped to the ground to join the fun. It wasn't till much later, when Tim and Danny came down out of the woods at the top of the hill, that Ellen remembered her errand. Then she got up, wiped her muddy hands on her dress and told her brothers their mother was after wanting them in the cookhouse this long time.

She then returned to the important work of building a small hill like the big one the fathers were building. The boys were quite willing to head for the cookhouse in the hope of a mid-afternoon bite of something.

"You took the devil's own time gettin here," was Mary's greeting. She was at the fire that was doubling the July heat, making a pot of thoroughwort tea for the canal fever that was on them again. She wiped her sweaty face with her apron and pointed at the paper.

"Look at that thing there, where it says 'land sale' and read me the rest of the tale."

Tim picked up the paper. Bridget and Tessa left their work, too, and came closer.

"'Land Sale,'" he began, "'And ap-ap . . .' I never seen this word before."

Danny leaned over Tim's shoulder. "A-p-p-r-a-i-s-a-l," he spelled out.

Tim jerked the paper out of Danny's line of vision. "I can spell it, and I can read it, too." He hurried over the unfamiliar word and went on.

"Aperaysale Notice. A sale of school lands will be held at the Coshocton County Courthouse on Saturday the ninth day of August at two o'clock. Thirty-eight lots in La- la- la-fayette Township will be sold. Lots are eighty and one hundred sixty acres in size. Terms of the sale: one-fourth cash down and the . . ." He paused.

"He's the grand reader, Mary," Bridget said admiringly. "Just like the school-master and him only a boy yet."

". . . the remainder in six equal in . . . in . . . somethin."

"Is that all?" Mary asked.

"That's all the readin. See all these? These is just numbers, one under the other."

When Tim had read it through once more, slowly, Mary cut a piece of bread for each of the boys and let them go.

"What do you make of it?" she asked Bridget but Bridget always lagged a step behind, waiting for Mary's lead.

Mary stared at the paper as if by the very intensity of her gaze she could pull the secrets out of it. "If Mr. Dent don't come back for it, I'll keep it for himself to read it."

Dan was sitting on the bed, taking off his boots when she came in with the paper. He walked to the door in his stocking feet to read it by the last glimmer of light. He leaned against the doorframe, holding the paper up as if, after all the heavy loads he had lifted this day, a scrap of paper more was too much to lift.

As he read, he straightened up. Mary moved toward him, sensing his excitement.

"I'll be goin to this sale to see what's in it," he said to her.

"To buy a piece of land?"

"It's yet to be seen can we get a piece for what's in the pouch."

"Where is it you'll go?"

"The sale is in Coshocton, where you went to the store with Mrs. Laurence. Where the land is . . . that's one thing there is to find out . . . There's others . . . Thirty-eight lots—eighty and a hundred and sixty acres." Those words wiped out all Dan's hesitations, all his thoughts of following the canal work farther down the road.

Land without rent! There it was, giving itself to them on the paper. Thirty-eight lots, next to each other. They would be next to each other, wouldn't they? Enough for all Dubliners who wanted farms, if they weren't out of reach? It looked to Dan like some of these lots were as high as two dollars and fifty cents an acre, twice what they had been told in Akron was the price of Congress land but some seemed to be as low as twenty-five cents.

Dan picked up the slate he had bought for the children and worked it out. Eighty acres at twenty-five cents would be only twenty dollars and a quarter of that . . . why he would need only five dollars in his hand. There was more than that in the pouch.

"Eighty acres is a big farm," he said to Mary. "The place in Carrignahown would be lost in it . . . I'll be goin to this sale. That's full sure."

At the end of the work next day he walked over to Buck who was unhitching his team. He pulled the paper out of his pocket.

"This notice here . . . you see this?"

"What notice?"

"Sale of school lands."

"Oh, yeah, yeah. I was talkin to Will Barnes about that. He done the surveyin. He reckons there's some good land in there and some that ain't worth a pisshole in the snow. I got a notion to go over and look at it myself come Sunday. You want to come along? It's in Lafayette Township. That's just east of here and mostly on the other side of the Tuscarawas."

"I'll come and my thanks to you for it. How much would the land be goin for?"

"Well . . . It depends, see. This list here, that's what it's appraised at. You can't get it for no less. But if more than one wants the same lot, they might bid it up. Some of it's been leased out and the folks that's on it will likely buy that. That's this here improved land. A dollar and a half, two dollars, two and a half an acre. What I'm gonna look at is the wilderness land. A hell of a lot of work in it and three-four years before you can make a good crop. Still an' all, you can get it cheap."

"For twenty-five cents an acre?"

"Well, yeah, but I reckon if they appraised it that low, it ain't worth buyin. That's what Will said. It's some a them steep hillsides that's more rocks than dirt. This here's what I want to look at . . . ." He put a dirty forefinger down on the list. "See that? This here's appraised at sixty to seventy-five cents. Some of them lots is a hundred and sixty acres. I might get me one a them."

Dan was already late for supper when he and Buck broke off the talk and Buck drove the team away toward the barn. Yet he walked very slowly toward the cookhouse, trying to do the figures in his head. He thought there might be enough in the pouch for the good land at sixty or seventy-five cents. He hastened his steps, wanting to get supper over and count the money and do the figuring on the slate. There was a smile on his face when Mary handed him his supper.

"It's good news?"

"If there's a farm in it, would that be good news? I'll be going with Buck to look at it Sunday."

As the word of the land sale spread, the people came crowding into the Griffen shanty, all talking at once. Mary smiled at them all.

It's like we cast out a handful of feed to a haggard full of hungry chickens. Each was scratchin away to get the day's wages but when a grain of promise come flyin through the air, all come runnin.

Tyrone was there first, reading the notice for himself. After that it had to be read out again and again by Dan or Tyrone and the minute it was finished, there would be someone else in the door calling for it to be read once more. Hugh was listening, but saying nothing.

"You'll be with us, surely?" Mary asked him.

"I doubt you could make a farmer out of me. I'm a seafarin sort of man, so I am. One day, I'm thinkin, I'll find me another ship."

Johnny was there and Molly with him, Bridget and Paddy, Tom Quinlan, all the Caseys—Kevin and Una, Mick and Aghna. Eileen Dawley came with her baby in her arms, saying Joe was down with the canal fever and couldn't get out of his bed. A few minutes later he was there, shaking till his teeth chattered, shaking out his own questions.

Even Dennis and Rose, Michael Kieran and Peg were drawn by the excitement, though they had no thought of buying land. As the news spread out from the heart of Dublin through the new shanties, more men came crowding in till there was no place for even one more in the hot airless room and Dan had to stand in the door with a candle to read the notice to those outside.

They were late getting to sleep but Mary was gay the next day. She sang at her work and when Bridget came they talked of being neighbors to each other.

Later, Tessa asked Mary, "You all makin it up to stay round here?"

"We are then. With our own farm, big as some of them grand farms in the valley . . ." forgetting that the valley of the Lee was as strange to Tessa as the valley of the Tuscarawas had been to herself until a year back.

"All your folks works on the canal be stayin?"

"No, not Jamie, not Simon and his masons, not all these young lads with no families, but Bridget and Paddy surely, Johnny and Molly, Eileen and Joe, enough others to make another Little Dublin over there on the other side of the river."

Tessa had followed Mary's list intently. "Not Donal," she said to herself. But was there, perhaps, a hope? She asked him that night when he lay beside her, satisfied, reluctant to go back to the comfortless quarters he shared with all too many other men.

He took his arm away from under her head. "Donal Shelley will never weigh himself down with anything but a toolbag. Once a man gets a piece of land, he's forever carryin it on his back. He's not his own master any longer."

In spite of the absence of Donal and the other skilled men, the gathering was even bigger that evening than it had been the night before. This time people clustered in small groups outside where a finger of cool air crept up from the river now and then. There was a question or an argument at the center of every group.

Was this the place to settle? Some had heard Si Maddox say all the good land in Ohio was gone already and the thing to do was go west to the Illinois country.

Wouldn't a man be a fool to load himself down with a hundred and sixty acres or even eighty with no one but himself and his family to work it? Anyone could see what it took to clear the land for the canal. But there would be no crew of axemen, no big canal plow with the team to pull it, no oxen to drag the logs away.

If there were good land and bad, how was a man to know which of those lots to bid on? More than one said he didn't come across the water looking for another hill to break with all the good land this country had.

Was there enough for all of them? The Yankees would be grabbing for it too, wouldn't they, if the land was good?

Some of the men new come from Ireland like Conn Mor couldn't seem to get their hands around the notion at all. They weren't yet accustomed to this canal camp and everything outside it was a chaos of strangeness. They hung around the edges of the groups listening, shaking their heads, exchanging a word or two with each other now and then.

Dan was asked to figure the cost at many different prices to the acre. Everyone talked as if he had enough for eighty acres, at least, but he well knew that some had it and some didn't.

By the end of the week, it was clear that some were as serious as Dan and Mary and some had a longing for it but the wish and the money didn't match. Dan suspected that the ones talking the biggest about going farther west were the ones needing something to hide their empty pockets. Kevin was like that. For all his swagger, he was still in debt to Jamie for bringing his wife over and his brother Mick the same.

It was agreed that on Sunday Dan, Tyrone, Johnny, Paddy, and Connie O'Riordan would go with Buck to look at the land that would be for sale. Connie was one just over from Ireland but it was understood that his father was a strong farmer and hadn't sent his son across the water penniless. The judgment of these five would be passed on to the rest.

The next morning, Mary was tossing her dreams of the farm into the air like birds, letting them swoop and whirl above her head.

"This big farm you gon have," Tessa said to her, "there'll be work aplenty."

"Plenty indeed, but we'll be workin for our own, buildin us a home we can stay in and our children after us."

"I done worked in the fields all my life till I got took in the house. Time comes you ready to leave the canal and go to farmin, Willie, he be near as big as a man.

Reckon you might need more'n just you and Mister Dan an your chillun to do all that work?"

It took Mary a moment to realize what Tessa was proposing, then she clapped her hand down on top of Tessa's and tossed another dream into the air.

"Think of us with such a place and hirin you like we was the Judge and Mrs. Laurence!" Then she added reluctantly, "But well I know that's years down the road. Dan says the money will go out like the rent the first six years and nothin comin in till we make our first crop."

Tessa's shoulders drooped. Donal wouldn't and Mary couldn't. It had been a small hope and it was soon gone.

A wind like this couldn't sweep through the camp without blowing Jamie's way. He said a word to this man or that, especially to those who came asking his advice. On Saturday, when supper was over, he kept all in the cookhouse.

"Now then." He stood up in front of them like a judge in the court, about to pass sentence. "This scheme you're talkin about, there's nothin but trouble in it. It wouldn't be a farm at all you'd be buyin. Nothin but a piece of rocks and trees with wild animals roamin through it, far from town, far from neighbors. You put out all your money to buy it and it will be years before you get a crop out of it. While you're fightin the trees to make a field, there'll be more payments to make on the place and taxes every year and not a goddamn thing comin in. What will you be eatin all them years? A smart man will do what I done, work for wages and save his money till he can buy a house in a city where there's things doin and jobs to be had."

He walked out without waiting to see if anyone had an answer, motioning Dan to follow with the paybook. The talk after they left was subdued. Mary could see his words had been swallowed like hard lumps of poor-cooked food.

After he looked over the paybook, Jamie had another speech for Dan. "It's your job to keep the men *on* the job, not give 'em these crackbrained thoughts about runnin off to Coshocton just because there's an auction goin on. You know there'll be no leavin the job for you to go to farmin. I got your word to stick with this job till it's over. If you ain't lost your wits entirely you'll go on from there to make somethin of yourself instead of gettin buried out in the woods."

"You have my word I'm stayin with your job till it's done. That will be soon enough to say do you want me for a foreman still and will I go on down the canal with you."

Already Dan felt that he had his own land at his back to anchor him in the new country. No longer was he a stranger to be blown here and there by a blast of words out of Jamie's mouth.

When a man had nothing but his hands, he had to reach for another man's tools and take another man's orders. When a man had land of his own, he got his own tools in his hands and took orders from no one.

"All I'm askin you now is a few hours out of Saturday next to go to Coshocton for the auction."

He didn't wait for Jamie to say yes or no but started out the door, saying, "I'll work the mornin through and be back in time to see to things at the day's end and mark the paybook."

There was no need to say anything to Jamie about going with Buck to look over the land. His time was his own on Sunday.

They left at sun-up for they had miles to go and all would be on foot except Buck. He would meet them at the Tuscarawas ford on horseback.

Sunday was a long day for those who stayed behind. Bridget and Molly began walking back and forth on the canal towpath in the afternoon, looking eastward. By evening, when the scouting party came back, there was a crowd to escort them to the cookhouse, where Mary had kept their suppers warm. It was quiet while they were eating but all eyes were on them.

Mary stared at Dan's face with the same intensity she had given the notice but this was a more readable record.

He's for it. He'll jump for it, he will indeed.

"The first thing is," Dan started the talk, "We made Buck a promise none of us would bid on the piece he wants. That's all he asked of us, to pay him back, like, for showin us the best places. The next thing is, no man could walk all over this land in a day. Buck had it from the surveyor, how there's parts of it has good water and from all that's growin there now, looks like good land when a man would get the trees down. All of it's hilly but his part has more level places ought to make good fields. That's what we looked at."

He's found a piece of it he likes. After all my worries, we're comin down the road to the farm.

Tyrone took up the tale. As he talked, Jamie strolled into the cookhouse and sat down, puffing on his pipe. Tyrone was saying he was ready to try for a one hundred and sixty acre lot but if the price went too high he would be satisfied with eighty.

"Better a small farm on good land than a whole mountain full of rocks."

"Better no piece of that wild tangle to deal with," Jamie gave his judgment. "That's well known to any man with sense in his head."

Mary wanted to throw his words back in his face but like the rest she kept quiet. Then Johnny picked up the talk where Tyrone had left it, as if Jamie were not there at all.

"For them that's got few dollars, Buck says there's not likely to be many biddin for that cheap land that's only twenty-five cents an acre."

"But if nobody wants it," Tom Quinlan objected. "Wouldn't that mean it's not worth buyin at all?"

"The way I look at it," Paddy spoke up for the first time, "Jamie is in the right of it. None of it's worth buyin. It's way off there in the woods, with no road to it. A man would have to stand there for the rest of his life, hittin at those trees with an axe. I don't call that a farm."

There was another silence. Mary looked at Bridget and got a sorrowful look back.

Without Bridget, without Maggie, who will be neighbor to me?

Johnny stood up with a motion of his hand as if to brush Paddy away. "All these farms around here, Judge Laurence's and all, they all looked like that once. If these Yankees can do it, a good Irishman can do it."

That brought cheers and yells, stamping of feet and pounding on the tables. Mary beamed. That was her old Johnny.

Paddy walked out with Bridget reluctantly following.

When the noise subsided, Joe Dawley, looking yellow from the canal fever but no longer shaking, asked "How many good lots is there? Enough for all?"

"There's four of those hundred and sixty acre pieces," Dan answered.

"One out for Buck leaves three and there's six eighty acre lots. There's more that could be good but we didn't have time to tramp around over them others."

"Only six? And look at all here," Joe waved his hand at the crowd of people. "How many of us is in it?"

"Maybe there's the full of a townland in it, if the price is low and none at all if the price is high," Tom suggested. "So how can a man tell if he's in it or not?"

When the day of the sale came, Dan had eighteen dollars and a bit more in his pocket and the number of the lot he wanted in his head. He had eleven dollars and thirty-seven cents of Joe Dawley's too. Joe's fever had him down again. Eileen had come to fetch Dan in the morning before work. Joe had given him the money with a trembling hand.

"That's every penny I got. Will you do what you can for me with it? I got to get a place and get off this damn canal. It's killin me."

There were a dozen men who headed for Coshocton after the noon meal. Bridget and Mary watched them go, Mary hopefully, Bridget sadly. Bridget's eyes were swollen from crying.

"It was my heart's wish, the two of us to be neighbors."

"It's neighbors we are now," Mary reminded her, "and neighbors we'll be till this job is done. And after? Who knows? Will Dan come back with a holdin or will he not?"

That was the question that was with her all the afternoon. As the hours passed, she went more than once to look out toward the job and see was Dan back. When she picked out his figure among the men she got a hollow feeling inside and her heart beat faster from then till he came in to the cookhouse after work was over. He pushed right up to the head of the line so he could say it to her.

"It's our land—eighty acres of it!"

Chapter 35

THERE WAS REJOICING in the Griffen shanty on the night of the land sale. Tyrone was there and Eileen and Joe. That was all that had come away with land.

Dan had to tell the story of the afternoon and then Mary prodded him with so many questions he had to tell it again in greater detail, leading up again to the glorious climax, the land that was now theirs.

"The big pieces of good land come up first. Buck wasn't the only man in Coshocton County that knew the best sections so one of 'em outbid him for the piece he most wanted. He had to pay a hundred and thirty-six dollars for his second choice. The prices went way up on the eighty-acre pieces too, and most of our folks dropped out when they saw the way the wind was blowin. Only myself and Tyrone and Johnny could stay in it. Johnny and his father-in-law O'Malley pooled their little money and borrowed from Michael who had it out of his stoneworker's wages."

"Things went so fast," Tyrone said, "a man could hardly keep up with 'em. When one piece went, a man had to put it to himself would he try for the next one and he better not be slow in givin himself the answer. One there I wanted, but before I could get my wits together, I lost it to a local man. And when another piece come up, there was Dan goin after it."

"My throat went so dry on me, I could hardly croak out a bid," Dan said. "It looked sure that, like the other good pieces, this one would get away from the Irish, too. There was two of them others after it. But at sixty-five dollars, one gave up. I said sixty-six. It crept up a dollar at a time between him and me an then by the half-dollars. I knew I had to show him I meant to stay with it till I got it, so when he said seventy an a half I jumped right up to seventy-two. If the other fella had knocked twenty-five cents more out of it, I was a lost man. I jumped up to seventy-two like I had my pockets full enough to go to eighty. But eighteen was what I needed for a quarter of seventy-two, and eighteen was what I had—eighteen dollars and fourteen cents. The man kept hollerin 'Seventy-two bid. Seventy-two.' The other fella didn't lay another penny on it."

"If Dan can do it I says to myself, I can do it," Tyrone took his turn. "There was only one of them good lots left and I could see Johnny wanted it too, but I got it for seventy dollars."

"I thought Johnny and O'Malley would come to blows," Dan said. "Johnny wanted to bid on that lot, but O'Malley was puttin against it. He's a cautious man, O'Malley is, very near himself, very near. He wanted to wait for a cheaper piece. But when the cheaper land come up and O'Malley wanted to try for it, Johnny threw up his head and walked off from it, so they come back with nothin."

Joe wasn't interested in what Johnny didn't get. He wanted to hear all about the buying of *his* land.

"When the fifty cents an acre lots come up, I tried twice to get one for Joe, but both times the price went to fifty dollars, more than twelve down. The third time I bid forty-six and got it. That took every bit of Joe's money and thirteen cents of mine."

Dan took a penny out of his pocket and slapped it down on the table. "There's our last penny," he said. "Will we buy a pig with it?"

"You'll have your thirteen cents back on the first payday," Joe promised. "And my thanks with it. Ah, now, I want to see my own place so bad I can taste it."

Joe tasted the whiskey in his noggin instead but he smacked his lips on it. "Would it be near yours, think you, Dan?"

"There's no knowin. We could be next neighbors, or we could be a mile apart. When the fever's off you, we'll go east there again where we was with Buck. You can set your feet on your own land and we'll see will it be a short road or a long one between our two places."

"I'll be on my own place the first day after the next payday," Tyrone said, "and then away with me to Cincinnati where my family is and bring 'em back. We'll have a cabin up before the winter and enough land cleared by the spring to do a little plantin. I got one big boy and a son-in-law to help with the work and my wife and daughter and the young ones to do their part."

He beamed around on all of them. "'Tis an ease to my heart now to have my own place at last."

That was the proud feeling they all had. They drank to it and gave each other a warm goodnight.

There was no rejoicing in the other shanties that night. The next day the camp was sullenly recovering from the euphoria that had swept in with the first hopes of the land sale. Work resumed on Monday and the old routine again dominated the life of the camp. It was made worse by the fact that this was the heel of the work year, the time of the unremitting heat, the mosquitoes and the canal fever.

Dublin had been the heart of the camp. The dream of a new Dublin had been its soul. Though the dream had been buffeted by the influx of new men, threatened by the defection of the stoneworkers and the loss of the Flynns, it had been there still. Now it was gone.

Bridget went around with the long face on her till Paddy answered the reproach in her eyes with his fists.

"You're the one has the luck, Mary," she said the next day, "with a man never lifts a hand on you. Paddy hardly ever hits me. He's been a good man to me, you know that. But he can't stand for me to cross him and when he starts hittin me, seems like he can't stop till he's wore out. Oh, Blessed Jesus, last night I wanted to crawl away and die."

Mary put an arm around her and she sobbed into her friend's shoulder, then wiped her eyes and turned back to the work.

"Now we'll be off down the canal somewhere when this job is over and you and Eileen will be neighbors to each other."

The reality of their own land diminished for Mary as the days of work went by without a chance for her to lay eyes on it and the dream of it was no longer the same.

*What storytellers will come in of an evening to sit by the hearth? What neigh-
bor women will there be to give help to in time of sickness, to call on in time of
need, to make a pleasant river of talk out of the trickle that will be comin from
each about the old days and the new ways, about the men and the children, about
the week's news from hereabouts and the little bits of the year's news that find
their way across the water? Only young Eileen and Tyrone's wife I never laid
eyes on.*

It wasn't only the future that was beyond the canal building that separated
them from the others. Already there was a difference in Dublin. The gaps that
had opened between Dan and some of his mates when he became a foreman were
widening. The landless ones looked on the lucky owners of land with envy.

"It's a sorrow to me, you not to have land with us," Mary said to Johnny, "and
you with us from the day we set foot in this country."

Johnny had come along as she sat in her doorway on a Sunday afternoon. Her
work over, she was trying to catch a breath of cool air as she watched the children
who had some kind of a game going in the shade of the big oak tree.

He was carrying a bucket of water and would have passed on after tossing her
a gay greeting but when she spoke, he set the bucket down and looked over at the
children without seeing them.

"Och," he said with a shrug. "Land is for the likes of Dan that's got the big pay
at the end of the month. Me and Niall and Kevin and Mick and the rest, we're
down in the ditch like we was back in Sligo, with the farmers up on top givin the
orders."

He picked up his bucket, saying his friend Niall, who lodged with him and
Molly, was perishing with fever and thirst. He hesitated a moment, looking at her
for the first time.

"Ah, well, go to your farm then and good luck go with you."

The canal fever came back on Dan that month and soon after, Danny got it too.
Each time someone went down, Mary was gripped with fear of the typhus. She
had an experienced eye for the difference but the canal fever was bad enough.
There was little she could do for the two of them. Tim had to carry the water to
the shanty. Ellen had to stay in the sound of her father's and her brother's voices
to give them a cup of Mary's thoroughwort tea or a cool rag to wipe the sweat
from their faces.

As for the other men that came down with it, one was lucky if a Dublin woman
would do him a kindness. Aghna Casey proved to be the one with the biggest
heart for helping the lone men. She was the mistress of the Casey shanty. She
took care of Mick and her own little one and was more of a mother to Una's two
than Una herself. The men downed by the fever were so many more children to
her and she did what she could for them.

There was a lot of working in the water now that the river was low. It wasn't
the hell it had been in the cold of the winter but it was hard and unpleasant and
was going slowly with some of the Dublin workers out with the fever and many of
the local men gone from the canal as they always were at harvest time.

When Dan was unable to make it to the job, Jamie got worn out with the added work on top of the worry and the heat. He was short of temper, cursing the men for a lazy stupid bunch of sluggards. They responded to the lash of his tongue with a show of speed when he was in sight and with curses of their own when he was out of hearing.

Bosses and men, women, and children all lived through each day and looked to the same future for relief: The cool days of autumn when the sharp frost would cut off the miasma that breathed up out of the mud and seemed to bring the fever.

The more distant future grew more and more hazy in contrast to the rock-hard reality and unremitting demands of the workdays. What was certain was that Mary and Dan would be alone with the children in the dark woods, away from the sound of Irish voices. There would be only the hostile trees, standing where they had stood for centuries, watching over the comings and going of wild things, the passing to and fro of Erie, Wyandot and Lenape, reminding newcomers that they were strangers to the land.

Part Three

Seed
of the
Fire

The Aqueduct

T HE WALHONDING AQUEDUCT was rising above the water and the surrounding land, an imposing product of the materials given up by the Ohio earth and of the labor assembled from as close as Tuscarawas Township, as far as County Cork.

The abutment on the Dublin side of the river was now a high curved wall, backed by great blocks of stone weighing hundreds of pounds. Though not yet finished, its size and its contours were unmistakable. The abutment against the opposite bank was well started and would soon match it. The way the two would hold back the crumbling earth behind them and resist the ceaseless motion of the water before them was plain even to those who had never before seen such massive stonework.

There had certainly never been anything like the aqueduct in Coshocton County. Even the settlers who had come here from the East had forded more rivers than they had ferried and ferried more than they had crossed on bridges. The unbridged Ohio was the boundary between the old lives and the new. Here at the Forks, there were no bridges over the Tuscarawas, the Walhonding or the Muskingum. A stone bridge of such dimensions would have been a wonder. This great structure that would carry boats above and across the river on a river of its own was a wonder greater still.

Rivers have always been barriers and boundaries as well as highways but no barrier was to stand in the way of the canal. No sudden force of storm or flood would be allowed to deter it, no accustomed ways of the ancient river would prevail against it.

Some men looked on the aqueduct with hostility. They resented the coming of changes planned and built by strangers. They distrusted fences and towns and courthouses and canals with their squares and straight lines crossing the curving land to hem men in or to channel their movements.

Others looked on the aqueduct with anticipation, seeing past the months of building to years of commercial dealings. Before the last stone was laid they were calculating the opportunities it would bring for wealth from sober business or daring speculation.

Caldersburgh had never been anything but a couple of houses, a store, and a dream in the head of its first settler, now long since dead. Now the building of a town was Joshua Laurence's dream to realize. He and Engineer Dent planned to buy land and plat the town that would surely grow as other towns were growing along the new waterway. Laurence was proud that his own land, the stone from his quarry, the timber from his woods, the labor from his workers were going into the canal that would make this possible.

Most Coshocton County men were fascinated by the work itself. Many of them had laid log on log or stone on stone but they had never worked with such mountains of cut stone and hewn timber. They had gathered together to raise a barn or a cabin but a group of neighbors was a mere handful compared to these swarming crews of laborers, carpenters and masons. Their own few axes, mauls and wedges, even the tool kits of the carpenters who built the new frame houses, were puny compared to these giant pile drivers and derricks.

Some local men came to work on the aqueduct for days or weeks, even months. Others came as often as they could, walking or on horseback or driving their teams, to observe its progress.

Pryor Foster, the black smith—always spoken of that way, with a separation between the words because he was a black man as well as a blacksmith—had his own way of looking at the aqueduct. He could appreciate the craft that went into the well-wrought ironwork that hinged lock gates and held the gates' planks together. There would be much more of such work when they put the wooden trough across from one abutment to the other. Foster looked at this new route from south to north, though, with something else in mind. Would it carry any of his folks who were fleeing? There would have to be a special way to load that cargo and handle that boat but he would keep it in mind.

Coshocton County women were not moved by the aqueduct in the same way as the men. There was no place for them on its crews, no way to relate its work to their own. They worked with different and less enduring materials. They cooked meals that disappeared more rapidly than they were prepared; swept, washed, scrubbed what would be dirty again in an hour or a day; churned butter that disappeared in a week, planted beans in the spring for summer picking; dried fruit and salted meat in the summer for winter eating; raised chicks from the shell to lay their own eggs before the year was out; made clothes that were soon worn threadbare and in need of patching. Their truly unique and most intense labor produced a new generation. The changes wrought by their greatest skills were invisible changes in growing children, unseen ties among people.

The women saw the aqueduct as a door out of isolation, a bridge to the civilized East, a road for the coming of more families, a magnet drawing together the scattered human fragments in town and country that might be molded into a community when the strangers who now labored here were gone.

To the women of Dublin, the aqueduct was a job for their men on such a scale that it was keeping them in one place for many months, a welcome pause in their ever-moving and uncertain life. It drew such numbers of men to the camp as to provide work for every woman in the cookhouse or in lodging and feeding as many as she could get into her own shanty. The very fragility and brevity of Dublin's existence made the women cling close to it, sheltering themselves against the world outside the camp, binding the little community together with the ways of living they had brought across the water.

The aqueduct would belong to the people in this part of Ohio when it was completed, when the disorderly manifestations of construction were gone and the canal boats were moving. It would remain as imposing evidence that Coshocton had settled into this part of the Ohio earth solidly, permanently. Canal boats would take their crops to market. In return, they could aspire to things that had always been too remote or too dear, things that would come from New York and Philadelphia, even from England, to be unloaded on the wharves of the Caldersburgh canal front. Coshocton County would be firmly part of the nation that stretched east to the Atlantic and west to the ever-moving frontier, a nation new enough that its permanence still needed affirmation and reaffirmation.

The aqueduct belonged to the Irish workers intensely in the present, not at all in the future. Now it was their job and their livelihood. They were making a little more of it every day. The river that had swept away some of their work in the winter flood had been mastered: Piles driven firmly into its bed, timber and stone raised above its now calm and rippling waters. The feel of its materials, the sight of its growth were part of their lives. It was the most tangible piece of the canal world that had become familiar, its driving purpose known, its values and its rules understood, its hierarchy delineated. Both masons and laborers saw it with pride as the work of their hands.

The Ohio men who worked with them shared that pride but they were farmers who would be back on their farms when the aqueduct was finished. When that time came, the canal workers would leave the aqueduct behind and go on working, building another part of this canal. Beyond that, the working future was too hazy for more than occasional speculation, half-formed hopes.

Only Jamie and Simon saw that future in terms of certain hoped-for contracts. Sections farther down the line would be let early in 1829. McCarthy and Lordon would have a good chance at the new contracts if they could get the foundations of the aqueduct's four piers in before winter and the first courses of masonry laid from pier to pier. That would show the Commissioner that the aqueduct could be completed during the following spring and summer, freeing them to go on to other jobs.

Chapter 36

WHEN HE HEARD the welcome blast of the noon horn on this sunny fall day, Dan leaned against one of the pile drivers and wiped the sweat from his face with his sleeve. His second bout with malaria had left him yellower, thinner, not quite so quick moving. More than two years on the canal had made him more confident, more deliberate. He would follow the men streaming toward the cookhouse in his own time.

He was in charge of building a cofferdam out in the river that was to be large enough to make the foundations of two piers inside it, two of the four that would hold up the aqueduct. Jamie was getting another coffer started for the other two, working from the opposite bank. October had come and the piers must be above the river before it began to rise again. Simon was shuttling back and forth between the two abutments, supervising the masonry.

It was Danny blowing on the horn. Still weak from the canal fever, he was back under Mary's eye. What reconciled him to it were the proud moments when he blew the horn that called the camp to rise in the morning to start the work and to come to meals.

A group of strangers was waiting for Dan on the river bank. He jumped from the scow holding the pile driver onto the dock that helped them carry their work out into the river. A closer look at the men showed that none were carrying tools. There were no carpenters or masons among them. All were diggers—laborers—general canal hands.

One stepped forward, taking off his hat. "God bless the work. You the boss on this job, sir?"

Dan headed for the cookhouse, telling them to come along. Jamie needed more hands and he could use a couple himself. This coffer was almost finished but there would be a lot of pumping to empty the pit inside it, then sixty-eight piles to drive within the pit for each of the piers.

The man who had spoken fell into step beside Dan and gave his name as Art Sheean. He was a rugged-looking fellow, the contours of his face obscured by a bristly stubble but the light smooth tone of his voice gave away his youth. When Jamie caught up to them he sized them up quickly, his eyes travelling from one to the other.

"Mr. Laughry would give us a character," Sheean said, "or Mr. Dent."

Jamie nodded. "Allright, I can use you."

"What's the pay?"

"Twelve and whack—and it's good whack."

"The pay when we go in the water?"

"We don't make no difference in the water or out but we'll keep summer pay into the winter. Work will be steady."

"We been gettin thirteen on Laughry's job up to the Tuscarawas aqueduct and seventy-five cents a day for work in water."

"I pay twelve. Come on, Dan, let's get some dinner."

He turned his back on them and walked off. Before they got to the cookhouse, Sheean caught up with them.

"We'll take twelve, do you make it seventy-five cents for work in water."

Jamie moved close to him and put a hand on his shoulder. "I don't like to pay you more than the other lads is gettin but I like your looks, I like your experience. You'll get seventy-five when you go in the water but keep it to yourselves, will you now?"

He pointed out a shanty where there would be room for them to sleep and sent them in to the cookhouse to get their dinner.

"Good strong lads," he told Dan, "but that damn Laughry pays too much."

"It'll get out, you payin them more and that'll be nothin but trouble."

Jamie smiled. "Keep them on the dry work and send the others in the water."

"You puttin them all in my crew?"

"You can have two of 'em. Cut out two-three of the sluggards. Them that didn't do nothin but lie in their beds and moan all through the heat. Draggin around now like sick cows."

Dan's brows drew together. "Who is it you called a sick cow?"

"Not you, man, not you. You're the same man you always were, barrin them few days the fever had you bad. You know which ones it is don't carry their weight."

"Where will you put the slow ones?"

Jamie was heading for his dinner. He tossed the words over his shoulder. "On the road out of here."

On the way back to the job after dinner, Dan noticed Tom walking with Sheean. It was damn full sure that with every tip of his head Tom was throwing a question up at the new man. And Jamie thought his promise of more wages for work in water would stay in his pocket! Ah well, time enough to bid the devil good morrow when you meet him. He had devil enough to deal with this day already.

He watched the men closely that afternoon with Jamie's orders in mind but he knew already which ones were lagging. It was Joe Dawley, Niall O'Dowd and Fat Seumas. Joe hadn't worked off his debt to Jamie yet so he was safe. It would have to be the other two. Jamie's words meant they weren't to be allowed to finish the month out. When Saturday came, Dan told them to get their pay.

He went to the Caldersburgh tavern that night with Paddy and Dennis. They got uproariously and then soggily drunk. Dan lay in bed the next morning, letting breakfast go by, sleeping long into the afternoon. Mary sent Ellen up with a plate of dinner for him. It was still untouched when Mary came in herself.

"Is it another bout of fever on you?" she asked.

"Nah." He pushed away the hand she had laid on his forehead and sat up. "It's nothin but the week's work and the night's drink."

She sat beside him at the table while he ate the cold food. "You know Jamie turned off Niall and that fat lad that was took so bad with the fever?"

Dan grunted. She took that for 'yes.'

"Och, poor Niall, it's only the day before the sickness struck him he sent off the money to bring his old people over. How will he keep them now?"

"Jamie's not the only contractor in the world."

"What boss will take him while he's still got the shakes?"

Dan finished his food and would have risen but she put out a hand to stop him.

"What some says, it was you turned them off and Joe would have gone too, but for bein a friend to you and havin the land beside you."

"Christ Almighty! What ninnyhammer says that? Joe better look lively or he'll be out on the road too, when he's got the dead horse killed."

When the cofferdam was finished Dent brought them two pumps to add to the four they had used for the previous operations. They would have four men for each pump, one on each of a pump's two handles till they tired, the other two to relieve them. Jamie, Dent, and Laurence were all there the morning the pumping began.

The pump handles went up and down, the pumps sucked up the water inside the dam and sent it splashing out over the outside wall into the river. Two hours later, when the breakfast horn sounded, the water inside seemed no lower than the river.

"Looks like that double coffer was a mistake," Laurence said. "Either that . . ." he looked over at Dan, "or it's faulty construction."

"It's a big pit." Jamie wasn't ready to give up on it. "Let half the men go to their breakfast," he told Dan. "Keep the rest at it till the others is back."

In mid-morning, Dent halted the pumping. As soon as the sand that had been stirred up by the action of the pumps had settled and the water was clear enough to see below the surface, Dent and Jamie walked the top of the cofferdam, looking below for telltale bubbles that would indicate leaks. They stamped on the fill between the two rows of sheetpiling and prodded it to test its solidity. Dan watched anxiously.

"It looks pretty tight," Dent admitted when they had been all around the dam. "I can't see it leaking in any place. Seems like it's coming in at the bottom as fast as you pump it out the top. We didn't get through all the loose gravel with the piling or else we've hit some loam or quicksand. You'll have to pump hard to get the pit emptied. Once the water is out, it will take one hell of a lot of pumping to fight the seepage while we're driving in the piles and cutting them off."

It was a relief to Dan that Dent was not faulting his work. He got the pumps started again and kept them going without a stop, even for dinner. Mary sent Danny down with bread and meat so each could take a bite when his turn came to let go of a pump handle. If someone faltered, Dan grabbed a handle himself till a replacement stepped in.

As it grew dark, the hands who had been working on the other cofferdam dragged up wood to keep a fire burning on the riverbank, held torches when the water was measured, took a turn on a pump handle when one of the others was ready to drop, or sat on the bank watching. When the watchers drifted away, the night grew quiet except for the thump-thump of the pumps and the gush of the water.

Mary and Tessa brought bread and tea down to the job in the middle of the night, then went back to the cookhouse to prepare early breakfast for the night workers and to set another batch of bread to rise.

Jamie went off for a few hours of sleep sometime after midnight. When he and Dent returned at daylight, the water level had been reduced but not nearly enough. The night's work was for nothing.

"Knock off, men." Jamie raised his voice so all could hear. "Knock off."

The pumps were silenced. The gushing of the water stopped. For the first time since the previous morning, the murmur of the river could be heard. The tired men went back to Dublin to eat and sleep.

Dan stumbled as he came off the dock and sank to his knees in the shallow water at the river's edge. He could barely summon up the strength to get back on his feet.

"We'll have to divide the cofferdam," Jamie told him as they walked away from the river, "and build the piers one at a time."

"That's more work in water. The Laughry men will have to be in it. There's bad feelin against 'em already, them bein dry since they started and against me too, for givin them the dry work when the old hands is in the water. This is the first time I didn't give every man a fair shake. Art wants to go in the water for the extra pay that's in it for him, so he thinks."

"If Laughry wasn't so soft in the head, givin in to the men every time they holler about gettin their feet wet, they'd be workin for the same as the rest and glad of it. And damned if you don't be just like him. Bad feelins they got, you're tellin me. We got a coffer to build. We can't stop for nobody's bad feelins."

So Dan turned a deaf ear to the complaints of the men who were getting their fill of the wet work. When Art pushed for a chance to get in it, Dan told him to shut his gob and do what he was told.

It was almost the end of a workday a week later when they finished getting the coffer divided. They tried the pumps just to see if they might succeed this time. The engineer and the bosses watched hopefully.

After two hours, Dent threw up his hands. "It's like trying to empty the river with a teacup."

The only thing to do was drive the piles through the water, meanwhile rounding up more pumps. It would be a harder and longer job than driving them in an empty pit but they would have to dewater only to cut off the piles and get the timbers and the first courses of stone on.

As the autumn days shortened, the workdays shortened but Dan was exhausted by each nightfall and so was his crew. There was no energy left for anything but the usual grumbling and cursing, sometimes at the job, sometimes at each other. Joe could no longer drag himself to work and was replaced by Toby Weaver.

Mary quietly slipped a little food to Eileen to keep life in the Dawley family till Joe could work again.

On the second Wednesday in November they had all sixty-eight of the big oak pilings driven in and were ready to begin pumping again. Jamie brought over his crew so they could have forty-eight men working twelve pumps, double the number they had before.

The drop in the water level was agonizingly slow. As one team gave up its place on a pump, the men would get something to eat or drink and fall heavily to rest on the ground. After an hour, they would go back while the other team rested. By the day's end, they were falling asleep in their rest periods. At sunset, Jamie gave out a jigger of whiskey to each man when the shift changed and told them they would continue all night but there would be another jigger for them at midnight. By morning they would certainly have the water far enough down to cut off the piles.

All the cooking was going on over the fire on the riverbank so no time would be wasted by the men going back and forth to the cookhouse. Mary had enlarged her crew so some could sleep while others worked. Dan had a few hours of broken rest, lying on the ground with his coat over him and his feet toward the fire. Even asleep his muscles were jerking like he was still at the pumps.

At dawn the pit was low in comparison to the river around it but still a deep pool with the tops of some of the piles sticking out. It was far from low enough. Dent and the bosses gauged the night's progress and talked about where they could get more pumps. While the bosses talked, the pump handles slowed.

"No, no, don't slack," Jamie yelled. "Keep it goin. We're close enough to it, we'll keep it up till we make it all the way down."

Something between a sigh and groan swept over the men on the bank but they began to move slowly up the plank onto the dock.

Asa McKendrie was standing by the fire warming his hands around a tin cup of hot tea. He swallowed what was left and tossed the cup away. It struck against a rock with a sharp 'ping' that turned heads in his direction.

"I'm goin home to sleep," he announced. "All you workin fools can go on jumpin ever time the Judge or Ol' McCarthy cracks the whip. Nobody's gonna tell me to work all day and all night and then all day again. If they want their damn puddle drained, they can drink it. If they had two bits worth of sense they'd know the river'll come back on 'em if they pump from now till Christmas."

The relief crew hesitated. Dan strode forward. "Come on, lads, give your mates a rest," he shouted. "Let the old man go if he can't work no more. We've got the daylight with us now and we'll have that water down in a few more hours. The harder we pump, the sooner we'll do it."

The relief crew surged forward and took the handles. Dan stepped into Asa's place till Jamie could get another man for it. The hope of seeing the end of this endless workday kept them going for a few hours but as the day wore on, the work lagged. At sunset Jamie admitted defeat, halted the work and let the men stumble off to their beds.

"Will we be eatin here by the waterside, comes the morn?" Mary asked Jamie. She got a curt "yes."

Mary and Dan were wakened next morning by a thundering knock at the door. Their limbs were so heavy they seemed to be fastened to the bed. They stared stupidly at the door till it opened and Jamie burst in.

"Are all of y' dead?" he demanded. "It's full daylight. Get that boy of yours out with his horn."

Dan sat up, pushed his hair out of his face, stared at Jamie. "What is it the day? Pumpin again?"

"Yes, yes. Up with you, damn it."

Dan got his two legs out from under the blanket and over the edge of the bed. "How is it we can do the day what we couldn't do yesterday?"

"Danny!" Jamie bellowed in the direction of the loft. "We can do it," he answered Dan, "the way Corny and me got two more pumps working and set up, ready. And the Judge ought to be back by night with more."

Danny came tumbling down the ladder with his horn and went outside to blow.

"Wouldn't you be steppin out too," Dan requested, "so decent people can get out of their beds?"

"That Jamie," Mary complained when he was gone, "breakin down the door like a bailiff's man. No manners to him at all, at all." She kept up a steady stream of invective while she got up and put her dress on over her shift.

"Hugh!" she called up the ladder to Cadigan, their only lodger since Michael and Johnny married. "Down with you now. I got m'self dressed. You too, Timmy." She got a rumble from Hugh and a moan from Tim in response.

"No horn for you, acushla," she said under her breath, looking down at Ellen who had slept through it all. "Sleep, sleep."

Jamie kept Danny blowing away. The Dublin people were slow to turn out this morning. One by one they began to emerge. Dan counted those coming out and went into one shanty to see why they were a man short.

"Come on, man," Dan said, pulling Connie O'Riordan out of the blankets. "Up with you."

"Yes, yes. I'm up, indeed," Connie mumbled without opening his eyes. He immediately fell back. Dan yanked him up again. "Up with you, damn it, or I'll give you a skelp will wake you."

As the reluctant force headed for the job, Dan saw there were still two missing. Worse than that, of the local men who had gone to their homes or their boarding houses for the night, most had not returned.

"You'll lose more men out of it, if you work us all day and all night again," Dan warned Jamie.

"You'll get your crew on the job with the sun on the morrow and not in the middle of the day like this or you'll answer to me for it," was Jamie's reply.

The day lasted till midnight when the Judge returned with four additional pumps. There was no way of keeping this force working while the new pumps were maneuvered into place and eight more men set to work. It would take every one of the men who had been working across the river. Again, the pumps were abandoned. Only Dan and a few others remained to get things set up for the following day.

When Mary and Dan got back to their shanty, they were surprised to see a few men still up and moving about the camp.

"A drink or two before they turn in," Dan said. "I'd do the same if I could stay awake for it."

Chapter 37

MARY RAISED her head and looked over at the fireplace. Weak daylight was coming down the chimney and spreading over the cold ashes. There was seldom a fire on their own hearth any more. All it was good for was to give her the bad news it was morning.

Danny didn't respond to her calls. She took a few steps up the ladder till her head was in the loft, reached out for Danny's leg and gave it a jerk.

"Up with you, Danny boy, or Jamie will be thunderin in here like yeomen after the guns."

She heard him rustling about while she shivered herself into her dress. Then his agitated voice called down that his horn was gone. Too sleepy to see in front of his face, she thought, and the loft dark as night. She opened the door wide to let more light in, roused Tim, looked under his blanket and Danny's, surveyed the loft. Unless Hugh was asleep on top of it, it wasn't there.

"You left it down by the river."

"I did not. Did I, Tim?"

"He did not. He dropped it on Ellen when we was comin up the ladder and she bawled like she was killed with it but there was no hurt on her."

The horn must be below somewhere. Mary thought. She searched around Ellen, waking her, and all over the cabin but there was no sign of it. Ellen sat up in bed, watching.

"Danny lost his ho-orn." She made a tune of it. "Danny lost his ho-orn. He won't never find it. Never, never, never."

Mary seized her by the arm and shook the tune out of her. "Where is it?"

"It's hidin. Danny won't never find it."

"Where is it?" Danny yelled down from where he and Tim were hanging over the edge of the loft. "If I don't blow, I'm in bad trouble with the boss. Where is it? Where is it?"

Ellen's eyes got big and she repeated wonderingly, "Where is it?"

By this time, Dan was awake and growling at the lot of them, not yet having it through his sleep-thick head what it was all about.

Ellen looked from mother to father to brothers and began to cry. "Danny hit me with it," she sobbed. "He threw it on me."

"I did not. It dropped out of my hand itself, like."

"Holy saints above." Mary was exasperated. "Pranks and quarrels in the dark of the mornin and the boss about to come down on us like a pile-driver. Keep the mouth on you shut, Danny, and let me get it out of her. Ellen. Tell your mother the God's truth. Where is the horn?"

"I don't know," Ellen wailed. "It went out the door."

"Out the door? On its own two legs? Someone snatched it? Who was it?"

Ellen opened her mouth, then clapped her hand over it.

Dan was standing beside Mary now. "You tell who took that horn, or Danny won't be the only one in trouble. Who was it?"

Ellen shrank back from the two angry faces. Father and Mother had to bend over to hear the whisper. "Johnny."

At that, Ellen was left staring as the storm that had been threatening passed over her head and out of the shanty.

Mary watched Dan and the boys go out into the foggy morning. What could Johnny be up to?

"This is the longest week God ever made. Come along, ma ghrianach, there's breakfast to cook. You won't be sleeping any more after all this pullalue. I wonder if Hugh slept through it all?" She raised her voice.

"Hugh! Hugh Cadigan! Suas libh! Daylight!" There was no response from above. She called louder till Hugh's face appeared at the top of the ladder.

"Stow it for the sake of Christ," he roared. "Can't you let a man sleep?"

"It's time to go to work."

"Go to work, then. There's no work for Hugh Cadigan the day." His face disappeared. The loft boards shook as he dropped back on his tick.

"Now what in God's name does he mean by that? There's no sense to this day at all." The only thing sure for Mary was that she had work to do, so she went off to it, Ellen trailing after.

Dan pounded on Johnny's door, loud enough to wake all of Dublin. Horn or no, some should be stirring but the camp was dead quiet.

"Johnny Brennigan! Out here with yourself and the horn. Brennigan! Johnny Brennigan!"

There was an answering grunt from inside. The door opened and Johnny stood there with his arms folded and his chin in the air. Dan threw a volley of 'fools' and 'scoundrels' at him, asking when would he stop being a gorsoon and make a man of himself, the way he picked such a day for a prank with the horn.

"Give it up, now. I well know it's you has it. We got the truth out of the girl, so don't bother yourself denyin it."

"No use for you to go barkin after the horn," Johnny said. "Danny here could blow all day and not a man would be comin. We made it up amongst us last night—no pumpin the day. We're wore out with it."

Dan was going so pell-mell after the horn, he began asking Johnny didn't he know it was past time to be on the job and the boss would be down on Danny and on Johnny himself. Before he had it all said, the words stopped tumbling out of his mouth, came slowly, one by one, stopped in mid-sentence with a question: "What is it you're tellin me?"

"I'm tellin you, you and Jamie can do your own pumpin the day. Day and night and night and day we've been at it till we're near dead with it."

"Give me the horn and I'll blow up a crew."

"Will you now?"

Dan made a move as if to pass through the door but Johnny barred the way.

"Forget the blasted horn. It was every man sayin he wouldn't pump decided it. I pinched the horn a minute before you come back from the job last night, thinkin the lads might as well have their sleep comfortable is all."

"If that's all, let me have it then."

Johnny laughed.

The laugh and the things Johnny had been saying rang in Dan's head till there was no way to get an understanding of them at all. Why was he suddenly alone in this unnatural quiet? He had come out to rouse his crew and march off at the head of them, as on every other day. Now his crew seemed to have evaporated into the impenetrable fog, leaving him behind.

"Don't you think I'm near dead with it m'self?" he asked Johnny.

"Like as not." There was agreement in the words, but none in the voice.

Dan pushed his hair back as if that would make room in his head to think about this thing being thrown at him and himself without a hint in the night or on the day before of what was coming. He could see Molly and her father moving up into the doorway.

Without turning his head, Johnny said to them, "You stay out of this. It's between m'self and Dan."

"It's between yourself and Jamie." Dan was putting some of it together now. "Isn't it what I was sayin to him? 'You'll lose more men out of it on the morrow, if you work the guts out of them today,' I says."

"That was the kind thoughts you had for us, was it? Kind thoughts for Niall too, when you put him out on the road. And kind thoughts for Johnny Brennigan, is it? When you tell Jamie who's at the bottom of his troubles."

They stared at each other like strangers. Dan was feeling the sharp pain of the knife Johnny was sticking into him with those words. His brows drew together. He said slowly and emphatically, "Don't you put that name on me, Johnny. I never turned in a man in my life."

Johnny bent his head, looking down at his foot where he was kicking dust with it. When he raised it again there was pain in his eyes, too.

"That was your days back in Cork. Many's the time I wished I was fightin along with you in them days. This here on the canal . . . I don't know. It's the big farmer you are now, or Jamie's man entirely. What I do know, wherever you are with it, it's not with us."

How could things get into such a brutheen that Johnny thinks me against them?
My own people! They don't know Dan Griffen. Jamie's man, indeed. If Johnny
knew how I pushed and shoved against Jamie to get the foreman's pay out of him . .

He walked away, the boys silently following but he had gone only a few steps
when he whirled and seized a shoulder of each.

"You never heard a word that passed between me and Johnny. You lost the horn
but you don't know what happened or who snatched it. Do you understand?"

They were bewildered but both nodded solemnly.

"Nothin to Jamie on it, nothin to Simon." Dan looked from one to the other, to be
certain they were getting the seriousness of it. "Nothin to no other boy neither."

The sharp pain had driven the night thickness from his head. He was thinking
fast of what was to come, what was to do, what was to be said to Jamie. He looked
up and saw Johnny still standing in the door. He walked back just a few steps, yet
it was as if he were returning from a long distance to the days when they were like
brothers. "How many knows about you takin the horn?"

"One only besides Molly and O'Malley and you."

"Good. Don't brag on it. It's the one thing could put the name of leader on
you. Stick together and don't push nobody up to the fore. Best be in your bed
now, like the rest of 'em. But wait . . . Is the stonies in it, too?"

"No, just us that's been at the pumps since Adam was a boy."

So the first thing was to wake the stonies or Simon would be down on him
along with Jamie. Did Dennis and Michael know what was up? What was left of
the embankment crew was mixed in with the other hands. He would have to bang
on every door anyway, to see were they together truly or was it Johnny and a few
of his mates, only. First there was a hole that needed a plug in it.

"Off with you to your mother," he said to the boys. "Tell her . . . tell her your
horn is gone and *no one knows who took it.* Tell her I sent that word to her and
the word to watch over Ellen's mouth."

"Breakfast here in the cookhouse and dinner by the river again," Mary was
saying to Tessa and Aghna when Bridget came in. "Not that we're much better
here, the way there's not walls enough to keep the wind out. When will Jamie let
us eat like Christians again?"

"I didn't know was I to come or not," Bridget said, standing there as if there
were nothing to do. "Paddy told me last night not to wake him and there was no
horn blowin the morn. It was beyond my knowin was there to be work this day.
What is it, Mary?"

"Danny wasn't ablowin of his horn," Mary began.

Aghna broke in on her. She had an answer for Bridget and couldn't wait to get
it out. "What's in it, the men pledged each other not one would be pumpin the
day. I told you, Mary, I'd be first up with Tessa, so I come. While men is men
they'll be eatin, pumpin or no, but sleep will be comin first for the men this day,
so it will."

"Who give orders for the work to stop?" Bridget wondered. "Wasn't Jamie after sayin last night the pumpin was to go on?"

Mary had no answer. In the quiet, she could hear Ellen singing her little tune again, "Danny lost his ho-orn . . ." She was sitting on the hearth, rhythmically striking on the stone beside her with a stick as she sang.

So that was why Hugh said there was no work for him, why Johnny took the horn so Danny couldn't blow the camp out of bed. Where was Dan in it? Did he know, even, what the men were about, the way he went pounding on Johnny's door?

"It's not the orders," Aghna was saying. "It's our own men took it in their own hands. Jamie won't be drivin them to the work day and night like cattle to market."

Mary walked out to the foot of the path and looked up. The O'Malley shanty wasn't in sight. She could hear the voices but not the words. Tessa continued with the work but the other two came out, thinking there was something to see, then followed Mary back in. Aghna was still talking.

"I told Mick when I was gettin out of bed, 'There's no horn blowin,' I says, 'and what could that mean but Dan is with you,' I says. 'A good friend he was to us always,' Mick says, 'A good friend he is still.'"

Aghna and Bridget both looked at Mary but her back was to them while she stirred the pot.

When our own people come together, there was never a time Dan wasn't in it. How could it be any way but that?

"Jamie McCarthy!" she exclaimed as she turned back to them. "That the devil may drive him to hell before he destroys us all."

Danny and Tim came running in, spilling out Dan's message.

"Danny lost his horn and no one knows who took it," she repeated, her voice uncertain at first, ringing out at the end as she got the meaning of it.

Bridget was smiling at the other part of the message. "What kind of a man is it you've got, sends you word to watch over the child?"

Mary smiled too. "He thinks the sun rises in her poll, don't you know it? . . . You, Ellen." She pulled the child up by the arm and off to the corner. Bending down, she looked into her face and said in a whisper, "Was you after givin Johnny a promise, you wouldn't tell it was him took the horn?"

"I was, but you . . ."

"You had to tell it to your mother. It's not right you should keep a secret from myself or your Da."

"I did tell you."

"You listen to me. You keep your promise to Johnny. You keep the mouth on you shut about the horn. You know and I know and Da knows and your brothers, but nobody else knows. You keep the promise you made to Johnny and don't tell *nobody.*"

Ellen clapped her hand over her mouth. "It's a secret is what I'll say."

"God save us." Mary shook her head. It wasn't likely anyone would ask the child, still . . . "What you say is, 'I don't know.' If Terry asks you, say 'I don't know.' If Bridget or Aghna or Hugh or even Jamie asks you, 'I don't know' is

what you say and that's all you say. You don't know who took it. No one knows
who took it."

She gave the child a final little shake and went back to her work. Two
stoneworkers and a few of the men who worked on the embankment had come in
for their breakfast, looking in wonder at all the empty places.

Ellen returned to her place on the hearth and began to beat it again with her
stick, singing very softly,

"Danny lost his ho-orn,
He won't never find it,
Never, never, never,
No one knows who took it."

Dan had made the quick rounds of the shanties and headed for Jamie's cabin.
Halfway there, he met all three of the bosses and Dent with them.

"There you are," Jamie said. "Have you got the hands on the job?"

"It's bad news." Dan turned and walked beside Jamie. "I've been this hour or
more gettin the straight of it. The men says they're wore out with the pumpin
night and day. There's no gettin 'em on the job at all."

That stopped all four men in their tracks.

"What?" Jamie yelled. "Blast! Damn and blast the lot of them and you, too.
You take that boy and his horn and blow in the door of every shanty in Dublin.
You get those men out there on the pumps."

"Will you listen to what I'm tellin you, Jamie McCarthy?" Dan said quietly.
"Some thief stole the horn in the night when Danny was sleepin and you and me
was gettin the day's work ready. I roused up every shanty, poundin on the doors."
He looked at Simon. "I got your masons up out of it and headed for the work and
the laborers that's helpin them."

"We'll put all them on the pumps, masons and all, eh Simon? Will that do it?"
Simon hadn't more than cleared his throat when Jamie answered his own question. "It won't do. It won't do. We got eighteen pumps, now. There's no use to
work twelve or fourteen. Seventy-two men we need. Goddammit, I'll get 'em out
of there, if I have to haul 'em out by the hair. The first one says no to me will find
himself out on the road with my boot in his backside."

He began to stride forward. "Come on, Dan. There's no man in this camp you
and me can't handle."

Dan didn't move.

Jamie looked over his shoulder. "Come on, dammit, half the mornin is wasted."

"Jamie, let me tell you what you'll be findin before you hit your head against it.
Some has got the shanty doors barred from inside and them that don't—well, it's
like pickin up a sack of potatoes. You can get it up but it won't stand by itself."

"I tell you and I'll tell them, it's work or get out of camp."

"Now let's give this another look," Simon said deliberately. "What think you,
Dan? If it was hit the work or hit the road would we get a crew out of it?"

"I put it to 'em like that. I asked did they know that might be what they was up
against. They just rolled over and went back to sleep . . . or made a show of it."

"It's a conspiracy!" The Judge was indignant. "We'll have the law on them."

"The law won't pump out the pit, Judge." Simon was thoughtfully pulling at his lower lip. "You know what it is, Jamie, you put enough of 'em out on the road and we won't have our seventy-two without we go out and hire more. That means more time lost and no knowin will we find enough. It looks to me like they got us by the balls. This is a Saturday, anyway. We'd be lucky to get the pit dewatered and a few piles cut before Sunday. Have to let the pit fill Sunday and start over Monday, work today or no. Unless you want to work Sunday?"

"I had thought to work into Sunday, if need be."

"No, no. No Sunday work," Laurence said.

"You know that's the Commissioner's policy," Dent added.

Jamie had simmered down and was thinking over Simon's words. "You want to let 'em tell us when they'll work and when they won't? There'll be no end to the trouble do we let 'em lie in their beds or be up eatin our food without a lick of work to pay for it."

"You might be able to get some more hands from Section One-sixty," Dent offered. "Green is finishing up there this week. It wouldn't be more than twenty-thirty men, though."

"The local men are on the job?" Laurence asked Dan.

"Them that's been pumpin? Some come yesterday and some didn't. There's a few today."

Jamie turned on Dan. "What are you hangin about here for? You give us your bad news, now off with you and get the work movin with whatever hands you got. We may as well put all on the embankment."

Dan went reluctantly. He looked back and saw the bosses heading for the Laurence house.

What will come out of that council? I'd give my last shilling to hear it. Will the men have a council of their own or will they sleep the day away while the bosses is wide awake? Will the bosses be down on 'em before they get their sleep out? Should I wake Johnny and tell him?

Johnny's sharp words cut him again.

Jamie's man! A man so low as to keep an ear to his mates and wag his tongue to the boss! Johnny, who knows me as well as any man in this country. How could he think it? I shoulda knocked him backwards for that . . . If I hadn't been too tired to lift my fist. The men has the right of it, it's time for a day's rest.

Dan's shoulders sagged, his feet slowed. Sleep seemed to be stealing over him while he walked. He stopped and shook his head to clear it. There was some thought he had by the tail and now it was escaping him. He looked up toward the shanties.

A council of the men. That's it. Who will be in it? Maybe they're havin it now . . . or last night. Is there plans beyond refusin the day's work? . . Och, there's no place for me in a council of the men neither.

"I don't know what for we're down here at the river keepin the pots boilin and the men so sound asleep it would take twenty horns to wake one," Mary said to the other women when it was near noon.

Dan had appeared at breakfast, snatched up a bowl of stirabout, eaten it standing, and disappeared again without a word to her which way he was going.

The women were all on edge. For every look at their work, they were throwing two over their shoulders toward Dublin and the road from that to Jamie's cabin and the farmhouse. There hadn't been a sign of any of the bosses. The masons were swarming around the abutments as if they were working as usual but it was clear they were standing as much as working, mixing the talk along with the mortar. Maybe the embankment crew would bring the news along with their hunger. Mary sent Tessa out toward the work with a pan and a spoon to bang out the signal dinner was ready.

When the men came in answer, Dan was with them. Mary served him questions along with his dinner.

"Why are you here at all? The word you sent by the boys, what were you sayin but you were in it with Johnny and the others that's stopped work on Jamie? I'd have wagered my soul you'd be to the fore."

"With all in their beds, how could I be to the fore?"

The men had questions for Dan, too. "When will the pumpin start again?"

"Ask them that's sleepin, do they ever wake up out of it."

"What did Jamie say?"

"You never heard Jamie cuss? What do you think he said?"

"What will the bosses do?"

"All they told me was, 'Get on with the embankment.' They're as near with the plans as they are with the pay."

That didn't satisfy the men. It didn't satisfy Mary either.

Jamie pushed all past what flesh and blood could stand, Dan with the rest. Our own men were in the right of it to say 'no' to any more of it. It isn't like Dan to be standin first on one foot and then on the other . . . There is a danger indeed in sayin 'no' when the boss says 'work' but Dan is the last man to fly from danger . . . Will Jamie do us all like he did Niall and Fat Seumas? Put us out on the road? If all is turned out of our shanties, will we be headin off to the farm? With winter comin and no roof over our heads? . . Och, Dan, poor man, with his head on his knees tryin to get two minutes of sleep.

The men were through eating and Thomas Noonan was getting the stonies back to work before Dan lifted his head. Then he called out to the embankment crew, "Go on. Get yourselves to work. I want to see some dirt moved when I get there."

He had a quiet word for Tim before the boy went off after the men.

"If Jamie comes to the job lookin for me, tell him I'm off there—" He jerked his head toward Dublin, "and you'll fetch me. Don't wait for him to say yes or no. Run for me. I'll be in my bed but don't tell that to Jamie."

"Tell me one thing before you go off," Mary said. "Are we in this with our own people? We're not against them. I don't need man or woman to tell me that. So where else is there for us but with them?"

Dan looked at her as if he had turned slow-witted. "Each of my feet is as heavy

as one of Simon's stones." His voice was slow and heavy too. "And my head's
weighin me down till I'll fall on the ground if I don't lay myself on the bed. God
knows whether I could have kept at the pumpin if the pumps were goin."

"Off with you then, before you go to sleep standin."

Mary put her hand out and gave a little push to get him started toward his bed
but he had a few more words to get out before he left. "Don't go waggin your
tongue to the women, we're in it, we're out of it, who's up, who's down. There's
more ways than two. They done this without me. How could I be in it? I gave
Johnny my word about the horn but I gave Jamie my word I'm his foreman while
the job lasts. Don't go flyin out at Jamie neither. If all's quiet the day and the
night and Sunday and all at work on the Monday, maybe that'll be the end of it."

"That you may have a quiet rest and a deep sleep, my sweet man."

He plodded off with an old man's walk. She sent another unspoken wish after
him. "That you may wake with a clear head and a clear road before you."

*Is it likely Jamie will take the 'no' the men were throwin in his face and let that
be the end of it? There's a fight comin surely. The good head Dan has on him,
with all the learnin in it, maybe he can show me more than two ways ahead.
Jamie's way taken will mean Dan destroyin himself on the pumps day and night
after day. He's havin a bit of a rest out of it now and isn't that thanks to the men
sayin 'no' to the boss? . . More than two ways? When our own people are up
there's only one way.*

Chapter 38

SUPPER IN the cookhouse that night was eaten in silence. Food always got
undivided attention first and talk came later but this time the silence was
heavy with consciousness of Simon. He was sitting in his accustomed
place but Jamie was not beside him.

It was a listening silence, receptive to any whisper of where it was Jamie and
the Judge had gone, and why. Jamie had been seen to go up the canal line in the
afternoon on horseback, Jim Dent riding beside him. The Judge and his son had
gone off in their wagon toward the town. None of them had returned.

It was a watching silence. Eyes were on Simon, on Dan. The stoneworkers
and the men who had worked that day on the embankment looked curiously at
those who had refused to get out of their beds. Furtive glances were cast at the
men thought most likely to make a move, if another move was to be made.

It was a considering silence. There had been a sudden drawing together, a
sudden facing off against the bosses. It had opened a yawning blankness in place
of the well-understood routine of next week's work, the time-honored relationship of men to foreman and boss. Each man was weighing the others he knew in
work, in the daily living of Dublin. How would this one or that one stand now?

When the meal was over, it was in silence the men got up from the tables. This was a restless silence. In unspoken agreement, most rejected the usual Saturday night exodus toward the Caldersburgh tavern but they were constantly in motion, as if seeking some other direction.

As they emerged from the cookhouse, as Simon went off alone to his cabin, as the Dublin men who ate in their own shanties came out to join the others, the silence was breached by many rivulets of speculation and rumor, of tentative questions and excited answers, of quiet agreement and loud argument, till the dam broke completely, accumulated resentments came spilling out and the camp was engulfed in a torrent of talk.

"Listen to 'em!" Johnny said, catching Dan at his door. "We got our courage up. There won't be no more of it now."

"No more what?"

"Workin us night like it was day, water like it was dry, winter like it was summer, men like they was dogs."

"How will you be stoppin all that?"

"Like we did last night."

Johnny followed Dan into his cabin, pouring out the story while Dan gathered a few sticks together and put the hot coal to them he had brought from the cookhouse fire.

For weeks, as Johnny told it, the usual grumbling had been sending up little puffs of bravado against working in water without more pay for it but it had come to nothing. In recent days, indignation at the unending hours of work had been building and a word had popped up here and there about making an end to such hours. Yet there was always one like Conn Mor to scorn such talk, saying he could work three days and three nights without stopping.

The night before, when they were slowly moving toward the shanties after the day that had begun at dawn and ended at midnight, Paddy O'Scanlon had raised his voice.

"I'm finished. They won't get *me* up on the morrow." This time the only response had been a grunt of approval from one and another.

"'I'm with you,' I hollered out," Johnny told Dan proudly. "'Flesh and blood can stand so much and no more,' I says. They come around me sayin 'True for you' and 'Enough and lavins of it' and I don't know what all. There was a bunch around Paddy, too. Conn Mor said he'd be off down the road sooner than let McCarthy and Griffen make a ox out of him and . . ."

Dan stood up. "McCarthy and *Griffen!*"

"Well, Dan," Johnny met his look squarely. "It was you pulled the men back to the pumps when Old Man McKendrie quit. And the orders . . . maybe the orders comes from McCarthy but it's you puts 'em on the backs of the men."

"You don't see how it is . . ." Dan began strongly enough but he couldn't find the words to tell Johnny how it was. He bent down to tend the fire and Johnny went on with the story of Friday night.

"They raised me up on their shoulders and I called out, 'No work on the morrow! Who's for it?'"

There had been a chorus of 'Aye' and 'No work,' Johnny said. Then the straggling collection of tired workers had become a purposeful procession, heading for the rest they had decided to take.

It had all happened so fast there had been no time to talk it over, to bind each other with strong oaths, to make certain there were no gaps of irresolution or weakness. Yet not a single man had risen up and gone to work against that decision. All together as one! It was as if they approached one of the stones that came out of the quarry, it looking so huge and heavy there wasn't the strength in the world to lift it, then all had bent together and found themselves unexpectedly strong, raising a burden unexpectedly light.

"We did it, man!" Johnny doubled up his fist and punched Dan's shoulder. "Not a pump moved! Not a one!"

"You stopped the pumps," Dan agreed, "damned if you didn't." He thought back to the morning, wondering whether it was the strength of their resolve or the weariness in their bones.

"You did it," he repeated, "but what's ahead? The foundation on that pier won't go in without some long days. You'll quit workin at sunset? You won't let Jamie get the foundation in at all?"

"We'll put it in, we will indeed, when Jamie comes round."

"No work till he comes round? Round to what?"

Johnny was uncertain for the first time. "I was thinkin . . . wouldn't we have to go to work on the Monday and we takin Saturday off?" Then with renewed confidence, "We'll swear every man in camp to stand together and go off when we give the signal."

"When who gives the signal?"

Johnny looked his surprise.

"I'm not askin the names," Dan said impatiently. "Don't you know it? I'm askin is there a Committee itself? Is it agreed who gives the signal? Is it agreed what every man will swear to?"

The door burst open and in came Paddy with a grin wide enough to reach from the jug in his left hand to the jug in his right. Hugh, the Caseys and three or four others crowded in behind.

"Come on, Johnny." Paddy lifted the two jugs up and down alternately. "We're pumpin whiskey the night. Come over to my place. You too, Dan, the grand pumper you are. Up-and-down and up-and-down." That brought snickers from some of the others.

Dan's sour look and Johnny's promise to join them later had scarcely cleared the cabin before Tom Quinlan was at the door, looking for Johnny. He went out and came back in a few minutes with Tom and Art Sheean.

"I give my word you was the man we could trust," Johnny said. "Am I right?"

"You are."

What else could he say, yet saying those two words cut down the space where he stood between them and Jamie. When he had laid himself down to sleep that afternoon it was a comfortably big space. By the time he got up, the space seemed to have shrunk. He had sat at supper with the silent men, their silence, their questioning looks pressing in on him, drawing a line across that space. While Johnny talked, he saw the men putting him on Jamie's side of the line, got a sense of their need for him on the other side. He wanted to give them some help on the one side but he still had one foot on the other.

Art and Tom and Johnny were staring at him like they had never seen him before.

"What Johnny was sayin outside," Tom began, "You got a good head on you. Don't we know it and don't we need another good head the way we better be diggin our spades into this if we're to make a move at all and this the Saturday night of nights after the day we took off the work."

"I'll put it plain," Art said. "Do we talk here, what ears hears it?"

"Dan Griffen's ears and no others. There's no hole in this house."

"Art ain't been here but a few weeks," Tom excused him. "It's a sound man you are, we know that, Dan. Now don't take it the wrong way around do I ask you, what happens when Jamie comes roarin 'Get the pumps goin. Drive the men to it, Dan Griffen'?"

"You're not goin back to the job on the Monday?" Dan looked from one to the other.

"We're tellin you nothin," Johnny said, showing that Art and Tom had put it to him, he shouldn't have emptied the bag for Dan. Johnny folded his arms and looked at Dan the same way he had done in the morning. "We're askin. Are you with McCarthy? Or are you with us?"

Dan looked back at him.

Did I say, 'I'm with you,' that would be the end of my foreman's job and my foreman's pay. Did I say 'I'm with Jamie' they'd turn their backs on me and walk out. Would there be a man in the camp would be a friend to me? Enemies, they'd be. Hatin me. Layin for me. Och, that wouldn't be m'self, goin against them all. If I tried to say 'I'm with Jamie' I'd gag on it.

"A sorry day it would be, did I ever go any road but all of us was on it together. I'm with you."

Johnny closed the half-open door behind him, pulled the bench in front of it and sat down.

"Now then. It's the thing you were askin, Dan, what's before us? Will we work on the Monday?"

There was a bang on the door and Art's name called. Tom threw up his hands. "In and out, in and out, how are we to sit down and put our minds on it and them shoutin at us and draggin us out every minute?"

Art was motioning Johnny to get out of the way of the door.

"All out then. Why not?"

"Because we need a tool got a edge to it," Tom answered. "We can sit here and hammer at it till we get it. Then's the time to see do the other lads like the heft of it."

Dan gripped Johnny's arm. "Over with you to Paddy's. Get Hugh out of it before he has too many drops taken. Let him stand sentry for us. We'll put an edge to it."

Hugh took his duties so seriously, he challenged Mary when she came up from the cookhouse. She made short work of that, slipped quietly in, got Ellen into bed with her prayers said in a whisper and herself settled by the hearth. Danny and Tim went up the ladder reluctantly and once up, hung their heads over the loft's edge.

When the four men were seated, looking at each other across the table in the firelight, Tom began, "I don't know did any notice what I was up to, puttin a question here and a question there . . ."

There was a laugh at that. Tom got red in the face but he joined in the laugh when he realized what he had said, for it was a camp joke the way Tom never opened his mouth without a question coming out of it. The laugh shook some of the tension out of the air.

"You can laugh all you want," Tom said, "My questions is hooks. I pull the thoughts out like fish out of the river. There's a lot of wild talk out there the night but what it is most all the lads would rise out for . . ."

He named the three things over on his fingers, to quick agreement from the others. It was the long days and nights with no rest; it was the short pay for the long days; it was the giving nothing extra for the work in water. But exactly what it was they were to ask instead and how they were to get it out of the bosses—it was not so easy to name those things off on one finger after the other, nor was it easy to get all in agreement. After a long struggle with it, Tom asked another question.

"Will we bring Dennis in on it? He was after bein in a turnout of the Dublin stonies—the big Dublin back in Ireland."

Dan was for it. "He'll give us a word worth listenin to, so he will. And won't we need him anyhow to get the stonies in with us?"

Johnny didn't see what they wanted with the stonies at all. "Simon don't work them the night through or send them into the water."

"Them stonies think they're the lords of creation," Art added. "We don't need them in it tellin us what to do."

"If we're slow to get 'em on our side, Jamie and Simon will be quick to get 'em against us," Dan told them. "Don't you know it?"

Johnny had a liking for Dennis and a respect for Dan's judgment but Art was harder to convince. At last he agreed and Tim was called down and told to bring Dennis.

"Don't go yellin 'Dennis' at the top of your voice through the camp,' Dan cautioned him. "Go quiet like to his shanty. If he's not in it, ask Rose where to find him. Put the word in his own ear that your father would take it as a favor if he would step in. If he puts you off with a 'later' or a 'maybe' or a 'on the morrow' you tell him I said you was not to come back without him."

"Off with you and don't be there till you're back again," Tom called out.

"And if you fall, don't wait to get up," Johnny added.

It did seem that Tim was back with Dennis almost before he had left. Dennis explained it. "The whole camp, barrin a few that's off drinkin, is outside your door, the same as m'self."

"And the whole camp knows who's in it, or it ain't day yet," Tom said grimly.

They looked at each other in silence for a moment, absorbing the meaning of that. There was no need to put it in words. Whatever the bosses had in mind, they would come down first and hardest on any that got the name of being a captain in this fight.

"Every man of them will have to be swore before the night's over," Dan said.

Dennis had more to tell them than the twice-told story of the Dublin turnout. Some of the stonies here in Little Dublin were of a mind to turn out. Although they had not worked the night through, their days had repeatedly been lengthened past sunset with no more pay for it. That wasn't the way of it on every section but Simon had been holding out the promise of work in his stoneyard in Columbus when the canal was done for all those who worked well and worked with a will on this job. There had been too many of those long days though. The promise of the future was wearing thin and looking remote against the hours they were paying for it in the present. If the canal hands were of a mind to turn out, there was a good chance the stonies would be with them.

The door opened, letting in Hugh's head and the sound of confused shouting that downed out his words. Mary ran to the door.

"I don't know can I stand 'em off," Hugh said. "Conn Mor and his lot says they'll break the door down and break Dan's head and any man else that's turned against 'em."

Mary passed the word to the men at the table. "That Conn Mor," she added. "He keeps his brains in his fist."

"All the same," Tom was quick with the thought, "Better we have him in than out. Come on, Art, me and you."

The noise subsided as Tom and Art went through the door, leaving it open. Conn was right there, backed by three of his friends. He pushed his face into Tom's.

"What you doin in there with Griffen and him a boss?"

Tom folded his arms and stared back at Conn. Hugh and Art moved in on either side of him.

"Conn Mor," Tom said, "How well it would be for you, were you to know what you're about before you start shoutin about breakin doors and breakin heads and throwin it up to better men than you, they ain't to be trusted."

Conn hesitated. The crowd surged forward, voices calling, "Outta the way, Conn." "Leave us hear Tom, willya?"

Conn and his friends reluctantly moved aside a few feet so they no longer screened Tom and stood there, glowering at him. It wasn't their black looks though, that suddenly overwhelmed Tom but the sight of the whole camp pressing in on him expectantly, waiting for him to speak. Hugh pulled the bench out of the cabin, so he could be up on it where all could see and hear.

"Lads," Tom began. "I . . . I . . . This here . . . What it is . . ." He threw a beseeching look over his shoulder.

Johnny gripped Dan's arm and spoke his name in an agonized whisper. What could Dan do but step out of the cabin and jump up on the bench beside Tom.

"Lads!" he called out. "Did you stop the pumps or didn't you?"

"We did!" "Aye!" "We stopped 'em!" came the answering shouts.

"Will you start 'em again with nothin gained but a day's rest?"

"No!" The shout was from many throats, but not from all. It was followed by a babble of individual voices.

Dan could feel Johnny and Dennis at his back. He raised his voice above the others. "Now then. We're in the same pot together . . ."

"How do we know you ain't in McCarthy's pot?" Conn Mor broke in.

"Because no boss on God's green earth can turn me against my own." He turned his back on Conn and spoke to them all. "We got some butter to carry to market here and a bargain to strike with the bosses on it."

Paddy and all who had been drinking with him had come out and joined the crowd while Dan was talking.

"We stopped the pumps on 'em once and we'll do it again," Paddy sang out, waving his drink in the air. "Here's to a day's work that has a day's end to it." He put the noggin to his mouth and drained it.

"I'll drink to that," someone yelled. "That's it." "We're with you, Paddy."

"We done it once. We'll do it again," Conn roared.

As the response to Paddy subsided, another voice was heard in earnest expostulation. "Speak up, man," several urged. Tim Sullivan was pushed forward. Tim was known for his silence, the way his wife Bet did more than enough talking for two. Whatever he had to say now, he was having trouble putting into words.

"The way I see it . . . well, I may not be in the right of it . . ."

"Spit it out before it chokes you," Art said.

"I will then. Now, you done what you had to do when you took your rest. But this here bargain Dan is talkin, I don't see it. McCarthy's notion of a bargain is 'Take what I'm givin or out on the road with you.' Winter's comin on and a cold road it would be."

There were some uneasy murmurs.

"Tell 'em, Dan," Tim urged. "Tell 'em what you was sayin inside about Jamie needin us."

"Tim, he's got the straight of it when one man bargains with the boss." Dan spoke loudly and deliberately so all could hear. "He left out one thing. McCarthy can send one man out on the road and get another but if he sends a hundred men out on the road, where will he get a hundred more? They can't pump out their pit without us. They can't build their aqueduct without us. If we all stand together, it's damn full sure they have to make a bargain with us."

That brought some hoarse cheers.

Then Kevin strutted forward. "You forgot one thing yourself, Dan Griffen, but don't you be thinkin I forgot. I'm just the boyo to put it away up here"—he tapped his head—"and bring it out when the time comes. What you forgot is that this winter just past, me and Mick threw McCarthy's job in his face and went off up the road lookin for another. And what was it we found? Winter's no time to be lookin for a job on the canal. That's the time the bosses is layin off, not hirin on. We told you that when we come back."

"Did you indeed? And do you tell me it's the dead of winter now? Bosses layin off now? Comes the snow and all, there might be more men than there is jobs, but now, *now*, every boss is pushin to get the work done before the winter closes in. Jamie and Simon and the Judge, they *got* to get the foundations in before high water. They *got* to. Could they get the pit pumped out with twelve men? Could they do it with twenty-four?"

"Twenty-four!" That was Johnny. "They couldn't do it with twice that."

"Seventy-two men they need," Dan said. "Seventy-two! Just on the pumps. *Now* is the time. We'll never have a better."

Tom finally found his voice. "I say we give the bosses notice no man will work a long day without he gets a long rest and a day's pay won't carry from midnight to midnight neither and we won't go in the water without seventy-five cents for it. Now then, who's for it?"

The answer was a cheer that started as each man's answer to the sound of his own purpose coming back to him in Tom's words. As each voice mingled with others it gained the strength of the common purpose.

"What I say," Johnny shouted. His voice was lost in the general clamor. He jumped up beside Dan. "What I say," he shouted again, more urgently. He had to give it to all of them, the way he had put it together for himself. His voice shook as he brought his thought up from the depths of him. "We won't let 'em work us night like it was day, water like it was dry, winter like it was summer, men like we was dogs."

A wave of excitement swept them all, cresting in a more deafening cheer. Dan felt raised up with it. The exaltation didn't blind him to the danger that could come when the crest broke and the wave receded. Something had to be done now to hold on to the power expressed in that cheer so a new wave would come thundering up when the bosses were in the way of it.

In the November night, he could scarcely see the edges of the crowd but he could sense restless movement there. As the cheer died, the cold and damp were creeping in.

"Brothers!" he called out, waited for quiet, spoke slowly and solemnly. "We're tight together. We know what we want. We'll put it on the notices. The bosses is to know what we want when they see them notices. We *stay* tight together till we knock it out of 'em, Brother United Men. Every man will be swore to it before the night's out. Any man that won't swear to it . . ."

A menacing growl from many throats threatened what was in store for any such man.

"One more word, Brothers. It's a dark night. Too dark to see the next man or the ones that's come to the fore. No one saw you here and you saw no one."

Yells and stamping of feet on the hard ground told him they took his meaning.

It was late when they were ready to write out the notices and the camp was subsiding into sleep. The Judge's wagon had rattled past, bringing him back from his unknown errand and quiet now reigned at the farmhouse.

Only in the Griffen cabin were men still up and talking. They had brought both Conn Mor and Connie O'Riordan back into the cabin with them; Conn Mor to bind him to the rest so he wouldn't be going off on some fight of his own making; O'Riordan for his lovely handwriting and the way he had of chasing the words across the paper almost as fast as you could say them.

When the writing was done, all put up their right hands and solemnly swore by the Holy Patrick and all the saints to stand firm on what they had put in the notices ". . . and do I betray my brother or the secrets of our society, that my ears may be cut from my head and my arms from my body."

They were ready then to start out through the camp to call the men out of the shanties one by one and swear each in the same way.

When Dan returned, Mary was still sitting by the fire. "Come and warm yourself," she said.

Dan sat down and held his hands to the flames. "We're in it now."

"There's no word of a lie in that. And there's no way but you must come to the fore."

After a moment, she asked, "How is it in this country with the law and the soldiers?"

"There's no king's soldiers in it. The only law I seen around here is the one sheriff, but who knows what the Judge brought back with him?"

Mary raked the ashes up over the burning log and they went to bed. There was no need for any more talk. They lay close to each other, very close and very quiet but sleep was a long time coming.

Chapter 39

THERE WAS a presence in Dublin on Sunday morning that made this different from all other Sundays. A notice proclaimed:

> Any person or persons who works here on the akkaduk any long day sunrise to sunrise or more without he take a day and a night rest follering may have his coffin for we are not to bear such a persecution. There is no man to work in water under 75 a day and no man to work the night sunset to sunrise without a days pay for same.

The notice was fastened to the door of Jamie and Simon's cabin, another like it on the Laurence barn and a third on the big oak tree between Dublin and the cookhouse.

The horn never called the men to rise on Sunday. Mary never rose before it was full day. This day, the Dublin shanties were still in the shadow of the hill but sunlight was already touching the valley when she stood in front of the oak tree with Danny and Ellen.

Danny read the notice out. Mary had heard it the night before but now it was out in the eyes of the world, fastened up with an iron nail filched from the carpenter shop, the black writing speaking out of the white paper for everyone to see.

Before Danny had finished reading, Johnny was bringing Molly and her father and her small brother and sister to see it and hear it.

Molly looked from the notice to her husband with admiration and O'Malley said, "Give me that bit at the end once more."

After the second hearing, he repeated it with relish, "No man to work the night sunset to sunrise without a day's pay."

Several others had drifted up by this time. When Connie's handiwork was admired, he blushed and muttered that "There wasn't hardly time to write it out proper."

Johnny turned to Old Fergus. "You for it?"

Fergus answered with his usual noncommittal grunt.

"What the bloody hell do you mean by that? When McCarthy hollers 'Fergus' you gonna come runnin?"

"Nah, nah. Spunky young feller, ain't ya? Give it to McCarthy right in the eye." He gave a little dry chuckle.

Danny would have liked to read it out again as more people were gathering but Mary pulled him away. There was water to fetch even on this day.

He came back from the well with more news than water. "Simon come out of his cabin. He tore the notice off the door. Then away he went like the devil was after him, to the Big House. Out of it again with the Judge and the two of them off to where all them others that sleeps in the barn were readin the notice on the barn door. I seen the Judge tear it down but I couldn't hear what he said with it."

Mary poured the water into her big pots and gave him back the two empty buckets. "Fetch me some more and don't slop it all over the edge this time. First, up to your father and tell him what you saw."

There was constant coming and going all the morning, with the cookhouse the hub of it. Dan sat a long time after eating, talking to Pat Flynn's son Egan and some of the other young lads. Long after the last spoonful of stirabout had been scraped from the pot, when Dan was gone and the women were busy with the dinner, there were still two little groups at table, talking and arguing.

Jamie came striding in, the notice from the oak tree in his hand, torn in two. "What's the matter with Dan, he left this trash up?" He threw the two pieces into the fire. "Where is he?"

"Why would you be lookin for him in here?"

Mary watched the notice burn to fluttering black leaves, its brave words destroyed.

"Danny," Jamie ordered, "Off with you and find your father. Tell him he's to bring all down here, and quick. Not just them that always eats in the cookhouse. All. All."

Danny looked questioningly at Mary and she gave him a nod.

"Have you found your horn yet?" Jamie asked him.

"No sir. No one knows who took it."

"You look for it and you find by nightfall, you hear me? Now get out of it and do what I told you."

He raised his hand but Mary was in his way. "Don't you be hittin my Danny. It wasn't him took the horn."

Danny slid out behind Jamie and ran up the path.

"Who took it then if you know so much about it?"

"I'm that busy with the cookin, would I be watchin after every prank these lads is up to?"

"No one knows who took it," Jamie repeated Danny's phrase savagely. He looked at Mary as if he would like to raise a hand on her too. "Don't you be thinkin I don't know what that means. It means everybody knows. Your Danny better find that horn and be ready to blow when I give the word."

He turned toward the table with something on his tongue for the men who had been there a moment ago but all were gone.

Simon and the Judge came in, and Jim Dent. The partners talked in low voices at the other end of the cookhouse while the engineer strolled back and forth along its open side, joined after a few minutes by Corny the smith, Donal Shelley the carpenter, and Thomas Noonan, Simon's right hand man among the masons.

Tessa's eyes strayed toward Donal. Where was he in all this? Not with the Judge, certainly, but not with Mary's folks either, it seemed.

Mary and Bridget exchanged looks but no words. When they heard the tramp of feet, they forgot the dinner entirely. A dense crowd was moving toward them with Dan a few steps in the lead. Jamie had said he wanted all, and all came, not in twos and threes and clumps as they usually came to the cookhouse on a Sunday, hungry and casual, thinking of nothing but food. They came all at once, the men and the women and children, too. All of Dublin moved into the cookhouse as one.

They left a respectful space in front of the bosses and packed tightly together in the room that was left, filling the benches, getting between the heavy tables, pushing them back to make more room. All couldn't get in under the roof; an unbroken mass extended outward along the open side of the cookhouse.

Not a word was said. They had come. They waited.

All the backs were to Mary. She couldn't see over the heads. She pushed against the man on the end of the nearest bench to get a foothold and climbed up on it. Ellen wanted up, so Mary reached back for her and set her on the table. Tim and Danny were jammed in the middle and wriggling back and forth, trying to see around those in front. She could just see the back of Dan's head and himself up there in front of all.

Jamie knows it now, it's Dan is the man in the gap. Or does he? The way he's sayin a word to Dan like all was well between them. Wasn't it by his orders Dan brought the people? Little he knows how much changed in Dublin the one day he was out of it. There he stands on the table above us all, Simon too, and the Judge.

Jamie was looking at them all as he had looked at Mary, as if he knew what was in their heads and would like to knock it out of them.

"We been gone out of here a day, me and Mr. Dent, and look at the stupid mischief you was up to as soon as our backs was turned. Now I'm tellin you we had enough of it. We got a aqueduct to build and we'll build it. You got one more chance to work on this job and if you don't want it, we got men comin here in the mornin, will do the work. There's to be no more crawlin off to your beds with your tongues hangin out like dogs that's tired of chasin the cows. And squealin for more pay on top of it. You're gettin more pay in a month than you saw in all your lives in Ireland. Me and Simon and the Judge gets the money from the Commissioner to do the job and we're the ones knows how little it is and how much of it can go in the wages. That ain't for you to know or for you to say."

Mary would have like to throw the words back at him.

Dogs is it? Squealin like a pig, is it? And yourself to hold the money and give it out a penny at a time.

"Some of you owes me a month's work or more and don't think I won't have it out of you. You pays your debts in this country or you goes to jail. There's the Judge who can sit in the court and send you to jail."

The Judge stood there, silent and severe.

That's the way he looks in his court, givin out the word to clap people into jail . . . or maybe hang them from the gallows? That does be Joe and Eileen he's givin over to the Law, and the Caseys, and God alone knows how many more.

Joe was standing near, one hand on Eileen's shoulder, leaning heavily against her, staring hopelessly at Jamie.

"And they ain't the only ones can be goin to jail over this. You don't put up notices on your boss in this country. Them that done it, take warnin."

Mary felt a rush of the old fear.

That's ourselves he's givin over to the Law. It's Jamie bringin back the old heart-scaldin. That's what Jamie McCarthy has come to, puttin himself on the side of the Law against his own people.

Her anger was rising now over the fear.

Jamie was leaning forward. They had all sat or stood there stunned while he was hitting at them. Now his talk poured out thickly, sweetly, like from the molasses jug.

"I know you men like you was my own brothers and I know it was only a few would rather fight than work. I know them kind. I got my eye on them. The rest of you is in it with me like you always was. You know I always favor my own but we got to get this aqueduct up and the hands got to come where we can get 'em. Them that's lived in this country all their lives, they know how things is done here and if we have to put a man like that in your place, that's your own doin. You know how many the Judge has got at his back right here, ready to go to work when he gives the word and more of 'em he got yesterday will be comin in."

Out of the corner of her eye, Mary saw several men coming from the direction of the river. There was a little stir at the edge of the crowd where they had joined it and the sound of voices. It was Toby Weaver and two of his friends. They were saying something to those near them but Mary couldn't hear it. The heads that had been turned so intently toward Jamie were turning away from him to see what it was.

"What's the matter with you, Toby?" That was the Judge, a crack of irritation showing on his stony face. "Don't interrupt Mr. McCarthy. I'll talk to you and the rest of my boys later. You just go over to Buck's and get all those fellows to come back with you. I'll meet you on my back porch . . ." He paused and pulled out his round watch with the long chain on it, "after dinner."

"Allright, Judge," Toby called out, loud enough for all to hear. "I just come by here to tell you me and Shad and Sam ferried five of the fellows across the river so they could go home. They says they like the job well enough, but not well enough to take a coffin along with it."

The Judge pointed his big nose toward Jamie angrily. "Now see what those ruffians have done. They're scaring men off with their threats. It's murder they're threatening. I won't have it."

"They didn't scare us off," Toby told him.

"Good. Good man, Toby."

"But we ain't workin no more of them long days without gettin paid for it."

The heads moved around as if pulled by a single string, watching as the three men walked off. Toby was whistling. The sound struck the glassy silence of the listeners like a pebble and shattered it. There was a rustling, a clearing of throats.

Dan said quietly to the man next to him, "Good man, indeed. Toby Weaver."

"We won't miss four-five of those men," Jamie said quickly. "We got plenty more comin. I been up the line, spreadin the word. Section One-sixty finished up yesterday. The whole crew will be down here by the mornin, ready for pumpin."

The heads turned in his direction again but the spell was broken. There were muttered threats about what would be in store for men from One-sixty, did they come looking for jobs that belonged to other men.

Dennis got up on a bench. "Askin your pardon, Jamie, could I put a question to Simon? . . You got any masons comin in here after our jobs?"

"Now Dennis, why would you ask such a thing as that?" Simon answered. "This ain't a mason's fight. It don't have nothin to do with layin stone."

"It's got this to do with it. There'll be no more stone laid after sunset on this job without we get paid for it."

"This ain't a mason's fight," Jamie roared. "Get down, there, and don't mix in where you got no business. I got one more word for every canal hand here. We're pumpin in the mornin and we're pumpin till the pit is empty and the piles cut. Don't matter how long it takes."

A low growl swelled out of the crowd.

Jamie roared still louder. "I'm givin *you* notice we don't feed nobody that don't work. Any man that don't figure on bein on the job at sunrise can take his bundle and go off out of this camp right now. Me and Simon and the Judge is right here and any of you that doesn't want to work, come up and get your pay if you got any comin and then be off with you."

Jamie caught sight of Mary's head sticking up in the back. "You hear that, Mary? Any that would rather sleep than work can sleep on the road and eat there too. They had their last meal in this cookhouse."

"I hear you, Jamie McCarthy. I hear you callin 'em brothers out of one side of your mouth and dogs out of the other."

All the heads turned in Mary's direction, the faces on them amazed, the bodies turning too, letting Jamie have their shoulders, their backs.

"I hear you turnin your brothers out of their houses like you was the captain of the king's soldiers out of Cork Castle itself. I hear you takin the food out of their mouths and out of the mouths of their wives and their babes, more shame to you. It's well for your sister she can't hear you across the water and her husband dead in the fightin. She'd die of shame, Peg would. It's well for you, your father can't hear you, the hard man he always was, but the fair one. Didn't he stand by his neighbors when the troubles come down on us? Not like you, Jamie McCarthy, no true McCarthy of them that was great chiefs in days past. You a chief! I get a right laugh out of that! More like a James Barry that grew fat out of cheatin the lord with his right hand and the rest of us with his left."

Dan's face was telling her she was in the right. Jamie was staring at her with his mouth hanging open.

"I hear you, Jamie McCarthy and I know you. I know you now and I knew you in Akron and you bringin shame on the name of McCarthy, makin a whore out of little Susan. I know you and you bringin shame to the name of McCarthy, leavin them you brought over the water to die of the fever in a strange place. I know . . ."

Jamie was roaring for sure now, drowning her out and herself not half through with the litany of his shame. He was yelling that she had cooked her last meal in that cookhouse.

"Out with you!" he bellowed. "Dan Griffen," he hollered. "Curb the vile tongue on that wife of yours!"

"Out with me, indeed," she shrilled it across the tops of the heads so it would pierce him. "And my dinner with me, that I cooked for all here. If we can eat by the riverbank like tinkers, we can eat by our own houses." Her eyes swept over them all. "The dinner will be in Dublin, I'm tellin you and all of us tight still in our own houses."

She jumped down from the bench, picked up her pot-rag and whipped the stewpot off the hook. She handed it to Tessa and stooped to shovel a bit of fire into the frying pan. Bridget picked up her little girl with one arm and the sack of bread with the other hand.

"Aghna!" Mary called, "the other pot. Bring my spoon, Ellen."

The Judge bellowed out Tessa's name. She put down the pot and stepped back from it as if it had burned her. Rose Farrell ran forward and picked it up.

"You set one foot outside this cookhouse, Mary Griffen," Jamie yelled at her, "and you'll never cook in it again."

"That you may do your own cooking, Jamie McCarthy," she yelled back, "and may you get the gripes from it."

They were out of the cookhouse in a minute, the four women and Ellen after them, waving the spoon like a flag. The crowd parted to let them through and closed in behind them. Dublin moved out as it had moved in. Even Shelley, Corny and Noonan melted in with the rest. The angry bosses were left staring at the empty and disordered place with only the engineer on their side and the lonely figure of Tessa by the fire.

Chapter 40

THE MASS of people that had streamed up the path broke into little groups in the road that passed in front of the Dublin shanties. The strong impulse that had held them together and brought them out of the cookhouse as one was being stretched and tested and pulled apart.

One group was talking over the threat of other workers coming to take their jobs. Another, the threat of the law coming down on them. The men who had met in the Griffen cabin the night before gravitated toward each other. It was clear they were the Committee. It was on them what to do.

Dennis was drawn away by Thomas Noonan and got into it with him over the place of the masons in the fight. Those who still had a dead horse to kill were seeking each other out, prodding tentatively to see was their own fear shared that they had jumped into water that was too deep for them.

The groups broke up and recombined, the one around the men of the Committee growing larger and larger. Dennis left Noonan and got into the center of it.

Mary and the other women made two circles of rocks at the road's edge and built fires inside the circles. They set the big pots over the fires to finish the cooking.

Eileen came up behind Mary and whispered to her, "Can they drive my Joe back to work and him shakin yet with the sickness? Or throw him in jail else?"

Mary stepped away from her task. Her head was high and her feet light from the march out of the cookhouse. She smiled into Eileen's worried face.

"Look at all here." She waved a hand at the crowd. "Is your Joe a lone horse then for Jamie to harness and drive to the work at his pleasure? All of us is in it together."

"It's like a whip he's got over us, the debt," Eileen complained, but she looked a little comforted.

The bosses came up the path and walked by toward the Laurence house. The many voices were silenced and all drew back to let them pass. They took the road with the certainty of ownership, the tread of authority. Their eyes looked straight forward as if no one were in the road at all. Tessa followed a few paces behind, her head bent. She looked up at Mary as she passed but Mary had drawn Dublin tight around her. Tessa was outside it. If there were a message in Tessa's eyes, Mary had no thought of trying to read it.

When the bosses had disappeared around the bend the talk resumed but it was subdued. Mary moved back to the fire and Eileen with her, looking more worried than ever.

Aghna gave Eileen a smile. "Did you hear the way Mary scorched Jamie? The tongue you've got on you, Mary, you had him smokin like a bad chimney."

That started Mary on her unfinished catalog of Jamie's sins. Drawn by her voice and the smell of the dinner, more gathered around. When she ladled out the stew, she ladled out another spoonful of shame on Jamie's head with it. The pity was, Jamie wasn't there to hear it. There were many to listen though, and many to add their voices to the chorus. It seasoned their dinner and took a little of the edge off their fear of what the bosses had it in mind to do and what power they had to do it.

The first thing was to keep all hands but their own off the pumps. Art asked Dan who was the contractor on the section where Jamie talked of getting the whole crew? Was it Green?

"That's it," Dan agreed. "I was after hearin it from Dent. Twenty? Thirty? Some such number of men they might get out of it."

"We're more than thirty. Let 'em come. We'll run 'em off," Conn said.

"Why would we sit here waitin?" Art had something else in mind. "I know one or two of them works for Green. Will I set off to meet 'em on the way? M'self and a few of the lads? If we can't make 'em see reason one way we'll do it another."

"I'm with you." Conn was quick for anything with a fight in it. Connie O'Riordan had been pulling away from Conn Mor of late but now he came in beside him. Egan was quick to follow. They soon had about twenty men, armed with heavy sticks, blackthorns from Ireland or stout oaks from the nearby woods.

"Don't be too quick to jump 'em," Dan warned Conn. "Let Art use his tongue first. Save the blows for the ones needs it."

He turned to Art. "It wouldn't be Green's section only. A lot of them sections above is done, like Laughry's job you was on and the men gone off, but not all of 'em. Jamie was ridin that way a-horseback a whole day and night lookin out for men, so *you* look out. Spread the word in all the camps that's still there. Hail every man you meet. Let all know there's no work on the aqueduct, whatever Jamie said. These is *our* jobs."

When they were gone it was like a hole had been made in Dublin, a hole that filled up with anxious thoughts of impending danger. Johnny walked up the road to see could he get a look at what might be doing.

"What about that?" he said when he came back, motioning with his thumb. "They're goin in there at the back of the Big House. That'll be the Judge talkin, like he said. Will he talk all them to the pumps?"

"Not Toby," Dennis said. "'We ain't workin no more of them long days,' he says. Didn't you hear him?"

"'We ain't scared off the job,' is what he says," Paddy contradicted. "The meanin of that is, they'll be workin."

While Dennis and Paddy argued it back and forth, Tom said to Dan, "What it is, we got to know will they or won't they."

Dan considered. "The Judge sent Toby out of it when we was meetin. I wonder would he send us out of it when it's them meetin?" He called Dennis away from Paddy and put it to him.

"I'll go," Dennis agreed. "I'll slip in quietly alongside of Henry. That's the Cincinnati mason. He sleeps with the other crowd in the barn since we come down from the quarry but he's strong for the Mason's Society. There's some other good men in there too."

Michael and Dan went with him, and a few others. It wasn't so easy to slip in quietly. The Judge hadn't begun talking yet, but all were gathered in front of him, where he stood on the porch. All heads turned to stare at the men from Dublin. Jamie and Simon jumped down from their places beside Laurence and came over to them.

"What are you here for?" Jamie challenged Dennis "Didn't I tell you to stay out of it?"

"The masons isn't to hear what the Judge says? Then what about them?" Dennis pointed to Henry and several stonies clustered around him.

Simon answered. "I'll bring them with me when the Judge is finished. We'll get all the masons together and get this thing fixed up. We'll be laying stone on the morrow, don't make no mistake about that."

"A meetin of the masons, is it? I'll just be waitin here till you're ready for it." He and Michael edged away toward Henry.

Jamie looked after them suspiciously, then turned to Dan. "Will you have your crew on the pumps on the morrow, or won't you?"

"Well, now." Dan tried to make his voice as bland as Dennis's. "Us here, we wanted to hear the Judge, the grand talker he is." The words came out smoothly enough but he couldn't keep the glint out of his eyes that told Jamie Mary's words were echoing in his head.

Jamie poked him in the chest with a hard forefinger. "You have your crew on the job. You hear me?" He poked again. "And you put a bridle on your woman's tongue or sorra word she'll say again around here. That's my last word on it."

He and Simon returned to the porch.

The men were not massed together, as in the cookhouse meeting, but were scattered loosely around the yard. The Irish filtered in next to those they looked on as possible friends. Dan and the Caseys joined Buck and Ike, Tom and Paddy moved over to the one they called 'Whiskers' from the way his bristly beard stuck out from his thin cheeks. Johnny and his father-in-law came in beside Toby. Toby's eyes were bright with excitement. He had his book clutched tightly in his hand. He gave Johnny a wink.

The Judge held up his hand for silence. This being Sunday, he said, he would open with a prayer. The Irish had felt conspicuous enough already. Now they were doubly uncomfortable. They hadn't bargained for a Protestant prayer meeting.

The Judge prayed for the poor ignorant Irish that had forgot their duty to God and man and asked the Lord to bring them back to the path of righteousness for his name's sake. He asked God to bless him and his partners and help them in the difficult task they had undertaken and to watch over the faithful workers who would not turn away from the work He had put before them to do, but would be hard-working and obedient, according to His word.

The faithful workers were getting restive. The Judge brought the prayer to an end and launched into a fine speech about the importance of the aqueduct to everyone in Ohio and especially to everyone in Coshocton County. With winter coming on, they must press ahead with it, hard though it might be, all working together, each in his own place.

"The day will come when we will show it to our children and our grandchildren. Think of it! You can tell them how you brought this waterway through the wilderness and across the river."

He stepped up to the very edge of the porch, looking from one to another. "We'll get back to the job at daybreak tomorrow. You have nothing to fear. We won't tolerate any riots or misbehavior from the Irish. We'll hire as many men as we need to fill the places of any that's foolish enough to stay off the job."

He repeated Jamie's claim of men coming from up the line and said he had spoken to more men who lived in Coshocton town and the county around.

In the cookhouse that morning, Dan had felt the changing responses to Jamie's words in the bodies of the men pressed closely around him. He had known did he begin moving out of the cookhouse after Mary, they would move with him. But here he was getting no signals from the scattered bodies and impassive faces.

Then Toby called out, "Judge!"

There was something in his voice that swiveled all heads in his direction. Now Dan felt some current running among these men.

"Yes, Toby?"

"You say we're startin at daybreak?"

"Yes."

"So we start at daybreak and when do we stop?" Toby didn't wait for an answer. "I ain't no preacher but I got as far as the first page of the Good Book and it says there, 'And God said, Let there be light in the firmament of the heaven to divide the day from the night.' What I want to know is, when you goin to start dividin the day from the night? We got a bellyfull of this here night work."

"Toby," the Judge said sharply. "I'm surprised at this coming from you. What would your father think? He was a good upright man and I thought you were a worthy son. If he were here, he would tell you that the Good Book also tells servants to be obedient to their masters."

"I'm tellin you right now, I ain't your servant. And you can leave my father out of it. Him and me, we heard you make some fine speeches on the Fourth of July. I guess you've forgot, but I ain't forgot. I can't make speeches like you but I got a book of words here." He opened the book at a place he was holding with his finger. "This here's about the unity of man and it says here . . ."

The Judge tried to interrupt but Whiskers spoke up. "Now Judge, we listened to you and now we'd kinda like to hear what Toby's got to say. You just hold your fire a minute, willya?"

Toby was reading out of the book: "'. . . by which I mean that men are all of one degree and consequently that all men are born equal and with equal natural rights.' What that means to me is that you and me and all the rest of us, whether we was born in Ohio or Virginia or Ireland or wherever we was born at, we all got rights. You got a right to ask me to go to work for you and I got a right to say I will or I won't."

He raised his voice, "And I say I won't lessen you give us the pay for goin in the water like the other contractors do and when we give you a day and a night workin you give us a day and a night restin."

"I'll vote f'r that," Buck said. "What d'ya say, Judge?"

"This is not a political meeting," the Judge said severely. "It is not a matter of voting. Ridiculous! Now Toby, I'm glad you remember my speeches because I was talking about this being free country, wasn't I? Don't you understand what that means? Every man is free to buy his own farm or make his own bargain. What they're trying to do here is a conspiracy against freedom, a threat of mur-der—*murder*—against a man who wants to make his own bargain on the work and the wages."

He called several by name, Whiskers being one, and said he knew they had too much sense to be swayed by a young hothead like Toby. Then he turned to Toby and pointed an accusing finger. "I want to know what book that is you were reading from."

"It's 'The Rights of Man' by Thomas Paine."

"Don't you know Thomas Paine is an irreligious atheist? If that's where you get your ideas, we don't want any part of them. You can leave now. I don't want to hear any more out of you."

Toby walked out with three of his friends beside him, Johnny and O'Malley along with them.

Buck and Ike looked at each other. "I ain't changed my vote," Buck said to his brother. "I'm with Toby."

"Yeah," Ike agreed. "What about you, Si?"

"I'm stickin," Si Maddox said. "You got a place to go now even if the Judge puts you off his place. I ain't got my stake together yet."

Buck looked like he was about to argue with Si. Dan was impatient. Didn't Buck see now was the time to make a parade of it? All over the yard, the men were see-sawing back and forth. The Judge was trying to make himself heard and was motioning with his arms to get the men closer.

"Wouldn't you be walkin with Toby?" Tom was saying to Whiskers.

Whiskers considered a moment. "Toby spoke up real good but so did the Judge. I got a right to say yes or no to the Judge. I say yes."

"Come on now," Dan said in a low voice to Buck, "Walk out boldly and you'll bring more with you."

But the moment was past. Only some of the men who had been boarding with Buck and his wife followed him. They gathered together at a little distance from the house, praising Toby for his grand speech.

"Did it sound pretty good? I don't know, it didn't come out strong like I wanted. Look at all them crowdin in around the Judge. I guess I'll get my stuff and be off home. I sure as hell ain't sleepin in his barn tonight."

"Don't go off." Dan put out a hand to hold him back. "We got a fight ahead, don't you know it? The Judge can preach all he wants. They still need us. Look at that bunch back there. That wouldn't be half enough to get the pumps goin."

"The Judge, he claims he got more comin."

"You have it in mind to let them walk in here and take your job?"

That took some more talking. The end of it was that Toby and his friends went over to the barn for their bundles and then off to Buck's place. They would be up before dawn, they promised, and over toward Coshocton to warn off any man from that direction.

"We'll talk Si over yet," Buck said, "and some of them others when they come back to the house, they can have their bundles or they can stick with us, one. If they want to be the Judge's hired men, they can sleep in his barn."

As the Dublin men walked back home, Dan said to Johnny, "They don't have the way of makin a Society like we always done it in Cork but they won't be on the job in the mornin, that's sure."

When Mary had served out the last of the stew, she looked at the empty pot, tapping it with her spoon, the emptiness of it giving her a twinge in the stomach with the recollection of other times and other empty pots.

How am I to fill it again for the breakfast? For the morrow's dinner? Where are we to get a potato or a piece of bacon and myself barred from the cookhouse? Those boarding themselves might have a bit and a sup to share but the shanties are full of single men, with a mouth on every one of them.

Her hand continued tapping with the spoon while her thoughts tapped here and there against the threat she knew all too well: hunger.

The sound of the wooden spoon against the iron pot gradually attracted attention with its regular, repeated, 'poom, poom.'

"You're playin us a tune?" Bridget asked.

It took Mary a minute to understand what Bridget was saying. "Och, beatin the pot won't fill it, will it now?"

The keys to the big chests where the food is kept is still hangin at my waist. The wonder of it is, Jamie wasn't snatchin them when I walked out with the dinner. As soon as the thought crosses his mind, he'll be after them. Who but myself knows what it is there in the chests? Jamie never knows till I tell him . . . Who is to help me? The men is gone off hither and yon. Bridget is too timid and Eileen too frightened. Peg and Molly. And Aghna's strong and quick. That's enough. It wouldn't do to leave the chests bare. We'll take the potatoes, for wasn't I tellin Jamie a few days past they was all gone to hurry him up, like, to get more. A sack of beans . . . a cabbage or two . . .

When the men returned from the Big House, the food was stored away, some in Mary's shanty, some in Peg's.

Chapter 41

W HEN THE STONIES gathered in the cookhouse in response to Simon's call, they found him sitting on one of the benches with his elbows on the table, talking in his usual slow way to Thomas Noonan about the backing stone that had been set dry in the west abutment the day before.

"It's got to come down from the derrick clean and square. There's no hammerin these blocks into place without crackin and chippin."

"Learnin how to quarry a stone don't mean you know how to set it, wet or dry. You got these quarriers on the derrick, never built a wall in their lives," Thomas complained. "When they got a stone in their grab-hooks, they're in too much of a hurry to let it go."

Dennis and Michael sat down across from them and were deep into the discussion before they realized it. Every journeyman had an opinion. The quarriers who had been turned into mason's helpers kept their mouths shut and their ears open. Simon laid out a change in the work, with Henry in charge of guiding the derrick.

"The last two stones was laid yesterday will have to be lifted and reset. You do that first thing."

There was a sudden silence, then Henry spoke up. "If we was workin in town, we'd have the rules of the Mason's Society to go by. Out here on the canal, seems as though everything's knocked six ways to Sunday. These men here . . ." He tipped his head toward the quarriers, "ain't exactly apprentices but God knows they ain't journeymen and most of us journeymen is masons and stonecutters both. But it's like this here, Mr. Lordon. You been takin advantage of us on this canal work out here amongst the trees. We had about enough of it. Let me put it to you like this: We'll lift them two stones the first thing in the morning *if* . . . if we can get it settled with you the day's work ends at dusk."

To everyone's surprise, Thomas Noonan chimed in. "You got a grand crew here, Simon. None better anywhere on the canal but we can't do a proper job without proper light."

Simon listened. That gave others the courage to speak but he held up his hand to stem the flow. "What it is you're doin, it's like you're puttin water in the mortar and forgettin the lime. It won't hold. If this was goin accordin to the contract, we wouldn't a laid a stone into mortar since the first day of October. It's only by the grace of God we have the weather with us and the Commissioner give us permission to go on with the masonry. We got to make the most of every day we got till the weather stops us and there's no more work for stonies. Wouldn't it be the best of your way for you to be makin the most of it while the work lasts? Don't forget, when October come and the sun risin late and settin early, we didn't take nothin off your pay."

"You get summer hours out of us yet. It's only right we should get summer pay," Dennis said. "No breakfast hour no more, eat in the dark of the mornin and the dark of the night and no time off in the day but for the dinner that comes down to the river and you hurry us through that. We want a proper hour for dinner and a day's work ends at dusk."

"Most days can end at dusk," Simon agreed, "but there's the task of layin the first courses of stone for each of them piers. That's ahead of us yet. You know the time they're havin with the pumps to get the water down. When they do get it down and the timbers laid, that stone must go on, whatever the time of day."

"*Every* day ends at dusk." Henry slapped the table with each word. "*Every* day. When the time comes we got to work after sundown for the piers or something of that, we're willin but we got to have a day's pay for it—or whatever part of a day's pay fits the part of a day's work we do."

Simon patiently explained how they got the money from the Commissioner for each perch of stone laid. The amount was already agreed on, he said, and no way to get more. No one had an answer to that. Was it the Commissioner was the devil in this and not their own bosses?

"There's money in it somewhere," Michael said. "The Commissioner don't be treatin you fair, maybe. There's a contractor buildin some of them locks over past Newark offered me twenty-four dollars. He do be gettin that out of the Commissioner somehow. You want to come with me on the morrow, Dennis? We could see is that master mason still in need of a good journeyman or two."

If it had been anyone but Michael, Simon might have looked on it as a bluff, but Michael always spoke out just what was in his head, openly and honestly. Simon began to bargain in all seriousness.

Dennis tried to bring in the laborers. "The sun rises and sets for them the same as for us. If day's end at dusk is right for us, it's right for all."

Thomas went over to Simon's side on that and Dennis could see the others wavering.

"I'll make it plain," Simon told them. "We got only so much money to do the job. Do we give the hands more pay for goin in the water or workin into the night, I couldn't be givin you the bargain like I'm doin it. Take it or leave it. I give you my word dusk is day's end, all work after to be paid accordin to hours worked and a full hour at noon for dinner. You give me your word to be on the job at sunrise and to give us the helpin hand when the aqueduct can't be built without. What could be fairer than that?"

"You got my word on it," Thomas said.

A few other voices echoed him but Dennis cut in. "What's the meanin of what you says there, 'a helpin hand when the aqueduct needs it?'"

"Do we need the work after dusk, you won't say no to it. I give you my word on the pay, I want your word on the work."

"That's all?"

"That's all, do all the hands be on the job, Monday sunrise. Do some of 'em fail us, might be we'd ask some of you to work the pumps a bit till we get the crew filled in." He stood up. "It's agreed?"

There was a moment of horrified silence, then Henry and Thomas both began to speak at once.

"You wouldn't put *me* on a *pump*?" Thomas couldn't believe it. "I'm a mason. I ain't a laborer." From the faces of the other journeymen it was clear Henry wasn't speaking for himself alone.

"No, no," Simon said quickly. "A few of the quarriers, most likely. Just to fill in, like. Only till we got all the hands back on the job."

"It be'nt laborers he wants to make of us," Dennis said bitterly. "It's colts." Seeing the puzzled expressions on the quarriers' faces he explained. "That's strangers to the job, brought in by the bosses to break up a turnout. I wouldn't a thought it of you, Simon Lordon. You wouldn't dare it in Irish Dublin."

"Nothin of the sort," Simon said. "How could it be, when there's no Mason's Society here? You're talkin like all the hands was masons."

"Now look you, Simon," Thomas said in a reasonable voice. "I'm bound to tell you it won't do. You got about half that other crowd . . ." He waved toward the Laurence house, "And that's all you got. Every man of us on the pumps wouldn't be half enough. And who would be layin your stone?"

"We got more than that. You heard McCarthy and the Judge."

"Maybe." Thomas was skeptical. "I see men goin but I don't see none comin."

"Do we lay stone in the mornin?" Henry asked. "Is it a bargain?"

"It's part of the bargain, you give us a hand on the pumps, do we need it. I had the devil's own time gettin McCarthy and the Judge to agree I could bargain with you. I can't give you half. You take it all or there's no bargain."

He began to walk away but turned back to add, "While you're chewin it over, don't forget, this ain't my last job but it could be yours."

As Simon walked by on the road to the Big House, Dan tried in vain to read his face. The stonies' meeting lasted so long, he began to fear for the outcome.

"They're talkin the sun down," Mary said, pulling her shawl around her against the increasing cold. "Will they talk the night through, think you?"

Dan sat down beside her in the doorway without answering and she went on, "Is it only the two days and the one night since the turnout began? I was sittin here countin over all the things happened. When Danny's horn was lost . . . That was truly yesterday in the mornin?"

"There hasn't been days like this since Captain Rock's time. I wish them stonies would come out with it . . . And Art, Conn, all them—how is it farin with them?"

He couldn't sit still and got up to build the fire high again now that night was coming. All that were left in Dublin gathered around it.

When the stonies finally came up the path, the others pushed and shoved to get where they could hear. Thomas gave them the story of Simon's bargain and what they had decided to do about it.

"What we'll do," he wound up, "we'll go to work in the mornin and lay stone but all are pledged not to work the pumps."

"They want that stone laid and they want it bad," Dennis added. "That's what knocked the bargain out of Simon. Can you see them takin the trowel out of my hand and sendin me off from the job just because I won't take a pump handle in my hands? Never in God's world."

"Will you hold fast, one and all, and you back on the job with Simon givin out the orders?" Dan was dubious.

"I wouldn't wager my life on every quarrier," Dennis admitted, speaking quietly and to Dan alone, "but the masons are solid. Any man that picks up a pump handle won't work with *us* again. He'll be a laborer from that out. We'll see to it."

Dan had to be satisfied with that. He didn't like the thought of the stonies marching off to work in the morning, perhaps drawing the timid and fearful among the laborers behind them. Much would depend on what piece of a crew Jamie could get together.

If the men around Buck and Tony held fast, all Jamie would have was a dozen from the barn. No new workers had come. Maybe Art and Conn had turned them back, or was their coming only halted by the coming dark?

While most remained around the fire, one Dublin man was sent to the bend in the road toward the Laurences' to keep an eye on the house and the barn and on Jamie and Simon's cabin but all was quiet. Another went up along the towpath beside the piece of canal they had finished, in the direction Art and Conn had taken in the morning. At first, these short sallies up the line were apprehensive, half in expectation of strange workers. Gradually, the concern shifted to anxiety for the fate of their own men.

"Jamie was on horseback and gone a day and a night," Tom reminded them. "Our men could well be all day goin. They could be sleepin on the road and comin back in the daylight."

Nevertheless, the longer the wait, the more uneasy they grew. Were their comrades bested in a fight? Fallen afoul of the law? Wandered away from the canal line and lost in the woods? It was all the young fighters in that company. What if they were needed here to repel some attack? None knew what might be coming.

Outside the circle of firelight, the dark thickened. There were no stars in the November sky. A chill wind touched their backs.

In a strange country, one steps softly with uncertain feet on the new paths, slowly lets go of old certainties and grows accustomed to what is expected, what is allowed, what is to be feared. How rashly they had stood on their little familiarity with the narrow strip of the new country that was the canal and the canal works. How daringly they had picked up the old weapons of struggle that belonged to a different time and place. When they turned their backs to the fire to warm them, they stared off into the dark, looking into an immense, a fearsome, an unknown country. How easily it might swallow up this handful of people, this cluster of shanties.

The people of Dublin were slow to leave the fire but at last there was no one left but Hugh and Paddy who would stand guard the first part of the night with Tim beside them to blow the horn and rouse all in case of need.

Deep in the night, Hugh woke Dan and Johnny. Tim sleepily handed over the horn to Danny who had stumbled down the ladder without fully waking and was soon asleep again on the ground. Dan stepped back into the shanty for a coat to throw over him.

The two men paced back and forth, out into the shadows and back into the firelight; along the road to the bend for a look at the farmhouse, darker than the dark around it with no light showing anywhere; a pause, then back to the cluster of quiet shanties.

"They won't be stirrin a thing up the night," Johnny said as they stood at the bend.

"No, but you can count on Jamie to be up and doin with the sun, whatever the thoughts he took to bed with him."

There was nothing said after that for a long while. It had been a day of much talk and the day was over. There was nothing to do now but wait the night out. They moved in step, their heavy work boots coming down on the hard earth together. After a time, it took only the exchange of a look to agree to a rest. Dan sat down beside his sleeping son, Johnny on the other side of the fire.

In the rare silence, in the near solitude, Dan went over the many things that had happened since Saturday was a morning, tried to push his thoughts forward to what Monday would bring. The silence swelled, the solitude grew enormous. His thoughts lurched into unreality. He shook himself awake and got to his feet.

"I'll walk a bit. It's keep movin or fall asleep."

"Walk then, and while you rest, I'll walk."

Dan went past the quiet shanties to the bend, looked at the dark hostile farmhouse, the hulk of the barn where the Judge's men were sleeping, the silent cabin that held Jamie and Simon. He turned and paced back toward Dublin.

Dublin is our place now. Let Jamie and the Judge try puttin us out of it . . . Carrignahown was ours and after all we held it. West Cork was ours to the top of its mountains.

He had kept a night watch on the mountainside once, raking the slope below and the road at the bottom of it with his eyes, east to west and east again, sitting motionless behind a rock.

In them days, we had to fight for every halfpence for the work and against every shillin for the rent and damned if it isn't the same here with different words to it.

He walked slowly, hearing his own steps, his eyes accustomed to the dark now.

There were stars out between the blowin clouds on those January nights . . .

He looked up, but there were no stars in the Ohio sky, only a dim radiance in one spot where the moon was behind the clouds.

This is a different sky, a different earth . . .

In the silence and the solitude, the loss of that other time and place swept over him. He stood at the bend, looking beyond at the dark wooded hills, heavy with night . . . turned with a sigh toward Dublin.

It is not ours as Carrignahown was ours, the way we were born into it and our fathers and mothers before us . . . Our houses dug into our hills, stone of their stone, clay of their earth, thatch of their fields . . . Here the shanties is made of ramshackly sticks, perched there, almost slidin off the hill, thrown up such a little while ago . . . How can we hold Dublin, frail shelter in this storm? And ourselves strangers to the land.

His steps sounded lonely to himself as he paced toward the bend. There was no sound at all as he stopped there, staring at the farmhouse—big, substantial, claiming all around it with the confidence of its size, its permanence.

The people in that house weren't born to it, no more than ourselves. No life-long, generations-long, thousand-year belongin for them neither . . . Strangers to the land themselves, if the truth was known. And who do they have at their backs? The law, indeed . . . People in Big Houses always have the law, but beyond that? A handful of men only, gathered from here and there . . . And Jamie? Who does he have? Not one, not one . . .

Back at the fire, he looked down at Danny, the youngest fighter, and again at the flimsy walls of Dublin.

Behind those walls are all those who grew from the same earth and crossed the same water as m'self, who have the same memories and the same tongue, who picked up the same tools for the same work and found the same need to stand together against the same bosses.

He stepped out firmly, for he had all Dublin at his back.

Chapter 42

MEN WERE plunging down the hill toward Dublin. In the dark before the dawn, they were unknown and threatening.

"Who comes?" The challenge from Dan was answered in Toby's cheerful voice. He and three others had climbed the hill from Buck's place and passed along it behind the Laurence house unseen. They were on their way to cross the river and stop any men coming to work from that side.

They had been gone only a short time when Thomas Noonan came along the road from the Big House. Johnny stopped him and waked Danny to blow the horn. The people came hurrying out of the shanties at the signal. Thomas had to give out the message from Simon before all.

The stoneworkers and anyone else ready to go to work were to come to the Laurence kitchen for their breakfast. As the stonies started off, Dennis and Michael, who ate in their own shanties, stood with the rest of Dublin, watching, hearing curses thrown after their friends. Dennis got red in the face and said there was no need for them kind of things.

"Not a hand of ours to a pump," he promised, "but any that puts the bad names on us is like to get a stone where he don't want it."

After that little flurry, all was unnaturally quiet for a Monday morning. In the shanties where the women cooked for their own families and a few lodgers, they filled the pots half full, not knowing how long their little stores of food would have to last. In the open, where Mary and Bridget fed those who usually ate in the cookhouse, the breakfast of stirabout came to the brim of the pot but it was a small pot for many mouths.

Dan paused in the eating of his, looked at it, looked a question at Mary. She motioned with her head toward the cookhouse. He gave her a nod, then ate the rest of the stirabout slowly, in small bites, the way one always did in the hungry months.

The morning dragged slowly by. There was a constant watch from a safe distance over the work and the size of the crew. All working were on the embankment or at the masonry. There was no effort to get the pumps going.

Late in the morning, the Judge was seen leaving the embankment with Robert and Whiskers, walking toward the barn. Shortly afterward, the Judge returned to the job and the Laurence wagon came rattling through Dublin with Robert driving the team. Whiskers sat beside him with his gun on his knees. The Dublin people pulled back from the road and watched them head up the canal line.

After the wagon had passed, some grumbled that it should have been halted.

Dan shook his head. "You want to start something with Whiskers and him with a gun?"

"They'll come back with a wagon load of pumpers. Then you'll talk out of the other side of your mouth," Kevin said.

"Never to the fore when there's a thing to do, always full of blather about how it should have been done," Mary muttered to Dan.

As noon approached, Bridget came into the Griffen shanty to see what could be conjured up for dinner. Mary was at the table with a heap of potatoes before her.

"Dan and Paddy and Hugh . . ." Mary took the potatoes from the pile one at a time, giving each the name of one of those who would be hungry for it, to see would there be enough to go around.

"Tom and Old Fergus . . ." Bridget continued with it. The pile was diminishing. Mary pulled out some small potatoes for the children. "My three and your two . . ."

"Conn Mor?" Bridget made it a question, reaching hesitantly toward the few potatoes left. The men who had gone up the line had not returned but neither had any other workers come from that direction, the way Jamie and the Judge had claimed they would.

"Let's see have we got a potato for each of them. Surely they'll be back soon. But we'll wait a bit before puttin 'em in to roast. One more meal is enough with the men not workin, so there's no need to hurry with it."

All Dublin watched the men from the aqueduct and the embankment being herded to the farmhouse for their dinner, the Judge in the lead, Simon and Jamie behind to see that no one slipped away. Even Dennis and Michael were not allowed out of line to have their dinners in their own shanties as usual. All Dublin watched again when they returned to the job. Still there was no sign of the absent Dubliners.

It was well into the afternoon when the women raked the potatoes out of the ashes. As if it had been a signal, here came Art and Conn and all, marching in victoriously, changing the meager meal into a celebration. The biggest potaotes had to be hurriedly cut in two and the children's share reduced for seven more men came back than had gone out. Rose and Peg brought out what they had prepared for Dennis and Michael or there wouldn't have been a mouthful left for the cooks.

Art told how the crew on Section One-Sixty had been hesitating between Jamie's offer and the lure of the Pennsylvania canals, where it was said wages were going as high as twenty dollars a month and pay given out at the end of every week. The word Art and Conn had brought had been enough to swing some toward Pennsylvania and bring four to this job—but sworn to the Brotherhood.

The story of the turnout had been carried well past One-Sixty and had been met with excitement among all the Irish they encountered. That was the way they had picked up three more. The newcomers were greeted with enthusiasm. A tall lanky youth called Phelim began telling his own version of the story till Conn's voice drowned him out, saying they had found a half-dozen Ohio men on the way back, heading for this job. It had come to blows that time but the Dublin men, with help from their new recruits, had sent the others limping away.

"It was our thought, the Judge's wagon was up the road to pick up a new crew," Dan said. "Did you get no sight of it?"

Art laughed. "We did, indeed. We come on the Judge's boy in the wagon and Whiskers with him. Let 'em roll on up the line as far as they want to go. They didn't have no one in the wagon when we saw 'em. Do they find one or two, that's about all they'll get. Most all the sections up that way is finished and the men gone. Where they ain't done yet, the contractors won't turn loose of a man."

"Here's aplenty happened while you was gone," Johnny told them. He had barely launched into the telling of it when Mick, who had been standing lookout came running to say the wagon was coming back, still empty.

"Will we give 'em a proper greetin?" Conn stooped to pick up a rock at his feet.

"No rocks!" Dan hit Conn's wrist, knocking the rock out of his hand. "They lost this battle. We'll let 'em know it. Rose! Give us some liltin! Quick now."

When the wagon passed the cookhouse it had to come to a stop, for the road in front of the Dublin shanties was full of people dancing. Others stood by, some lilting the tune and the rhythm for the dance with Rose's sweet strong voice leading. The dancers were encouraged with shouts and clapping. No one seemed to see the wagon at all or hear Robert yelling to them to get out of the road.

After a few minutes, Dan appeared to catch sight of the wagon for the first time. "Och! Look at us now, blockin the way," he called out. "Stop the noise!" The lilting died down to a subdued murmur and the dancing feet slowed.

"Isn't it ashamed of yourselves, you are?" he continued sternly. "Can't you see little Mr. Laurence here, drivin his horses like a man and Old Whiskers with his gun was out huntin and come back with a load of nothin? Let 'em go by now and take it to the Judge and Jamie that's waitin for it beyond there."

No sooner were the horses in motion than Rose had the lilting started again and the dust had not settled behind the wagon before the road was again full of dancing people.

They kept it up till Toby and Buck came down the hill. Why they had come that way instead of across the river was a puzzle.

"When we crossed the river in the mornin," Buck explained, "We left the raft on the other side and the masons couldn't go to work till they got some of the fellers works on Lock Twenty-Six to come down and bring it back. So when we was ready to come back, damned if Simon didn't keep us off the raft. We had to go upriver to the dam to get back acrost. That was round about noon."

"Noon?" Dan was surprised. "You been back over to this side since noon and no word to us what happened?"

It had not occurred to them to bring their news until they began to wonder what was happening in Dublin. When the stories of the day's doing had been exchanged and they were about to leave, Dan held them back. There were the next day's plans to make.

"If they come round, we'll go to work. If they don't, we won't," Toby said. "What kind of plan do we need for that?"

"And if they bring the soldiers down on us?" Tom asked, "Or the law?"

"Soldiers?" Buck looked at Tom as if he were crazy. "This ain't a war."

"What was them soldiers marched around Coshocton one day back in the summer? The Judge couldn't bring them down on us?"

"You're talkin about the militia," Toby realized. "Hell, you can forget it. My uncle's the captain of it and Buck and Ike and me, we're all in it. The Judge can't call us out and the Governor over to Columbus ain't callin us out neither, to fight our ownselves. Come on, Buck, let's get back while there's still light to see by."

"Goodnight to you. You'll be at your post across there—" Dan waved his hand toward the river—"tomorrow again?"

"What for? We got those fellers from Caldersburgh and Coshocton told not to come back to the job till we give the word. They might come along to see what's goin on but they won't pump."

"And if they come along to see what's goin on and there's no one there to tell 'em but Simon?" Dennis asked. "They got me and Michael and Henry all on this side where we couldn't give 'em a true word."

"I'll go over across," Conn Mor volunteered. "Me and my lads, we can throw Si in the river and take the raft."

"No-o." Dan didn't trust Conn, who was altogether too quick to start a fight. "There might be some talk in it and Toby can talk to the ears on those Ohio men better than any of us. What about it, Toby?"

Toby agreed but suggested that one of the Irish should come too. "We told the fellers that was comin to work and the crews on the locks below the aqueduct and up to the dam, but all them is Ohio men. Wouldn't hurt to spread the word on the sections below that's most all Irish."

Conn volunteered again, so Dan had to come out with it that he was too slow with his tongue and too fast with his fist. That sent Conn off, muttering about Dan giving everybody the orders when he hadn't done nothing himself but sit by the fire while others was out fighting.

With Conn out of the way, it was soon agreed that Tom and Johnny would go and go now to be ready to cross with Toby and Buck upriver in the morning. Much of the next day went by without a sight of them.

In midafternoon, all four and two more of Buck's friends came tearing down the west bank, passed Simon and his crew in a rush, knocked Si and his fellow guards aside, jumped on the raft and polled across as if the devil were after them. At the first sight of them, Danny's horn summoned Dublin to stand together in front of the shanties.

By the time they were across the river, a group of men on horseback appeared on the other side, three with guns slung over their shoulders. Dennis and Michael took one look, dropped their tools and pelted after Buck and his company toward Dublin. Both of them had wives there and Dennis children. Thomas called after them in vain.

Jamie left the embankment with two others to take the raft back across. With the boss gone, the diggers leaned on their shovels to watch the horses being led onto the raft on the other side. As it came closer, they could see it was Judge Laurence, Sheriff Bixel, and three strangers.

They saw the men remount on their side of the river, unstrap their guns, hold them across their saddles and ride toward Dublin. Jamie followed on foot. One of the diggers, then another, moved after them, then all were hurrying to see what would happen.

The men and women of Dublin were gathered together with the children among them, the Ohio men on the edge of the group. Most of the men had cudgels in hand and a few had guns. The Judge's party faced a silent, hostile crowd.

"Men," the Judge began. He stopped to clear his throat. The Irish had never looked like this to him before. They had always been rough but that was commonplace on the frontier. They had their own queer ways but they had been obedient on the job, deferential off the job and full of laughter and merriment among themselves. Even Sunday in the cookhouse, they had not looked so grim.

"Men," he began again, "you were hired to work for me and Mr. McCarthy and Mr. Lordon. You are to come back to work immediately. Your houses are to live in while you work for us. Any man not at work has no right to stay here. Do you understand? No work—no house—no food."

Surely that made it simple enough for even the most stupid. Yet there was no word and no movement except a slight drawing together more solidly as Dennis and Michael edged around the mounted men and joined their wives. Some of them didn't know English, of course. He caught sight of Dan Griffen, toward the back.

"Dan Griffen, do you understand what I'm saying?" There was no answer. "Griffen! I'm talking to you."

Dan had been on the lookout a short distance up the line. Tim had run to get him with the word the Judge was bringing the Law on them. He had come in at the back of the crowd as the Judge began speaking. Those in front now moved aside a little, making room for him to come forward, but he stayed where he was, folded his arms across his chest and said, "I hear you."

"You're the foreman on this job. You can explain to the rest. I want you to get every man here on the job in the morning."

He wouldn't speak to the Ohio men. If the Irish conspiracy could be broken, they would come back to work. Just thinking of the way Buck, his own man, and Toby, William Weaver's son, had let themselves be sucked into the plot enraged him.

He rose up in his stirrups and bellowed, "You work for me or you get off my place. Do you hear?"

There was a stir in the crowd at that; people exchanged looks with one another. The Judge sat back in the saddle. "Now the Sheriff has something to say to you."

Sheriff Bixel urged his horse forward a few steps. Johnny, Phelim—the new man from One-Sixty—and the others who were in front pushed against those behind to get out of his way. Bixel aimed a stream of tobacco juice at a rock at Johnny's feet. It splashed up on his trousers.

"Get to work or get out," Bixel said. "That's all I got to say. This here is Judge Laurence's place. You don't stay lessen he says so. If you ain't goin back to work, you better pack up now. You better not be here tomorrow, that's all I got to say."

There was another stir in the crowd as Dan and some of the others who had been toward the back began to shoulder forward.

"Now Judge, you listen a minute," Dan began, but they had not come to listen. Bixel was already turning his horse. Laurence and the two deputies followed.

Conn dropped the stick he was holding in his left hand, the better to make use of the rock in his right. It sailed through the air and hit the rump of the sheriff's horse. While Bixel struggled to get the hurt and frightened animal under control, one of the deputies raised his gun and fired at the crowd.

There was a woman's high-pitched scream, screams and cries from the small children, one hoarse shout and a shower of rocks came from the Dubliners. Then the Judge's party rode off with a thunder of hoofs. The watching masons and diggers melted away before them. Halfway to the river, the sheriff dismounted to look at the injury to his horse. There was much talking and gesturing toward Dublin.

There, some were gathering around Peg who was still screaming, her face white, blood showing on her sleeve. Others gathered around the Committee who were exchanging hurried words as to how to repel another attack. Then they saw the sheriff and his men moving toward the river and the Judge cutting off across the field, back toward his house.

Michael got his arm around Peg and helped her into their cabin, calling frantically for Mary who was quieting the frightened children. She left that for Bridget and the other women and came quickly, Rose with her.

"Keep the rest of them out," she said to Dennis who was just behind her. So he stood in door and talked, now to those outside, now to Michael inside who was beside himself with fear for his wife.

"Och, she's all bloody," Dennis announced. "The scoundrel hit her in the arm! What is it they're sayin, Michael? There's no bullet in it? Poor woman, poor Peg, did you hear her cryin out? That's with the whiskey Mary was pourin on it . . . Now then, Michael, it wasn't you got hit. Quiet yourself . . . See there, what a brave woman you got. Hardly a sound out of her now while they tie it up."

Michael was holding Peg's right hand while Mary and Rose bandaged her left arm with the kerchief Rose took off her own neck.

"They could have killed her, they could have killed her," Michael kept saying, "and the babe with her."

"Whisht now," Mary said impatiently. "It's only a scratch itself. Don't be scarin her any more than she's scared already with the bullet flyin at her. Rose, did you find the scarlet thread? Tie it then, while I say the words . . . Will you quiet yourself, Michael? How can we staunch the blood and you makin such a noise with it? Are you ready, Rose?"

While Rose tied a scarlet thread around Peg's throat and another around her wrist, Mary laid her hand on the bandage above the wound and spoke so loudly her voice could be heard outside.

"There came a man from Bethlehem to be baptized in the River Jordan; but the water was so muddy it stopped flowin. So let the blood! So let the blood! Let it stop flowin in the name of Jesus and by the power of Christ."

Mary told Michael to let Peg lie on the bed and keep her arm quiet till the charm could do its work and the babe she was carrying be at peace.

"Don't leave us," Michael begged.

"I'm only a step away, do you need me," she soothed him and went out to see to the children. They were all standing around Terry who had found the bullet that had hit Peg. There was a hot argument going as to who else was to be allowed to hold it.

"Mary, Mary," Bridget hurried over to her. "Wherever are we to go? Turned out of our houses in the cold of the year and no friends to turn to this side of the water."

"Is any here coward enough to go crawlin back to the job?" Conn's loud voice turned all toward him. "I say we leave out of here and don't leave a stick standin. Torch the shanties and the cookhouse . . ."

"And the barn," one of his friends took him up, "and Jamie's cabin."

"That's easy enough for Conn," Joe said to Paddy, "He can go off down the road without thinkin twice. What about us that's got families?"

"I got my rest out," Paddy answered. "If it's back to the pumps, it's back to the pumps."

"What do you want to burn it all down for?" Buck asked Conn. "What will that get you?"

Conn moved toward him threateningly. "You takin the Judge's part?"

"I didn't hear the Judge throwin *you* out of *your* house," someone else yelled at Buck.

The Ohio men drew together. Several of Conn's gang fell in behind him. Everyone else pulled back, waiting for the first blow.

"For the love of Christ," Tom said in exasperation. He walked out between the belligerents and up to Conn who was twice his size. "Conn Mor, will you listen to me? Who was it brought the warnin the Sheriff was comin? It was Johnny and me and Buck and Toby and Shad and Sam. It was us was together last night in Buck's house and the whole day over across the river, spreadin the word to the other sections. The thing I got to ask . . ." He turned away from Conn and sent his question out toward all of them. "Is it back to the pumps or leave out of here? Wouldn't there be another way? A way to hold on?"

"That's it," Johnny said eagerly. He and Dan moved up beside Tom, ignoring Conn's still threatening stance. "My own thoughts, entirely. Why wouldn't we do it like the stonies? Go back to the job but off again at sunset, whatever they say about pumpin through the night?"

"Here's another thought . . ." Dan was putting it together in his own head and took a minute to bring it out. "When all of West Cork was up and the soldiers come, they never found man, woman or child in the houses. We was up in the hills. And when the soldiers was gone, we was back in our houses. There's hills here too . . ."

Heads turned to look at the hills, dark in the late winter afternoon. The thought of heading into those strange woods was worse even than the thought of going out on the road.

"Whatever it is, we better get about it," Art said. "Who knows when the Law will be back and more with 'em."

"Is that what's in it, Buck?" Tom asked. "Will they be back tonight yet?"

"I dunno. I don't hardly think so." Buck looked suspiciously at Conn's gang, then shrugged and turned to his friends. "What do you fellers think?"

"Naw," Shad spoke up. "Bixel won't come back without more men, you're right there, but he won't hardly get none between here and Coshocton. We seen to that. And who can he get in town? A couple more of them clerks like whatshisname out of Campbell's store that was with him today."

"We got more too, is in it with us," Johnny told them.

"That's right," Toby chimed in. "The men on the locks next to the aqueduct. Last night they told their contractor they wouldn't go in water for less than seventy-five cents and he agreed to it. He don't want them quittin on him like we did."

"The Irish on the section next after the locks, they'll be up at the end of the day," Johnny continued, "to hear more of what's in it. You know who's the boss on that section. The Judge's brother-in-law."

Dan brought his hands together with a loud clap. "That puts a different face on it."

The fear and the confusion were by no means over. Those for holding out were pulling this way and that over how to do it, while others began to talk quietly, one to another, saying how foolish of the Committee to think they could stand against the bosses and the Law too.

Chapter 43

E LIZA LAURENCE had rushed to the door when she heard the shot, fearing for Joshua. Even when she saw him, she could hardly be persuaded that he was unharmed. Joshua paced back and forth across the room, telling her the story. He finished by passing judgment on the guilty. "This has gone too far. Bixel will be back tomorrow as soon as he can get enough men together to get that scum out of here and take the rascal who threw the first rock."

"And the one who shot at you?" Eliza asked. "You could have been killed."

"No, dear, no, that was Chance Sadler. It was his gun you heard. He was the only one shooting."

"What was that boy doing with a gun? He didn't hurt anyone?"

"I don't think so, no," Joshua answered almost absently. He went on talking, his voice rising. "I saw him with my own eyes, that big fellow, Moore or More or whatever his name is. He's the ringleader. Robert saw him in the lead of that gang that went up the line to stop us getting any hands. We should have got rid of him then and there. When he hit Bixel's horse, that was the signal for the rest to attack us. Right here on my own place! They're worse than savages. We have to get rid of them, every one. There's no other way."

He held on to the back of a chair with both hands, his voice rising, then moved the chair around and sat down on it. "I think I'll have a drink. This has been very upsetting."

He sipped the whiskey Eliza brought, growing more calm. It had been his idea, bringing the sheriff to make the rebellious hands understand that what they had been told on Sunday had not been idle threats. Lordon and McCarthy had been against it but he had insisted, confident that this would end the turnout. It was men of property and education like himself and Commissioner Kelley who could manage such affairs. They might need the assistance of tradesmen in handling some of the actual canal work but these two Irish fellows knew very little about the rights and wrongs of things, nothing at all about the law.

The workers' place was to work according to the orders they were given. That they should cling to their shanties without paying for them with their work was a threat to his ownership, his control, the unassailable rights that were the very foundation of his world.

He held out his glass to Eliza to refill and began to tell her all about it again, in greater detail. She had to get back to her work and could not stop to listen. Now that the cookhouse was empty, she had a first table and a second table for every meal. Emma hadn't come to work today and Tessa couldn't handle them alone.

The first table was already eating when Thomas Noonan came in with the news of what had happened to Peg.

"Who?" Simon asked, "not Kieran's wife?" He threw his fork down on his half-eaten food and stamped out.

Joshua wasn't pleased to see him go. He was impatient to tell his partners what was to be done in the morning. As it was, he had to wait through the second table before he could speak to Jamie without others hearing. He went into the front of the house and paced the hall. As soon as he heard the men leaving he was back in the kitchen, pouring out the story as if Jamie had not seen most of it himself.

Jamie listened in silence, every word out of Laurence's mouth irritating him almost past endurance. He was as determined as the Judge to break the back of the turnout but he had told Laurence bringing in the Law might start more trouble than it ended and the event had proved him right. What they needed was not a bludgeon to drive the people together but a lever to pry them apart and a knife to cut the leaders away from the body. It would have been better to wait another day or two till hunger began bringing some of them around, precious as each day was. He had been open with the workers about how desperate they were to make each day count and now they were using it against him. It was no accident they turned out now. Someone in Dublin had put their complaints together with the urgent need of the bosses. He thought he knew who that was.

He had been all action and all confidence on the first day of the turnout, all anger on Sunday. When Monday came and no crew with it he had been suddenly without action, without plan, with an unaccustomed feeling of helplessness.

When a man has made a tool for himself out of material he knows and understands, sharpened its edge to do his work, shaped its handle to fit his hands, there is a feeling of loss if the tool is taken from him. Now Jamie could no longer grasp the crew he had made out of his own Irish. If he did get a hold on it and swung it into the job again, could he have confidence in its being always at hand to serve his purpose? He had risen above his poor West Cork peasant boyhood but he knew that part of his success was that he came from the same world as his crew. The roots of his authority were in that world. Somehow they had been pulled up.

"After you've emptied out Dublin, who is it will do the pumpin?" he asked when the Judge paused for breath.

The Judge stared at him as though this were the first time he had ever heard of a pump. "We'll just have to cross that bridge when we come to it."

"That's the bridge we're at now," Jamie tried to keep the heat out of his voice. He wanted Laurence to stop blathering because someone threw a rock at him and get his mind on the real problem. If Laurence and the sheriff had put a scare into Dublin, why wasn't there a stream of workers running down here to say they would be on the job on the morrow? Not even a single one sneaking in to whisper it.

Simon came in and Eliza set before him the supper she had kept warm on the hearth. He ate without a word. The others waited impatiently for him to finish. When he pushed his empty plate aside, he turned on them before they could come out with the questions both had been holding back.

"Now that you've near destroyed my crew, will the two of ya's tell me how I'm to put it back together?"

This was so unexpected coming from the usually soft-spoken, even-tempered Simon that neither had anything to say.

Eliza had a question and took this opportunity to slip it in. "Is the woman badly hurt?"

"No ma'am, not bad, but she's carryin a babe and the way they talk you'd think we killed the woman and the babe too." That was all he had to say to Mrs. Laurence but he wasn't through with his partners.

"You've gone and lost me two of my best men, maybe more. If you woulda give your hands a small piece of what they wanted, you could a talked 'em back to the job like I done the masons. But no! You wouldn't listen to me. Now they're puttin the blame on me for the shootin and they're goin off, Kieran and Farrell and God knows who else."

"Masons only, or others too?" Jamie asked.

"Masons only! Only! How will we build a aqueduct without masons?"

"Christ Almighty," Jamie snapped back, "Don't I know we need the masons and don't I know we need pumpers too. What I'm askin: Was the pumpers scared out of it like the masons? Comes the Judge on the morrow, will he find empty houses?"

Simon thought about that for a moment and then shook his head. "Them said for sure they was goin was Kieran and Farrell and they won't go till Peg is able but they won't work tomorrow or any day till they leave. Don't dare go on the job, they say, the way the Law might come back and put their families out with the rest and maybe shoot 'em besides. So what is it you've got a mind to do?"

Jamie didn't have an answer, only another question. "Was there no talk like back to work in the mornin?"

"The only talk was how I went back on 'em after they stayed on the job for me and how I turned the law loose on 'em. Wasn't nobody but the stonies talkin to me." Simon stopped abruptly, remembering something. "Now I think of it, there was one of the hands at Kieran's door, sayin he wanted a word with me but when I turned around he was out of it again."

"Who was it?"

"How could I see in the dark?"

"You don't have no idea what's goin on over there?" Jamie was getting irritated with Simon now.

"What's goin on over there," Simon said grimly, "is a dozen hands from down the line, poundin our lads on the back and callin 'em heroes."

"From down the line? How did they get across the river?" Laurence demanded.

"As near as I could get it, they hollered for the raft and said they heard we was hirin so Maddox brought 'em over and tried to send 'em up here but as soon as they was on this side, they made for Dublin."

"You see what they're doing?" Laurence asked. "They're spreading this conspiracy to other sections. We've got to put a stop to it. It might hold us back on our finishing date but the Commissioner would back us up. I'm sure he would. If we don't end it here and now, it will be a matter of the whole canal."

"So how do we cork it up," Simon asked him, "without another bloody mess?"

"You can bring your masons and their families, those few that's got families, down to the barn the first thing in the morning before the sheriff comes back. They'll be safe enough here till we get the rest rooted out and get that Conn ruffian tied up."

"The longer this goes on, the worse it gets, true for you," Jamie said thoughtfully. "If we bring 'em out, the rest would know it's a danger to stay. Some of 'em must be near scared enough to give up already. We could give 'em a chance: Stay and face the law or come back to work. Eh, Simon?"

"They wouldn't come to work when you threatened 'em Sunday. They wouldn't do it when you threatened 'em today. What makes you think they'll come when you call tomorrow? And if you root 'em out with the Law, who you got to pump?"

They were still arguing it when Dent came. He had taken advantage of the lull in the work here to look at the progress on a few other sections. He refused Eliza's offer of food but accepted a drink and stood with his back to the fire, warming himself and bringing them an unwelcome message from the neighboring contractors. Those who had been holding work in water down to sixty or sixty-five cents had gone up to seventy-five for fear of a turnout and were blaming Laurence, McCarthy, and Lordon for it. They were also incensed that hands from this camp had come down where they had no business, interfering with the work and talking wild.

"When I heard your hands were still out, I thought of getting Thomas Van Dorn to bring his crew up to pump for a day or two. With the ones you got still working, that might have been enough . . . enough to put an end to the turnout, anyhow. But Van Dorn said 'no.'"

"What's the matter with Thomas?" Joshua was surprised at his brother-in-law.

"He said to tell you he'd like to help but claims he's got all he can do to keep the men on the job. If he tried to bring 'em up here, he couldn't vouch for what they'd do. I think some of his men were up here tonight. I met a dozen or so on their way back. Van Dorn and Wilcox and the rest wanted me to press you to get this thing over."

"They want us to get it over but they won't raise a finger to help," Joshua complained. "Look here, Dent. What would the Commissioner think . . ." He put his proposal of evicting all of Dublin before the engineer. Dent listened in frowning concentration.

"I can't speak for Mr. Kelley. I don't know as he's had anything like this happen before. I do know when there's trouble, he likes to come down hard and quick on it or either hush it up, like when they had that outbreak of smallpox around the Licking summit in the summer. He hushed that up good so we wouldn't scare off any workers. If you put the whole Dublin bunch out, they'll be going down the line, talking all the way. If you're thinking about Mr. Kelley giving you another extension . . . I wouldn't count on it. He give you a big one after the flood. He wants to see those piers above the river before Christmas. He's not going to be happy about all those pumps sitting there at the river and nothing happening. Not happy at all."

Joshua wasn't satisfied with this. He wanted Dent to start off the next morning to consult Kelley.

"I've written to the Commissioner about it. There's no use for me to go chasing after him when I'm not sure where he is."

"What should we do then?" Joshua asked.

Dent came over to the table and sat down. "I was thinking about that all the way here and I got to wondering just how much it would cost you to give those fellows what they're hollering for."

"What? Give in to that scum? After they attacked me on my own place?"

"Now just a minute, just a minute. Have you ever figured it out? Take the business of a day's pay for a night's work. How many nights will there be? Now that you've got eighteen pumps, I figure you shouldn't have more than two or three nights on this pier and certainly no more—probably less—on the others."

"We still have a lot of work in water ahead of us," Jamie reminded him.

Now that the problem was before Laurence, he wanted to get the answer. "Let's see what it works out to." He got out his records and Eliza brought paper and ink. The clear clean certainty of numbers was soothing. Jamie contributed his estimates of what was coming.

Joshua worked away at it while the others kept a respectful silence. When he finished, he frowned at the final number. "It's a very considerable sum, very considerable."

Jamie looked at it and whistled. "It is, indeed, but I was thinkin here while you was figurin. If we was to pay past sunset like it was a new day, we wouldn't be keepin up the summer pay on top of it. What would it look like if we brought the pay down to ten a month?"

Joshua worked at it and gave them the answer that it would be a little more reasonable.

"It may look reasonable to us, but will it go down with the men, dropping their monthly pay two dollars?" Simon asked.

"They don't have to know till the payday," Jamie said quietly.

"Ah . . . exactly so," Joshua agreed. He frowned at the paper, still not liking the look of it.

"Give one or the other of the two things they're wantin," Simon suggested, "but not both."

"There's another number you ought to put in there," Dent said. "What will it cost you if you don't get the piers up before high water?"

That wasn't a clear and certain number and it was one none of them liked to think about.

"It would likely break us if we had to run over another season." Jamie put the gloomy thought into words. "Unless the Commissioner . . . ."

Dent shook his head.

The Judge was hitting the table and shouting again. "We're sitting here talking like nothing happened today. I will not pay wages to that Conn rogue. He's a murdering bastard. Don't forget Sheriff Bixel is coming tomorrow to arrest him and throw all those sons of bitches out."

He saw Eliza's surprised face and asked her pardon for the language he had used but he was glad he had made his feelings clear to the others.

"No one here has any thoughts of payin another day's wages to Conn Mor," Jamie said.

"Agreed," Simon said promptly.

"Good, good." Laurence looked at McCarthy with a pleasant word on his lips but he met such a hard stare the word remained unspoken.

"The next thing," Jamie said, "is for you to meet the sheriff before he gets here and tell him our hands is back on the job and we don't want 'em turned out of the houses."

"But they're not."

"They will be. We'll have them back on the pumps tomorrow one way or t'other."

"No!" The Judge hit the table again. "I won't have that scum on my place one more day."

Jamie leaned toward him. "It's your place, indeed it is, but my name is on the contract and Simon's name. We do this job and we need workers to do it and the plain truth is there's no others but the ones we got here, scum or not."

Laurence looked at Simon and got a hostile stare in return. He looked at Dent but the engineer was opening and closing his clasp knife, with his eyes on what he was doing.

"What do you mean, you'll have them on the pumps tomorrow 'one way or the other?'"

Jamie swallowed his anger and spoke softly. "The meaning of that is, you maybe put the scare into 'em today, so when one or two of their leaders is gone, might be they'll be fallin over themselves to come back but maybe they won't. If they still hang together, well, you give it to us there on the paper. We'll have to give 'em what they're hollerin for."

He paused, his face closing up around the bitterness of possible defeat. "That's for now. When we get 'em back on the job, howsomever, we'll find a way to pry 'em apart and teach 'em not to pull any more of them kind of tricks."

"Yes, yes. We'll do that. We'll certainly do that." The Judge sighed and added reluctantly, "Allright then. You take care of the hands. I'll take care of the sheriff."

As they got up from the table, Dent turned to Jamie. "You said one or *two* leaders. You think Conn ain't the only one?"

"I know it."

Dent continued to look his question.

Jamie bit off his answer. "Dan Griffen."

That surprised Dent.

Jamie spilled out his anger at his old friend. "Do you think that woman of his would have loosed her evil tongue on me and Dan not in it? I know him. If he's in it, he's to the fore. But he's got Jamie McCarthy to deal with. He's had his last day's pay out of me."

Once outside the Laurence house, Jamie growled about the Judge. "Fat-assed fool. God help us if he gets out of bed in the mornin callin for the sheriff again."

"I think we got him wedged in pretty tight." Simon's good nature was returning. If all Dublin were back at work in the morning, he had hopes of holding on to Kieran and Farrell. One thing was still making him uncomfortable though. "God alone knows what will happen when the sheriff busts in to grab Conn."

"True for you. It could be a right mix-up."

They walked slowly in silence, then Jamie suggested, "What if a message was to find its way over to Conn in the night to give him a warnin the jail and maybe the gallows is on its way to get him? Wouldn't we be rid of Conn quiet and easy and no reason to have the sheriff at all, God blight him."

There was another thing in it for Jamie besides getting rid of Conn. Such a message from him would say he was with his people against the Law. It would open the way for him to walk into Dublin in the morning, send Dan and Mary out on the road and pull the rest back on the job.

Simon laughed out loud. "The devil himself couldn't get the better of you, Jamie."

Chapter 44

DONAL SHELLEY brought Jamie's message to Dublin. He found only a few still standing around the fire, listening to Conn Mor. Conn had basked in the praise of his bravery from the men up from Van Dorn's section. A couple of his faithful lieutenants were still egging him on. He was in a roaring good humor, unwilling to put an end to such a day. He had forgotten all about burning Dublin and now saw himself as the general of its defense. Dan and Tom tried to hold all together and lay out some kind of plan for the morrow, though neither knew what it should be. Conn's idea of a plan was to brag about the fight he would lead against the Law, did they dare to show their faces here again. The more he went on about it, the fewer he had to hear it.

Throughout these days of anxiety, a warmth of comradeship had been growing among the Dublin people, a satisfaction with themselves and each other. None wanted to give up those feelings or break their solemn oaths but the suspicion was creeping in that survival might demand such a price. They had no deep roots in Dublin to hold them firm, no love for it, no known and friendly hills around it where they could flee if the fight went against them. Defending Dublin wouldn't give them the job back. It began to appear that the only way back to the job was the bosses' way. No one wanted to say it out loud but few were ready to commit themselves to battle. Quietly they slipped away from the fire.

Donal was scarcely well launched on his warning to Conn when they began to return. The word seemed to seep under the shanty doors and in through the cracks that Donal was up with a word from below.

Conn listened without losing a drop of his bravado. "I take it kindly in you but I was after knowin already, they'd be back. Let 'em come. They'll get more than they bargained for."

"It's a grand fighter you are surely," Donal agreed, "but the morrow will be another thing entirely from the day. A whole troop on horseback with guns and all and rope to tie you up and drag you off to rot in the jail or swing from the gallows."

That was a sobering picture. It stopped Conn's mouth and sent shivers down many backs.

"Is it Conn only they're after," Kevin asked, "or all them throwing the rocks?"

"The Judge himself saw Conn heave the rock at the sheriff. I'm thinkin he's the one they're after, unless fingers gets pointed at others."

"Who told you this tale?" Conn demanded.

"It's Jamie himself sent the warnin," Donal said impressively.

There was a murmur of surprise.

Donal took in the sensation he had created and went on, "The way of it as Jamie gave it to me, it was the Judge brought the Law down on you. Him and Simon was against it. 'I was against it the day and I'm against it the morrow,' Jamie says to me. 'I'm determined,' he says, 'not to give up one of mine to the Law. You tell Conn Mor,' he says, 'to be off out of it before day. The sooner he goes, the farther he'll get before it's known he's gone.'"

"There now," Paddy exclaimed. "Isn't Jamie a good man at heart?"

"Maybe it's the good in his heart." Dan was skeptical. "And maybe it's some scheme in his head. He wants Conn out of it before day maybe, and no waitin for the Law to take him."

Conn seized on this. "He wants me out of the way, that's what's in it. Don't he know I'll give 'em a fight if they come tryin to take me?"

"Or maybe what it is," Connie O'Riordan suggested, "they don't have a good law case against him. Wouldn't all here swear Conn was out of it entirely and none of us knows who threw one of them rocks?"

"We would," Dan agreed and 'ayes' came from all sides.

Toby Weaver, who had remained behind when Buck and the others had gone, looked at Dan in amazement. "You would?"

Conn heard him. "And you wouldn't?"

"Who's to ask the likes of us," Mary put in her word, "when the Judge himself and all three of them law men will swear it was Conn. All that was up from the embankment seen what happened too, and Jamie himself." A thought suddenly came to her. "I wonder would that be it. Jamie wouldn't want to swear Conn's life away but he wouldn't swear against the Judge neither."

"Donal," Joe Dawley broke into the speculation, "is it all the men and the horses and guns comin after Conn only or is it to put us all out on the road?"

There was a dead silence. All drew in closer. Donal looked around at the anxious faces in the firelight. He hated to be the bearer of bad tidings, yet he enjoyed being the one who had the answer.

"Here it is, what Jamie said on that. If all is on the job on the morrow, workin for him, you'll be secure in your houses. If you're not, there's nothin he can do against the Judge bringin down the Law on you."

"Conn Mor," Tim Sullivan said gravely, "many a good man has had to go on his keepin before now. My advice is, make the best of your way out of here. Whosoever comes askin, not one here will know where you went or when."

Conn looked at him and around at the others. "Not a one here is man enough to make a fight of it?" No one answered. He took off his cap and flung it on the ground with a curse. "The lot of ye be damned for a bunch of cowards."

"Go now and godspeed," Johnny said, "or stay here and throw any more a them 'cowards' at us and you'll have all the fight you've got stomach for."

Conn made a move toward Johnny but one of his friends halted him. "Aw, wouldn't you be off out of this hole and m'self with you?"

With another curse, Conn picked up his cap and looked defiantly around at them all, his eyes searching out those who had been his followers. Connie O'Riordan was carefully looking the other way. When Conn turned to go, only two of his friends went with him.

"Conn!" Toby called and ran after him. "If you head for Pennsylvania," he whispered, "that's another state. I think you'd be safe there."

Conn looked at him with suspicion. "Wherever I'm off to, the likes of you won't be in the secret."

"It's the bad luck on us, Conn to go off," Egan Flynn said. "The beat of him isn't in it."

"He's got a powerful arm on him," Mary agreed, "but I'll sleep better with him out of it. He's one would walk into the bog without feelin what's underfoot, draggin the rest of us after him."

As soon as Conn was gone, people began to move back from the fire, to fade into the shadows, to disappear into the shanties.

"Well," Donal said after a few minutes, "it's off to bed with Donal Shelley. Goodnight all."

Dan reached out and caught him by the arm. "You brought us the message from Jamie. What's the message you'll be takin back?"

"Why . . . a . . . I'll be sayin I gave Conn the warnin and he's out of it with two of his mates. Jamie won't like that."

"He won't like what?"

"That Conn took two with him. He wants a full crew on the job, I could see that. 'Get Conn out of it,' he says to me. 'If he don't go, they'll take him, so I've lost him off the job anyhow. But I don't want to lose no more,' he says."

"He needs every man on the pumps, he does indeed. Yet he'll let the Law put every man out on the road?"

"So he says."

"So he says, but what Jamie says and what Jamie does is two different things."

Dan brought his face close to Donal's in the dim light. "What is it with you? With Jamie or with us?"

"I'm with you. Don't you know it?"

"No, I don't know it. You're the grand one to have a smile and a kind word for everyone and I got nothin against that but sometimes I think you're a friend to anyone that's got a smile for you." He tightened his grip on Donal's arm. "There's times you can't be the friend to everyone. When you tell Jamie them words you said, he'll be askin for more. What will you say then?"

Donal tried to pull away. "How do I know what I'll say when I don't know what he'll ask?"

"I know what he'll ask. He'll ask what's the talk in Dublin about goin back to the job."

"Ah, that's it. If Jamie knows the fear is in Dublin now. . ."

"You emptied a jug of fear over them with that message from Jamie. To my mind, that's what he sent you for. If it was for Conn only, you would be for putting the word in his ear and no other."

"Well now, that's exactly what I says to Jamie. I says it's m'self knows how to slip a word to a man and not another the wiser."

Dan let go of Donal's arm but held him with his eyes. "And what did Jamie say to that?"

"'No need,' he says. 'Let all hear,' he says. 'None in Dublin will give the Law a word where Conn is off to,' he says. Now you're sayin he had reasons for wantin all to get the warnin?"

"And the fear."

"And the fear," Donal repeated.

"So what will you be sayin to Jamie?"

"What I'll say," Donal kept his eyes on Dan's face to see how his words went down. "I didn't hear nobody talkin about goin back to the job and that's the God's truth."

"True for you. Now what you was sayin before, Jamie won't like it two went off with Conn. A man like yourself could count the thousands in the daylight but wouldn't it be hard for you in the dark of the night?"

"Well nigh impossible. I couldn't see how many was leavin, I'll tell him, 'but Conn didn't go alone,' I'll say. 'I couldn't swear was there four with him or six or . . .'"

"That's enough. He'll see with his own eyes, Dublin isn't emptied out. Just give him somethin to sleep on. And don't let him pour you out too many drinks or he'll have it out of you, what you don't want to give him. Like, 'who's to the fore?' he might be askin."

"Dan. Don't think it of me."

Dan watched Donal go, then turned to the few still left around the fire. Too few. Most of Dublin had taken the fear back into the shanties with them.

Chapter 45

ANNY AND ELLEN looked curiously at Willie, Tessa's oldest son, who sat on the hearth, shivering a little and holding out his hands to the fire.

"You come all the way in the dark by yourself?" Danny asked.

"That ain't nothin. I can see in the dark." He looked around the cabin. "Where at's Tim?"

Danny and Ellen exchanged a look. Danny put a finger to his lips. "He ain't here."

The men who had come up from Van Dorn's section had taken Tim back with them. If they caught sight of the Law next morning, or got wind of any danger to Dublin, they would send him back with the message.

"It's like when Danny's horn was lost," Ellen explained. "No one knows."

"What did you come for?" Danny wanted to know.

"Can't tell what for. My Mammy tole me not to say nothin to nobody 'cept your Mammy."

Danny went out to find his mother. While he was gone, Ellen and Willie sat in uncomfortable silence, their mouths stopped by the secrets. Danny came back with mother and father too.

Willie gave them Tessa's words, so low they had to bend their heads to listen. "My Mammy say, you come to our cabin. Don't let nobody know you comin. Don't show no light. Don't make no noise. She gon tell you how all them mens in the Big House gon do you."

"I'll go," Dan said at once. "Nobody's out there now but Hugh and Toby. It's no matter if they see me."

"Miss Mary come, Mammy say. She say don't tell nobody or she won't tell you nothin. Nobody got to see us. I come thout nobody seein me."

"So you did. How did you do it?"

"I knows the back ways in the bushes. It's black dark all over, 'cept your fire. I slides in here when you all lookin the other way."

Mary said she would come and Willie reluctantly accepted Dan too. When they reached Tessa's cabin behind the farmhouse, she opened the door and motioned them inside. Here in her own tidy little room, the light of the small fire on the hearth showed a different woman from the workaday Tessa.

"You all welcome to my house. Take a chair." She waved toward the two stools she had set before the fire.

"God bless all here," Mary responded as they sat down.

"You, Willie," Tessa said, "Watch out the door. Anyone come, say so quick." Willie cast one longing look at the warm fire and went out.

Arden wanted to follow. "I can watch, too."

"You stay right where you is, on that bed. I don't want to hear nary word outta you."

She stood quietly for a moment, smoothing down her apron, collecting her thoughts, then she spoke softly to Mary, almost as if Dan were not there. "I hearn

what they done to your folks. Shootin at Miss Peg an all. I was scared they gon
put you out and I wouldn't have a friend left. So I listen and listen. They think I
made outta wood or somethin, can't hear nothin, can't feel nothin, but I listen, I
hear. I had Willie to bring you so I could tell you, you better watch out. That Mr.
McCarthy, he got it in for you," she looked briefly at Dan, then back to Mary,
"and you. And all them bosses mad with that fella threw a rock at somebody."

"Conn?"

"That's him. They gon throw him in jail sure. What they schemin bout you, I
wisht I knew. I mighty near didn't hear nothin bout it. Mr. McCarthy, he tell Mr.
Dent, 'Dan Griffen in it deep,' but Griffen got him to deal with, he say."

Dan and Mary looked at each other. "How? What kind a deal?"

"I wisht I knew. All he say, you not gettin no more pay outta him." She shook
her head mournfully. "It look like a bright mornin for you all till that come
along."

"No more pay," Mary said it over. "Out upon the road by Jamie McCarthy's
hand in the cold of the winter."

She and Dan were both so intent on this personal disaster, they missed the
significance of Tessa's last remark. "Out upon the road," Mary repeated. Elbows
on knees, head in hands, she rocked back and forth. "Och, ochone. Out on the
road."

Dan put his hand on her shoulder. "Maire, Maire. Don't, acushla. Jamie's
not the only contractor on the canal. I'll have a job in a day the same as before
when Jamie wouldn't pay me foreman's wages."

Mary straightened up and wiped her tears away with the back of her hand.
There were tears of sympathy in Tessa's eyes.

Dan was biting his lips, chewing on this message. What a night for messages!
"Tessa," he said abruptly. "Did Jamie tell you . . . Did he say for you to take us
this word?"

Tessa stepped back as if he had struck her. "Miss Mary, what he askin? He
askin am I carryin some kinda tales?"

"No, no." Mary reached out and gave Tessa's hand a squeeze. "We thank you
for givin us the word, we do indeed." She threw a reproachful look at Dan. "The
anger isn't on you, it's on Jamie."

"Mr. McCarthy, he never hardly speak a word to me. I hear what he talk to the
Judge and them and I tells myself, you off there, no way a knowin what they
plottin and plannin." She looked searchingly at Mary and then at Dan. "You
won't tell ary man or woman who told you?"

"Never!" they said almost in unison.

"That would be the poor thanks for your kindness," Mary added.

"Iffen the Judge knew bout me havin any truck with you folks, tellin you his
business and like that, he like to put me out on the road or either send me back
down south. You all don't know the Laurences like I know 'em. All them
Laurences is stubborn and this place don't belong to McCarthy. It belong to the
Judge."

Dan woke up to the risk Tessa was taking. He stood up. "A thousand pardons if I spoke rough. Would we be puttin you in danger bein here in your house? We'd best be goin, Mary."

"I thinks they sleepin over there to the Big House. I think we safe if we talk quiet. Willie let us know do anybody come prowlin round."

Mary hadn't moved. "Tessa, Jamie and the Judge and Simon . . . What was they after sayin about the Law? The Law to come down on Dublin and put all out on the road on the morrow? Or me and mine only?"

"I just fixin to tell you. I hears a heap of things in that kitchen tonight but Mis' Laurence, she talkin in my ear so much I couldn't hardly get it all straight. If you set down again, Mr. Dan, I try to rake it together."

Dan sat down and Tessa smoothed her apron again, folded her hands in front of her and launched into her tale.

"What you just say, Miss Mary, that what the Judge want. 'Clean 'em all out,' he holler, 'Get 'em off my place' and all like that. But seem like Mr. Lordon and Mr. McCarthy don't want it like that nor Mr. Dent neither. 'Who gon pump? Who gon build that there akeduck?' they kep sayin. I never thought I live to see the Judge done like they done him. The end of it was, Mr. McCarthy tell the Judge he have to call off the sheriff from all your folks 'cept Conn. Everybody go to work tomorrow, he say. Nobody get put out. I so happy to hear that, I most broke out laughin. Mis' Laurence, she would a thought Ise crazy. And then Mr. McCarthy, he spoil it, say he gon deal with Dan Griffen. Then I don't know what to think."

"Everybody go to work. Nobody put out." Mary said it wonderingly.

"A different story entirely from Donal's," Dan muttered.

"How come Donal to give you any kinda story? He wa'n't there. What he know?"

"What Donal knows is what Jamie tells him," Dan said, "and that would be what Jamie wants him to tell us."

"That's it," Mary agreed. "Tessa's the one got the full of her ears with listenin."

"But if they don't bring the law down on us," Dan put one word after the other slowly, "how is it they're sure of gettin all back on the job? Did you hear a word of such as that?"

"One way or tother, Mr. McCarthy say. You know what he mean?"

"He's got some kind of a scheme but it's beyond me what it is."

Tessa racked her brain for a helpful clue. "The Judge, he figger and figger on the paper bout the wages and things. I couldn't get much of that part. But seem like Mr. McCarthy want you all back on the pumps so bad he can taste it."

"I knew it, I knew it." Dan clapped his hands together. "I knew they had to have them pumps a pumpin."

Tessa frowned and put her finger to her lips.

"Pardon, pardon," Dan spoke lower, but more urgently. "I'd give my last shillin to see what was on that paper."

"What was on the paper!" Tessa was triumphant. "That what Mr. McCarthy tell the Judge. I knew I'd dredge it up did you dangle out the right question. Mr. McCarthy he look like he eatin sour apples but he say, 'You give it to us on the paper, Judge. Might be we have to give 'em what they hollerin for.'"

"Give us what we're hollerin for!" As low as Dan's voice was, it was rich with the sound of victory.

"And ourselves out on the road, leavin hearth and friends behind us, just when the battle's won," Mary mourned. "If it is won at all."

Tessa looked doubtful. "That McCarthy, he all the time talkin like he got some nasty trick or 'nother."

"We can't light the bonfires yet," Dan conceded. "He sent us one of them tricks already, makin out like we'd have the soldiers down on us come sunrise. I fear me there's many a sheep in Dublin now, ready to run to the job when Jamie barks after 'em."

"Turn Miss Mary loose on him. She scorch the hair on that dog once. He still sore from it."

They had a stifled laugh over that, then Dan and Mary got up to leave.

"Slip right round to the back, the way Willie brung you so you don't have to cross the yard."

Dan opened the door a crack and peeped out. "All's quiet and the Big House dark."

Tessa pushed the door closed again. "I think they sleepin over there but sometimes the Judge, he come out on the porch in the night and piss all over the yard. Make Mis' Laurence mad but it don't make me mad. I hates to empty them chamber pots. He just better not do it tonight. And you just better not take no chances."

"No chances," Dan agreed, "and nothin said to nobody, we was ever inside your door."

"God bless you for what you did the night," Mary whispered before she followed Dan out. "May the Blessed Virgin keep you in her care."

Chapter 46

O
UT OF THIS place and no hearth of our own till heaven knows when." Mary watched while Dan mended the fire. The flames licked the new sticks and began to toss up brightness and warmth.

"You knew surely, we wouldn't be here our lives long." Dan straightened and stood beside her, near the warmth.

"I did. I did, so. On a summer's day or in the harvest time, with the sun on us, we'd go, that was the way of it in my thoughts. With many months pay to buy a horse and wagon like Buck has and time enough before us to build a bit of a house before the cold."

"That's what we will. What difference if we're gettin the months' pay we have need of on another section?" That was to cheer her and himself. He well knew the difference.

They stood with shoulders hunched forward around the warmth that was reaching in through the damp that clung to their clothes after the walk from Tessa's. Cold still fingered their backs.

"You wouldn't be goin off up the canal again without givin me the where of it and the why of it?"

"I would not. Why would you think it of me, I would do such as that?"

Men has short memories, Mary thought, but this was no time to rake up old quarrels. "What of the promises you and Jamie give each other, you to be foreman till the job's done?"

"If Tessa's in the right of it, Jamie don't care no more for a broken promise than a broken stick. How is it he knows I'm to the fore? Is it the scorchin you gave him in the cookhouse?"

"I wouldn't take back a word of it."

"I wasn't askin it, was I? I'm thinkin only, must we leave all behind in the midst of the turnout, not knowin will they go back to work? Is the Brotherhood all for nothin? Or will they win over him, and ourselves not here to see it?"

Mary had gradually become concious of a rustling in the loft. "Danny must be wakeful up there. Whatever the sun brings, we'd best sleep, late as it is."

The rustling above increased. A pair of legs swung over the edge of the loft. A pair of feet in gray stockings reached for the rungs of the ladder. It was not Danny. It was a full grown man. After a startled moment, they saw it was Toby.

"Hugh sent me in to his bed," he explained. "Do you mind?"

"Sleep the night out here and welcome," Mary answered.

Toby looked at them uncertainly then down at his feet, feeling inadequate without his boots on. He muttered something incomprehensible, then blurted out, "Why are you goin away? What does Tessa have to do with it?"

They had to tell Toby the whole story.

"Not a word of this to nobody," Dan ended it. Then he looked sharply at Toby. "You never swore the oath. How do we know you'll keep the secrets?"

"I promise."

"Promise, promise. Will you swear like all of us in Dublin done?"

Dan repeated the oath.

"I don't get the sense of it, swearing by the Holy Patrick. I'll swear by the Good Book if you want. You got a Bible here?"

How could they explain the oath to Toby? There had been no need to explain it to any of the Dublin men. Generation after generation, struggle had required organization. Organization had required a bond that would hold it together to withstand hard blows against all or against one. The bond was there to hand in the religion that was denied and despised by those against whom they struggled. The oath combined the sanctification of the cause, the commitment to obey chosen leaders and the reminder that retribution would descend on any who failed his brothers. Retribution would come in this life from the Brothers betrayed, in the next life for being false to God and St. Patrick.

"Aren't we all in this together?" Toby asked. "I trust you."

Mary heard in Toby's voice that he felt himself being left outside. She heard it because she had felt it herself. That was being a woman, always to help, never to be in the center of such things as the Brotherhood. How could a woman be a brother at all? But if Toby and Buck and the others were left outside, they would not be at the edges like herself. They must be full with the Dublin men or they could be against them.

"What makes you brothers in the Brotherhood?" she asked Dan.

She could see he didn't understand what she was asking. "All on the one job, isn't it? And Toby workin the night through on the pumps like you. Didn't he stand against the bosses the same as yourself? It was his own words he threw at the Judge. Let him swear in his own words to the Brotherhood."

"Let's hear then, what class of words you got."

Toby raised his right hand. "I swear by the Holy Word of God," he said slowly, "as true as if it was here under my hand. Now, what was the rest of it?"

He repeated the rest of the pledge after Dan all the way through. Much of it seemed queer and unrelated to their business. Why was he swearing "not to have carnal knowledge of my brother united man's wife, sister, or mother," when there wasn't a man in the camp had a mother here and there were few women? The mystery of it though, added to the solemnity.

". . . and do I betray my brother or the secrets of our society that my ears may be cut from my head and my arms from my body," he finished.

Dan and Toby clasped hands. That was solemn too, almost too much so. Toby scratched the calf of one leg with the toes of the other foot and put his thumbs in the waistband of his pants.

"Now I'm in it to my ears, you might say. I want to know how we can get all to hold one more day. It sounds like what they were talkin in front of Tessa means we damn near got what we want if we can hold out, but if you're gone, I just don't know. They all look to you, Dan."

"We need more heads on it. We need the Committee. But we don't tell the brothers about Tessa. What it is we'll say . . . the two of us picked up a word here and a word there, like from the stonies or Corny or Donal but we don't name no names. Let 'em think it might be from one of your lads, that knows the peelers." Seeing Toby's perplexity, he added, "or whatever it is you call 'em in this country that brings the Law down on you. Come on, we can't wait till sunup or Jamie will be up before us and down on us with another of his tricks."

Mary sat long by the fire after they went out, with the heaviness that had been in her since she got the news she was to be cut off from hearth and home, from friends and neighbors. At last she stirred and looked over toward the corner. There in the shadows were what was left of the supplies from the cookhouse.

Our last meal in Dublin most likely. The last meal before the cookhouse will be full of people again, without myself at the head of the women. I'll make this a hearty meal, at least. Och, that it will put the heart into the men to stand up to

Jaime. What a blessin it would be to win over him. If we have to go out on the road it would be a thing to take with us . . . Look at the small size on that pot, what a pitiful mouthful for each from that one. I may as well be hung for a sheep as a lamb. It's down to the cookhouse this minute for the big pot and whatever I can find to put in it.

Danny was blowing on the horn.

"Again!" his father said to him each time the air in his puffed out cheeks was used up in the sound. He took another gulp of air and blew again and yet again.

Ellen came out of the cabin behind them, pushing her tangled hair out of her sleepy eyes. It was dark as midnight out in the world with Danny pointing his horn at the faint strip of light between the top of the hill across the valley and the clouds above it. Dublin was lit up though, by the fire that was flaming high. Mary was bending over a big pot that had another small fire under it. Bridget held a long stick with pieces of bacon impaled on it. Drops of fat sizzled into the fire and sent up an entrancing smell of plenty.

The people were pouring out of their shanties. Toby and Buck were coming, leading another bunch of men. The air was so charged with excitement and anticipation that Ellen wondered were they going to dance in the road again.

There was panic in some of the faces that emerged from the shanties. "What is it?" they were asking. "Is it the Law?"

"No fear!" Dan called out and Johnny ran on his long legs from one shanty to the other with the same words. Egan and Connie faced off toward the Ohio men, seeing a menace there but Toby was smiling and waving his hat in greeting.

Mary banged on the pot with her big spoon. "It's the early breakfast we're havin the morn and plenty in the pot for all."

Dan walked into the thick of the people, talking to them as they crowded around to get the food. A call cut through the confusion, a call to Dan to get up where he could be seen and heard. Hugh pulled the bench out of the cabin as he had done on Saturday night. Some of the stonies pushed Dennis to get up beside Dan. The stonies were not sharing the food but they were not going off to breakfast at the farmhouse either. Dan motioned to Toby to join them.

"Brothers!" Toby sang out in a high excited voice. "We got the news for you all the way from Coshocton. The sheriff won't be comin to put anybody out."

The air was filled with questions and exclamations. "Is it so?" "Is that the truth of it?" "Good news!" " Listen to that, would you?"

Toby grinned at them, pleased with them and himself but he felt uncomfortable up above the rest and jumped down. Dan waved the questions aside and hurried into speech. Jamie might appear at any moment and there was much to be said.

"All of us together, we're goin to the bosses."

That brought a hush, a stop even to the movement around the fire. Then the movement began again but quietly, each person taking a full trencher from Mary or Bridget and moving back to make room for the next without a word said. Dan made his voice boom out over the little stir of activity.

"We tell Jamie and all we're ready for the work if they're ready with the right pay, like we put it on the notices. There's been three days besides Sunday without a pump pumpin. They can't stand another. They need our hands on them pump handles. They see we're all together on it, I'll wager my life we'll get what we want."

Art and Johnny roared out approval. A few other voices joined in.

"Will you speak for all?" Connie asked.

"Will I?" Dan put the question. There were scattered 'ayes'. No one said nay. All knew that to step forward out of the protective mass and stand alone in front of the bosses would put that one in danger.

"Let's go!" Egan shouted.

"Wait a bit," Tim Sullivan motioned Egan back. "Not so quick. You, Dan, you can make a wager and you can lose one. Jamie can tell us to get on the pumps and damned if he'll pay us another cent for it."

"He'll say such as that, he will indeed, don't you know it, Tim? Wantin us to run like sheep when the dog barks. But listen! Who will pump if we don't? Did he get one man on the pumps Saturday?"

"No!"

"Did he get one man on the pumps Monday?"

"No!"

"Did he get one man on the pumps yesterday?"

"No!"

"Will he get one man on the pumps the day, without we get what we want out of it?"

"No!" Perhaps that last 'no' was not as strong as the others but Dan could feel them coming together.

"The likes of us isn't so easy scared. We'll show Jamie each and all is men will stand by their oath and stand by each other. If he don't give us what we want, one more day with no pumpin will bring him round."

That brought a hearty cheer. They were drawing warmth from each other, feeling the strength of the common purpose. But as the cheer died down, a cold breeze seemed to strike the outer ring of people and move toward the center. The light of the fire was in Dan's eyes. He strained to see into the dark beyond it. Heads were turning. The crowd was parting to open a way for Jamie and Simon. Simon moved off toward some of the stonies but Jamie came walking straight toward Dan.

"What's this?" Jamie shot the words out like bullets. "What is it you're up here for? You think you're the priest, maybe sayin the mass?"

Dan folded his arms across his chest and opened his mouth to speak but Jamie turned his back and faced the crowd. "I see all of y' is up before the sun and ready for work. Let's get to it then."

Dennis spoke from behind him. "Nobody's settin foot out of here till you tell us, are you bringin the Law down on the ones we leave in it while our backs is turned?"

Jamie only half turned his head to hear Dennis. "I am not. I am not."

"And the Judge? Is he bringin the Law?"

"He is not—if all are back on the pumps."

"If all here was to pick up the pump handles again," Dan said to Jamie's back, "what would be the pay for the night's work and what would be the pay in the water?"

Jamie whirled, his hand lifted as if to push Dan off the bench but Hugh and Johnny were solidly behind him. Jamie had to hit Dan with the words only. "The wages is nothin to do with you. You're no foreman of mine no more and no laborer neither. Get out of it now while I talk to my own men."

Dan stared down at him. "All here wants me to speak for 'em. That's the job they give me. You can't take it away. I'll be off out of here soon enough and down the line to superintend another section. I could a done it before and I can do it again. Was I askin *my* wages? I was not. I was askin for all here. Do I speak for all, lads?"

There was a chorus of 'ayes.'

Jamie gave Dan his back again with his characteristic twitch of the shoulders. "I'll speak to any man here that's ready for work," he said. "I'll call out the names and them that wants to work, give me your word. Them that don't can come forward and get what pay is owed and get out on the road, along with this misshapen piece of a man behind here."

Dan made an involuntary movement at the insult, felt Johnny's hand from behind restraining him, then saw what Dennis was doing. He was pointing downward at Jamie and imitating him as he had done so often by the fire of an evening. The twitch of the shoulders was exaggerated, the pushing out of the chest made ridiculously pompous.

Some of the tense faces in front of them relaxed into smiles. Winks and knowing looks were exchanged. Unconscious of what was going on behind him, Jamie began to call out the names. "Fergus."

"Err . . . aye."

"Joe."

Joe was looking at the ground, rubbing his sweaty hands nervously against his pants legs. There was a little commotion around Fergus.

"I answered to my name," Fergus was protesting. "Can't a man answer to his name? It wasn't no 'yes' to the pumpin."

Art moved close to Joe.

"You ready to pay me what you owe, Joe Dawley?" Jamie pointed his finger. "If you ain't, you better be on that pump the day."

Joe went white but he kept silent.

Jamie's eyes swept across the faces, "Kevin."

"Now Jamie," Kevin said, looking from side to side apologetically, "You know how it is with me and Mick, here." Mick and Aghna were standing next to him. "You got work or money comin from us for bringin over Una and Aghna."

Aghna jabbed Mick with her elbow. "Speak up, Mick, lad. Speak up," she whispered.

"We wouldn't deny it," Kevin went on. "Never let it be said the Caseys don't pay their debts . . ."

"But we ain't pumpin," Mick spoke up loud and clear.

Jamie caught sight of a clump of strangers. "Who are you? What are you doin here?"

There was a brief silence then Phelim was nudged forward to answer for all. "You come up to Section One-sixty, offered us a job."

"You want to work?"

"We do."

There was a gasp from the Dubliners and a move toward Phelim.

"What's your name?" Jamie asked, a note of triumph in his voice. He took out his paybook and a stub of a pencil.

Phelim took a quick look at his friends to be sure they were still with him. "Phelim I was christened and Phelim you can put in your book. And put in there that I work for seventy-five cents in water and a day's pay for a day's work and a day's pay for a night's work."

There was a murmur of approval. Jamie got very red. His eyes searched the faces, finding no response. He looked from side to side, wanting something to stand on, so he could speak out to the whole crowd. There was nothing except the bench on which Dan remained, his feet planted firmly wide apart, his arms folded, Dennis beside him, Hugh and Johnny backing them up.

"Let me tell you how it is." Jamie was still speaking loud but the tone of his voice was different. "We got more pumps out there than any day or night you was pumpin. There won't be many nights work in it and when there is, we'll give a day's pay for a night's work."

That brought a cheer. What he had said was tossed from one to another to make certain all knew.

"And the work in water?" Dan called out.

"Now you know," Jamie said persuasively, still speaking as if to everyone but Dan, "we couldn't put the work in water up to seventy-five . . ." He hesitated. Had he given enough to bring them back? Could he risk another try at getting them to move? He fixed his eyes on Paddy O'Scanlon who shifted uncomfortably from one foot to the other. "We couldn't put it up to seventy-five . . ."

"Why not?" Paddy asked.

"The other contractors was holdin it down . . ."

"Some was and some wasn't." Dan's voice had all the authority of his commanding position and his firm support. "Now Wilcox has gone to seventy-five and it was on account of our turnout he done it. If Van Dorn don't do the same, he's like to have a turnout on his section."

Jamie gritted his teeth. "What I was after sayin, did that ill-mannered spalpeen there let me speak a plain word, is this here: Now that the other contractors is goin up on it, we'll do likewise."

"Seventy-five?"

"Seventy-five."

The word was repeated from front to back in the crowd. Relief, joy and triumph burst out in a cheer.

"Let's go to work!" Art yelled.

"What about a day's rest after a day and a night on the pumps?" O'Malley asked.

Jamie wouldn't hear it and Art only laughed. "If they don't give it, we'll take it."

Dennis left Dan and joined Michael who was listening to Simon's persuasions to stay on the job, but was shaking his head. Laughing and talking, the rest of the men began to turn toward the river and the work. Jamie quickly got out at the head, leading them back to the job.

Dan sat down on the bench. That suddenly, it was all over and himself left behind.

"Here," Mary handed him a trencher full of stirabout with a lump of bacon on top. "You haven't had a bite, nor m'self neither." She sat down beside him with her own breakfast.

Ellen wiggled herself in between. "Won't there be dancin?"

"Dancin? After the work maybe, there'll be dancin for some but it's many a day before we find a place for your feet to dance . . ." Mary's voice trailed off and she drew in her breath sharply, bringing Dan's head up from where it was bent over the food. "Will you tell me what's that? Who is it stirrin up a new commotion?"

The movement toward the job was slowing. Some kind of counter-current was at work. They could hear voices raised, see arms gesticulating. Egan and Connie broke away and headed back toward them, a third man took the same direction, running to catch up. Johnny and Art were not far behind, in a hot argument with each other. Jamie hurried through the crowd, calling out to Egan.

The dense mass changed its shape, a thin broken line stretching toward Dublin, away from a lump that swayed hesitantly, followed watchfully. Jamie was moving from one to another of those in front. Was he ordering? Pleading?

"Looks like there's some stray sheep and the dog can't get 'em back in the flock," Dan remarked.

Egan came breathlessly up to them. "We're with you, Dan Griffen. If you go off, we go off, the three of us." Connie and another young fellow were right behind him.

Michael and Dennis broke away from Simon. Dennis strode over and put a hand on Egan's shoulder. "You're a son of your father. Was Pat here, he'd do the same."

"I'd be proud . . ." Dan had to stop and clear his throat. "I'd be proud to have the three of you on the road with me but I'm bound to tell you, it might be a long road for all my braggin to Jamie."

"I'm with you too," Dennis declared. "You know that surely."

Michael found his voice and faced off at Simon with a long speech. "I was after tellin you the night, I don't work for no man shoots at my wife. Now here's Jamie breakin his word, Dan to be his foreman to the job's end. Was I ready to lay stone here at all, I wouldn't be doin it now with Dan and Mary put out on the road. Why here's Mary saved my life and me dyin of the fever and bound up my Peg's arm when them peelers you brought in was like to kill her."

Jamie came up while Michael was talking, but before he could get a word out, Simon seized him and spoke vehemently into his ear.

Johnny was there now, and got his word in. "True for you, Michael. We was together in Akron, together on the road from Akron to this place, together in the

ditch and in the water and beside the fire and all. We'll be together on the way
out of it."

"I'm in your company," Phelim added his word. "I doubt we would a made it
without you, Dan. Is it right us to get the sweet and leave the bitter to you?"

"Stop it, stop it." Simon was saying frantically to Jamie, "while we got a man
left."

"Stop it!" For once Jamie had no words of his own and had to use Simon's.

Mary didn't care in the least what Jamie had to say. The faces of the friends
crowding around shimmered strangely in brightness as she looked at them through
her tears. Bridget was beside her, holding her hand.

"Since it's such great friends we got here," Jamie had found some words though
he clearly didn't like the taste of them. "We'll keep all on the job. That's if all
stays. Dennis and Michael too."

The two masons consulted each other with a look and a nod. "We keep Dan
with us?" Dennis asked.

"We do."

"Dan to be foreman?" Connie asked.

"No. He can pump like the rest. I'll do my own superintendin, like I done
before I had the misfortune to bring Dan Griffen over the water, thinkin him a
friend to me."

Connie looked doubtfully at Dan.

"I will, I'll work with you," Dan said to his brothers.

Chapter 47

THERE WAS to be a goose for Christmas dinner. Ellen was the first to know.
"Myself goes with Maimie to make the bargain for it," she told Danny.
"There will be aplenty to do from this out till Christmas."

Indeed there was enough for Ellen to do every day now that her mother was
taking in lodgers again, besides being often called to the sick. Pat's Egan and Art
Sheean were now in the loft. Four more came for every meal. The time Mary was
all night with Rose Farrell, helping Rose's third child into the world, Ellen cooked
the breakfast stirabout all by herself.

In the cookhouse, her mother had been absorbed in the tasks and the talk she
shared with the other women. Now it was Ellen who shared the talk as well as the
tasks. All the while the preparations went on, Mary was telling her of Christ-
mases in Cork where Christmas began days before the birthday of the Lord Jesus.
Here, there would be just the one day off from the work but they would make the
most of it.

Preparations for a feast were going on, not only in the Griffen shanty but in
every shanty that had a woman in it and in the cookhouse as well, where Aghna

now presided. Mary had been sure everything would be in a brutheen with herself out of it but Aghna was doing well with Tessa's help and Una in Bridget's place. Bridget had thrown up her job in resentment at the preference given Aghna when it was herself who had been longest at the work. She too was taking lodgers.

All the men and boys were out in the frosty air on Christmas morning. They had a small bundle of straw perched up on a stump to serve as a target. The young ones were hurling stones at it. After each round, the winners were moved back a few paces to see could they still knock it down. The older ones jeered the losers and cheered the winners.

Into this scene, to the surprise of all, walked Pat Flynn. He had left his two little ones with Kate in Cincinnati and come back to work with old friends and his son, Egan.

The noise of the welcome brought Mary to the door. "You'll have Christmas by our fireside. That will make a pure holiday of it for your Egan and ourselves too."

The food at the Griffen table was well seasoned with the story of the turnout. They weren't half through the telling when others came in to greet Pat and add their own word to the tale. The part Egan had played in the great events made Pat beam with pride.

"Och, that I had come back a bit earlier to be in it with all of y'. . . And isn't such a thing needful all along the line? The lads would give me a place to sleep in their shanties as I come along and tell me the way of things on their sections. Wasn't hardly one where they wasn't complainin about the low winter pay they was gettin or the poor food or not enough extra for goin in the water."

"True for you," Dan said. "Lads has heard the rumor of it and come from sections miles off to get the whole of it told by ourselves."

"Is Jamie hirin? Will he take me on?"

"A man like yourself that's been with him since the Erie?" Hugh rumbled his assurance. "He will then."

"Likely he will," Dan agreed, "but not for the sake of old friendship. There's little value Jamie puts on old friendship. It's the need he has for good workers. That bastard of a pier that nearly broke the backs on us is done now and the second one too. We're not finished with the third and there's another one after that."

Pat shook his head over the way Jamie had driven them day and night on the pumps. "And myself givin him the character of a good boss to men on other sections."

"It's this long time I knew him for what he is," Mary said. "Ourselves would be out on the road in the cold of the winter was he our only friend on this side of the water. But look there at your Egan. He's a true friend. And all here, the same. It's them kept us here in our own place and Dan on the job."

"That Maggie could be here to see the man we've got there for a son," Pat said quietly to Mary, not wanting to brag out loud but too full of pride to keep it from bursting out of him.

"She'd have the right to be proud, she would indeed. And look at Tim, the way he's forever followin after Egan. Thinks he's St. Patrick returned to earth, so he does."

"Some of the men thinks that of Dan." Pat was watching fellows he didn't know who had just come in and were gathered around Dan.

The door couldn't be kept closed with all the people coming in or leaving for a look at what was going in the other shanties. A whole group came when the cookhouse dinner was over, those who couldn't get in crowding around the doorway with something new to tell.

"See that tall one?" Mary pointed to one of the newcomers. "That's Phelim. A good lad and him comin in with us when we turned out."

"We put it to Jamie about the cookhouse wall," Phelim announced, looking triumphantly around.

"Time you did," Mary said. "Didn't Jamie promise there would be a wall before the cold? If it was m'self in the cookhouse, Jamie would have heard about it before now, I promise you."

"He heard about it this day."

Half a dozen of them began talking at once. They had told Jamie the Christmas feast was grand but how could a man enjoy it when he was shaking with the cold wind?

"When is it you'll be shuttin out a bit of the cold?" Phelim had asked him, "or are we to have snow in our stirabout and wind in our stew from this out?"

"What did he say to it?" Dan asked when the laughter at Phelim's words had subsided.

"That got a right laugh from Jamie himself. He says he was after tellin Donal already he didn't like the cold neither. Donal will be gettin at the wall on the morrow, so Jamie says. 'He's been waitin only to be free of the other work piled up on him,' Jamie says."

"What is it I'll be doin on the morrow?" Donal had heard his name.

"Buildin us a wall to the cookhouse to keep the wind out."

Tom had one of his questions: "Is it the truth, Jamie's been tellin you this long time to do it?"

"Not a word did I have from him on it since we put up the roof and that bit of a wall that's there now."

"What it is," Dan said, "we get from Jamie what we knock out of him and that's all we get."

"You didn't leave off knockin things out of him when you ended the turnout then?" Pat wondered at it.

"Nah, nah, we did not."

"The very day we went back to work," Tom told Pat, "he had us at it like we never stopped pumpin. We got to the bottom of the pit by sunset but we pumped into the night while they was sawin off the piles. 'Will we knock off comes sunrise?' I asked Jamie. 'What? Let the pit fill again and all to do over? We'll work through the day,' he says. Well, then, we passed a quiet word from one to another till all had it, 'A night's rest and a day's rest when the work is done.'"

"What did Jamie say to that?"

"Not a word, not a word. He knew we'd turn out on him again, did he try to drive us to work without the night's rest and the day's rest after."

"We put that on the notice," Connie explained, "and we was stickin to it."

"Jamie didn't say nothin," Dan took up the story, "but he done somethin. When we come back to work, all Van Dorn's men was loaned for the time we was on the pumps. There was no more long days from that time out. The work went on without stoppin but it was twelve hours work and twelve hours rest for all. We got it dewatered one last time and kept it like that with some pumpin and some in the pit sawin off the piles and layin the timbers and some restin till their turn come. Will we walk down and look at it while there's still daylight? The stonies has got the masonry up above the river on it now."

Mary and Ellen soon had the shanty to themselves. Mary waved her hand at the disordered table and the food still left on it. "As sure as we put it up, someone would be in askin for a bit and a sup and we'd have to drag it all out again. I'll just have another sliver of the goose myself, the way I've been too busy stuffin it into the men to make a proper meal . . . if I can find a sliver at all. They stripped it to the bone, they did indeed. Did you hear Pat's word?"

"I did, Maimie." Ellen clapped her hands. "'I didn't have such a feast since Christmas in Ireland,' Pat said."

"It's the taste of home in the food and the good friends eatin it with him. That's what Pat was sayin."

Bridget came in, then Rose with her new babe, bringing what was left of her Christmas loaf to give them a taste of it. Ellen heard the children outside and ran out to play. Soon nearly every woman in Dublin was beside the Griffen hearth. Peg would be the next to give birth and Molly wouldn't be far behind her sister. The two of them hovered over Rose's babe.

The women in the cookhouse who now did the cooking weren't looked for in this gathering. There had been hard feelings between Mary and Bridget on the one side and Aghna and Una on the other since the two Casey women took the cookhouse jobs. The feelings were made harder on Mary's part over Kevin being always hat in hand to Jamie, going after Dan's old place as foreman. And Tessa had never been part of these gatherings.

When Dublin talked of the turnout, Tessa's part in it could not be included and as the weeks passed, Mary had become so accustomed to the story without Tessa in it that the midnight hour in her cabin was almost forgotten.

In preparing for Christmas, she had been lavish with the money taken in from the lodgers. Not the least of it was a nice lump of sugar from the store. She made them a drop of hot punch with it and all the friends were comfortable and merry together.

Pat and Dan were walking toward the river, the others strung out before and behind.

"How is it with you now you're not the foreman?" Pat asked.

"It's short pay and hard pumpin and the rough side of Jamie's tongue. The truth of it is, Jamie is tryin to drive me off the job."

"But you won't let him do that surely?"

"I will not."

"Who was it got put in your place?"

"No one but Jamie himself. What will be done when there has to be a crew on the embankment again and one at the river and the Judge gone lawing around the country, nobody knows. I'm well out of it. After what we was through together, me and the Brothers, I couldn't drive them no more like Jamie wants 'em drove."

Dennis caught up to them with some questions for Pat about the stone work he had seen as he came along the line. Dan hardly listened while they talked of it. His thoughts were on the half-answer he had given to Pat.

How is it with myself? It's all well and good to make light of the changes, tellin 'em to Pat. What I wasn't tellin was the way I got to swallow my pride every day along with the bitter taste of the words rollin off Jamie's tongue. If I don't keep the mouth on me closed and the hands busy, I wouldn't be gettin even the short pay at the month's end. But there's more in it than the pay. Them hard words he's hittin me with, they're like pebbles. They sting but I don't need no kind words from Jamie. What would bring me kind words from him? Nothin but goin against the men and them lookin to me like I was Captain Rock all over again. I'm their man and I'm my own man. He can't touch that. So how is it with me? It's well. It's well.

Dark was falling by the time the men returned. They found the fire warm and the punch hot and the children coming in from the cold. They crowded in for a drink then broke up into smaller groups and drifted back and forth among the shanties.

The men in the Griffen loft had agreed they could make room for Pat but he lingered a little longer with Dan and Mary when the rest had climbed the ladder.

"Where's Joe and Eileen? I knew there was some I was missin but it took me till now to know who it was."

"We said good-bye to them after the last payday." Mary sighed. "Poor Joe, he had the canal fever that bad, the wonder was he could work at all. When he got the dead horse killed they went off to Philadelphia. Eileen has a mother's brother in that place. We cried over the partin, Eileen and me. We thought to be neighbors on the farms but Joe had to sell their piece of land for the money to get to Philadelphia."

"This is the first word I heard about the farms this day. You was buyin land, was you? Who was after buyin besides Joe?"

"Ourselves and Tyrone. That's all. And Tyrone is out on his land already."

Nothing more was said about the farms. It was a subject that had no interest in Dublin. Mary and Dan no longer talked about it between themselves. It seemed to fit nowhere into Dublin the way it was now. The land on which they lived was not their land but this section of canal line was theirs in a new way. They belonged with the people who worked on it. The signpost pointing toward the farm which Mary had always had in view had once looked like a signpost to a new

Dublin. Now it had the look rather of a road to a second exile, if none of their people would be traveling it with them.

The signposts pointing down the canal line, to other jobs when this one was finished had once looked to Dan like a road he could walk a step behind Jamie, with himself a kind of boss like Jamie at the end of it. Now it showed the way that would be taken by the rest of the Dublin people who had been with them in the living and the dying, the feasts and the fevers, the struggle and the survival. Yet it pointed the way down a hard road and one without a rest at the end of it on their own land, the land without rent for which they had always longed.

They were not at the crossroads yet. They turned their thoughts away from the choice they would have to make.

Chapter 48

THE GRIM FACE Jamie had on him since the turnout was gone on the December payday. He was giving out jokes along with the pay in his old way.

Dan peered around those ahead of him in the pay line to see was Jamie greasing the wheels to take them over a bump in the road.

When it was Dan's turn, he looked down at the money in his hand in surprise. Jamie said brusquely, "Move along, move along."

Dan stepped aside and stood there counting his money. "Here, Jamie," he said, "I'm more than a dollar short."

"You're not a penny short. You're a digger now, don't you know it? I never cheat a man on his wages."

It was true that unlike some contractors, Jamie and Simon had that reputation. The men who were slow at the figuring could take their pay without count or question, yet there could be mistakes. Dan always figured his own pay and often helped others to do the same.

"It's near sixteen dollars I was due. Two days not worked in the bad weather and one out for Christmas brings it down from twelve dollars, and six days in water brings it up again and there's three and a half for board now I boards myself."

"Get a more knowin man to figure your pay for you, seein as how you can't do it yourself."

Jamie put money in Kevin's hand and Kevin sniggered at his jibe. Other men who had been paid were gathering around Dan, questioning or complaining that they, too, were short. Jamie stopped the line and raised his voice. "You all got what's comin to you. It's winter pay now. We would a give you summer pay all through the winter to make up for the long days and so we told you. It was you wanted the extra pay for the long days. You can't have it both ways, don't you know it? You'd be better off did you stay with the job and the pay we was givin. You didn't gain nothin with that turnout. You lost with it."

"Is that the truth?" Paddy asked Dan, coming off the line with his pay in his hand.

"Let's get out from under Jamie's eye and figure this for ourselves."

Everything was in confusion. The men were telling each other how many days work there had been and how many nights. Tim Sullivan and Mick and some others had so much pay, some thought they weren't cut like the rest, but it was the more days they had worked in water.

"Jamie's in the right of it," Kevin said. "Any man can see twelve dollars a month is better than ten."

When supper was over, Dan, Connie and Tom sat at the table in the Griffen shanty and worked at the sums till their heads cracked. All others were pushed out so they could have some quiet for the task.

When they could see the pattern, the others were called back. All were better off this payday, they explained, except the few who had been in the water less than five days.

There were few with exactly the same pay, some differences having to do with the number of days missed, some with the number of days in water, some with the difference between those who boarded in the cookhouse and those who got board money along with the pay. Differences were not new and had once been accepted without question. Now that they had taken their own part in determining the pay, each was counting his own and comparing with others.

"Look here now," O'Malley said. "The way it was before the turnout with summer pay but nothin extra for my five days in water, I'd be after gettin near the same as this here. Only ten cents more I got. All that trouble and worry and losin three days pay over it and all for ten pennies! Is it worth it? I ask you."

He held out his hand with the ten pennies in the palm of it and pitiful they looked indeed.

"If your ten cents ain't worth nothin to you, give it to me," Art called out.

O'Malley tightened his fist around the money and glared at Art but that was only one of many contentions. The men butted against each other in the crowded shanty and got things more mixed up than before. On top of everything else, the Saturday night drinking had started, adding enough fuddled heads and raucous voices to the general confusion that they finally had to give up.

By Sunday afternoon, some of the drunk ones had sobered up and with all the talking the Committee had been doing to a few at a time, the confusion had lessened. They built a big fire outside with all gathered around with Dan up on the bench again.

"Since we got the pay, there's not been a word spoke about nothin else but what was it we turned out for most of all? It was against the pumpin through the days and the nights and the days again without rest. Did we put a stop to that or didn't we?"

"Aye, aye. We did. We did."

"If there's a man got cut down on the pay, it's m'self, and I say it was worth it for the end of them long days. The next thing is, all know now it was a dirty lie, us to be better off for the pay without the turnout."

There was some assent to that too, but Paddy asked "Why wasn't keepin up the summer pay on the notice along with them other things?"

"Did I hear you askin it?" Tom challenged him.

"Even a good man with the figures like yourself, Dan, can't make ten dollars look like twelve." That was Kevin.

Tom, who was sitting on one end of the bench, banged on it with a stick to bring silence.

"This cut in the pay Jamie brought down on us," Dan resumed, "sent us barkin after the wrong hare. He was makin out it was the turnout brought the pay down. Was it?"

"It was not." For once, Tom had an answer instead of a question. He jumped up on the bench beside Dan. "Them that wasn't here last winter don't know it but here's how it was: Jamie give us the same story about keepin summer pay through the winter, but comes the flood, we was cut down to eight dollars—not ten, eight!— and we was after bein so scared we took it. The bosses would a cut the pay down this winter, turnout or no. That's my guess on it."

"Tom's in the right," Dan agreed. "And here's another thing that's in it. We made Jamie pay us for them days that went on into the night, but them times we got the Van Dorn men up here and the pumps never stopped, we worked twelve hours. That's well past the sun's time from its risin to its settin in winter. I say that's summer hours and damned if it shouldn't be summer pay."

"Will we turn out for it?" Egan called out.

"For what?" O'Malley asked. "We got things some better and I don't know as I want to lose God knows how many days' pay turnin out for a little more and maybe losin what we got."

They argued it back and forth. In the midst of it, Toby came up with a couple of the other Ohio men and not long after, several of the Van Dorn crew walked in. They had been cut down to winter pay too. What was to be done about it?

"We could put another notice on the bosses," Phelim suggested. "They had a taste of how we can do when we get together on it. Maybe we wouldn't have to turn out at all."

"The farmers around here always bring the pay down for the hired hands in the winter," Toby said. "Our folks is used to it being like that. I don't hardly think we could bring but one or two out."

"There's still the third pier to finish and the last one to build," Tom reminded them. "If they don't have all four done, they might as well not have any, the way they'll have to wait for low water again. They need all hands as much as they did before. Phelim may be in the right of it. A notice might be enough."

"That could be," Dan said. "But there's no use to put a notice oñ 'em unless we're ready to back it up."

The meeting began to break up into half a dozen separate discussions. Voices were raised and cold feet were stamped as they talked. The young ones around

Johnny and Egan were talking of other threats they might put on Jamie, short of a turnout. O'Malley and Tim Sullivan were pulling the more cautious around them, arguing for putting their pay in their pockets and taking no more chances.

Men from other jobs had been here in the last weeks, looking for work. All knew it would be easier for the bosses than it had been in November to fill their places.

"It looks like you won't be doin nothin against the cut." Timothy Manrow, a Van Dorn man, was disappointed. "Was you ready to put a notice on your bosses to give back the summer pay, we might could get ours in behind you, doin the same. The way it is . . ." He shook his head.

"If we was to try, we couldn't carry more than half with us," Johnny answered him. "That's what it looks like. It's the way Tom said about the aqueduct. They can't put up the bridge part without all the piers under it. We can't put a notice on the bosses without all the men holdin it up."

"Why wouldn't you lead the way this time?" Tom tipped his head to the side and squinted up at Manrow. "You got your seventy-five for work in water out of our turnout. Wouldn't you have a right to be to the fore this time?"

"Our lads look to you and if you're doin nothin, they'll to the same."

Some of the men moved off and those still seeking a way to act drew closer around the bench where Dan, Tom and Connie were now sitting.

"To my mind, the winter pay ought to be more than summer, if there's any difference," Art said. "The wet cold it is and gettin colder day by day."

"Was Conn Mor still about, we'd have some action," another one of the young fellows declared.

"We would so," Egan agreed. "And why not without him? I'm for it."

"Was Conn Mor here, we'd have some broken heads or it's not day yet." Dan frowned at them. "Is this a faction fight, with nothin in it but to see how many heads can get broke?"

Egan wasn't so easily silenced. "Have we got a Brotherhood at all? Then let's move it."

"Have we got a Brotherhood?" Dan repeated the words thoughtfully, looking from one to another. "Have we got a Brotherhood? We got one here but it isn't yet on your section, Timothy. The men that was workin for Wilcox isn't in it. What if we was all in the same Brotherhood? Did we stand against the winter pay we'd have some chance then."

"Never was a truer word spoke," Pat said solemnly. "Like I told you, I come across from Cincinnati to Chillicothe and followed the canal line from Chillicothe here. I seen many a section where the Irish was in it and hardly a one where they wasn't complainin the winter pay was down on 'em."

Art pointed at Pat. "The days it took him to get here, how would we get the word up and down the canal to bring all in?"

"Not so hasty, not so hasty," Tom objected. "Look down the road a bit farther. If we can't stop the pay comin down now, could we have a thing or two to say in the spring, when does it go up and what does it get put up to? We could put heads together beforehand and all come down on the bosses at once."

"Don't you see you started already?" Phelim pushed others aside to come forward in his excitement. "Art and them with him brought the Brotherhood up to Section One-sixty and that's why you had us with you instead of against you. And some of your other lads took the Brotherhood down to Van Dorn's section. Without that would the turnout be won at all? Don't you see it?"

The men from Van Dorn's had been talking among themselves. Now Manrow held up his hand. "We're ready for the oath. We'll bring in our men and take the word down as far as the locks at Adams Mills. Peter McNally works down there. He's a good man. He'll carry it further."

"It looks like we got our foundation laid," Dan said. "The days without work in the winter we can build on it like we done in the winter days when we wasn't plantin or harvestin in Cork. That's when we made the uprisin."

Before the day was out, Timothy Manrow and his mate, John Joice were added to the Committee and Phelim put in Dennis's place. Dennis said masons and laborers should each have their own society the way their fights mostly came at different times and for different reasons, which wasn't to say they wouldn't be a help to each other.

The word of the Brotherhood spread to the Irish camps from Caldersburgh to Frazeyburgh and from Frazeyburgh to Newark. No effort was made to bring in the Germans. None of them had the Irish and few had the English. The Irish workers looked at them across a wide gap, perceiving only strangers. The Ohio men were less strange but even at the aqueduct few of them could see the need for the Brotherhood or the hope in it, nor were they comfortable with its words and its ways. The canal would provide work and cash wages for a few more months. After that, they would have no more part in building it and no interest in hours worked on it or wages paid. Buck and Ike, Toby and Shad were all rooted in Coshocton County. Only Sam and one or two of those who had been learning the stonework had any thought of following the line into other camps and other counties.

The Griffen shanty became the headquarters of the Brotherhood for the whole canal world. One Irish camp got the word from Manrow's friend McNally just when their job was closing down for the winter. Five of them came all the way up to Dublin, spent a Sunday in talk before the Griffen hearth and squeezed into the shanties to sleep that night. They were heading for one of the Ohio River ports, hoping to pick up a little work and find some shelter till the spring. They would carry the word along the line as they left and as they returned in April. They were sworn in and Connie wrote out a copy of the oath so they could swear in others.

"Look to it you don't bring in nobody you can't trust or we'll have our Society wiped out before it gets started," Dan warned. "When you come into a new camp, ask how the work is and the pay and what kind of a boss is it. Ask has they heard about such a thing as the Brotherhood like you don't know about it yourself. It's answers to such as that will point you to the ones is ready to be sworn."

Chapter 49

ONAL WAS SEEN coming from Tessa's cabin in the night. Far from denying it, he bragged that it had been going on these many months under their noses. It was well talked over when the women gathered for a cup of tea after the noon dinner. The colloguins were now in Mary's house or Bridget's, not in the cookhouse.

"Didn't Donal fool us all?" Bridget said. "Makin out like he was sleepin with some woman in Caldersburgh. We was after knowin in Akron already, he wouldn't stay with the Irish but would it enter anybody's head, that one would take a black woman for himself?"

"He's a sly one," Peg chimed in. "Remember my weddin, him dancin around them Ohio girls?"

"All knows the Judge is the father of her boys," was Bet Sullivan's contribution. "What all should know, she'll lift her skirts for any white man that comes along, like all her kind. Look at the fancy dressed-up whores in Caldersburgh. Two of 'em's black. They parade up and down in front of the tavern, not a scrap of shame in the lot."

"The Judge is not the father of her boys," Mary said. "Who it is, that's Tessa's secret."

"You bein in the know of her secrets, was you knowin about her and Donal?" Bet asked.

"I was not."

"Then you don't know neither, what others has been into her."

Bridget laughed. "You don't know Donal, if you think he's content to be one of many."

"I always said it was a shame to have such a one in the cookhouse," Bet reminded them. "Flauntin herself in front of our men. I wonder at Mrs. Laurence, allowin her on the place at all. You was always one to put her above your own, Mary. Even you can see what she is now."

"When I was in the cookhouse, Tessa did her work and behaved like a decent woman, not like one I could name."

That turned the talk to Una, but Una's behavior in the cookhouse was an old story and there was nothing new even in the way she was now making up to Jamie. The talk soon drifted back to Tessa and Donal.

There was something about that talk and her own part in it that nagged at Mary the rest of the day.

Well then, why did she keep it from me, she was Donal's woman? Talkin the way there was no man in her bed since the father of her boys. But I was lettin Bet put the name of whore on Tessa just because she has the same color on her as two of them Caldersburgh whores. Doesn't the rest of 'em have the same color as Bet? That would have stopped her mouth, did I think to say it . . . It's hard for a woman with no man, year in and year out. Didn't Maggie tell us how it was for her and herself seven years without Pat? Poor woman, she didn't have long to enjoy him when she followed him over the water.

If Maggie could wait out the seven years without lyin on her back for another man, couldn't Tessa do the same, till she could have one of her own to wed? She wouldn't think Donal would wed her surely? Not if she knows him at all, the sinner.

Tessa became a presence beside Mary as she went about her work. The way she told her old life over while they plucked the turkeys. The way she stood proudly by her own hearth, giving them the word that helped win the turnout.

Mary stood at the door one evening with her shawl wrapped around her, waiting for Tessa to pass on her way home from work.

"If you like the cold so well, why don't you go out in it?" Dan called out, "and not be freezin the bones in the rest of us."

She closed the door behind her, gave Aghna and Una a cool goodnight when they passed. Then Tessa came along and both of her boys with her.

"How is it with you the night? It's been this long time since we had a word together."

"Well, thank y' ma'am."

"Willie and Arden workin in the cookhouse?" Mary was surprised to see them, since Aghna's Brian had taken Danny's place.

"No, ma'am. I has my boys to meet me, it so dark and all. Some a these mens been gettin mighty rude lately. Miss Aghna don't keep 'em in order like you done."

So, it was just as she thought, things were not the same in the cookhouse without herself there. She shivered, watching Tessa and the boys go down the dark road, then went slowly back into the warm shanty.

The talk among the men about Tessa was that Donal shouldn't have kept a good thing to himself when the rest of them had let Tessa alone, thinking her to be the Judge's woman. Art and a couple of others, having a Saturday night load of drink in them, knocked on Tessa's door. When the cabin remained dark and quiet and a push on the door proved that it was barred from within, they made such a racket the Judge came out on his porch with his gun and chased them away.

Art came lurching into the Griffen cabin where all were asleep. He couldn't make it up the ladder to his bed in the loft, so he sat down on a stool by the dying fire, muttering drunkenly to himself till Dan and Mary woke and Dan got him put away for the night.

Sunday was a rare mild day for January and all were out in it except Mary when Art came down the ladder the next morning. Mary set some breakfast before him. He leaned his head on one hand and picked idly at the food with the other.

"The food has no taste to it when you've had too much to drink, is that the way of it?" Mary sat down across from him. "What was it you was grumblin and groanin about the night?"

"Did I wake you? I ask pardon."

"It wouldn't be a Saturday night, did one or another of you not wake me. What I have to say—it's a pity you didn't heave up the drink before you got in the house and the nasty thoughts with it."

"Aw now, Mary, don't come at a lad this early with the foolish things he said when he had the drink in him . . . What did I say?"

"It was a woman was on your tongue and what you'd be doin to her could you get at her and what you will do some night when you catch her out from behind her door. What woman was that?"

"Mary! You wouldn't think I'd lay a finger on you?"

"You may be a fool but not such a fool as that. Was it Tessa?"

"What if it was?"

"And myself thinkin you the fine young lad."

The silence after that lasted till Art looked in her face and saw there were tears in her eyes.

"Art Sheean, didn't I sit here in this room itself and hear you swear not to betray any of your brothers and not to do wrong to our women neither?"

"That's you and Rose and Peg and such. Tessa's no woman of ours. She's a nigger. Do you mean she's Donal's woman? We never swore him in."

Mary continued to look at him.

He hastened to justify himself. "Maybe you wouldn't be knowin she's the Judge's woman. Donal might a got him a piece but it was the Judge come out with his gun after us. I'll take the Judge's fancy woman any time. I'll show him he can't chase me with his gun. I'll make him suffer." Art's nostrils flared and he drew his lips back from his teeth.

Mary stared at him. "That I have such a beast in my own house. Not a thought in you, you'd be makin the woman suffer. Or is it that her sufferin makes a man of you? Is that it?"

"I shouldn't be talkin to you so. It's men's talk. You don't understand."

"It's too well I understand. Not that all men are like you, thanks be to God."

Art started to rise to get away from her.

"Sit you," she said sharply. "Sit! You wasn't alone, was you?"

"I'm not tellin you who . . ."

"Don't then. Did I ask? Be loyal to your brothers, the fine true man that you are. How many is all I asked."

"Three."

"Three of you after a lone woman. I have this to say to you and for you to say to the other two heroes. You wouldn't touch a woman belongs to a brother. Is that it?"

He gave a reluctant bob of the head.

"Tessa belonged to a man once. A man who could buy her and sell her and beat her and kill her child. She don't belong to him now. She don't belong to the

Judge neither. For all she's been too kind to Donal for her own good, she don't belong to Donal. She don't belong to none of the brothers but there's no woman took the Brotherhood's part better than Tessa. I can't tell you that story but it's the God's truth. You got a right to look on her the same as if she was myself or Rose or Bridget."

"She done something when we turned out?"

"She did."

"What could she do? And myself without a hint of it? Likely she give you some made-up tale."

"You think you know all, do you now? I'm losin my patience with you, Art Sheean. I give my word no one was to know but myself and Dan. Could I tell you the whole of it, you'd sing another tune."

She stopped talking and looked at him while he looked everywhere but back at her, looked at him till he felt a weight settling down on him, holding him to the bench with her eyes on him.

At last he mumbled, "I'm sorry. Did I know it before . . . How could I know?"

"You could have acted like a man, not a beast, knowin it or not. Now you know, will you tell the other two? Will the three of you bar the way do any more brave men draw their weapons out of their pants and charge after her?"

He gave her his promise. Then he climbed to the loft and a few minutes later came down with his bundle, walking out without a word or a look, going back to his old place in another shanty. She wasn't sorry to see him go but she worried could she trust his promise and there were others . . . She told the whole story to Dan.

"It will be a risk to Tessa, the word gettin about she was with us," Dan warned.

"See what a risk to her it was, keepin the secret."

"It was. I'll see all know she's to be left alone. It was not knowin was at the bottom of it. Art's a good lad, barrin when he has the drink in him. Damn all, why couldn't she leave Donal alone?"

"You wouldn't ask, why couldn't Donal leave her alone?"

She waited for Tessa again that afternoon. It was broad daylight still when the Sunday dinner was done and Mary saw at once the troubled look on Tessa's face.

"Don't worry yourself, Tessa, don't now. I'm that ashamed for those drunken louts, the way they was after you in the night. They won't do it no more, I promise you."

"Oh, Miss Mary, the troubles and sorrows all come to onct. I got to have somebody to talk to. I got to."

She looked uneasily at the other Dublin people who were out of their houses. Curious looks were being cast in their direction. Bet was at her door, saying something over her shoulder that brought Tim to look out at them too.

"Will we go to your house?" Mary suggested. "With all the comin and goin here, my house is the last place in God's world for a quiet word together'·

"Good day to you, Bet Sullivan," she said as they passed the Sullivan shanty. "Gettin the full of your eyes of what's passin?"

"That one's tongue wasn't quick enough this time." Mary gave a short laugh. "She'll be waggin it as soon as we're out of sight but all knows she can jabber the day long without sixpence worth of sense in it."

"I hope you right, they won't do it no more," Tessa said as they walked into her cabin. She turned to bar the door behind them. It was a new stout piece of wood that dropped into place. It had the look of Donal's work about it, Mary thought.

"I was mad 'nough last night to kill 'em," Tessa went on. "On top a the things they been sayin and the way they been grabbin at me in the cookhouse. They come at me again, somebody gon get killed, me or one a them, don't matter. I had bout all I can stand."

"Was you alone last night?"

Tessa folded her arms and looked at Mary defiantly. "Donal was here."

"And what did he do?"

"Him and me pick up pieces a that firewood in our hand. If they bust down that door, they be sorry. When they gone off, the Judge come to the door and ask is I all right, does I want to come and sleep in the kitchen. When he gone, I still so mad I most hit Donal with the piece a wood."

"Donal didn't do right by you neither."

"That ain't it. Donal, he been right nice to me. It was like I had to hit some-body. The Judge and Mis' Laurence, they gon find out about Donal now, sure as you're born. And that ain't all. What I wants to tell you, the Judge he got a letter from Master. No free papers in it."

"No papers for the boys?"

"Nothin for Willie and Arden. Nothin for me. Nary word bout no papers. He got two babies by that woman he marry. Don't care bout these boys no more, I reckon. She die birthin the last one and soon as he can get crost the mountains, he comin here. He fixin to take me back. Want me to take care a those babies. I knows it, sure as you sittin there, that's what he fixin to do."

She leaned close to Mary as if to pull some help out of her. "What I gonna do? If I stay here till he come, he gon get me, sure."

"The Judge . . .?"

"When he read me them things outa the letter, I say, 'Judge, he comin after me. You gonna let him take me back?' 'Now, Tessa,' he say, 'Ain't nothin in the letter bout takin you back. Don't be thinkin the worst, now. We'll just wait and see.' We wait and see and what he and Mis' Laurence gon see is what I been up to with Donal and they gon want me outa here. I knows that."

Tessa jumped up and paced back and forth "Ain't had hardly a wink a sleep since the letter come," she said in a tormented voice. "It's makin me crazy in the head."

"You tell Donal?"

Tessa threw up her hands. "I tries but he don't want to hear it. He say he won't low nobody to take me away from him, but I ain't lost all my sense yet. He might fight one a these Irish for layin a hand on me but he ain't gon fight the Judge and Master Paul."

Small wonder Tessa felt trapped and she didn't even know the danger that the Judge might find out about her role in the turnout.

"Miss Mary, does I tell you somethin, you won't let on to a soul, will you?"

"I will not."

"Pryor Foster, he tol me long ago, did push come to shove, he help me run off."

"Who's Foster?"

"I tol you bout him. He the blacksmith over to Coshocton. One a our folks. You musta heard bout what he done here a few months back. Everybody round here talkin bout it. He help six a our folks come up crost the river, runnin outa slavery. I say this for the peoples round here, lots of 'em know he had them folks but when the slave catchers come, none of 'em told. Thing is, he got 'em outa here right enough but they got caught a coupla days later." She put her hand over her eyes. "Oh, Lord, I hates to think what happens when they gets 'em back south. Oh Lord have mercy."

"Where is it you'd go, did you run off?"

"That scare me. I never been one step north a here. Don't know nobody. Got no place to go." She jumped up again. "Pryor, he say some a our folks up thataway free like him. They gon help me. You think that so?"

"Peter Hobbs. Could be there's more like him."

Tessa stopped her restless pacing to seize this crumb of hope. Then she sighed heavily. "Whenever I most gets my mind made up to run off, I thinks, what if Master keep his promise when he come and give the boys they freedom? If I carried 'em off, they never get them papers."

Mary still had her mind on Peter. "Peter, he's free the same as ourselves. No papers neither. Some kind of trouble over it but Dan and him hushed it. I never seen his farm but the milk that come from there when the fever was on us! The eggs! The potatoes! The Indian meal!"

Tessa's boys banged on the door. She brought them in, gave them something to eat and shooed them out again.

"Don't dare talk about runnin off in front of Arden," she explained. "Willie, he big enough to keep his mouth shut but Arden, he think everybody his friend."

They talked a long time. At last Tessa said, "I most got my mind made up to run off but how can I get outa here long nough to get it planned out with Foster?"

Mary thought this over and proposed sending Pat's Egan with a message this very night.

"Egan's a lovely boy," she assured Tessa. "He's not one a them come botherin you. I'd trust him with my own life. He can tell Mr. Foster to meet you in one a them shanties in the section cross the river, next after the aqueduct. The work's all done and the men gone but the shanties is till there. Egan can tell him to meet you there tomorrow's a night. You know the place? You knock on my door in the mornin before you go down to the cookhouse so I can give you the word did Egan find Foster and is all well."

Tessa looked dubious. "What you gon tell Egan?"

Mary considered. "Three words only." She held up three fingers and pointed to them one by one. "He to tell Foster it's a message from you. Foster to come to the first a them Wilcox shanties. The time to be about two hours after sunset."

Mary whispered the whole story to Dan after she had sent Egan off and gone to bed.

"Why Egan? Why not myself?"

She couldn't sleep, thinking it should have been Dan. Young Egan might have stumbled into some trouble. It was almost morning when he returned.

She raised up in bed and he bent over to say softly, "I found Foster. He'll be there the night."

A nod and a smile to Tessa when she knocked on the door a few hours later told her that all was arranged. The following morning Tessa knocked again and gave Mary back the same signal.

"When?" Mary's lips just formed the word.

"He say it take time to fix it," Tessa whispered. "We meet again yonder in a week."

A week later, Mary walked a piece of the road with Tessa one evening to get the news.

"Not yet," Tessa told her. "Lord, Lord, it gotta be soon. One a your folks musta tol the Judge bout me and Donal. Judge mad as a hornet. I say it all lies but he say he catch ary man in my cabin, that the end a me on this place. I tell Donal not to come no more but that Donal, he reckon to slide in thout the Judge knowin."

The next night, something happened in Dublin to take Mary's mind off Tessa's concerns. There was a row in the Casey shanty. As close as the shanties were to each other, everyone in Dublin knew it but on a cold night no one put an ear outside to listen. In the morning, it was a surprise to see the marks of the row on Kevin's face. Mick was slow to anger, always taking care of his brother. What could have got into him, to give Kevin that black eye?

Whatever it was, Kevin was sulky and unnaturally quiet the whole week. Mick was beside him or behind him more than ever. Aghna and Una did their work without a word about it. The biggest surprise came on Sunday when the Casey brothers went to Jamie for their pay and their wives' pay while the women wrapped up their bundles.

"Why are you goin out of it in this weather?" they were asked, but they gave short answers with no meaning to them.

Mary was in her own shanty, sitting over the breakfast after the men had eaten and gone over to Van Dorn's section to meet Manrow and Joice. The Sunday laziness was on her. The door opened and Aghna stood there.

"Mary Griffen, not one good word did I get from you since I took your place in the cookhouse and you knowin it was no fault of mine you was out of it. I'm not askin for a good word now. I come to say when you call a curse down on the Caseys, remember brothers has to stand by brothers and wives by husbands but the shame shouldn't be called down on all alike."

Before Mary could collect her wits, Aghna was gone. What had she meant by it?

Toby's mother and another Ohio woman were put in the cookhouse to take the places of Aghna and Una. Mary waited for Tessa one night to ask how things were with the new women there. Tessa shrugged indifferently.

Since she had nothing to say and a cold wind was blowing snow at them, Mary turned back to her own door.

"Don't go, Miss Mary." The undercurrent of excitement in Tessa's voice brought Mary to her side.

"You're off?"

Tessa nodded, her eyes shining. "We goin. I mighty glad to see you tonight. I wants to say goodbye."

Mary took both of Tessa's hands. "Goodbye then, and good luck go with you."

They stood together on the dark road, reluctant to part, in spite of the snow falling on their shawled heads and the wind blowing their skirts against their bodies.

"Give me the blessin again, like you done before," Tessa asked.

"God bless you and may the Blessed Virgin keep you in her care." Mary's voice shook a little.

Tessa pressed Mary's hands, dropped them, and walked quickly off into the night. That was Mary's last sight of her.

"What's happenin in this place?" Mary said to Dan uneasily when she was in by the fire again. "I don't like it the way people are up and disappearin out of it. Who's to go next?"

Chapter 50

THIN ICE EDGED the river most mornings. Each day the men were more reluctant to go into it.

"Seventy-five cents a day is not enough for this," Dan said to Johnny. "We should be askin a dollar."

The aqueduct foundations were almost finished and the winter was on them, mild though it had been this year. Eyes were turned anxiously toward the January payday. If the bosses had it in mind to cut down this big work force till the spring, payday would be the time for it. There were sighs of relief when the day passed without a single man being sent down the road.

The Commissioner came early in February while they were driving the last piles. He shook his head over Simon's intention of laying the first courses of masonry on that final pier in the cold weather but agreed at last that it could be done. He stayed the night in the Laurence house.

"How well it would be for us, was Tessa still in it," Dan remarked to Tom, "the way we might be knowin what the talk is."

They finished laying the timbers on that last pier one Saturday. Dan had been in the water again that day and was too cold even to stand in line for his jigger of whiskey. He made for his own shanty, dropped his clothes in a soggy heap on the floor and settled himself by the fire, wrapped in a blanket. Mary gave him a noggin with a more generous portion than those Jamie was handing out.

"Ah, now I'm gettin warm on the inside of me with my own whiskey and warm on the outside of me with my own fire and warmer still with knowin that was the last of my days in the water on the piers, blast 'em."

The other lodgers were gathered around the table while Mary filled their plates. Johnny walked in and sat down across the hearth from Dan without saying a word.

One look at his face and Dan exclaimed, "What is it, man?"

Johnny held out his hand for Dan to see money in it. "Paid off. Paid off and sent down the road. And you the same."

Mary left Pat holding out his empty plate and walked over. "Dan too? You and Dan paid off?"

"There's dozens in it, depend on it," Pat said. "What we feared on the payday. It's down on us now."

"No, Pat, that's not what for. It's my part in the Brotherhood. 'I got no place on my job for mischief makers like yourself,' Jamie says. 'Call yourself a Committee man, don't you?' he says. 'You can tell your Committee to pay your wages. You won't get no more from me.' Then he says, 'You can tell Dan Griffen to come get his pay. His last pay.' Now I'm off to give Molly the bad news."

Dan's wet boots squelched as he walked along the muddy road to Jamie's cabin. With each step his body came heavily down. It was an effort to raise his leg for the next step. His head was quite disconnected from his plodding body. It was light with the weariness from the week's work and the hunger for his supper, floating with the fumes of the whiskey. It hardly knew where his body was taking it, on what errand.

Jamie was sitting behind the table when Dan came in. He pushed a little pile of money across the table. "There's your pay and your boy's pay. I got no more work for you and your gang. We're done with your kind here. Send Quinlan down. He can have his pay the same as yourself."

Dan picked up the money, counted it with exaggerated care and plodded toward the door. Then he stopped. The thoughts that had been skittering wildly, trying to stay upright, falling over themselves, now focused on the door. Out the door? Out of it all for the last time? He turned and came back, looking at the man who had been his friend.

"Go on, go on now, I'm done with you." Jamie waved his hand like he was brushing a mosquito away.

"Jamie McCarthy." Dan spoke slowly, wonderingly. "Is it yourself? Or is it another man entirely?"

As he stared into Jamie's face the wonder changed to contempt. "Done with me, is it? No work and no pay for my kind, is it? We was the same kind once, but we're not the same kind no more. No, no. The money that's in it is for your kind only, the kind can't see nothin but the money. You was a good sound man once but I seen it happen before. Good sound potatoes and them turnin rotten in the field."

Jamie was half out of his chair, his mouth open, but Dan was gone.

Dan stopped at the O'Scanlon shanty where Tom lodged to give him the bad news. For once, Tom was without questions. Paddy and the others watched him put down his spoon and leave his beans half eaten. When he was gone they looked covertly at each other. This was a blow—at Tom, certainly, but not at Tom only.

Back home, eating his supper, Dan still felt heavy in the limbs but the lightness was gone out of his head.

Myself was to the fore in front of Jamie but him knowin Tom and Johnny . . .
Someone in Dublin has a long tongue.

When Tom returned he had the word Art was to go. Art returned with the same word for Dennis. Dennis returned with the news for Connie. By this time, supper was over and all of them were together, waiting for the axe to fall on Phelim, asking each other must they indeed leave Dublin on the morrow. Egan was sent to bring Timothy Manrow and John Joice from the Van Dorn camp. Had they been paid off too? Or was it only Dublin men that were hit?

When Connie came in, Phelim clapped his cap on his head and moved to go but Connie stopped him. No one else had been called for. All eyes turned on Phelim who stood there with his mouth open, staring at Connie in astonishment, turning to his mates and seeing their surprise turn to suspicion, feeling the silence fall.

Dan got up and came so close Phelim backed away. Dan came closer still. Those behind Phelim moved out of the way. Dan backed Phelim up against the wall.

"Phelim, was it you talked?"

All movement in the shanty ceased, all voices were hushed except for Phelim's agonized cry, "No, no. Dan, how could you think it of me?"

Art and Johnny came up on either side of Dan, moving in on Phelim who pressed against the wall, looking at them in horror.

Tom walked over and put a hand on Art's arm, raised to strike. "Wait a bit. Why is it you're thinkin it's Phelim?"

"Why is Jamie leavin Phelim only on the job if it wasn't him talked?" Dan answered. Art pushed Tom's hand away.

"Who knows the names of every man on the Committee but the Committee itself?" Johnny demanded.

"As God is my witness," Phelim said solemnly, fastening his eyes on Tom, "Not a word out of my mouth, not a name."

"With all we was tryin to keep things secret," Tom said, his matter of fact tone easing the tension. "You well know how few secrets there is in Dublin. And wasn't it Phelim come to the fore when we put it to Jamie about the cookhouse wall? Leave the boy get his breath while we worry this over a bit more."

"All knew I was in it, even Jamie himself," Dan admitted. "But all?"

"How could you think it?" Phelim was almost crying. "How could you think it? My curses on the one that did it, bringin such a thing down on me. A hundred thousand times rather would I be out on the road with the rest than you to think such a thing of me."

Art stayed in front of him, his fist still doubled up but Dan moved back, frowning, beginning to doubt that it was Phelim. But if not him, who then?

It was the question all were asking.

Mary said to herself that a traitor's name didn't fit on Phelim. It wasn't only that he wasn't the poor kind of man for it. It was that there was someone else she could fit it to, someone who was just around the corner of her knowing.

Phelim was leaning against the wall, looking hopefully from one to another. Suddenly, Art turned away from him and smacked his own hand with his fist.

"One a them Yankees!" he exclaimed. "That's who done it. They been out of it since the turnout but they was knowin who was in it in them days. Dennis was one of us then and Phelim was not."

"Let's hear Timothy on it," Tom said as the men from Van Dorn's came in. People squeezed together to make room for them. "Was none from his section put out on the road that might tell us is Art in the right of it. None of those lads was in it when we had the turnout."

Timothy told them neither him nor John had been paid off. All the Brotherhood were still on the job on his section.

"It was one a them Yankees." Art was sure of it now. "We never shoulda brought them in. Didn't I say so? Toby Weaver, he was the one most in the know."

"Not Toby," Mary said. "Kevin Casey."

Everyone looked at her, waiting for more. She thought for a few moments, each moment becoming more certain.

"Wasn't Kevin cap in hand to Jamie from the time you went back to work after the turnout? Pushin for Dan's job, he was, and wouldn't he give anything for it? What did he have to give but the names? You was all to the fore where Kevin could see you in the turnout. Any man not blind in both eyes could know who the Committee was then. But nobody was trustin him with nothin when you put the Brotherhood back together. He wouldn't know Dennis was out and Phelim was in. Nor that Timothy and John was in."

"Kevin Casey," Dan repeated, looking from one of the Committee to another, seeing in their faces a reflection of his own thought: Why had they not thought of Kevin at once?

"Kevin was after askin me this and that about the Brotherhood," Johnny remembered. "Did I think this one was with us and wasn't Dan too much the friend to Jamie to be on the Committee at all. I give him short answers or no answers but I never thought . . ."

Mary pointed to the door. "Aghna stood in that very spot and all but told me. 'The time will come,' she says, when I would call down a curse on the Caseys, but it was Kevin she meant. I was to know Mick stood by him only that they was brothers and her and Una only that they was wives."

Art couldn't hit at Phelim now, and Kevin was beyond his reach. "Would

Kevin betray his own people? Them Yankees, any one of them could a done it like I was sayin. Besides, if it was Kevin, why wasn't we paid off back when he was yet here?"

"Jamie was in need of all when there was the piers to get up before the water rises," Dan said. "And look what happened when he tried to turn me off—half the crew come in at my back. He wouldn't chance that again. But now—now he can throw us off like we was broken tools."

"Why would Kevin go out of here and him gettin close to the boss?" Pat wondered.

"It wasn't Kevin's wantin," Mary said. "Remember the black eye he got from his brother? Mick must a found out or Aghna found out and they wasn't leavin him stay here, doin the dirty on us. Or they had the fear for the word gettin out and all the Caseys sufferin for it."

Phelim's long thin legs wouldn't hold him up any more. While the others were cursing Kevin, he let his back slide down the wall till he was sitting on the floor. Glad to be forgotten, he could recover from his fright and nurse the good name restored to him.

Timothy and John said goodnight. "And good luck go with you on the road. Pass the word up the line to us when you find a job, the way we'll know where at you're workin, if it don't be till spring. You might have to winter over in a town, the poor time this is for the hirin on the canal."

"I'll back you like I done before," Egan declared. "Would Jamie take you back did it look like he was losin half his crew again?"

"Good man, Egan." Dan considered the question. "My fear is, Jamie would turn you out along with us. He don't have the same need of a big crew now."

"You wouldn't be off to your farm?" Johnny asked Dan.

"In the dead of winter and no roof overhead?"

Dan looked around at the shanty full of friends, then away from them, away down the canal line where they might be together on another job. Jamie wasn't the only boss on the canal but putting the tales together that had been drifting back from other sections, all bosses were much the same. They would have to make a fight of it if all were not to be thrown out on the road whenever they spoke up for themselves.

"We got Brotherhood business in the spring," he said to them, "and I'll be in it, so I will."

"We'll be headin off down the canal line in the mornin?" Mary asked. "As soon as we can wrap up our bundles?"

"What else?" Dan could see no use talking of it.

"Where will you be off to?" Pat asked. "There was some sections where I could have got put on when I come along at Christmas time. A big job is goin at Circleville, do you find nothin before."

Tom opened the door to look out on the weather. A blast of cold wind swept in on them, with rain in it. He slammed the door shut. "A pitiful bad day for the road."

Molly began to cry. Less than a year married, she was big with her first child. "It will be on Peg to care for the family without me, along with her own babe. M'self will be off with Johnny, leavin father and sisters and brother and never knowin will I see them again."

"It's no kind of weather for my babe to be out in it," Rose said.

Mary looked at her own three. Tim's legs were almost as long as his father's but Danny was thin and yellow yet from the canal fever and Ellen was still small for the road in the cold of the year.

"I'm not leavin here without knowin where in the world I'm to go. With the childers and all it would be a slow wanderin with many nights on the road, likely. Why wouldn't you, Dan, and you, Johnny and Dennis and the rest go lookin till you have the place for us on the canal like Pat says it or in the town like Timothy says it?"

"A hundred miles down the line maybe, before we find a place and then a hundred miles back after the women?" Art objected.

"That's on me and Dan and Dennis, comin back to fetch them," Johnny answered. "Not on you at all."

"And does Jamie come puttin the women out when our backs is turned?" Dan asked.

"Nah, nah," Pat said. "Jamie's a hard man but I wouldn't think it of him to be doin such a devil's trick as that. And did it come to such evil doins there's enough of us here to say 'nay' to him."

Egan was still for going with them and Pat proudly backed him. Phelim was quick to agree to it. Hugh couldn't be left out. That lifted the spirits of all and they had a drink on it.

Then Tom had another thought. "Wouldn't we like to have you with us, indeed. But the best thing out of Egan's mouth was the thing he had there a while ago of pushin this nasty bit of work back on Jamie and makin him swallow it. Wasn't we too soon leavin that? Could we do it at all if the best of the Brotherhood is all out of Dublin?"

They talked that back and forth and left it at last that only those Jamie had turned off would go down the line in the morning. They would keep the others in their thoughts as they looked for jobs. Could they get places for themselves? Could they get places for these friends so the threat could be held over Jamie? When they had the answers to these questions it would be the time to put their heads together and see whether they could say to Jamie: "Put all back on the job or lose another piece of the crew."

The days passed slowly with the Committee gone and no knowing what they were finding. The absence of Dennis left a hole in the masons' crew that had been working so well together. There was nothing Simon could put a finger on, just one little thing after another going wrong.

"I'm gettin a bellyfull of this job," Henry said to Michael as they returned from dinner one day. "I'll be glad when it's over. I don't know why I ever left Cincinnati."

"I should have gone off when they shot at Peg. Simon hasn't had my trust since that day and now look at him, turnin off near about our best mason."

It was worse on the embankment where all diggers were now concentrated. Four of theirs were missing. Jamie, roaming up and down the line of diggers, found everyone working steadily but sullenly.

"I'll be damned if there's not some bad apples in that barrel yet," Jamie told Simon. "I'll get who it is out of Fergus."

All he got out of Fergus was a noncommittal grunt.

There was more drinking than usual after work. A fight broke out with it on Tuesday. When Tim Sullivan came out bellowing at them to stow it for the sake of Christ and let decent people sleep, he was driven back in a hail of rocks and dirt.

"Who will help me do I have another child or the sickness comes to my shanty again?" Bridget mourned.

When Pat broached the plan of backing the Committee with a threat to Jamie, Paddy said they were fools to talk of such a thing. Bridget came crying to Mary over that. That made Ellen cry too.

"Bridget, acushla, will you dry your eyes? It's a dry eye and a clear head I'll be needin for what's comin and no need to drown the little one in tears till she thinks it's the end of the world itself."

When all was quiet at night, Mary sat long by the fire. She sent her thoughts out into the dark after Dan and the others.

Are you findin shelter the night or lyin under a tree in the cold and the wet? Are you findin a place for all of us? Will all be together in the one camp or broken and scattered? Does it come to spendin the heel of the winter in a town, is there enough in the pouch to keep us till spring? What strange places will be in it for us at the end of the journey? . . Another journey . . . Will it ever end with a hearth of our own and our own people around us?

It was near dark on Thursday, the men just breaking off the work when Tim and Danny came running with the news that Dan was back and all with him on the other side of the river. Fergus was polling the raft across to get them.

Mary was on her way to the river before the words were out of their mouths. She didn't give the bosses a look as she passed them coming away from the job but she was conscious of the men strung out behind them. Some followed the bosses closely, their eyes on the ground, others moved more slowly, with looks over their shoulders. A few stood on the bank, waiting. Pat and Egan were in that group, Phelim and Hugh, Buck and Toby.

All gathered around while Dan gave the news. "There's no jobs on the canal for the likes of us. The Commissioner has give papers with our names on it to every contractor. More than one would have hired Dennis. Another wanted two diggers and there was one ready to hire all. It was askin what was our names destroyed it every time. We went on from section to section, tryin all together, tryin one only askin a job, or two, leavin out of it that we worked on the aqueduct. It was no use. The last one, he showed us the paper, with our names on it, where it said, 'These men not to be hired for work of any kind on the Ohio and Erie Canal by order of Alfred Kelley, Commissioner.' That's when we turned back."

Chapter 51

W HEN BOOTS were off the tired feet and hot food inside the bellies of the returned travellers, then it was time for the question, "What are we to do now?"

"Head for Pennsylvania where there's canal building goin on," Tom proposed. "The Commissioner, he got no say in what happens way off there."

"I had enough canals," Dennis said. "There's work aplenty for a good stone mason on the National Road or in the cities."

Connie and Art were for Pennsylvania with Tom. They pressed Dan to join them but the blacklist had put the cap on the mountain of refusals. On the long way back to Dublin his thoughts had begun to turn away from the canal work.

"Wasn't we headin for a farm of our own all the years since we come across the water?" he said to Mary quietly under the babble of the others' talk. "Jamie can't put us out of it nor Kelley neither."

Mary savored the thought, trying not to bite on the hard kernel of loneliness in it. "No more journeyin, is it?"

The words were no sooner out of her mouth than Johnny and Michael came in with another journey to offer. "We're out of here on the morrow, all of us," Johnny said. "Here's Michael, his name was never on the Commissioner's paper and himself the fine stone mason. Here's Molly's father, the name of O'Malley was never on the paper neither. They're makin an O'Malley out of me and who's to know the difference?"

"That's comin around the blind side of 'em." Dan smiled but he added a word of caution. "Don't be askin for a job till you get down past where we was, lest some boss remember this big fellow with the red top to him."

"The Commissioner, now, what about him?" Connie asked. "The way he's forever roamin up and down the line, he's after seein Johnny many a time."

"Not a bit of it." Dan brushed that aside. "Don't you know there's hundreds of men workin the line? Thousands maybe. We're all hands to him. He don't know the men fits the names. Johnny'll walk into a job like his name was never writ down."

"That's it," Michael agreed. "Now here's what we come for. I'm offerin you the name of Kieran, do you and Mary go with us. You to be the brother to me, with the same name on both of us."

That was a great gift for one man to offer another. Dan was quick to give thanks for it but slow to accept.

"We'd be in Ohio still and not so far from our own place, not like goin off to Pennsylvania." That was what Mary liked about it, yet she spoke hesitantly. "Ourselves to be with friends, Johnny that's been with us since we come over the water, Michael since Akron, all the O'Malleys since we got to Dublin."

That was the best of it. The worst of it she couldn't say out loud, the way it would be an offense to Michael. What it was, they would be losing their own name, turning themselves into the tail of another family. She looked at Dan to see what he was thinking.

"Ourselves on the Ohio canal yet." Dan looked from Michael to Johnny and back again, "The three of us together, we wouldn't be torn off from the Brotherhood altogether. Comes the spring, we three would be helpin to put a push in it for a dollar pay in the water and the same pay the year round like we been talkin of it with the men from the other sections."

Johnny and Michael exchanged a look. "Well now, Dan," Michael said. "What's in it . . ." He couldn't find the words.

Johnny had to say them. "O'Malley, he calls it a disgrace and a danger, my name to be on the Commissioner's paper. I give him my promise to stick to the work and not to do nothin to get the O'Malley name put on the paper."

Johnny looked at Dan to see how this was going down and not liking what he saw, hurried on. "Me and Molly's got a little one comin, you know that. Was I without work, how would I keep the two of `em?"

Dan turned his eyes on Michael. "And the name of Kieran? Is that to be wrapped up in silence and kept off the Commissioner's paper too?"

"Wouldn't it be better for all?" Michael urged. "To do the work and not harry the bosses till they forget you was in it?"

"My thanks to you, Michael Kieran." Dan spoke with deliberation to put all the necessary weight into what he had to say. "My thanks to you and to you, Johnny, for the friends you are to us. It would please me to go the road with you, and Mary too, you heard how she spoke on it. But the Griffen name is mine the way I got it from my father to keep it like he kept it. When our people in Cork was up, a Griffen was in it. When our people on the canal is up, a Griffen has to be in it. I can't give it away for the sake of the name of Kieran. Not but that Kieran's a grand name."

He held out his hand, clasping Michael's and then Johnny's. Mary went with them to the door saying the morrow would be soon enough and too soon for the farewells. A sob rose in her throat with the words. She stood at the door for a moment to let it die.

Behind her, she could hear all breaking into talk again. Phelim and Egan were saying how sorry a loss Dan was to them, the way they would be keeping the Brotherhood on the canal, more shame to Michael and Johnny for turning their backs on it. Tom and Connie were trying to persuade Dan to come with them to Pennsylvania.

It was still going on when Dennis and Rose came in. "I talked with Henry," Dennis told them. "Cincinnati bein the biggest city has the most work for a mason like myself."

They would travel like gentry, by stage to Marietta and riverboat down the Ohio to Cincinnati. Dennis felt confident enough of work to pay out the money for the fares and said Henry himself would be going back there when the aqueduct was finished.

"He told me of a master mason there and a journeyman that's a friend to him. Now here," he held out a piece of paper to Dan, "is the name of Henry's friend and where he's to be found. Do you come to that city, find him and he'll tell you where I'm to be found. Whatever help I can be to you, Dan, to find work, I will. Don't you know it?"

"If we have a roof over our own heads," Rose added, "there will be a place under it for you till you have your own."

Mary put the paper away carefully in the sea chest that stood open for the things they would be taking with them wherever they were to go.

"We'll treasure that," Dan said. "Do we come to Cincinnati soon or don't we, it's well for us that we don't be losin you altogether."

"The Good God will give us the sight of your faces again." Mary seized on the hope.

"It will not be soon," Dan decided. "Cincinnati bein an unknown city, the likes of New York and myself not a mason nor any other kind of a city man."

Dennis and Rose could not linger, with all the preparations they had to make for the journey.

When they were gone, Mary looked down into the chest. "What do I put in this at all? . . without knowin whither . . . how long on the road . . ."

She looked questioningly at Dan. There was no answer in his eyes but both knew they had come to the crossroads they had so long been avoiding.

"One way is the farm," Dan said. "That's our own and less than a day's journey."

"The farm? A piece of the forest and but one Irish family somewhere else in the same forest."

"Company we'd have on the road, did we take the road to Pennyslvania " Dan offered the other way.

Mary didn't have the same feelings for those three that she had for Johnny and Michael. Connie and Tom were a shorter time known and she couldn't look at Art without seeing the bestial face he had on him when he threatened Tessa. This was no time to renew that quarrel, so she said only, "The three of them is single men, like to go off any time one way or another."

There was a long silence between them while each weighed the good and the bad of the two roads.

"Might be we'd get so far off, goin to Pennsylvania," Dan said at last. "We'd never find the way back to our own piece of land."

"There's no way but all of us is to be scattered." Mary reluctantly faced it. "Well then, does there be no roof over us in our own place, was there a roof over us when we come here?"

"We can build us a roof," Dan agreed.

So it was decided.

The three who were heading for Pennsylvania were off early in the morning.

The dark was leaving the sky, showing there was not a cloud in it. They would have the sun on them for the first day of their journey, at least. The longer-legged Art and Connie matched their steps to Tom's shorter stride, their boots striking the frozen earth together. Mary and Dan stood in the door and watched till the three figures with bundles over their shoulders were blurred by the morning shadows, were almost lost in the distance, were gone around the curve of the hill.

All the sounds of a Dublin work day beginning came between them and the friends who were gone: The clatter of the cookhouse, the men emerging from it and from the shanties, the distant clop and rumble of Buck's wagon coming down the road past the Laurence house with its load of workers. They were no longer part of this purposeful movement. It would go on without them.

"You'll be here the night?" Pat asked before he went off to the job.

"We will."

Dan would have to go to the town to get a pair of wheels and put a cart together to carry their things.

Some of the men greeted them as they passed, some never had a word for anyone till after the sun was up and their sleep out of them, but when Paddy passed with only a twitch of the head instead of a good morning, Mary realized how few and subdued were the salutations.

Dan noticed it too. "Paddy's got the fear in him, and others besides Paddy. They don't want Jamie to see 'em too friendly with the likes of us."

"So, some of our friends is goin off from us one way and some another."

"Hey, Dan!" Buck called out, whoaing his horses where Dan and Mary were standing. "Still here, are ya? Y'know, I took a notion to go over to that quarter section I bought, this Sunday comin. It ain't far from your place. If you folks want to come along, I got plenty room."

Dan gave his thanks and Mary blessed him for it.

Buck leaned forward with his elbows on the front of the wagon box, the reins slack in his hand as if he had the whole day to talk. "It ain't the best time a year to get started, but it ain't so settled up that way but what you can keep the family in meat. You got a gun, ain't you? Enough powder and shot?"

"Come on, Buck, let's get to work." His passengers were getting impatient.

"Yeah, yean," but he lingered to give Dan advice about tools.

As he started off again, he said, "Me and Toby, we'll be along 'fore sunrise Sunday. We'll give ya a hand to get your leanto up. You keep a good fire goin in front of it and you'll make out alright till spring."

Saturday night all was ready except for rolling up their blankets and shoveling some fire into a bucket to carry to their new place. They sat around the fire, all the Griffens and the friends who had been their lodgers.

"Our last night at this hearth," Mary mused. Thoughts had been coming up in her mind these last few days like flames from the fire and words coming to her to shape them, almost like a keen for this hearth.

"Our last night at this hearth. It was Michael laid the stone. He's gone and ourselves goin. Johnny sat by this fire many a long evenin'. He's gone and ourselves goin. You, Pat, stayin. Egan, Phelim, Hugh, all stayin, and ourselves goin."

All were still, listening to Mary's quiet voice, watching the fire wrap the log in flames.

"I'll smoor the fire for the last time tonight but it will blaze up for you on the morrow. It will dry you when you're wet from the work, warm you when you're cold from it. When you sit by it talkin, you'll maybe have a word for us that's gone from you."

"We will, indeed."

Mary looked from one to another. Her voice rose and sharpened. "There will be no place for Jamie at this hearth?"

"Nah, nah."

"No place for the likes of Kevin Casey?"

"Never."

"All others, all others in Dublin welcome still at this hearth?"

"Aye, all welcome."

They were all silent, looking at Mary, knowing she had more to say.

"We're gone from our own hearth in Carrignahown these many years. That was a sad day for us. How could we carry a seed of that fire? It would die on the wide water, so we thought. But is this another fire entirely? No, not entirely. We had a thing inside us, a burnin that blazed up again."

Dan got up and laid another piece of wood across the burning log. They watched it catch fire and blaze up. Then Mary spoke again.

"It's a sad day for us, leavin hearth and home and fire and friends behind us again but I've had a thought the day, along with the tasks of the leavin. There will be another cabin. Dan will build it with the new neighbors helpin. There will be another hearth. Tim will lay the stone the way Michael and Dennis showed him. There will be another fire started from the seed of this. Danny will swing his axe and cut the wood for it. Ellen will hang the pot over it and cook the stirabout. If their time comes to go a journey, they will carry a seed of that fire . . . of this fire . . . of the fire from the old home across the water."

The End

The Making of *Seed of the Fire*

The Making of *Seed of the Fire*

"All art is a collaboration," as John M. Synge said in his preface to *The Playboy of the Western World*. The active involvement, generous assistance and sustaining encouragement of many collaborators through the nine years I worked on *Seed of the Fire*, enriched it with many insights and kept me from making mistakes. Those mistakes and weaknesses that remain are my responsibility entirely.

Work and Life in Ohio Canal Camps

Of the many books and journal articles that put a foundation under my structure, Harry N. Scheiber's *Ohio Canal Era* came first. The text provided essential information while chapter notes and bibliographic essay pointed me in the direction of additional research. Prof. Scheiber also answered many questions and brought other sources to my attention.

The Canal Papers in the Ohio Historical Society Library and the assistance of its staff were invaluable. The Cincinnati and Western Reserve Historical libraries and librarians were also helpful. Nancy Lowe Lonsinger, then historian of the Roscoe Village Foundation, provided me with material relating to the local history of the Forks area and its part of the canal. (Roscoe is the Caldersburgh of the story).

Pick, shovel and wheelbarrow were still major construction tools when R. B. Scales began his forty years of work in that trade. He recounted personal experiences and reviewed an early draft of the work chapters.

David L.Wright, Chairman of the History and Heritage Committee of the Pittsburgh Section, American Society of Civil Engineers and a member of the Board of the Pennsylvania Canal Society, was my consulting engineer. David and I walked the line of the old aqueduct and embankment together. He assisted me with additional research and reviewed all the chapters dealing with construction. My canal crews could hardly have done their work without R.B. and David.

Mrs. Frankie Johnson grew up in the backwoods of Arkansas when conditions there were very much like those of Ohio seventy years earlier. The vivid memory and dramatic story-telling of this ninety-year-old African-American friend gave me a feeling for the life and for Black-white relationships in a frontier community.

Lumber camps were most recent of the long series of temporary work communities that began with the canal camps. Loggers of the lumber camp era helped me "see" canal camps.

Gordon ("Brick") Moir of Hoquiam, Washington, had just retired after many years of working in the woods when I first met him in 1977. He answered many questions and shared many recollections with me. His friendship is one of the rewards of working on this book.

Brick also introduced me to George Katzamanis, whose life as a logger began in 1916, and to Walter Ballew, who went to work in the woods of North Carolina even earlier. I taped long interviews with both and regret that neither lived to see the book to which they so generously contributed.

Anna Hildebrandt shared logging camp life with her husband, a donkey engineer, in the twenties. Beatrice Fotland was a waitress (a "flunky") in the cookhouse of a large camp a decade later. They helped me to get a sense of what logging camp life looked like to women.

Irish workers struck on the Pennsylvania Canal in the winter of 1828-29 and a few years later on the Chesapeake and Ohio. The history of the Canadian Canals includes strikes by Irish canal workers in the 1840s. I drew on accounts of all these strikes as well as on other early Irish-American labor history in creating the turnout at the Laurence-Lordon-McCarthy camp. Labor historian Philip Foner (1910-1994) made helpful research suggestions on this aspect of the book and reviewed the chapters dealing with the strike.

For answering medical questions and reviewing my "cases," I am grateful to Doctors Linda Rosenstock and the late Malcolm Peterson. Thanks, too, to these scholars who responded helpfully to inquiries in their fields of expertise: Dr. Elizabeth Fee, The Johns Hopkins School of Hygiene and Public Health; Prof. John C. Messenger, Dept. of Anthropology, The Ohio State University; Prof. Philip Jordan, author of *The National Road*; and Prof. Harry R. Stevens, Dept. of History, Ohio University.

Dr. Francis Jennings, Director of the Newberry Library Center for the History of the American Indian, reviewed "The Forks." He is not to be held responsible for the simplifications inevitable in compressing so much history into so few pages.

The Irish Background

I visited Cork and Dublin in 1980 in pursuit of a greater understanding of the circumstances in which Mary and Dan Griffen lived before emigrating. My guide was Criostoir de Baroid, a lover of County Cork, its people and its struggles. He introduced me to the countryside, to people of Cork's present and to stories of its past.

The highlight of our stay was an evening with Miceal O'Suilleabhain, his wife and his artist daughter at their home near Ballyvourney. His book, *Where Mountainy Men Have Sown*, had first introduced me to the hills of West Cork and to "Cath Cheim an Fhiaidh" (The Battle of Keimaneigh) by Maire Bhuidhe Ni Laoghaire, a poem written shortly after that battle, set to music, and still sung in that part of the world.

Patrick O'Connell, Reference Librarian at University College Cork and other members of that library's staff were most helpful and hospitable. The resources of the National Library and State Paper Office in Dublin and the British Museum in London were also invaluable.

While I was in Cork and by mail after my return, significant help was also given by Ann Barry, Archivist and Secretary, Cork Archives Council and by Tim Cadogan, Reference Librarian, Cork County Library. Prof. Joseph J. Lee, historian and Dean of the Faculty of Arts at UCC and Miceal O'Suilleabhain of the Music Department (same name as the O'Suilleabhain above; different person), were encouraging and helpful, as was Sean Daly of the Tower Book Store. A fellow explorer among the old books and documents in the University library, Declan McCormack, then working on his doctoral dissertation, assisted me in pursuing research leads after I left Cork.

The discovery of the keen for the dead as a women's art form was an exciting aspect of my research. More on this subject was one of my goals in Ireland. Rionach Ui Ogain of the Department of Irish Folklore, University College, Dublin, assisted me with the keens from County Cork in the Folklore collection. These keens were translated for me by Maire Harris, then a student in the Department of Early and Medieval Irish at UCC. Leo Corduff, also of the Dept. of Irish Folklore, discussed the keens with me and directed me to the few available on records.

Sean O'Tuama, Irish poet and scholar, read successive drafts of Mary's keens for Owen and Maggie and helped guide them into the Irish mode. He also made helpful suggestions about the dialog, as did Robert G. Lowery, then editor of the *Sean O'Casey Review*.

James S. Donnelly, Jr., brought me into the Rockite struggle of which the battle of Keimaneigh was a part. He was then studying the rural uprisings of the 18th and 19th centuries and generously shared his work with me prior to its publication in *Irish Peasants, Violence and Political Unrest, 1780-1914*, published by the University of Wisconsin Press.

The Birth Chapter

Patricia Hadfield permitted me to be present at the home birth of her daughter, Leah. Rebecca Harless, R.N., who was part of that experience, helped me see birth from the point of view of a midwife. Additional help came from Susan Meyers and Margery Mansfield of the Seattle Home Maternity Service and Brigitte Jordan, medical anthropologist, author of *Birth in Four Cultures*. I attended Prof. Jordan's lectures during her 1981 visit to the University of Washington and saw her videotapes of birth in Yucatan. She generously shared other work in progress and reviewed both the childbirth chapters.

People Real and Imaginary

Dan Griffen's return to his village to bring his small daughter to the port is based on a family legend but the Griffen family is otherwise entirely imaginary.

Commissioner Alfred Kelley stepped onto my pages from history. I tried to make the words I put in his mouth characteristic of him. The "Letter to Laborers on the Canal" is a real document. The blacklisting letter is not, but is based on similar incidents of the time on other canals.

Pryor Foster, the Coshocton blacksmith, who appears indirectly, was also a real person. The episode of the escaping slaves appears in *Ohio Annals. Historic Events in the Tuscarawas and Muskingum Valleys* by C.H. Mitchener. It was said to have "occurred about the time of the construction of the Ohio Canal."

Peter Hobbs and Zeke Johnson were suggested by anecdotes of men with other names, recounted in Ohio county histories.

Although the characters of Peter Hobbs and Tessa are not portraits, I would never have been at ease in creating these characters had it not been for our long and loving partnership with Walter and Essie Johnson. Brodines and Johnsons lived together from 1951 until Walter's death in 1992, and Essie is still with us.

My Most Important Collaborators

Throughout the years I was working on *Seed of the Fire*, my husband Russell built my work rooms, cooked most of the meals I ate, and took on more than his share of household drudgery. He read every chapter as it came out of the typewriter and was the first barometer of how far accomplishment had risen toward intention. He accompanied me on research trips, proofread manuscripts, suffered with me through the dry spells and celebrated with me the passing of each important milestone.

Cynthia Snow read the manuscript with the eyes of a competent editor and the heart of an intensely partisan daughter. She lifted the burden of typing from my shoulders and carried it with unflagging patience through what must have seemed endless changes. Marc Brodine has been one of my most perceptive and helpful critics. A strike strategy session with Russell and Marc was a turning point in the development of the final section. The work my daughter began, my son picked up at the end. Marc and his computer did the final job when publication was imminent.

Gerda Lerner's work as theoretician and historian of women has been an influence and a stimulation. A talented writer herself, she is also a brilliant critic. What she has given me as historian and writer are only two of many gifts of a friendship that has lasted more than fifty years. Gerda has read this work in progress six times, always with comments which gave me new insights and reinforced my confidence in the book.

I owe a special debt to my Irish-American brother-in-law, the late William J. Corr. When I broached the idea of this book he immediately supplied books and suggestions for further reading. He made helpful comments on a draft of early chapters and maintained his interest all the way to a review of the finished manuscript. I include here, in his memory, a few lines from the keen I wrote for his wake on November 17, 1984:

Bill knew where the well is

That has many springs feeding it,

One coming from Ireland

Where his fathers and mothers drank from it. . .

We will drink from that well

In remembrance of Bill.

He will always be part of the long past

Of the working class

And part of its great future.

I am fortunate in having a large extended family and many good friends whose interest in my book sustained me through the years. I have warm memories of readings and discussions in Bellingham, Roslyn, St. Louis, Cleveland, Santa Cruz, San Francisco and Laguna Beach. I will mention only two: an evening with Gloria Gordon and Hilary Sandall to celebrate their approval of the first seven chapters with a bottle of Irish whiskey and a dinner of Irish food. And the family pot-luck, when ten sisters and brothers and nephews and nieces brought comments on the completed manuscript to the home of Peter and Debbie Corr.

My profound gratitude to all my collaborators.